"You and Buzz need bedroom. Now. Lock the doors, and don't come out until I tell you."

Colton pulled out the gun from his waistband, his jaw set with steely determination.

Sarah didn't argue. She scrambled away, hardly able to breathe.

But as she locked the door, Buzz beside her, she pressed her ear there, trying to hear what was going on.

It was silent as Colton waited, seeming to prepare himself for battle.

Sarah waited. The moments felt like hours.

Flashbacks from earlier hit her, making her flinch. Images of seeing that man in Loretta's room. Watching as Loretta took her last breath.

Sarah remembered running. Fearing the man was following her. Fearing what he would do if he caught her, too.

Now Colton was in danger.

She stood and pressed herself into the wall, resisting the urge to look out the window and see what was going on.

She didn't have to.

She heard tires crunching on gravel in the distance.

Someone was here.

USA TODAY Bestselling Author

Christy Barritt
and
Hope White

Chasing Danger

Previously published as *Trained to Defend* and *Mountain Hostage*

LOVE INSPIRED
INSPIRATIONAL ROMANCE

LOVE INSPIRED®

INSPIRATIONAL ROMANCE

Recycling programs
for this product may
not exist in your area.

ISBN-13: 978-1-335-41858-6

Chasing Danger

Copyright © 2021 by Harlequin Books S.A.

Trained to Defend
First published in 2020. This edition published in 2021.
Copyright © 2020 by Christy Barritt

Mountain Hostage
First published in 2020. This edition published in 2021.
Copyright © 2020 by Pat White

This edition published by arrangement with Harlequin Books S.A.

For questions and comments about the quality of this book,
please contact us at CustomerService@Harlequin.com.

Love Inspired
22 Adelaide St. West, 40th Floor
Toronto, Ontario M5H 4E3, Canada
www.Harlequin.com

Printed in U.S.A.

CONTENTS

Christy Barritt's books have won a Daphne du Maurier Award for Excellence in Suspense and Mystery and have been twice nominated for an RT Reviewers' Choice Best Book Award. She's married to her Prince Charming, a man who thinks she's hilarious—but only when she's not trying to be. Christy is a self-proclaimed klutz, an avid music lover and a road-trip aficionado. For more information, visit her website at christybarritt.com.

Books by Christy Barritt

Love Inspired Suspense

Keeping Guard
The Last Target
Race Against Time
Ricochet
Desperate Measures
Hidden Agenda
Mountain Hideaway
Dark Harbor
Shadow of Suspicion
The Baby Assignment
The Cradle Conspiracy
Trained to Defend

Visit the Author Profile page
at Harlequin.com for more titles.

TRAINED TO DEFEND

Christy Barritt

God is our refuge and strength, a very present help in trouble. Therefore will not we fear, though the earth be removed, and though the mountains be carried into the midst of the sea; Though the waters thereof roar and be troubled, though the mountains shake with the swelling thereof.

—*Psalm* 46:1–3

This book is dedicated to Rusty, Sparky, Molly and Buttons. My furry companions are faithfully by my side every day as I sit down to write. Thanks for the inspiration and letting me be your person.

ONE

Sarah Peterson quietly opened the back door to her new, temporary home in Spokane, Washington, and slunk inside. The warm glow of delight spread inside her as she reflected on her evening. Maybe things were finally starting to look up for her.

She'd been at an art show this evening, and two people had shown interest in her work. All she needed was one big break, and maybe all of the hardship of these past several years could finally be in her past—and stay there.

Behind her, the freezing rain pounded relentlessly as a mid-January storm claimed the area. Forecasters had predicted the precipitation would soon turn to snow and conditions outside would become perilous.

But now, inside the house, everything around Sarah was dark and quiet with the stillness of the evening.

Good. Loretta must be sleeping.

And, if Sarah was smart, she'd remain quiet so the woman could continue sleeping.

Loretta Blanchard wasn't the type of woman you wanted to wake up—or even look at the wrong way, for that matter. She was a force to be reckoned with, and if she didn't like you, she would make your life miserable.

Sarah left her damp coat on a hanger by the door in order not to track any water inside. As she crept through the kitchen, she looked around for Buzz, Loretta's emotional support dog. The husky always greeted her at the door.

Strange. Where was he?

Buzz was one of Sarah's favorite parts about this job. She'd never met an animal with such intelligent eyes, and his wagging tail was just the welcome she needed on most days. Her muscles tightened as she wondered where the dog was.

Sarah headed through the dark house toward her bedroom so she could change out of her dress and heels. Her bag slid from her shoulder as she slipped her heels off and carried them up the massive staircase.

Her boss was a scientific genius who'd created a new medication to help people with arthritis. She'd been at the top of her game until ALS, also known as Lou Gehrig's disease, had claimed her body and weakened her muscles. However, her mind was just as sharp as ever.

Sarah stepped into her room, flipped on the light and paused.

Something felt off.

Her spine tightened, and she glanced around her room. Everything appeared in place. Her ivory quilt was neat. Her curtains were drawn. Her dresser drawers closed.

But something was different. She was sure of it.

Her mom had always said that Sarah had an eye and an ear for detail. It was probably what made her such a good artist today. She noticed things that others didn't. Slivers of light hidden beneath barren trees. A shy bird singing among the throng of boisterous ones. The way the sky still turned different colors for nearly an hour after the sunset.

So what had alerted her senses that something was wrong right now?

Sarah's eyes went to the closet. Was someone in there?

She grabbed the scissors from her dresser. She'd used them to trim her bangs this morning. Holding them like a knife, she stepped closer to the door.

Her lungs froze as she reached for the knob.

This was probably nothing.

Dear Lord, please don't let this be a mistake.

After lifting the silent prayer, she jerked the door open.

Something leaped toward her. Sarah swallowed a scream and threw herself back.

An oversize ball of fur nearly knocked her off her feet.

Buzz.

Buzz?

As the dog pounced on her, Sarah rubbed his head, sensing something was wrong—desperately wrong. "Why are you in my closet, boy? And you've been so quiet."

Buzz whined.

The only reason he'd be in her closet was if Loretta put him there and commanded him to stay, Sarah realized. But if Loretta, who was in a wheelchair, had gone through all of that trouble, she had to have a really good reason. There was an elevator in the house, but Loretta hated using it.

Buzz whined again, trying to tell her something.

"What is it, boy?" Sarah murmured, leaning toward the canine.

Her words seemed to give the dog permission. He charged toward her bedroom door, nuzzled it open and ran into the hallway. Still gripping the scissors, Sarah took off after him.

The dog ran down the stairs and toward the opposite wing of the house—the wing where Loretta's bedroom was located.

"Buzz!" Sarah whispered, urgency lacing her voice.

She didn't want the dog to wake up Loretta. Then again, maybe Buzz knew something she didn't.

She swallowed hard at the thought.

Sarah didn't have much time to think. No, she could barely keep up with Buzz.

She caught sight of the dog as he pushed his way into Loretta's bedroom and disappeared.

The knot in her stomach squeezed tighter.

This wasn't like Buzz. The dog was usually regal and reserved.

A groan emerged from the darkness, then a loud, hard crash.

Something was wrong. Really wrong.

Sarah flung herself into Loretta's room, fully expecting to find Loretta having a medical emergency of some sort. She froze in the doorway and gasped.

A masked man stood over Loretta as she lay on the floor, her wheelchair shoved to the side.

Fear rippled through Sarah.

What was going on here?

The intruder glanced over at Sarah—but only for a second—before Buzz charged at him and knocked him off Loretta and into the wall. The man's head hit the wall.

The man groaned before his eyes closed and his body went limp. Had he lost consciousness?

Either way, Buzz still growled on top of him.

With her heart beating out of control, Sarah's gaze slid across the room and stopped at Loretta.

She moaned on the floor, her chest rising and falling too quickly. Rapid gasps sounded at her parted lips.

Sarah hurried toward her, kneeling at her side. Blood gushed from a puncture wound in the woman's neck.

Tears rushed to Sarah's eyes. That man had hurt her. She and Buzz had gotten here too late.

"Loretta, hold on," Sarah whispered, grasping her boss's shoulders. "I'll call 911. Help will be here soon."

"Sarah…" Loretta's voice was so faint that Sarah could hardly understand it.

The woman tried to sit up, but Sarah gently pushed her back down. She was in no condition to move right now.

"It's okay," Sarah said. "Just stay still."

Loretta's sixty-year-old face wrinkled with pain that whispered across every feature, a face that had only recently developed fine lines. The woman was always so strong. Seeing her like this…

It made Sarah's heart twist into knots.

"You've…got…to…go," Loretta rasped.

"No, I need to stay here with you." A shiver went up Sarah's spine as she said the words. There was more at stake here than just Loretta's wound.

The man who'd done this to her was still in the room. Still passed out. For now.

But he could wake up at any time and try to finish what he'd started.

Loretta might be hurt, but her grip was strong as she grasped Sarah's arm. "Take… Buzz…and…run. Far away. Danger."

Her eyes closed. She was fading, Sarah realized. Near death. Delirious maybe.

Had Sarah understood her words correctly? Run? Why would she run? She needed to stay here with Loretta.

"Ms. Blanchard—"

The woman squeezed her arm again, her gaze coming alive with a spark of intensity. "Go. Now. He'll… kill you."

"What?" The breath left Sarah's lungs. Hearing the words out loud made a fresh round of panic swell in her.

"Don't…trust…the…police."

"But—" What did she mean? If she couldn't trust the police, then who could she trust?

Loretta's gaze suddenly locked on to Sarah's. "Buzz…"

"What about Buzz?"

"Take…him…"

Before she could finish her sentence, Loretta shut her eyes, and her grip loosened—went limp.

She was gone, Sarah realized.

"Oh, Loretta." Grief stabbed at Sarah. But she didn't have time to dwell on it. Urgency pushed her on.

That man was beginning to stir. His limbs jerked, and soon he'd be awake. She felt certain of it.

Sarah stood, dropping the scissors from her hands. She needed to go. If Loretta had given her those instructions, there was a good reason. The woman was smart, and she must know something that Sarah didn't.

"Buzz, come on."

Looking back at the man in black one more time, Sarah tore through the house.

She and Buzz had to get out of here. Now.

And there was only one place she could think to go. However, it was the last place she wanted to be.

Colton Hawk froze as a strange sound pulled him from his sleep.

It was a car. Coming up the gravel lane that led to his home. At four thirty in the morning.

He jumped out of his warm bed and threw on some clothes. After grabbing the gun from his nightstand, he peered out the window. Adrenaline pounded through him.

Unexpected visitors in the middle of the night usually meant trouble.

As a former detective, Colton had a whole list of people who might want to track him down and exact revenge. Apparently, not even moving out here to ten acres in northern Idaho was enough to keep people away.

He watched as the driver cut the headlights as he neared the house. He didn't recognize the beat-up sedan. But the fact that the driver was being secretive set off all kinds of warning alarms in his mind.

Colton hurried down the stairs to his front door. He stepped out onto his porch just as the vehicle rolled to a stop behind his truck.

With his finger poised on the gun, Colton waited to see what would happen next.

Snow pelted down from above, and the darkness obscured the landscape around him. Nightfall out here in the middle of Idaho's Rocky Mountains was unlike any Colton had ever experienced. The blackness was so deep, a person felt like they could be swallowed by it.

The isolation was both a friend and a foe.

Colton knew one thing: someone had to be desperate to head out in slick, treacherous weather like this, especially in a sedan like the one in front of his house. The vehicle looked like it could break down at any minute. The front bumper was dented, the driver's side door was faded, and the tires looked tiny and worn down.

He glanced beyond the car to make sure no one else had followed. He saw nothing, no one—just a dark, empty lane lined with pine and fir trees.

Colton sucked in a breath when a dog hopped from the backseat and into the knee-high snow. A husky.

Why would someone bent on revenge have brought a dog with them?

And then he saw the biggest trouble of all.

Sarah Peterson stepped out and stared across the expanse at him.

He sucked in another breath.

Sarah. His Sarah.

Colton never thought he'd see the woman again, not after the way things had ended between them two years ago.

But there she was. Even in the darkness, he could see that she looked just as beautiful as ever with her shiny blond hair and petite figure. But something about her body language was different. Gone was the light-hearted, carefree vibe that Colton had loved so much.

In its place was…terror. It was the only word he could think of to describe the look.

She staggered toward him and collapsed into the mounds of white, icy flakes that covered his front yard.

Colton jammed his gun into his waistband and rushed toward her. The dog barked at him, urging him on, telling him he wasn't moving fast enough.

When he reached Sarah, snow already encased her limp body.

She was…barefoot? In a knee-length dress?

What was going on? Why would she be dressed like this in such frigid weather? Something was seriously wrong.

Colton gathered her in his arms and carried her inside his house. Despite the craziness of the moment, he still caught of whiff of Sarah's honeysuckle-scented lotion.

At one time, it had been one of his favorite aromas in the world. It brought back memories of watching sunsets in each other's arms. Of dreaming about the future while hiking their favorite trail. Of good-night kisses and long hugs on the porch.

Shoving aside the bittersweet memories, Colton lowered Sarah onto his leather couch. She was freezing and had to warm up. He'd call an ambulance, but it would take twenty minutes to get here.

Before grabbing a blanket, his eyes skimmed the light blue sweater covering her arms. Was that…blood on her sleeves?

Colton sucked in a breath.

What in the world had happened to her?

He quickly checked her for wounds but saw nothing. That meant the blood wasn't hers.

Wasting no more time, he grabbed a blanket and covered her. That blanket wouldn't be enough, though. He went to the fireplace and added wood, waiting until the blaze fanned and filled the room with more heat. Then he turned up his thermostat, hoping it kicked in quickly.

Colton went back to check on Sarah. He felt confident she just needed to warm up. He'd let her rest for a few minutes before deciding his next step.

His breath caught as he gazed at her. Beautiful Sarah.

He hadn't expected to see her again. Ever. Not after the way things had ended. Not after she'd chosen a job over a future with him. Bitterness tried to claw at him, but Colton pushed it away. There wasn't time for that now.

The dog nuzzled his hand, and Colton looked down at him. The husky sat directly in front of Colton, almost as if telling him that he had to answer to this canine.

"What happened, boy?" Colton murmured.

The dog let out a soft growl and stared at Sarah.

"Something bad, huh?" Colton's stomach tightened. If only the dog could speak.

Colton double-checked Sarah's vitals. Her pulse was good. She was breathing and didn't appear feverish.

She must have passed out from exhaustion or shock.

Lord, be with her. I don't know what happened, but I know she needs You now.

Just as he said "Amen," Sarah began thrashing on the couch, and her breathing quickened.

"He's coming," Sarah murmured, her eyes still closed. "He's coming."

Colton's back stiffened. Who was coming? What exactly had Sarah gotten herself mixed up in?

He didn't know. He only knew that the woman he'd once loved had somehow found herself in serious trouble.

TWO

Sarah jerked her eyes open and startled at the unfamiliar space around her.

Where was she? Was that man here—the man who'd killed Loretta? Had he caught Sarah and taken her somewhere?

She sprang up, swinging her gaze around as panic seized her. Movement caught the side of her vision.

The killer. He was here.

Sarah raised her hands, ready to give every last ounce of her strength to stay alive.

Her arm jerked toward him. But, before her fist connected with the man, he grabbed her wrists.

The action immobilized her. She thrashed, trying to get away. It was no use. The man…he was too strong. He overpowered her too easily.

"Sarah, it's okay." His voice sounded surprisingly calm and soothing—not at all like Sarah had imagined.

But she wouldn't let that fool her.

"No, it's not okay." With one last burst of strength, she began fighting again.

"Sarah, it's me. Colton."

Slowly, her ex-fiancé's face came into view.

Colton.

That was right. She'd fled to Colton's house. She barely remembered making it here.

She only vaguely recalled driving around as if on autopilot. Of deciding to come here but changing her mind. Of wandering country back roads in the dark, worried about running out of gas.

She remembered the panic. Remembered not thinking clearly.

As more details from last night flooded back to Sarah, she gasped.

Details about Loretta. Of the woman's final moments.

Tears sprang to her eyes, and her limbs shook uncontrollably.

Loretta was dead. She'd passed right there in Sarah's arms while her attacker had lain collapsed against the wall.

As Colton released her hands, Sarah leaned back, desperate to hold herself together. Yet she couldn't.

No, she'd been so frantic that she'd run to the very man who'd broken her heart—only he refused to acknowledge that he'd been the one to pull away. Colton refused to understand why Sarah had no choice but to leave, refused to understand that this was never about her art.

Buzz appeared beside Sarah, and his cold nose nuzzled her hand. She smiled and rubbed the dog's head, finding comfort in his familiar scent.

Her smile faded quickly.

Poor Buzz…he must feel worse than she did. Buzz had loved Loretta so much.

And now she was gone.

Another guttural cry escaped.

Colton leaned toward her, his gaze intense and concerned. "Sarah, you need to tell me what's going on."

She studied Colton a moment. Glanced at the perfect lines of his face. His messy light brown hair.

The man always got her pulse racing.

But he was off-limits. Sarah needed to remember that. He'd already broken her heart once. If he broke it again, she wasn't sure it could ever be repaired.

Which was why coming here had been such a horrible idea. Sarah definitely hadn't been thinking clearly. Otherwise, she would have gone anywhere else.

She gathered the blanket around her and stared at the fire in front of her. Buzz lay down beside her, his icy blue gaze on Colton, as if daring him to make one wrong move.

She needed to tell Colton why she was here. But first she needed to collect her thoughts. Besides, she wasn't sure she could say the words aloud.

Every time she remembered what happened it felt like a punch in her gut. Maybe this was a nightmare. Maybe she would wake up. Sarah wished those things might be true and, even more, she wished she believed them.

But she knew the truth. She just didn't know if she could find her voice long enough to share.

"Can I…can I have some tea?" Sarah asked, buying herself time. "Please. I… I just can't get warm."

As if on cue, her teeth chattered. The reaction had little to do with the cold, however. No, it felt like someone had rammed an icicle into her chest and shattered her emotions.

"Of course." Colton stood. "But then we need to talk."

Why *had* Sarah come here? Why couldn't she think of anywhere else she'd be safe?

She knew why. Colton had always been a protector. Even if he had been distant and withdrawn toward the end of their engagement, he was still, in some way, her safe place.

The drive here flashed back to her.

There had been headlights behind her. They'd appeared about fifteen minutes into her escape.

Sarah had tried to lose the driver, fearing it was the man who'd killed Loretta.

But what if she hadn't lost him?

She jumped to her feet and pulled the blanket around her as she walked toward the window. She had to know if she was truly safe here or not. Sarah had to see if anyone lingered outside, waiting to make his next move.

Buzz followed beside her, keeping a watchful eye on her.

"What are you doing?" Colton asked from across the open expanse of the room. His hands froze on the teakettle, as if he braced himself for action.

"That man…" Sarah started, fear seizing her again.

She couldn't get the image of Loretta's dying figure out of her mind. Couldn't forget the horror of finding that man standing over her.

"What man, Sarah?" Colton stepped from around the breakfast bar, coming toward her. "Who are you talking about?"

Sarah shook her head, battling the memories and hoping this was all a bad dream. She knew it wasn't. "I'm afraid… I'm afraid he followed me."

Colton took her elbow and led her back to the couch. "If that's the case, the last place you want to be is in front of the window."

She felt stoic as she sat back on the cushions and stared at the fire. The kettle whistled.

"One minute," he murmured. "Then we need to talk."

A moment later, Colton handed her some tea, complete with sugar and cream. He'd remembered what she liked. The thought shouldn't bring her so much delight.

"Sarah, you need to tell me what's going on." Colton stood with his hands on his hips. "Tell me why you have blood on your clothes."

At his words, she glanced down and gasped. He was right. Loretta's bloodstained her sweater.

A new round of tears welled up in her eyes. She jerked the sweater off, unable to stand the thought. She tossed it on the couch out of sight, wishing she could discard her memories as easily. But life didn't work that way.

Colton's intelligent, compassionate gaze remained latched on to hers. He sat on the chair near the couch, leaning toward her, waiting to listen.

He'd positioned himself at a place where he could also see the windows.

Sarah didn't miss that fact. Colton was always the cop, wasn't he? He was ever vigilant, kind of like Buzz.

She sucked in a deep, shaky breath. She wanted to forget about tonight. Erase it from her mind. Yet she realized that she couldn't do that. She was going to have to go back and revisit those dark moments.

As she opened her mouth, words wouldn't escape. "I…"

Where did she even start?

"It's okay," Colton prodded. "What happened last night?"

She drew in a deep breath, praying for courage as she shared the truth. "I've been working for a woman, Loretta, and living in her home. I returned to her house last night and found her on the floor in her room. Bleeding." Her voice cracked.

Colton's eyes widened. "What happened next?"

"Buzz knocked out the man who attacked her. I tried to help Loretta, but she told me to take Buzz and run and to not trust the police. And then she…" Sarah swallowed hard. "Then she died. She was gone."

"I'm sorry, Sarah."

She nodded stiffly. "So, I did what she told me. I didn't know what else to do. I didn't even put my shoes on. I just… I wanted to get away."

"What happened to the man?"

"He was still in the house when I left. Buzz had jumped on him, and I think the man hit his head and was knocked unconscious. But then, on the way here, I was certain someone was following me."

Colton stiffened. "Why do you say that?"

Sarah shivered at the memories. "There were headlights. And they always seemed to be there, even when I turned off the main highway. I lost him… I think. I mean, I didn't see the car for the last thirty minutes of my trip."

"Why did you come here, Sarah?"

She swallowed hard, downing every last ounce of her pride as her gaze met Colton's. "Because I didn't know what else to do or who else I could trust. Please help me, Colton. Please."

* * *

Colton tried to process everything that Sarah had told him. He had so many questions but most of those could wait until later. Right now, he was concerned about Sarah. About how frail she looked. About how her arms trembled so badly she could hardly drink her tea.

"Sarah, I need to call the police—"

"No!" She nearly jumped off the couch, and Buzz followed her, standing on guard. "You can't. Loretta said not to."

"Why would she say that?" What sense did it make? The woman had been murdered. If Sarah had called the police, maybe the guy who'd committed the crime would be behind bars right now.

"I have no idea. But if she said it…she had a reason."

"But the police could catch this killer. Time is of the essence in situations like these and—"

Sarah glanced around, as if looking for her keys or purse or whatever she would have brought with her. "I should leave. I'm sorry. I shouldn't have come here. Some part of me thought I could trust you, though."

Colton touched her arm, ignoring the electricity that came from feeling her soft skin. "Don't leave. That's not what I'm saying. Please, sit down. We'll figure this out. I'm just asking questions right now."

She stared at him. Said nothing.

Finally, she nodded and lowered herself back onto the couch across from him. Buzz jumped up beside her and laid his head on her lap.

"Let's just talk." Colton spoke softly, trying to put her at ease and alleviate some of her caginess. "Okay?"

Sarah nodded, but her eyes looked strained and unconvinced. Instead, she leaned forward and rubbed Buzz's head.

"Do you have any idea why anyone would want Loretta dead?" he asked.

Sarah shook her head. "No. And…the more I think about it, the stranger it all is."

"Why do you say that?"

"Because I found Buzz locked in my closet upstairs. He couldn't have gotten himself locked in there. It wouldn't make any sense."

"Okay. You think Loretta put him there?"

"It's the only thing that makes sense. If the killer had put him there, Buzz would have been a wreck, clawing to get out. But he was sitting there obediently." As Sarah talked, she continued to rub the dog's head.

"So, he's well trained."

Sarah nodded. "That's right. But the thing is… Loretta could hardly get up the steps. She had ALS. If she went through all that trouble…"

"Then she suspected something might happen."

"Exactly." Sarah trembled again. "I don't know what's going on, but I don't like it. I hope I didn't lead trouble here, Colton. I didn't think I was going to make it. The roads were so icy. And the drive was long and dark. I barely had enough gas. So many things were not in my favor."

"It sounds like God was watching over you to bring you this far," Colton said.

"I agree." Her gaze met his, her brief moment of gratefulness at their spiritual connection replaced by fear. "What am I going to do?"

"We'll figure something out, Sarah." Had he just said that?

Colton had taken time off from law enforcement, even though he'd been offered a job in investigative services with the Idaho State Police.

One day, he thought he might go back into that line of work. But, if he ever had hopes of doing that, the last thing he needed to do was harbor someone who might be wanted in a police investigation. And if the police weren't looking for Sarah yet, they would be soon.

Still, one look at Sarah, and Colton knew he couldn't refuse helping her. She'd always had that effect on him.

Sarah rubbed her hands against her dress and frowned. "Colton, is there a way you could... I don't know. Maybe call someone? Maybe use some of your connections to find out if there are any updates? Maybe the police caught this guy. Maybe those headlights I saw were just another traveler headed in the same direction I was. I just don't know. Nothing makes sense, and nothing will make sense until I have more answers."

He didn't say anything for a moment and instead sat there, letting her words settle.

She frowned. "I'm asking too much, aren't I? I'm sorry."

"I'll see what I can do," Colton finally said before nodding toward the hallway. "Listen, first, why don't you take a shower?"

"A shower sounds nice."

"I'll find you something to wear and you can leave what you have on now outside the door. I'll wash everything for you and leave you something fresh. Once you've cleaned up, we figure out a plan."

Sarah continued to stare at him, as if trying to gauge his thoughts, to figure out if he was still trustworthy.

"You're not going to call the police while I'm in the shower, are you?"

"I won't. You know I'm as good as my word."

Finally, she nodded. "Okay then."

But just as she stood, her phone buzzed. She pulled it from her purse and looked at the screen. Her face went pale.

"What is it?" Colton moved closer, sensing something was wrong.

"It's a message…from Loretta."

The killer must have grabbed the woman's phone, Colton realized.

"What does it say?" Colton asked, glancing over her shoulder. As he read the words there, his blood went colder than an Idaho winter.

I know who you are, and I will find you. You have something I want.

THREE

Sarah's heart raced as she sat on the couch and stared at the words on her phone.

The killer knew who she was? How? What did this mean?

Fear rushed through her. Exactly what was this man planning to do when he found her? Sarah didn't even have to ask that question. She *knew* what he planned on doing.

He would kill her.

She should have pulled up his mask and looked at his face. At least then she would know what the man looked like.

But it was too late for that now. It didn't matter.

Her head spun as reality again hit her and left her reeling.

"It's going to be okay, Sarah," Colton said beside her.

His voice snapped her back to the moment. His platitude was meant to bring her comfort but it failed. Nothing was going to be okay. Nothing.

Why couldn't Colton see that? Why did he always think things would be okay when they clearly wouldn't?

Sometimes people couldn't change their circumstances, no matter how hard they tried.

Sarah's life had been a case in point.

Nothing had gone the way she'd planned—including her relationship with Colton.

She put her hands over her face. Why had she ever come here? What had she been thinking?

This was just one more bad decision in a long line of them.

Colton leaned closer, still staring at her phone. As he did, his arm brushed hers, and a surge of old memories rushed through her. Memories of when life used to be happy. When the future had seemed bright. When it looked like her future wouldn't be a repeat of her past.

Sarah had been wrong then. As much as she wanted to believe and trust in God's plan for her future, she'd accepted the fact that her future was meant to be full of struggles. Other people might cruise through life and find happiness. But not Sarah.

Her father had left. Her mother had been arrested. She and her sister had grown up with a string of foster care families—and they hadn't been together in most of those homes.

No, life had never been smooth sailing. Even now as an adult, life had been full of financial and career struggles, all of which had led her to this point.

"Do you have any idea what he's talking about when he says, 'You have something I want'?" Colton asked, his gaze still laser focused on her phone screen and that text she'd received.

Sarah's mind raced, charging back to the present. What *did* the man mean? What exactly had he come to Loretta's to get this evening?

"I have no clue," she said, her voice shaky. "I left with nothing. All my things are still at Loretta's. It was just me and Buzz and a few of Buzz's essentials that were in a bag by the back door."

She leaned down and patted Buzz's head. The dog leaned into her, but Sarah noted how his eyes remained on guard as he scanned the room.

She felt sorry for Buzz. He'd cherished Loretta so much and had been such a faithful companion.

The dog was truly beautiful. White with gray spots. His eyes were an icy blue, and he had a matching collar. Despite his regal demeanor, the dog also had a playful side. Loretta had trained him well. All she had to do was cluck her tongue once, twice or three times, and he would immediately obey whatever command corresponded.

In fact, in some ways, the dog had been like a child to Loretta. Buzz had been raised to act as an emotional support canine for her.

"Is Buzz special?" Colton asked, staring at the husky.

Sarah looked at the dog again. "I mean, he's special in the sense that he's a great dog. But he's not of a championship bloodline or anything."

"That's strange that the man would say that then." Colton reached over and rubbed Buzz's head also. "Whoever killed Loretta must think you have something—something worth killing for."

Sarah wrapped her arms over her chest. "I agree. But it doesn't make sense. What am I going to do, Colton?"

Colton stood. "You should take that shower. Maybe it will help you clear your head."

She rose to her feet. "You're right. I need to get this blood off me."

Loretta's blood.

Nausea churned in her stomach.

Everything still felt surreal, like a nightmare.

Only Sarah knew she wouldn't wake up and everything wouldn't be better this time.

Colton waited until he heard the door to the bathroom open and close before he peered around the hallway.

Sarah's clothes were on the floor, neatly folded, just as he'd asked.

His heart twisted as he quietly stepped from his room, carefully picked the dress up and slipped it into a bag.

The clothing would most likely be needed as evidence. Though Sarah didn't want to tell the police what had happened, Colton hoped to make her come around. And, when she did, these clothes would need to be examined.

Though Sarah wanted to stay far away from the police, they would only help her. That was their job—to find the truth. Colton had no idea why her boss had told her not to talk to them. Was there more to that story? Or had the woman been delirious during her final moments?

Colton left the bag on the washing machine for the time being and then went into his bedroom. He opened the door to the attic and stepped inside, a musky smell enveloping him. He searched for a moment before finding what he wanted.

An old burgundy trunk. With a touch of trepidation, Colton opened the lid.

Sarah's old clothes stared back at him.

She'd left them at his old place when they thought they were getting married. She'd needed somewhere to store a few things, and his place had seemed like a logical choice. When he'd moved, he'd thought about getting rid of them. Why hadn't he?

He wasn't sure. It didn't matter now.

He rummaged through several things before pulling out some choices for Sarah.

Colton deposited the clothes for Sarah outside the bathroom door. He could still hear the water running on the other side and steam seeped from beneath the doorway.

He pulled out his phone, remembering that call he'd promised to make to find out more information on Loretta's death. He glanced at his watch. It was early—too early to make any inquiries without bringing attention to himself, which was the last thing Sarah would want.

But there was one person Colton could call. Fred Higgins. The man was his closest neighbor and one of the most vigilant people he knew. If there was any suspicious activity in this area, Fred would know about it.

The man always woke at the crack of dawn, and it was already past 7:00 a.m. Quickly, Colton dialed his number and waited for an answer. Mr. Higgins didn't disappoint.

"What I can I do for you, Hawk?"

"Morning, Higgins. Listen, did you hear anyone coming down our road last night?" Colton got right to the heart of the matter, knowing the ex-military man would appreciate his directness.

"Funny you ask that. As a matter of fact, I did. An

old beat up sedan came through about four thirty, taking it real slow."

Sarah. That had to be Sarah's car. "An old friend is here visiting me."

"Good to know. Strange thing is that a few minutes later, another car crept by."

Colton's spine stiffened. "Is that right?"

Colton walked to the window and peered out, looking for any sign that someone was there. The sun hadn't risen yet, and everything was still clothed in darkness, making it nearly impossible to see.

"That's right. But it turned around and left a few minutes later. Figured someone got lost."

Colton wished he felt as confident about that. But at least he knew more now. "Thanks, Mr. Higgins."

"Everything okay?"

"It's fine. I know you like to keep an eye on this mountain. My friend thought she saw someone behind her."

"Well, she was right. But, like I said, that other car turned around."

But that also meant that someone knew where Sarah was. Most likely, the killer. The thought made Colton's stomach churn.

"Will you let me know if you see anyone else?" Colton asked.

"Absolutely."

Colton ended the call and leaned against the wall as the impact of this early morning's encounter hit him. Sarah…he never thought he'd see her again, especially not like this.

The two had met when he'd been a detective in Seattle. Sarah had worked in a coffee shop he liked to frequent. They started talking about some of the artwork hanging on the walls, and Sarah had finally admitted the paintings were hers and that she'd been working as a barista just until she got her big break in the art world.

After a month of coming in every day for coffee, Colton had finally asked her out. They were inseparable after that first date. They'd gotten engaged six months later and planned for a spring wedding.

But one night on a case, Colton had been forced to shoot an intoxicated, belligerent man who'd put innocent people in the line of fire. Guilt had haunted Colton ever since—especially when he remembered the rage the man's wife had toward him afterward. He wasn't a hero to her. No, he was the villain.

It wasn't long after that that Colton had decided to move from Seattle to northern Idaho. He wanted a slower pace of life in a more peaceful area. He wanted a lot of land and clean air and fewer demands.

Sarah had seemed onboard at first…and then she'd taken that job at an art gallery in Spokane, saying it was too big of an opportunity to pass up.

Apparently, that opportunity was bigger and more important than he was. His stomach clenched at the memories.

His life looked so much different today than it had two years ago. Colton had taken a break from police work. Instead, he built live-edge tables out in his barn.

His friend with the state police called him every month, asking when he wanted to come work for him. But Colton had refused. He'd know when the time was right to go back—if he ever did go back.

Despite all of that, sometimes he wished he could turn back time and go back to those days when his life had seemed so full. Back when he'd had someone to share his sorrows and joys. When his dreams of having a family had seemed close enough to touch.

There was no use dwelling on all of that now. He had other more pressing concerns to think about. The first thing he wanted to do right now was move Sarah's car out of sight—just in case.

He grabbed Sarah's car keys—she'd left them on the table—and then went outside and climbed into her sedan.

Colton cranked the engine and slowly pulled around to the back of his cabin.

As he did, he glanced around. This car was old. It was the one Sarah had back when they'd been engaged. And it had been unreliable then.

In fact, Colton was surprised the vehicle had even made it this far. It was probably fifteen years old, one of the seats was ripped and the engine made a puttering sound.

Colton put the car into Park and shook his head. Just what had happened with Sarah in the past two years?

His jaw tightened. It wasn't important. That wasn't his business. Nor was what kind of car Sarah was driving or what kind of condition it was in.

As he took the keys out of the ignition, he glanced on the floor and saw a bag there. It seemed out of place in the vehicle. The leather looked expensive and new.

Colton started to reach for it and then stopped himself.

No, he wouldn't look inside. That was too intrusive. But his curiosity was sparked.

He glanced down at it one more time and saw a tag

on the side labeling the bag as Buzz's. This must be dog supplies.

At that thought, he unzipped it, checking to see if there were items inside that he needed to take into his house for Buzz.

Instead, he saw money.

A lot of money.

Carefully, he prodded the bag open more. His eyes widened.

Just by looking, Colton would guess there was at least fifty thousand dollars there.

Where had Sarah gotten that money? He couldn't even begin to imagine.

Had she gotten in with the wrong crowd? Had she done something illegal?

Colton didn't like the conclusions that his mind started to form.

But he needed to be more cautious now than ever.

FOUR

Colton climbed out of Sarah's car, locked the doors and went back inside the house. He wandered into the kitchen and pulled out what food he had in his refrigerator. Maybe something to eat would help them sort out the situation.

He put some water on to boil for rice and found a can of gravy. This would work as dog food until he could get something else.

A few minutes later, Colton heard the water stop and the bathroom door open. The clothes disappeared from the hallway.

Colton's pulse pounded at the thought of talking to Sarah again. It had been so long, and there was so much he wanted to say to her, to ask her. But he needed to keep himself in check. The last thing he wanted was to get hurt again.

Buzz lay at his feet, keeping a watchful eye on the house. "Long night, huh, buddy?"

The dog stared back at him, seeming to take everything in.

"Your food is almost ready," Colton continued. "Maybe you could use something in your stomach too."

Buzz raised his nose to the air and sniffed his approval.

Just then, Sarah emerged from the hallway, her hair wet and her skin flushed. Yet she looked adorable. She always did.

"Thank you for the clothes... I can't believe you kept them." She stopped at the kitchen counter, looking a touch self-conscious.

"I meant to get rid of them. I guess it's a good thing I didn't."

"I guess so."

Colton nodded toward the kitchen table. "Look, why don't you sit down? I'll fix some breakfast."

Her lips twisted down in an adorable half frown that Colton often thought about. It wasn't just that expression. He often thought about Sarah. He thought about her too much, for that matter.

He knew he needed to move on—to find someone who'd be more committed to him than a career. But there was no one else like Sarah. Despite that, she was off-limits.

"If you don't mind, then that sounds good. Thank you." She glanced around. "This place looks really great, by the way. It's rustic, but it's got a bit of style to it. Did you make this live-edge table yourself?"

He nodded and began scrambling some eggs in a bowl. "As a matter of fact, I did."

He liked working with his hands. It was quiet work that helped him to sort out his thoughts. He had a barn out back that he used as a workshop. He'd thought on more than one occasion about how much Sarah would enjoy a space like that to paint. The view of the mountains out the back was amazing.

As he poured the eggs into a sizzling pan, the timer went off. The rice was ready. He put the food in a bowl and waited for it to cool.

Buzz scooted a little closer, and Colton smiled, tossing down a small piece of egg for the dog to eat. A few minutes later, the omelets were finished, and Colton set the plates on the table so they could eat.

"Green onions, cheese and ham," he said. "Is that still good?"

He was rewarded with a smile.

"It's perfect," Sarah said. "Thank you."

He placed a bowl of rice and gravy on the floor for Buzz and then sat down. "So, how did you meet this Loretta woman?"

Sarah forced herself to swallow a bite of her breakfast, not hungry but trying to eat anyway. "It's kind of a strange story. I was actually participating in an art show in Spokane. It was outdoors. I saw Buzz near my booth. He'd stepped on something. I went over to help him and found a rock had gotten lodged in his paw."

"Poor guy."

Sarah flashed a bittersweet smile at the dog. "Yeah, he wasn't feeling too great. I decided to wait with him until his owner came back. Loretta showed up. Apparently, Buzz had gotten away from her. She was in her wheelchair and had attempted to take him out to the show. She offered me some money for my trouble. I told her I couldn't accept anything. She ended up coming over to my booth and purchasing a painting instead. She talked to me a little about my work, and genuinely seemed to like it."

"How did that lead to a job?"

Sarah put her fork down. "At that point, she knew my name and even my number—I'd given her my business card. She called me two months later and offered me a job as Buzz's caretaker, as well as part-time personal assistant. She said the job would still allow me time to work on my art. It was like an answer to prayer."

"It sounds like it."

"It wasn't always easy. Not at all. Loretta wasn't the easiest to get along with. But I really respected the work she was doing in the medical community, and it was an honor to work for her. She was a medical researcher, and she developed a drug to help people with arthritis."

"That's great, Sarah."

She picked up her fork again but looked uncertain. "I know this sounds weird, but could we turn on the TV? I want to see if they're reporting Loretta's death yet and what they're saying about it if they are."

"Of course."

Colton flipped on the morning news. Breaking news aired over the station.

All the blood drained from Colton's face when Sarah's picture appeared on the screen. The headline proclaimed that Sarah Peterson, twenty-seven, was wanted for the murder of famed medical researcher Loretta Blanchard. The news anchor continued, saying that there was now a manhunt to find Sarah and warning viewers that she could be dangerous.

Sarah exchanged a look with Colton.

This was much, much worse than he'd imagined it would be.

Because not only was a killer potentially looking for Sarah, but so were the police.

* * *

"The police think I killed Loretta," Sarah murmured, her head spinning. "Why would they think that? I would never hurt anyone."

"Someone could have seen you run from the scene," Colton told her. "It would be a natural assumption."

She put her fork down, her thoughts clashing inside her until her head pounded. "You're right. Of course I look guilty. I was the last person seen with her. Her blood was on my sweater."

Colton squeezed her arm. "Don't panic yet. We could talk to the police, explain what happened—"

"I told you, no police. I can't risk it." Especially now that Sarah knew they thought she was guilty.

"The police aren't your enemy, Sarah." Colton's voice was quiet and calm—but also full of conviction.

"I didn't say they were. But Loretta had reasons for everything. There was a reason she said that. She…she was one of the smartest women I've ever met."

Colton frowned, looking as if he was trying to find the right words. "Not coming forward will only make you look more guilty."

Sarah shrugged, knowing his words were true but unable to verbally agree with him. "I just don't know what to say or do."

Colton opened his mouth, like he was about to say more. Before he could, his phone buzzed. He glanced at the screen and frowned again before answering.

Sarah tried to interpret the one-sided conversation but couldn't. She only knew something was wrong. Colton's voice sounded stiff, and he glanced at the window.

He ended the call and stood. "You and Buzz need

to go to the back bedroom. Now. Lock the doors, and don't come out until I tell you."

Alarm raced through her. "Why? What's going on?"

"My neighbor saw someone coming up the lane toward the house." Colton walked toward the window.

"And that's strange?"

Colton looked back, locking gazes with her. "There are only two places they could be going—his house or mine, and neither of us are expecting anyone."

Sarah's heart rate surged. It was the killer, wasn't it? Or the police. Either way, her future looked bleak enough that nausea rose in her so quickly that she grasped her stomach.

"You need to go. Now." Colton pulled out the gun from his waistband, his jaw set with steely determination.

Sarah didn't argue. She scrambled away, hardly able to breathe.

But as she locked the door, Buzz beside her, she pressed her ear there, trying to hear what was going on.

It was silent as Colton waited, seeming to prepare himself for battle.

"Buzz, what's going on?" She reached down and wrapped her arms around the dog, relishing his soft fur.

The dog let out a whine and licked her cheek. Buzz knew something was wrong also.

Sarah waited, praying for safety and favor. But the moments felt like hours.

Flashbacks from earlier hit her, each one making her flinch. Images of seeing that man in Loretta's room. Watching as Loretta took her last breath.

Sarah remembered running. Fearing the man was

following her. Fearing what he would do if he caught Sarah too.

Now Colton was in danger.

She stood and pressed herself into the wall, resisting the urge to look out the window and see what was going on.

She didn't have to.

She heard tires crunching on gravel in the distance. Someone was here.

Sarah braced herself for whatever would happen next.

Colton rushed to the window, reaching for the gun at his waistband. Who would be coming here at this time of the day?

No one—unless it was an emergency or unless it was trouble.

His breath caught when no vehicles emerged at the end of the lane.

Someone had started this way and stopped.

Colton's instincts were finely tuned from years of law enforcement—finely tuned enough not to believe in coincidences, especially given the circumstances right now.

No. Someone had scoped out this place. Seen his cabin. And then returned.

That person was most likely the one who'd sent Sarah that threatening text.

He wanted whatever it was he thought Sarah had.

Colton couldn't let that happen. He *wouldn't* let that happen.

Without thinking about it anymore, Colton stepped

outside. He glanced around, listening for any signs of trouble.

He heard nothing.

Cautiously, he walked down his road, his gun still in hand.

He was never one to cower away from trouble, and he wasn't going to start now.

With every step, Colton listened for any clues that someone was near. Stalking. Waiting.

He anticipated hearing footsteps. Twigs cracking.

All was silent except for the occasional rustle of wind or the crackle of icy snow beneath his boots.

He still didn't let down his guard. If this criminal was in any way trained, he would know to disguise his presence. And based on everything Sarah had told him, this man very well could be someone who hadn't killed in the heat of the moment but in premeditated murder. The thought wasn't comforting.

As Colton turned the corner, he spotted a dark sedan tucked away at the end of the lane.

He froze. His heart pounded in his ears as anticipation built inside him. What was the driver doing?

The car didn't move, and the windows were too tinted to see inside. The driver could be there...or he could have slipped out.

Colton's gaze traveled to the front of the car, but the license plate was concealed by the brush.

Quickly, he scanned the woods.

Was the driver waiting behind one of these trees, watching Colton's every move?

Colton heard nothing around him.

Cautiously, he took another step.

He wasn't leaving here until he knew who was inside that car or until he at least got a license plate.

With every step, he listened, keenly aware of everything around him.

Suddenly, the car's engine revved.

A moment later, the car charged toward him.

FIVE

What was taking so long? What was Colton doing out there? Sarah wondered.

A few minutes ago, it had sounded like the front door opened. Had Colton gone outside?

What if he was hurt right now? Hurt because Sarah had brought danger into his quiet life, the life that was supposed to keep him from situations like this one.

She glanced down at Buzz. The dog stared at her, as if trying to communicate, before letting out a bark.

"Something's wrong, isn't it?" she murmured.

Buzz barked again.

Sarah shushed him, trying not to draw any more attention to them than necessary. Buzz's barking could alert an intruder that they were here. Since she had no idea what was going on outside this room, she had to be cautious.

Taking a tentative step, Sarah went to the window and peered out. Just as she shoved the curtain aside, she saw a car careen toward Colton at the end of the lane.

She braced herself for whatever would happen next while frantically praying.

Please, Lord, help him. Keep him safe. Please!

Just before the car hit him, Colton dove into the woods. The black sedan did a swift U-turn. Then it sped off, leaving a trail of dust behind it.

Was Colton okay?

Sarah couldn't stay in here any longer. She had to check on him.

If he got hurt because of her, then she'd never forgive herself.

"Come on, Buzz," she called.

The dog remained on Sarah's heels as she ran outside. Her bare feet crunched in the thick snow, and a painful ache began because of the cold. Her wet hair slapped her face before the strands froze together in clumps. Icy air invaded her lungs.

She didn't care.

Colton could be in danger right now.

Moving as quickly as she could, Sarah hit the gravel road. Her feet were already numb now as they hit the rocky soil.

All she could think about was Colton and whether or not he was okay. That driver had tried to run him down.

The seriousness of the situation hit her again. Whoever was behind all of this wasn't playing games. He'd rather kill again than risk being exposed.

Sarah pushed down a sliver of fear.

Just as she reached the end of the lane, Colton emerged from the woods. He rubbed his head and his eyes were narrow with irritation, but he otherwise looked okay.

Thank goodness.

She rushed toward him, stopping just short of touching him. She paused there, a bone-chilling wind sweeping around her, sending clumps of snow from the branches above down on them.

"Sarah, you shouldn't be out here."

"Are you okay?" she asked, still worried about him and studying his features for any sign that something was wrong. "I couldn't leave you."

"I'm okay. But I don't want that man to see you if he comes back." He took her elbow and turned her around. "Come on. Let's get inside. Besides, you're going to freeze out here."

She ignored the charge of electricity she felt rush through her at his touch.

This was no time for electricity. Besides, she and Colton were finished. Done. There was no going back to fix what had happened between them.

Colton might forgive, but he didn't forget.

Not that Sarah would ever want to get back together with him. It didn't matter that she'd missed him and his companionship. Missed the kisses they'd shared. Missed the possibility of spending the future with someone.

But everyone she'd ever loved had disappointed her. Why should Colton be different?

Sarah had so many questions she wanted to ask about what had just happened. But she held them in.

For now.

Instead, she listened for a minute. She didn't hear the car. Didn't hear footsteps or yells. Buzz seemed calm.

Those were all good things, but she didn't know how long they would last.

As soon as they stepped into his cabin, Colton locked the door and then peered out the window again. His entire body looked tense and on alert.

"Is the man still there?" Sarah demanded, a surge of

anxiety rising in her. What if he came back? What if he killed all of them, just like he'd killed Loretta?

Colton's gaze remained focused out the window. "I don't see him. Was that the car that followed you?"

"I... I don't know. Maybe. It was so dark that I could really only see headlights. But whoever was driving the car just now left. What does that mean? If he knew I was here, wouldn't he have stayed?" Sarah walked toward the fire, unable to ignore just how cold she was and how badly her feet hurt.

"He may have been feeling this area out. If he lost you as you came down the road, then he may have come here looking for your car. He may be looking for confirmation."

"My car..." Sarah's heart skipped a beat. It had been out front, hadn't it? She hadn't been paying attention, but that was where she left it.

Colton looked back at her, his gaze softening. "I moved it behind the house, so he didn't see it. I don't think he saw you when you ran out either."

"He could have killed you." The words caught in Sarah's throat. No matter what had happened between the two of them in the past, she couldn't live with herself if something happened to Colton because of her.

"He could have. But, most likely, he doesn't know with certainty that I know you. If he knew you were here, he would have kept on going right to the house to find you and complete his mission."

"You think?" She shuddered. That had been close. So, so close.

"He was aggressive. He wouldn't have let me stop him."

"Maybe he'll move on now..." Sarah walked over

to the window and glanced out also, half expecting to see the car again.

Instead, the peaceful woods stared back, the early morning sky stretching above the frosted evergreens.

Colton's expression remained grim, as if he didn't want to give her false hope. "If he suspects you're in this area, then he'll keep on looking."

Sarah trembled again. "So what should I do?"

His jaw tightened with resolve as he continued to stare out the window, not saying anything for a minute. "We don't have any choice but to get out of here. We have to operate as if this is a worst-case scenario. That guy could come back—we don't want to be here if he does."

"We?" The words came out as a squeak, and Sarah's hand flew to her throat.

Colton nodded. "I can't send you out there alone, Sarah."

"I… I don't want to put you at risk." She'd pulled him into danger with her. What had she been thinking? Why had she come here? She would have been better off driving until her car couldn't make it any farther.

But when she'd thought of safety, Colton was the first person who had come to mind.

Colton stepped closer and lowered his voice. "You're not. I'm going with you, Sarah. Nothing you say will change my mind."

She didn't want to feel pleased. Didn't want to feel the shiver that rushed down her spine. Didn't want to find benefit in the thought that someone else was in harm's way.

But Sarah did feel relief wash through her.

Because she knew she couldn't do this on her own.

And Sarah *could* do it with Colton by her side. But their history was going to be their biggest obstacle.

Colton's eyes continually scanned the road as he traveled from his cabin into the majestic countryside. Snow-capped peaks surrounded him, along with rocky terrain and what in the summer months was a rollicking river.

These were the things he'd moved to the area for—the peace and serenity of wide-open spaces and clean air.

But right now, he found no joy in his surroundings. Not knowing what he did. Not with everything he'd learned that was going on with Sarah.

He hadn't seen the dark-colored sedan since he'd left his cabin twenty minutes ago, but he still didn't let down his guard. Someone who was determined to kill Sarah wouldn't give up that easily.

They'd left quickly. Sarah had packed up some of her old clothes, as well as a few extra supplies for Buzz, including a water dish. Colton had also packed a bag, as well as some snacks and water. He'd slipped Sarah's bloody clothing into the bottom of his duffel, just in case. He didn't want to leave them there for just anyone to discover.

Glancing in the backseat, he also saw that Sarah had grabbed the bag from her car. She didn't act suspicious, like she felt guilty about whatever was inside.

But Colton couldn't stop thinking about it. Maybe Sarah had sold a painting. Maybe she had a good explanation for having that kind of cash.

But what if she didn't?

He would ask her. Soon. When the time was right.

"Where are we going?" Sarah's arm snaked into the

backseat of his double cab, and she rubbed Buzz's head. She'd done that often since they left, and the dog's presence seemed to calm her.

She wore some old jeans and a blue flannel shirt. Her hair—wet when they'd left—had been pulled back into a bun. She had no makeup on, but she didn't need any. Her skin looked perfect just the way it was. Colton had given her an old jacket of his—a thick black one that would keep her warm outside. She'd also found some old boots in that trunk, back from when they used to go hiking together.

Colton glanced at Buzz again. He liked having the dog with them. The canine had perceptive eyes, and he always stood on guard. Without ever witnessing it, he could tell that Buzz would do whatever it took to protect Sarah.

"I think we should go back to Spokane," he told Sarah.

Sarah's wide eyes focused on him. "Spokane? Why would we go back there? Shouldn't we get as far away as possible?"

"A couple of reasons. First of all, I doubt this guy would think you'd go back."

"That could be true, I guess." She shrugged, still looking uncertain.

"Second, I think we need to figure out what happened to Loretta ourselves."

"Why would we do that?" Sarah's voice climbed with anxiety. "I mean, the police are looking for me. Won't they be more likely to find me there in Spokane?"

"I realize that, so we'll need to be careful. But I think the only way we're going to put this behind us is to find answers ourselves."

She gasped and paused before she said, "You think we should find the killer? Is that what you're saying."

"Yeah, I guess that's what I'm saying." Colton knew it sounded crazy, but he'd worked in law enforcement for more than a decade. If he trusted his instincts, he knew this was the right plan.

"How are we going to do that?"

Colton stared straight ahead as the sun peeked just over the trees, the new day settling in for a while. "We need to talk. I need more information."

"I can do that but…what about your work? I know you have a job. You can't just leave." Sarah sounded halfway panicked and halfway guilt ridden.

It was kind of her to be concerned about him. Sarah had always been sensitive and intuitive. It made her a great artist. She picked up on things that others didn't.

At one time, Colton had loved that about her.

"I'm just doing some woodworking right now, Sarah. I'm on sabbatical from my work in law enforcement."

"But—"

He glanced at her and shook his head, trying to nip this conversation in the bud. "No buts about it. Now, tell me more about your boss."

Sarah shifted, pulling her arm back into her lap and staring straight ahead at the road. "Loretta? I hardly know what to say. She was…she was esteemed in the medical community. She was a real genius."

"Did she have enemies?"

"I… I don't know. I mean, I didn't work for her that long, so I didn't get to meet many people who knew her. She was demanding and a perfectionist. I guess that's why she was good at her job. But she also had ALS. She was in a wheelchair. She didn't even have a chance to defend herself..." Sarah's voice broke as tears streamed down her face.

"I'm sorry, Sarah." Colton's heart squeezed with compassion. This situation would be a lot for anyone, but for someone as tenderhearted as Sarah it would be devastating.

"I just keep picturing her. I keep seeing her in her room, on the floor, with the man standing over her. It was so horrible, Colton." She sniffled again and used her sleeve to wipe beneath her eyes.

He reached over and squeezed her knee. Colton hadn't intended on touching Sarah, but he couldn't stand to see her looking so alone, especially considering what she'd been through. No one should have to be so isolated in their suffering—not when they had someone right beside them.

"Seeing that would be hard on anyone," he murmured.

Using her sleeve, Sarah wiped beneath her eyes again. "I've always known that there's danger in the world. But seeing it firsthand... I just can't stop thinking about it."

"We're going to get through this, Sarah." There Colton went again, promising Sarah things. Promising a future—no matter how potentially long or short. Their paths were intertwined, for now, at least.

Just as he said the words, a black sedan came into view behind him.

Colton pulled his hand back from Sarah's knee and gripped the steering wheel, his law enforcement training kicking into gear.

"What is it?" Sarah asked, glancing behind them. "Is that the car?"

"I don't know. But I'm not taking any chances."

SIX

Sarah gripped the door handle, her lungs frozen as she waited to see what would happen next. Would the driver try to run them of the road? Would he shoot? Try to kill them?

She had no idea. But each possibility made her head pound harder.

How had her life turned into such a nightmare? Things had just seemed to be getting back on track. She finally found a better place to live. Another job. All her mistakes seemed to be haunting her less and less.

And now this?

She glanced over her shoulder again. The sedan was still back there, but it wasn't close. No, the driver kept a decent distance behind them.

Maybe that was a good sign, an indication they'd be safe for a while longer. But Sarah knew the interlude wouldn't last for long. If Sarah had to guess, they were still forty-five minutes away from Spokane. The town was almost two hours from Colton's house, which was just north of Coeur d'Alene, Idaho.

Expertly, Colton began weaving in and out of traffic. The closer they came to Spokane, the more congestion they'd encountered. It was mostly commuters, some logging trucks and a few semis.

"What are we going to do?" Sarah couldn't seem to stop asking that question.

"We're going to lose them." Colton sounded so confident as he said the words. He always had that calm, soothing way about him. While everyone else panicked, he calmly assessed a situation and became the hero.

She gripped the door harder as her thoughts continued to race. "How did he even find us again? He wasn't back there when we left. I've been watching, and I know you have also."

Colton glanced in the rearview mirror. "He must be tracking you somehow. It's the only thing that makes sense."

"How in the world would he track me?"

"I only have one guess. Your phone."

"My phone…?" It made sense, Sarah supposed. The man had her number—he'd called her using Loretta's cell. The device had a GPS locater that he could have somehow tapped into, if he had the right skills or knowledge. "What should I do? Throw it out the window?"

"No, I have another idea. I don't think he knows for sure that we're in this truck." He eased into another lane.

"Why do you say that?"

Colton glanced in the rearview mirror again and pressed the accelerator harder. "It's just a hunch. He seems to be keeping his options open and staying behind several vehicles. I'm going to play a little game with him so I can know for sure."

Sarah nodded, her throat tight. She was going to have to trust Colton on this one because she had other ideas about what they should be doing.

* * *

As the road curved up ahead, Colton hit the accelerator and sped just out of sight. He turned at a large gas station and parked beside a semitruck. Moving quickly, he took Sarah's phone, instructed her to stay in the car, and then rushed out.

As Colton walked past the back of the semitruck, he nestled the phone in the back bumper of the vehicle. Based on the snug fit, it should stay there for a while.

He glanced around.

No one looked his way.

Moving quickly, Colton headed back to his car, jumped into the driver's seat and sped around to the back of the building to wait.

"Why are we staying here?" Sarah's voice sounded breathless with fear.

"I need to see what happens." The semi was just in his line of sight. He had to keep a careful eye on it. Otherwise, his plan would be all for nothing.

"If your guess is wrong, then we're sitting ducks," Sarah whispered.

Her words were a somber reminder. She was right. The stakes were high right now—it could cost them their lives. But he had to rely on his gut instinct at the moment. It was all he had.

"You're right," Colton said. "So let's hope I'm not wrong."

"Comforting." Sarah crossed her arms and slunk down lower.

Though Colton was just out of sight, he could still see the truck where he'd planted Sarah's phone. He watched carefully, waiting for the black sedan to appear.

His breath caught when he saw the car slowly creep into the parking lot and pull into a space.

Part of Colton wanted to get out and confront the driver right here. But he couldn't do that. The man could be dangerous—could have a gun and put other people at risk. No, Colton had other ideas right now—ideas that required patience.

"Colton?"

He raised a finger, asking for silence. "Just a minute."

He could feel the tension—the fear—in the car. Even Buzz seemed to notice. The dog stuck his nose into the front seat and sniffled, like he smelled danger was near.

A minute later, the semitrailer pulled out of the lot. Colton waited, watching to see what would happen next.

The sedan pulled out after it.

Sarah gasped. "Wait…"

"Someone *was* tracking the phone."

After giving the driver a good head start, Colton followed as he headed down the road. He wanted to follow this car. See who was inside.

Because the driver had some answers—answers they needed.

But there was also more than one way to figure out who was behind that wheel.

With his eyes on the car, he pulled out his phone and called a friend, Jim Larsen, with the highway patrol.

"Colton, what can I do for you?"

"Hey, Jim. I need you to run some plates for me for a case I'm working," Colton said. "Would you mind?"

"Not at all. What do you have?"

Colton rattled off the license plate.

"I'll do it right now. One second."

Colton waited, anxious to hear what Jim found out.

A moment later, his friend came back on the line. "Car belongs to a Randolph Stephens in Spokane."

"Randolph Stephens?" Colton repeated, glancing at Sarah.

She shrugged, indicating the name wasn't familiar.

"Anything else on this guy?" Colton asked.

"I don't see any priors. Not even a parking ticket."

"That's great. Thank you, Jim."

Colton ended the call. At least it was something. He'd take whatever information he could get right now.

Randolph Stephens?

Sarah turned the name over in her head as they continued down the highway.

Had Loretta ever said the name?

Sarah didn't think so. She'd probably remember a name like Randolph. It was unique enough that she didn't hear it often.

Colton handed her his phone. "Do me a favor. Do an internet search for me for this Randolph Stephens guy. Tell me if anything comes up or if he looks familiar."

Sarah took the device from him and stared at the screen a moment. "I need your code."

Colton swallowed so hard that his neck muscles pulled taut. "It's 0521."

"0521?"

"Yes," he confirmed.

That was supposed to be their wedding date. Sarah kept the thought to herself, not wanting to make this situation any more awkward than it had to be.

"I never got around to changing it," Colton muttered, his jaw muscle jumping.

"I get it." It was nothing, Sarah told herself. No, like

Colton said, he'd just gotten comfortable with the numbers and left them. That news didn't mean that he still cared about Sarah or that he still felt any heartbreak over their split.

Pushing aside her thoughts, Sarah typed in the name.

Only one person with the name Randolph Stephens popped up in Spokane. Sarah stared at the man's picture, hoping for a light bulb moment. But there was nothing. The dark-haired man with a receding hairline was unfamiliar to her.

"Here it is," Sarah told Colton. "Randolph is fifty-two years old, and he's an engineer. He volunteers for numerous organizations. Has a wife, three children and one grandchild, it looks like, according to his social media. This guy doesn't look like a killer."

"That doesn't mean anything. Is there any resemblance to the man you saw at Loretta's?"

Sarah shook her head. "In this picture, Randolph's wife looks taller than he is. The man I saw was big and burly. Not like this."

Colton frowned. "I see."

"But according to that state trooper you called, that car belonged to Randolph…"

"We'll have to look into it more a little later." Colton wove around some cars, trying to keep the sedan in sight.

"What?" Colton muttered, his gaze flickering to the right.

"What's wrong?" Sarah asked.

"He just turned off the highway," Colton muttered.

He accelerated back into the right lane, trying to get over before he missed the exit. The cars behind him laid on their horns. Colton wasn't swayed. He continued to follow the man who had once been following them.

Just then, another logging truck pulled in front of them. Sarah gasped as Colton pressed on the brakes and leaned to the side, trying to see around the truck.

"Is he still in eyesight?" Sarah asked.

Colton's jaw tightened. "It's no use. The whole lane is now blocked."

"You can't get around?" As Sarah asked the question, she glanced beside them. The road had a sharp drop-off.

There was no wiggle room to ease onto the shoulder.

And the logging truck had slowed as the road became an incline. As Colton slowed also, Sarah knew that they were losing the sedan.

Finally, they reached the top of the hill, and the road opened up again. Colton pulled his car into the left lane to pass the other vehicles.

But the sedan was gone.

Colton hit his hand against the steering wheel.

"We lost him," he muttered. "The driver either got off this road, or he's so far ahead that we won't be able to catch him."

"I'm sorry, Colton." Disappointment spread through Sarah. They'd been close. So close.

"The good news is that he also lost us."

"So we're safe?"

Colton frowned. "For a minute."

Sarah glanced at Colton and studied his expression— the set of his eyes and jaw. "But you don't think this is over, do you?"

He turned to her. "I think this is a long way from being over."

SEVEN

Colton's jaw tightened as he stared straight ahead at the road. He couldn't believe he'd lost the sedan. If only that logging truck hadn't cut in front of him. If only the road hadn't narrowed. If only the incline hadn't been so steep. But it had been.

And somehow the driver—along with their best lead for finding answers—had gotten away.

Sarah cleared her throat beside him. "Did you ever call any of your police contacts and see if you could find out anything about what happened? I know it's asking a lot but—"

"No, I haven't made any calls yet. But I will. Now." He had nothing to do but drive, and the sooner they had answers, the better.

"And, I hate to bring it up, but I'm going to need a restroom break before too long. Could we stop somewhere?"

"Yes, let's do that." Colton had planned on doing it sometime, but now, as they were getting closer to town, seemed like just as good a time as any.

He pulled up to a convenience store, a larger one that sold various items, and paused. "How about you go in alone, and I'll wait out here, keeping an eye out? Maybe I'll let Buzz stretch his legs also."

"That sounds good." She grabbed her purse. "I won't be long."

He watched as Sarah went into the store. There were several cars in the lot, so she wouldn't be the only person inside. Hopefully, no one would recognize her. Either way, Colton felt like he would serve her better by remaining lookout near the door.

It would also give him the chance to call one of his contacts and to speak freely.

He stepped out of the truck, Buzz's leash in hand, and wandered to a grassy area to the side of the building. As Buzz sniffed around, Colton dialed the number for Detective Ben Simmons, one of his contacts in Spokane. He'd worked with Simmons back in Seattle, and the two had a good relationship.

"Hello?" his friend's voice rang through the line.

"Hey, man. It's Colton."

After a couple minutes of chitchat, Colton swallowed hard. "Listen, I have two questions."

"Shoot."

"First, I was hoping you could do some research for me on a man named Randolph Stephens. He's from the Spokane area."

"What do you need to know?"

"Could you see if he's reported any vehicles that have been stolen?" Colton's gut told him that was what had happened, but he needed confirmation.

"Sure thing. What else?"

Colton shifted, entirely more uncomfortable with his next question. "I was watching the news, and I saw a story about that medical researcher who was killed in the area."

"Loretta Blanchard. Yes, it's a huge loss for our community. The woman was brilliant and respected."

"That is quite the loss," Colton said, watching as another car pulled into the lot. A woman with a young son scrambled toward the door. Still no signs of trouble. Good. "But I also heard that someone named Sarah Peterson was a person of interest."

"That's right. You sound like you know something…"

Colton shifted, still scanning everything around them. "I was actually engaged to Sarah. She couldn't have done this."

As he said the words, he knew they were true. Sarah was many things—but she wasn't a killer.

"How long ago did you say it had been since you were engaged?" Ben asked.

"Two years." Sometimes it seemed like just yesterday, and other times it seemed like another lifetime ago.

"Well, a lot could have changed in two years. Apparently, Ms. Peterson worked for Ms. Blanchard, but from everything I'm hearing, the two of them didn't really get along."

Colton sucked in a breath at the news. "Why do you say that?"

"That's the word from people who knew Loretta. Loretta was always fussing about her newest employee, saying she wasn't tidy enough. That she stayed out too late. That she got things done too slowly."

"Maybe Loretta was just a fussy type of person."

Ben let out a chuckle. "She was. I can assure you of that. But this woman—your ex-fiancée—comes on to the scene out of the blue and then Loretta was murdered. That in itself is suspicious."

"That doesn't mean she's guilty," Colton reminded him, the tension in his shoulders growing by the minute.

"Ms. Peterson's prints were found on the murder weapon."

"What murder weapon is that?"

"Some scissors. And about fifty thousand dollars of Loretta's money is gone. Loretta made a cash withdrawal earlier today, and it's no longer in her house. No one in her inner circle knows what she would have done with it."

He remembered the bag in Sarah's sedan. Could that have been…?

Colton shook his head. No. She wouldn't have done that. Sarah wasn't the type.

"The real killer could have taken it," Colton said.

"That's right. The real killer. And that may have been your ex-fiancée."

"There are a lot of assumptions here."

"We also found some of Loretta's jewelry in Ms. Peterson's room. We think she fled so quickly that she forgot to take it."

The killer had to have planted that jewelry. He was the one who'd taken that money. It was the only thing that made sense.

"Thanks for your help," Colton finally said.

"I appreciate you calling to offer your perspective. But your ex-fiancée is still our prime suspect."

"Good to know." He ended the call just as Sarah began walking back toward the truck.

He had some hard questions to ask her. He really hoped that the conclusion that wanted to form in his head was incorrect. Because he didn't want to think that Sarah had anything to do with Loretta's death... but the evidence was stacking up and becoming harder to ignore.

Sarah climbed back in the truck. As soon as she saw Colton's face, she sensed something was wrong.

He lowered his phone. What exactly had the phone call turned up? Whatever it was, it wasn't good.

"What happened?" she asked hurriedly. "Is something else wrong?"

Colton pressed his lips together, the same way he always did when he dreaded something. "Sarah, I have to ask you something, and I don't want to waste any words. Did you take money from Loretta?"

The blood drained from her face. "What? Colton—"

"I'm just asking." His eyes were level, as was his voice. He seriously wanted to know.

"You saw that threatening message," she reminded him. "You know I didn't do this."

His gaze locked on to hers. "Then why aren't you answering my question?"

"I did answer it."

"What was that bag in your car?"

"That bag in my car—" Sarah stopped short.

She'd grabbed Buzz's bag, only because it had been by the back door. She'd given it little thought since she'd taken it before leaving Loretta's house.

"What were you going to say, Sarah?" Colton asked her.

"Nothing of importance. I kept a backpack by the back door, and I always took it with me when I walked Buzz. I grabbed it on my way out."

"Have you looked inside?"

"Why would I? I haven't needed the treats or anything else. I've had other things on my mind."

"Look inside." Colton's words left no room for argument.

Sarah reached into the backseat of the truck, grabbed the bag and unzipped it. She gasped at what she saw inside. Reaching in, she pulled out a stack of one-hundred-dollar bills. "Where did this come from?"

"You didn't know it was there?"

"I had no idea. Why would Loretta put money in Buzz's bag, especially such a large amount?"

Colton stared at her.

Sarah's mouth gaped open as she realized what he wasn't saying. "What? You think I stole this and put it here?"

"I didn't say that. I'm just gathering information."

"Colton, you've got to believe me. I had no idea."

"Why *would* Loretta give you that much money? That much cash? There are thousands and thousands of dollars in there."

"I have no idea. To take care of Buzz, maybe? Buzz was her baby. She didn't have children, so the dog was her life."

"Is there anything you need to tell me?"

The pointedness of Colton's question caused a jolt of alarm to shoot through Sarah. "No, there's not. Why? What are you getting at?"

"Did you take some of your boss's jewelry?"

"No!" Her jewelry? Sarah sucked in a breath as she realized the truth. "I mean, yes. I mean—"

"What is it, Sarah?" Colton's tone made it clear he

was losing patience with her and beginning to doubt her story.

"It's not like that. I did have some of her jewelry. I was supposed to take it in to be cleaned. It was actually on my agenda for today—back before everything went haywire. I had the appointment at Goodwind's Jewelry. You can call and ask them. I had an appointment set up and everything."

"I may have to do that." His voice held a sharp edge and he turned away from her. He put the truck into Reverse, backed out and took off again down the road.

Panic began to rise in her. Sarah started to reach for Colton, but she stopped herself and swallowed hard instead. She had to convince him she was telling the truth—because she was.

"Colton, I know how this looks. But I didn't want her money. I'm not that kind of person."

"But you were having trouble. With your job. With making ends meet."

Heat rushed to Sarah's cheeks at the starkness of his words. "But I wouldn't steal. You know me better than that. Do you really think I would do that?"

"It's been two years, Sarah. I have to ask these questions."

She shook her head and looked away, unwilling to let Colton see her tears. She didn't think it would hurt this much to have Colton doubt her, but it did. "It's been two years, but you still know who I am. You know my character. At least, I thought you did."

Colton touched her knee, jolting her. "I'm sorry, Sarah. I'd be foolish not to ask. I really don't know what's happened in the years since I've seen you. That's the truth. People change whether we want to admit it or not."

"It's like I told you—I moved to Spokane and got a job at that art gallery. I don't have much money, but what I do have is mine and no one else's. I earned it rightfully."

"But you're not there anymore, are you? Or are you working more than one job?"

"No, I'm not working at that gallery anymore."

"Instead you moved in with someone and took on the side job of being her personal assistant and a caretaker to her dog. What happened?"

She frowned. "Let's just say that my boss at the art gallery didn't exactly hire me because he respected my knowledge of the art world."

Colton's eyes widened. "Did he proposition you?"

"He made it clear that he hired me because he thought I was nice to look at and that he hoped our relationship might grow into something more." Her stomach roiled as the words left her lips. "And, if it didn't, well... I couldn't expect my career to progress."

"What did you do?"

"I quit, of course." Her voice rose with outrage. "There was no way I could work for him anymore."

Colton's shoulders visibly relaxed. "It sounds like you made the right choice."

She nodded, heaviness pressing on her. "I know I did. But it was hard to find another job. John Abram—that was his name—called the other galleries in town and made up some lies about me."

"What kind of lies?"

"He said that I stole from him." She let out a bitter laugh and shook her head. "I know it sounds unbelievable that two people would say I'm guilty of stealing. But I didn't do it. At Loretta's or at John's. I was trying to do whatever I could to make ends meet and that's why I took a job working for Loretta."

"I'm sorry, Sarah." Colton's voice sounded soft and concerned.

She ignored the warm feelings that Colton's reaction brought—memories of better times. Of feeling loved and protected.

Those days were over, and she'd be wise to remember that.

"Life doesn't always turn out the way we expect, does it?" she murmured.

Colton shook his head. "No, it doesn't."

His words hung in the air, and neither was able to forget them.

Never in a million years would Sarah have thought she'd be running for her life. That such simple life choices could have such disastrous effects.

But now her life was on the line—and so was Colton's. Deep down inside, she wasn't confident either of them were going to get out of this alive.

EIGHT

As Colton continued to head down the road, he couldn't stop thinking about what Sarah had told him.

All he'd ever wanted to do was take care of Sarah. Yet she'd pushed him away. Made up an excuse about being unable to pass up her job offer. Said she couldn't see herself living in the country and away from life as she knew it.

Colton's heart had been crushed. He'd tried to talk her into staying, but her mind had been made up. She'd given him the engagement ring back and said goodbye.

But she'd been crying as she'd driven away. Colton had seen the tears.

Colton couldn't—and didn't—try to make Sarah do anything she didn't want to do. If Sarah stayed with him, then he'd wanted it to be because she chose to do so.

She'd made her choice two years ago. Once she'd walked away, Colton was done. He wasn't going to beg someone who didn't want to be a part of his life to remain a part of it. Colton's heart had been broken; he knew there was no going back.

He wasn't the type who easily forgot the sting of rejection. Sarah had made her choice.

But, as hard as all of that was and as resolute as he felt to stick with his convictions, he did want to be there for Sarah now.

Colton continued down the road, at once remembering how much he and Sarah had loved road trips together. On his time off, they'd taken trips to see the redwoods, to explore waterfalls, to marvel at mountains. She'd helped to open his eyes to the wonders around him and reminded him to take time to breathe.

Those times were behind him. A bittersweet memory.

Instead, he glanced at the road ahead. They were almost in Spokane now. Behind him, he could see the mountains where his home was nestled in his rearview mirror.

"So, what are we going to do when we get to Spokane?" Sarah asked, still looking shaken.

"I've been thinking about that. We're going to have to talk to some people who knew Loretta. We need to find out who her enemies were. It's the only way we'll get to the bottom of this."

"It makes sense."

He glanced at Sarah again, watching as the mountainside blurred past her window. "So, who did Loretta talk to? Did she go into an office? Did she have a circle of friends?"

Sarah wrapped her arms across her chest and frowned. "Loretta was a bit reclusive—at least, she was in the time I knew her. But…well, she worked in the office up until six months ago, from my understanding."

"What happened then?"

"Her health started to go downhill. She's had ALS for several years, but it took a turn for the worse recently. I think she was really struggling with the change and felt like she should be able to push through it. Finally, she realized she couldn't."

"Did she ever mention anyone from the lab?"

Sarah stared out the window and narrowed her eyes with thought. "There was one woman…her name was Debbie Wilcox. If I remember correctly, Debbie was the CFO of Loretta's company."

"Did you ever meet her?"

"No, I didn't. I only heard Loretta talking about her. Apparently, she was Loretta's right-hand woman. The two seemed close."

It was a starting place, at least. "What was the name of her company?"

"Blanchard Pharmaceuticals. Why?" Sarah turned toward him, her wide eyes searching his.

"I think we should start there. See what Debbie knows."

"What are you going to tell her? You're not officially on this case…"

Colton's jaw tightened as he thought through the legalities of everything. "I'll tell her that I'm investigating Loretta's death."

"What about me? When she sees me, she'll know the truth. My picture has been on the news." Sarah's voice cracked as she said the words.

"You're going to have to stay with Buzz. I don't like the idea of it, but we don't have any other choice. Yes, you are recognizable. But Buzz? Everyone's suspicions about you would be confirmed if they see him."

Sarah nodded and turned back toward the window. "I understand."

Sarah might understand, but Colton didn't like this situation any more than she did. But there was little he could do to change it at this point. No, they needed answers and they didn't have time to come up with a Plan B.

Sarah's life depended on Colton keeping her safe... and that was a task he didn't take lightly.

Apprehension continued to rise in Sarah as they drew closer to the Spokane area. What if someone here recognized her?

If the wrong person found her, she could be put away. For life.

It had happened to her mother. She'd been arrested for stealing money from her boss. She'd claimed she'd only done so in order to buy groceries, but prosecutors hadn't cared. She'd been given a five-year prison sentence, and Sarah and her sister had been put into foster care.

Sarah's mom had appealed. But, before anything could go through, she'd had a heart attack while in prison and died before ever seeing freedom again.

Sarah and her sister were forced to live alone in the system. Their dad had left when Sarah was six, and he hadn't reappeared in their lives.

Since all of that happened, trusting people hadn't come easily for Sarah.

When Colton had begun to pull away after a particularly heart-wrenching case, she'd seen the red flags. He'd never acknowledged the change in himself. No, he'd been in denial. But he'd become withdrawn. Aloof.

He still said he loved her, but Sarah knew the truth: love could turn on a dime. What one minute seemed like happily-ever-after could fade into a nightmare.

So it had been better that Sarah had just left. Gone away to start a safe life without anyone to hurt her.

But the decision still haunted her every day. Every day Sarah wondered how life could have turned out differently. If Colton would have bounced back from his last case. If they'd be happy together now.

It didn't matter. Those times were behind her now.

Colton put his truck in Park in front of the six-story building where Loretta worked. He reached into his glove compartment and pulled out a hat and sunglasses. "Put these on. Just in case anyone sees you."

A surge of panic rushed through Sarah. "What if the man in the sedan comes back…"

"He shouldn't have a way of tracking you right now. If you stay low, you should be okay." Colton thrust something into her hands. "But if someone approaches you, I want you to drive away."

"What about you?"

"I'll be fine."

"But—"

His gaze locked with hers. "No buts about it. If you see trouble, you leave. Understand?"

She nodded, though she felt anything but okay. His look didn't leave much room for argument. "How long will you be?"

"I have no idea, but I'll try to be quick." Colton lowered his voice. "We're going to figure this out."

He kept saying that. But Sarah had little hope that would happen. She knew how these things worked. She didn't have money to defend herself if the cops pressed charges.

She was going to end up like her mom. In jail until she died.

Her throat ached.

Instead of expressing those fears, she simply said, "Okay."

Colton stared at her one more moment before nodding. "I'll be back as soon as I can. Buzz, keep an eye on her for me, okay?"

Buzz nuzzled his hand in response.

Sarah watched as Colton disappeared inside the building. Then she slunk low in her seat and watched everyone around her. The office building was located in the downtown area so plenty of people were out and about, going to and from their office buildings.

No one seemed to be staring at them. Thank goodness.

She'd been to this area many times. Mostly there were offices but, just two blocks away, there were some restaurants. One block in the opposite direction there was a little park with some trails cut through small wooded areas, a playground and a breathtaking view of the river.

She'd taken some walks there when she'd worked for the gallery. She'd gone there often to clear her head. To get away from the terrible John Abram who'd hired her not for her brain but for her looks.

Minutes ticked by.

Sarah glanced at her watch. It was just after eleven.

Behind her, Buzz let out a whine. She turned toward him and rubbed his head.

"What is it, boy?"

He whined again.

That's when she realized that he probably had to go to the bathroom. They'd been in the truck for a long time. And Buzz had eaten the same dog food every day without change for the past four years. The unexpected change in his meals was bound to upset his stomach.

Sarah frowned. "Can't you wait for Colton to get back?"

He barked.

"No, hush." She tried to silence him by rubbing his head. "Don't draw any attention to us."

He barked again, louder this time. The canine probably sensed her panic, which only added to his anxiety right now.

This wasn't good.

Sarah glanced around. One person—a businessman with a briefcase—glanced their way.

"What are you doing, Buzz?" she murmured. "You're going to have to wait. You can do that, can't you?"

He barked even louder.

Buzz couldn't wait, Sarah realized. He was going to keep barking until he got out to relieve himself.

With a tremble raking through her hands, Sarah knew she was going to have to leave the truck for a moment. She couldn't risk Buzz drawing too much attention to them with his barking. Besides, it was cruel to make him hold it.

She glanced around and still saw no one suspicious.

With trepidation, Sarah opened her door, bracing herself to venture out for a few minutes.

She hoped she wouldn't regret this.

NINE

Colton waited for a moment in the lobby as the receptionist called up to Debbie Wilcox.

The office of Blanchard Pharmaceuticals had spared no expense with this building. The walls appeared to be marble and all the decorations were slick. The atmosphere contained an air of professionalism—and mourning. Numerous people had walked past with tissues in their hands, whispering quiet condolences to any and everyone they passed.

As he waited, he put in a call to Goodwind's Jewelry. Though he wanted to believe Sarah, he wanted to verify what she'd told him. Sure enough. She did have an appointment there today.

Relief swept through him.

Good. He felt better knowing Sarah was being open with him.

A few minutes later, Colton was called up to Debbie's office. The mood around him seemed even more somber on this floor. Was everyone here mourning the death of their CEO? Were they trying to regroup? Were they theorizing about what had happened?

At the direction of a receptionist, Colton walked

down a short hallway, knocked on a door and then stepped into an office. A woman sat behind a desk there, a pile of tissues filling the trash can beside her chair.

Debbie Wilcox was probably in her late thirties with dark hair, stylish glasses and a trim business suit. She looked up from her desk and offered a professional smile. But her red eyes showed she'd taken Loretta's death hard also.

"How can I help you?" she asked, lacing her fingers together.

Colton stood in front of her and paused. "I'm looking into the death of Loretta Blanchard, and I'm hoping you can help me."

Debbie balled another tissue in her hands before raising an eyebrow. "And you are?"

"I'm Colton Hawk. I'm a former Seattle detective." He pulled out his ID and showed her. "I don't have a badge, but I can assure you that I'm legit."

She took his ID from him and examined it a moment before handing it back. With a touch of weariness in her voice, she asked, "What do you need to know? I thought the police already had a suspect. That's what the news is making it sound like."

"They do have a person of interest, but I believe they should look into other possibilities, as well."

She leaned back in her leather chair and crossed her arms, almost seeming resigned. "Whatever you need to know. Loretta was a good woman, and she'll be missed by everyone here. Her death is a huge loss to the medical community."

It sounded like a standard public relations script. Colton needed more than that. "Did she have any enemies?"

"Any enemies?" Debbie thought about it for a moment, ignoring the phone as it rang on her desk. "I think *enemy* would be a strong word. Loretta was a hard woman to love. She was smart, confident and brisk. She didn't let people into her inner circle. People admired her, but I'm not sure many wanted to be her friend."

"I see." Colton could easily picture the kind of woman Loretta was. He'd met the type before. And the description matched what Sarah had already told him.

"Did she make anyone mad?"

Debbie shrugged. "There are people she's fired throughout the years. But more recently, she had other people handling those kinds of unpleasant situations for her. Although, I can make you a list, if that would help."

"It would."

"I suppose she also had competitors. I wouldn't say enemies, but as I'm sure you probably know, the drug business is big business."

"So I've heard."

"I'd say our biggest competition here at Blanchard Pharmaceuticals would have to be the folks over at Danson Tech."

Danson Tech? Colton vaguely recognized their name. Maybe from a commercial on TV or something? "Where is Danson Tech based out of?"

"It's funny, actually. They're based out of Coeur d'Alene. It's unusual to have two companies so close together, but the company's founder, Yvonne Warner, was actually Loretta's roommate while in college."

"Isn't that interesting." Colton had no idea they had such a personal connection. That very well could lead to Yvonne being his number-one suspect.

Debbie raised her eyebrows. "It is, isn't it? And if

you're wondering if Yvonne is responsible, you should know that she was out of the country helping sick children in Africa. It's been documented all over the web."

"Good to know." He had thought about seeking her out next. At least he could save some time and not do that—after he verified the information.

She sat up and straightened some papers on her desk, a silent cue that she was ready to wrap up this conversation. "Other than that, I'm not sure. Loretta didn't talk about her personal life very often. Now I can see I should have pressed more. Maybe if I had, this wouldn't have happened." The woman's facade cracked as her eyes filled with moisture.

"What do you mean?" Colton asked, his curiosity spiking.

"I just mean that it's a shame the woman had to hire someone," Debbie said. "Loretta paid that woman to do things a friend should have been able to do for her— help with groceries, housework, act as a companion. She worked hard for her entire life, but it boiled down to her having no one. It's sad, really."

"It does seem unfortunate, especially for someone who was so esteemed in the community."

"She told me one time that I should hold my friends close but my enemies closer. It's an old saying, I know. But when Loretta said it, she looked like she meant it. Like she'd lived it."

That was interesting. Just what kind of enemies did Loretta have? And which ones had been disguised as friends? "That's good to know. Thanks so much for your time."

Colton had stepped away when Debbie called him back. He paused and turned toward her.

Debbie's gaze locked on to his. "I hope you find who-ever did this to her. And if you need anything else, don't hesitate to call. Everyone here wants to figure this out and see Loretta get the justice she deserves."

Sarah tugged on Buzz's leash and glanced around the city sidewalk.

No one appeared to be watching them—that she could see. Still, she had to play it safe. There was too much at stake right now.

She pushed her sunglasses up higher, tugged her baseball cap down lower and led Buzz to the park.

She wished she could call Colton and tell him where she was going. But she no longer had a phone. Hope-fully, she'd let Buzz go do his business and then return before Colton got back.

There were no green areas around here, which only left the park. It wasn't far away—it was a block away. And although the day was brisk, thankfully she had her coat on.

Colton's coat.

When she pulled it close, she caught whiffs of his scent. His leathery aftershave.

How she missed that scent. How she missed Colton.

The thought nearly stopped her cold. No, she didn't miss Colton. She missed the *idea* of what they could have been. But she was better off alone. Better off not getting her heart broken again.

Sarah and Buzz reached a lovely park filled with walking trails, a river and a little playground.

"Go ahead, Buzz," she murmured. "We don't have much time."

As the dog sniffed around, Sarah remained on guard for any signs of trouble.

She'd seen that man standing over Loretta. Sarah had gotten to her room too late—he'd already given her that fatal wound. Sarah knew he wouldn't hesitate to do the same to her. Her only comfort was that she was in public. Certainly there was some safety to be found in that.

Despite her reassurances, her arms still trembled.

It was too bad, really. This place was so beautiful.

Sarah had always wanted to come here and practice her watercolors. At the time, she'd felt like the future was flung wide open ahead of her with grand possibilities waiting at every turn. No longer.

Now, her future seemed bleaker than the gray day around her.

Buzz sniffed around the grass, around a tree.

Sarah silently willed the dog to hurry up. But she knew it would do no good. Soon enough, Buzz would do his business, and they could return to the truck, to safety.

Buzz pulled her farther down a walking trail and finally paused beside a tree.

As Sarah waited, her skin crawled, and she swung her head around.

Was that her internal instincts telling her that something was wrong?

She didn't know for sure, but she didn't want to take any chances.

"Come on, Buzz."

Sarah glanced around again but saw no one suspicious. A businessman strolling with a phone to his ear.

A mother chasing two young children. Another man walking his dog.

Everything seemed normal.

Just as the thought entered her mind, Buzz let out a low growl.

Even Buzz knew something was wrong.

But what? What—or who—was the source of this danger?

Sarah tugged on Buzz's leash, suddenly anxious to leave. "We need to get out of here, boy."

But as she started back toward the truck, she heard a bullet whiz past her.

Someone was shooting at her, she realized. And the shot had narrowly missed her.

That time.

TEN

Colton glanced around as he left the building for Blanchard Pharmaceuticals.

While his talk with Debbie Wilcox hadn't been overly enlightening, he had gotten some insight as to Loretta's personal life—or lack thereof. The woman was brilliant but lonely. A genius yet difficult. A force to be reckoned with and someone a person didn't want to get on the bad side of.

He still needed to remain on guard right now. Though he'd lost the person following them earlier, this guy who'd killed Loretta and who was now chasing them obviously had resources. It was the only way he'd be able to track Sarah's phone and follow them.

Colton knew they needed to stay on the move if they were to stay alive—which was why he was anxious to get back to Sarah right now.

As soon as he saw his truck parked at the curb, he sucked in a breath.

Why didn't he see Sarah or Buzz? Were they slumped down low?

His gut told him no, told him that they were gone. But he needed to confirm before acting on anything.

Colton quickened his steps even more. As he reached his truck, he peered inside. It was just like he thought: empty.

What had happened to them?

He glanced around the sidewalks at the crowds who wandered from place to place. The businesspeople. The shoppers. A few college students.

There was no sight of Sarah or Buzz. Sarah might blend in, but Colton would spot that husky anywhere— yet Buzz was nowhere to be seen.

Jogging, Colton hurried to the intersection and glanced down the street.

They weren't there either.

Sarah and Buzz couldn't have gone but so far. Colton was only inside the building for fifteen minutes, and there was no sign of a struggle in his vehicle.

His gaze scanned the signs in front of him.

The Riverfront.

Would Sarah have taken Buzz there? It was worth checking out.

Colton's jog became a run as he hurried down the street. With each step, his apprehension grew until his muscles felt tight enough to break.

Please, Lord, let Sarah be okay. Buzz too. I don't know why You brought Sarah back into my life, but whatever the reason, don't snatch her away yet. Please.

Colton dodged across the street and stopped in the middle of a grassy area. He desperately hoped to find Sarah and Buzz here.

Still not spotting them, he darted toward a walking trail in the distance. As he did, he heard barking.

Buzz?

It had to be.

He quickened his steps, but another sound sliced through the air.

Gunfire.

People around him screamed and ran away.

He had to find Sarah.

Now.

Just as he stepped onto the other side of some bushes, he spotted Sarah. Terror stretched across her face as she turned toward something in the distance.

Just as another bullet rang out, Buzz jumped on her, pushing Sarah to the ground, to safety.

But Colton had a feeling this wasn't over yet.

Sarah hit the icy ground just as another bullet whizzed past. Her heart pounded out of control as she waited for what would happen next. Buzz stood on top of her, a low growl emerging from deep in his chest.

People around her ran, scattered, fled for their lives.

She needed to run, but she was too scared to rise. Fear paralyzed her. Fear of running. Fear of staying.

She should have never left the truck.

"Sarah, are you okay?" someone whispered above her.

She looked up.

Colton…he'd found her. He knelt beside her now, but his gaze remained fixated on something in the distance.

The shooter, she realized.

She nodded quickly, fearing for Colton's safety. "I'm fine."

"Buzz, stay with her," Colton said. "Meet me back at the truck in five."

He took off in a run toward the trees.

He was going after the shooter, Sarah realized.

Oh, dear Lord. Watch over him. End this nightmare. I beg You.

As she heard frosty foliage rustling in the distance, she realized the shooter was running.

She nudged Buzz off from atop her and stood, wiping the snow from her knees.

"Are you okay?" a woman asked, keeping her distance yet her eyes filled with concern.

Sarah nodded, trying not to draw any attention to herself. That was the last thing she wanted—for someone to recognize her. "Yes… I'm fine. Thank you."

She had to get out of here. Now. Before the cops showed up.

She couldn't go to jail for Loretta's murder. Not right now especially. She needed answers first, and she wouldn't find them in a cell.

Colton had said to meet at his truck. That's what she needed to do.

With another nervous glance around, she grabbed Buzz's leash. They began walking at a brisk pace down the sidewalk. Sarah wanted to run, but stopped herself, giving a silent reminder that she should attempt to blend in.

The Riverfront area felt strangely normal and unaffected considering what had just happened. A few people still fled from the scene. Others were clueless about the gunshots that had rung out. Others moved on briskly, acting as if their schedules were too busy to be bothered by a crime that they had no direct involvement in.

Sarah couldn't see the area where Colton had run.

Had he caught the man? What if the man had caught Colton?

Panic tried to swell in her, but Sarah attempted to hold it at bay.

Instead, she glanced again at the winter wonderland around them. Her breath came out in icy poofs in front of her face.

It appeared the situation had de-escalated. People's panic had quickly receded, other than a few who had been right there.

No one looked at her now. All the people who'd been there during the shooting seemed to have scattered.

In the distance, sirens wailed louder.

The cops were on their way. If they saw her...

Sarah picked up her pace.

She walked the first block, each step feeling safer. She knew she couldn't let down her guard, though. Too much was at stake.

Finally, she reached the truck without incident. She and Buzz climbed into the front seat and ducked down low, so they wouldn't be spotted. But, at any minute, Sarah half expected the gunman to find her. To knock at her window. For a bullet to shatter the glass above her.

No, she couldn't think like that. She just needed to wait for Colton.

Where was he?

What would Sarah do if Colton didn't get back? She didn't care about the man romantically anymore, but she didn't want something to happen to him.

Or *did* she still care about him? Had she ever stopped?

Her heartbeat sounded like a deafening throb in her ears.

She'd have to think about that at another time. Right now, she needed to focus on surviving. She petted

Buzz's head as he lay in the back of the truck beside her. Thank goodness the windows were tinted, offering another layer of concealment.

The police sirens wailed closer.

Sarah held her breath, desperate to know if the police were coming for her. If someone had secretly been watching and reported her. Panic climbed higher and higher until she felt like she couldn't breathe.

In only a few seconds, she'd learn whether the police were coming for her or not.

The sirens wailed closer...and kept going.

Sarah released her breath.

Thank You, God.

As she shifted on the floor, something pressed into her side.

The truck keys Colton had given to her. He'd told her to leave if she had to.

Would that be now?

But she didn't want to leave Colton behind. What if she couldn't find him? What if he was hurt? Arrested?

Jitters filled her stomach.

She needed to make a decision and quickly.

Just then, the driver's side door jerked open.

Sarah craned her neck to get a glimpse of who it was, fearing it might be the killer. The police. Instead, it was Colton.

Steely eyed. Jaw set with determination. Movements confident but urgent.

And he looked okay. He was alive and unharmed.

Her shoulders sagged with relief.

She handed him the keys, and he jammed them into the ignition.

Two seconds later, they took off, headed away from trouble…hopefully.

ELEVEN

Colton pulled off from the curb where he'd parked, desperate to get away before anyone saw them and pointed them out to the cops. His hands were white-knuckled on the steering wheel as he wove between cars on the street, his mind racing as he processed what happened.

"Why in the world did you get out of the truck, Sarah?" As the question left his lips, Colton glanced in the rearview mirror, searching for police cars or the black sedan from earlier.

He saw nothing.

"Buzz…he had to go to the bathroom," Sarah said, stroking the dog's head. "He started barking, and I was afraid he was going to draw attention to us. I didn't know what else to do, and I couldn't call you. I'm sorry."

Hearing the sincerity of Sarah's words eased some of the tension in Colton's shoulders. "It's okay. I'm not blaming you. I just… I just thought you were gone."

"Thank you for actually looking for me when you could have easily just let me go."

There was something in Sarah's tone that made Colton pause.

Did she think Colton had let her go too easily before? Did she think it was easy to watch her walk away? Because it had torn him up inside—torn him up for months until he'd lost weight and hardly been able to sleep.

But this wasn't the time to talk about those things, not when their lives were on the line. Their past could wait.

"Did you see the man who shot at me?" Sarah asked.

Colton's jaw clenched tighter as he remembered the chase. As he remembered rushing across the icy ground, trying to capture the shooter. For a moment, he'd felt so close. "There was a car waiting on the other side of those trees. He jumped inside and sped off."

Sarah frowned. "Same car that followed us?"

"Yes, it was."

"So he somehow found us."

"Or maybe he assumed you might come here." Colton's words rang out in the truck.

"I don't even know who this person is. I don't know how he can predict anything about where I am." Sarah glanced at Colton, her eyes full of questions. "What about Debbie? Did she tell you anything?"

Colton wished he had more to share, that they'd made more progress during these first few hours. "Just that Loretta was a bit of a loner."

"That's right. She was. She enjoyed being by herself. That's what she said, at least."

"Now that you've had more time to think about it, did Loretta talk about anyone? Talk to anyone?"

Sarah shrugged, then shook her head. "The landscaper maybe. She loved talking about flowers and herbs with him."

"Who's the landscaper?"

"His name is…" Sarah paused again and then snapped her fingers. "Frank Mills. He was always working outside. He would probably have some insight into things—into Loretta."

It was a place to start, at least. "Any idea where this Frank Mills lives?"

"Actually, I do remember. He lives in Bellamy Acres on the north side of town. I only remember because one of the artists at the last gallery I worked at lives there. Despite the name, it's full of little craftsman-style houses on small lots."

"Maybe we should pay him a visit," Colton said. "See what he knows."

"I think that's a great idea. But if he sees me…" Sarah's voice grew distant, and Colton heard the tremble there.

"We need to convince him you're not guilty."

Sarah nodded. "I'm game. I just want this to be over. I want answers. And I want to stop living in fear."

"Then let's do this."

Sarah's hands felt sweaty as they pulled into Frank's neighborhood. It was just like she remembered it—full of character yet understated. She always thought that if she was able to buy a house, she'd like one like this. She wanted something cozy and warm.

Or like Colton's place with its high ceiling, log beams and natural stone fireplace.

The thought surprised her. But his cabin had felt homey, and it had been nice to breathe the fresh air. To see nothing but mountains. To feel like the world wasn't closing in on her.

Sarah never wanted a lot in life. She didn't care about

being rich or acquiring material things. But she did value security. Having a safe place to live. She'd had so very few of those things.

Everything Sarah held close—what little she had—had been turned upside down. Or stripped away. It was like she'd always known that she only had herself to depend on.

"Looks like Buzz was a lifesaver back there," Colton said, glancing behind him.

Sarah followed his gaze and rubbed Buzz's head as he panted beside her. "Yes, he really was. It was like he sensed danger was close. In fact, I might not be around right now if it wasn't for Buzz. He pushed me out of harm's way."

"He's a smart dog. You can see it in his eyes."

"Loretta picked him, and she was a smart lady."

"She picked you too." Colton stole a glance at her.

Sarah shrugged, wishing she could believe Colton's words. But she felt so worn down. Like she'd made so many bad decisions. And now everyone thought she'd killed Loretta. When would she ever catch a break?

"I mean it, Sarah," Colton continued. "Loretta chose you for a reason. She saw something in you."

"Thanks." Her throat ached as the words left her lips. His words had touched her more than she anticipated. Just having someone who believed in her, it meant more than she wanted to acknowledge.

Why was Colton being so nice to her now? It reminded her of when they'd first started to date. She'd been over-the-moon happy to be with him. Those months were some of the best of her life, leading right up to the moment Colton had proposed to her.

Then Colton had been forced to shoot the intoxicated,

belligerent man on his last case. Colton had become withdrawn. Distant. He stopped opening up to her and wanted to spend more time by himself. And he always got that distant look in his eyes, like he was physically with her but not mentally or emotionally.

Sarah was able to see the writing on the wall. She'd sensed the change.

It wasn't that he was mean. Colton wasn't that kind of guy. But he'd definitely pulled away.

Just like her dad had pulled away before he left Sarah's life forever. She couldn't put herself through that again.

She *wouldn't*.

Colton pulled to a stop in front of Frank's home—they'd looked up his address on the way here—and put the truck in Park. Sarah glanced over at the house. The cozy-looking home was painted white with blue shutters. Snow surrounded the structure, and all it needed was smoke puffing from the chimney, and it would have looked like it belonged in a storybook.

Behind the house, she barely caught a glimpse of the snow-capped mountains that she so dearly loved. They could inspire a thousand paintings, and then some.

"I think you should come with me to talk to Frank," Colton said.

Surprise raced through her. "If the police see me with you, your career could be in jeopardy, Colton."

"I can handle whatever is thrown at me."

She raised her eyebrows, surprised that Colton was willing to risk so much. Should she even let him? She didn't know. Instead, she said, "Thank you, Colton."

"It's no problem." He nodded toward the door, always

the perfect gentleman—the ideal mix of tough and tender. "Now let's go see if we can find some answers."

She climbed out behind him and called Buzz. The dog trotted out from the truck and fell into step beside her, nuzzling the snow before sneezing.

Buzz had always seemed to love these conditions. Sarah remembered him frolicking outside on more than one occasion. But not now. Buzz seemed to know—to sense—everything that was going on.

Another rush of nerves went through Sarah as they climbed onto the porch and a chilly breeze swept over the landscape, invading her clothing until she shivered again. Colton rang the front bell, and they waited. Sarah glanced around, anxiety continuing to rise with every second that passed.

Frank's truck was in the driveway. He was obviously home. So why wasn't he answering the door? Had he spotted them through the window and called the police?

Sarah glanced at Colton. He didn't seem nervous.

She really should follow his lead and try to remain calm in this trying situation.

Except she and Colton were opposites. They always had been. Sarah was the emotional, intuitive one. Colton had been the calm, logical thinker. At one time, she'd thought they complemented each other perfectly.

The sound of the doorbell chiming inside drew her attention back to the present. Two more attempts later, no one answered.

Colton turned to her. "Let's check around back, just in case."

Sarah glanced at the beautifully manicured flower beds as they passed. Frank definitely had a gift for working with plants. Even in the winter, they looked lovely with the evergreens he'd chosen and artfully arranged.

She knew the man was single, but she wasn't sure if he had any kids or not. Frank never talked about them, and gardening seemed to be his life. He'd come across as nice and friendly—more welcoming than most of the people in Loretta's world.

Sarah followed Colton on the sidewalk to the back of the house, her boots crunching on the icy snow.

The only other prints out here were hers, Colton's, and Buzz's. However, a fresh snow had fallen last night, so maybe Frank hadn't left his house all day. Maybe he'd heard about Loretta and had taken some time to mourn.

Sarah paused just for a minute as she stepped into the backyard. This area looked just as lovely as the front, including a gazebo and a little bridge that crossed what must be a man-made pond that had now frozen over.

"This is fabulous, isn't it?" Sarah murmured aloud, her artist's mind already painting pictures of it.

"Yes, it really is. He has a gift, for sure, and I can see why Loretta chose him." Colton kept walking toward the garage on the other side of the yard.

"I think that's why I liked Frank so much. He and I both had an artistic side to us, you know?"

"I can see that." Colton paused by the garage door. "Let me just check inside. If he's not there, we'll move on."

"Okay."

Sarah followed behind Colton, but nearly collided with him at the garage door.

"What's wrong?" Sarah asked, trying to peer over his shoulder.

Colton held his hand up, stopping Sarah from going any farther.

"No wonder he didn't answer the door," Colton said.

Sarah scooted around him, desperate to see with her own eyes what he was talking about.

Frank lay on the floor of his garage, blood seeping from what appeared to be a bullet wound in his chest.

Her hand went over her mouth to cover the O of horror there. No, not Frank...not another person who'd lost his life...

Nausea roiled in her gut as the direness of the situation hit her full force.

How were they ever going to get out of this alive?

TWELVE

Colton's stomach tightened as he knelt on the frigid cement floor of the garage beside Frank's prone body. He touched the man's wrist, feeling for a pulse. As Colton suspected, there was none.

His skin was cold—ice-cold. Based on how the man looked, Colton would guess that he'd probably been dead several hours already. Even his blood, pooled on the floor, had frozen.

A gun lay beside him, near his hand, almost like he'd dropped it.

Frank looked like he was probably in his early sixties with gray hair and a fit build. He didn't have the face of a killer—not that that meant anything. No, he looked like a grandfather.

"Did he kill himself?" Sarah asked, her hand still over her mouth, covering the horror on her face. She'd seen two dead people within the past twenty-four hours, and she'd probably never seen a murder victim until then. This was bound to be hard on her.

Colton stood and stared down at Frank, his chest tightening at what seemed like such a senseless act, whether it was suicide or murder. "I don't know. The gun makes it appear that way, doesn't it?"

Sarah cast a sharp glance his way. "Wait, do you think someone set him up?"

Colton's jaw tightened. "I'm not assuming anything right now. But I need to let the police know what's going on."

"The police?" Panic laced her voice. "But you can't call the police."

Colton knew how delicate this situation was, and he was torn between his duty as a former cop and his loyalty toward the woman who'd broken his heart. Above all, he had to do the right thing. That was most important.

"I'm going to have to take you and Buzz somewhere safe," Colton finally said, after thinking things through for a minute. "But, Sarah, I can't not report this. Every second counts when it comes to a crime like this. If someone killed Frank, time is of the essence."

"I understand." Her voice sounded compassionate and resolute but also fearful.

It was understandable. Anyone in her shoes—falsely accused of murder and the target of a killer—should feel a good dose of fear.

"I'll make sure you're secure first, okay?" Colton told her.

He would do everything within his power to make sure that Sarah didn't get hurt. To ensure that she was protected and safe. Heartbroken or not, he couldn't live with himself if he allowed harm to come to her.

Sarah nodded but looked unconvinced.

This wasn't the way Colton liked to do things, but he didn't have much of a choice right now. He had to protect Sarah—but he also had to act as an officer of the law.

"The sooner we go, the better," Colton said. "I want to keep things on the up-and-up as much as I can."

Sarah's gaze remained fixated on Frank, her skin growing paler every second she stood there. Buzz nuzzled her hand, as if trying to cheer her up.

Colton needed to get her out of here before the trauma of the situation hit her even harder. The sooner they left, the better. "Let's go."

He placed a hand on her back to lead her away, afraid she might pass out. But she kept moving, one foot in front of the other—almost robotically—until they reached his vehicle.

They climbed back in Colton's truck. He'd find a hotel for her to stay in, and once he knew she was safe, he'd come back out here.

For now, he started the ignition and pulled out of the neighborhood. He'd need to go somewhere secluded, somewhere Sarah would be a safe enough distance from this whole mess, just in case things went south.

"I can't believe he's dead," Sarah said as she sat beside him, looking dazed. Maybe even in shock.

But at least she was talking. It was when Sarah stopped communicating and started to bottle everything up inside that he got worried. That was what had happened right before she'd left. It was like she'd made her mind up, that she'd buried her fears and concerns, and self-preservation had won out.

Against Colton's better instincts, he reached over and squeezed Sarah's hand. He tried to let go, but he couldn't. Something about feeling her fingers in his brought back better memories of their past—the memories that he missed. Memories of the good times. Memories he should try to forget.

"I'm sorry you had to see that, Sarah," he said softly.

"This is bad, Colton." She squeezed his hand also, not looking the least bit inclined to let go. She probably wasn't thinking clearly or she would have.

In the meantime, he wouldn't argue. It felt good to feel her soft fingers intertwined with his—if only briefly. He'd never admitted it, but he missed these moments.

He missed Sarah.

"I know," Colton finally said. "It is bad."

There was no need to skirt around the truth. They were both in an impossible situation right now, and it was going to take every ounce of their strength and wits to get through it.

"I didn't want any of this," she continued. "All I wanted was…"

"What did you want, Sarah?" Colton honestly needed to know. He'd asked himself that question about Sarah for two years now. He just couldn't figure out her endgame.

"I wanted a safe place," she said quietly.

"I wasn't safe?" Colton hadn't meant for the question to slip out, but it had.

"Colton—" She started to explain.

Before she got any further with whatever she was about to say, Colton realized what a mistake that might be to continue this conversation. "Never mind. It's okay. I don't know why I asked."

He pulled into the parking lot of a cheap motel with outside entrances for each room—which would probably work in their favor—especially with Buzz.

Sarah opened her mouth like she might respond but shut it again. It was just as well. Because there was nothing she could say that would change things. No, the damage had already been done, and there was no reversing it as far as Colton was concerned.

Sarah leaned back on the bed, biding her time until Colton returned. Buzz seemed to feel the same way. He looked rather mopey as he lay at her feet. He wasn't relaxing; it was almost like he was pretending to for her sake.

"You're a good boy," she murmured, stroking his head. "You've been my saving grace. What would I do without you?"

He nuzzled her hand.

"You've always been there for me." Her words were true. Throughout everything that had happened, Buzz had been the one she shared her deepest secrets with as she took him on walks and brushed his fur. He'd almost become like a best friend.

"You know about all my mistakes and you still love me," she continued. "And you know what? I can't see you ever leaving me. I can't say that about many people."

He let out a long sigh.

She rubbed his head once more before glancing around.

She hated this hotel already. It smelled old, like a mix of dust and mildew. The quilt on the bed was probably thirty years old with an orange-and-brown pattern. The carpet was matted, beige and stained.

At least the location was off the beaten path. Woods and mountains lined the back of it, and a small stream, now frozen, had at one time cascaded along the edge of the property.

There were more glimpses here of God's majesty. They were everywhere when people just opened their eyes to it. But even despite that reminder, Sarah still felt an unrest at being here alone while Colton went out to take the bullets for her.

She wished she had a cell phone or computer or… that she could do something.

But there was nothing to do but wait.

Every time she closed her eyes, she saw images of Frank. Dead. With blood on his chest.

Poor Frank.

Poor Loretta.

Whatever was going on here, it was bigger than Sarah had ever imagined.

And now she was in the middle of it.

She glanced at her watch. Colton had been gone an hour. What was taking so long? What if he never returned? What if he turned her in and told the police she was here?

No, Sarah couldn't think like that. Because no matter what their past history was, Colton wasn't that kind of guy.

Although she would still love to know what was going on.

But she didn't have her phone anymore. She had no way of communicating or even checking in on the outside world.

At the thought of it, she straightened. A memory hit her.

Loretta had sent her an email yesterday evening. Sarah had been at the art show. She'd only glanced at her inbox and had seen the email come in. She hadn't bothered to check it and had told herself she would do so later.

What if Loretta had emailed her something that would give insight about what had happened to her? This could be the breakthrough they'd been looking for.

But how was Sarah going to get that email?

She nibbled on the inside of her lip as she thought through the question.

There had been a computer in an office beside the reception area of the motel. It was the kind meant for businessmen and women or travelers who needed to print tickets and such.

If Sarah could get there and hop on really quick, then maybe she could discover something.

She glanced at Buzz. "What do you think, buddy?"

He stared at her.

He clearly thought it was a bad idea.

But that didn't deter Sarah.

Maybe she just needed something to do to keep her mind occupied. Maybe this was the clue they'd been looking for.

"I can't take you with me," she muttered, rubbing the dog's head. "Can you stay here and be a good boy?"

Buzz whined, as if he understood.

"I'll only be a minute. I promise."

He whined again. Even Buzz thought this was a dangerous plan.

She wanted to read that email. And what better time than now while Colton was occupied?

Sarah had been checking out the window. No one was here. No one knew she was here. Besides, she'd only be a minute, and this could help with their investigation.

With a new resolve, Sarah stood and grabbed the key card to the room. She gave Buzz one last pat on the head and then stepped outside.

Looking both ways, she saw no one.

Carefully, Sarah hurried across the sidewalk toward the lobby. She pulled her hat down lower as she stepped inside, nodded at the man behind the desk, and then she slipped into the room with the computer.

Perfect. No one else was here.

Quickly, she pulled up her emails, desperate to see if there was a clue there she'd missed earlier.

But as soon as the screen filled with her messages, her eyes went to the newest one.

It was from the storage facility where she kept her paintings. The building flooded after the recent snow and rain, and she needed to go check on her items.

Her stomach clenched. Had her paintings been ruined?

Tears pressed at her eyes. She didn't want to cry. There were far more important matters to cry about. But those watercolors represented years of work.

If they were destroyed, then Sarah really wouldn't have anything left, would she?

As she noticed movement out front, she glanced over at the glass doors.

A black sedan pulled up.

Was it the man who'd been following them?

She didn't know for sure. But Sarah did know she had to get out of here. Now.

THIRTEEN

Sarah found a back exit and slipped outside. Woods and a small creek lined the back side of the building. Here, she was concealed—but also more isolated if the man found her.

Careful to remain out of sight and moving quickly, she skirted around the side of the building until she reached the corner. She pressed herself against the wall and peered around to the front parking lot.

The sedan was still there, outside near the front door.

Had the man gone inside? Was he questioning the clerk, asking if he'd seen her?

Sarah knew the most likely answer was yes.

She didn't have much time.

She had to get to Buzz.

Sarah darted to her room. Her hands trembled as she jammed the key card into the lock. She glanced back one more time as the door opened.

A man stepped out of the lobby. Sarah couldn't make out much about him except that he was large—muscular—and he wore aviator shades. His dark hair was slicked back from his face.

She didn't think she'd ever seen the man before.

That had to be the person following her. He was large enough to be the killer.

He hadn't seen her. Not yet.

But Sarah knew he'd probably check all of these rooms until he found her and killed her.

She locked the door. And then she shoved a chair in front of it. Adrenaline pulsed through her blood.

Buzz rushed toward her, his body on alert as his canine intuition reared to life.

Sarah glanced around.

How was she going to get out of here?

There were no windows other than those at the front of the room.

They weren't a possibility. And there was no other way out.

Fighting panic, she glanced out the window. The man was walking toward her room.

He'd seen her. Knew she was here.

And he was coming for her.

"Buzz, we've got to do something," Sarah whispered, her head swirling with adrenaline and fear. "But what?"

Buzz walked toward the interior door by the TV and he sat there. It was the passageway leading to the adjoining room for families or groups that needed more than one area.

"I should go into the connecting room?" It seemed like a good enough idea. Besides, it wasn't like Sarah had many other options right now.

She opened the door on her side of the space and listened for a moment. It was silent on the other side. Maybe that meant the room was unoccupied. She hadn't heard any noises coming from the space since she'd arrived.

Moving quickly, Sarah grabbed the other knob.

It was locked.

How was she going to get this open?

Could she charge the door and knock it down? She doubted she was strong enough. Besides, it would be too noisy. Certainly the man would hear her.

There had to be something else she could do.

She pulled out her key card. She'd only ever seen this done on TV. Would it work in real life?

Someone banged on her door just then. "Maintenance!"

Sarah had no choice but to find out if her theory would work. The man was here and only moments away from killing her.

She jammed the card where the lock was, praying it would release.

Please, Lord. Please. Let this work!

Her hand still shook uncontrollably. That didn't stop her. She continued to jam the card into the lock mechanism, hoping—praying—it would catch.

The man knocked again. Then something crashed into the door.

He was trying to get into her room, she realized. And nothing was going to stop him.

Sarah gave the card one last shove.

Something gave.

She sucked in a breath.

It had worked, she realized. The card had released the latch!

Sarah pushed the door open, hoping no one else was on the other side who would alert the man about what she'd done.

Quickly, she scanned the space. The room—identical to her own—appeared empty.

"Come on, Buzz," she whispered. She clucked her tongue once. It was Loretta's command for him to come.

As trained, the dog ran inside. Sarah grabbed Buzz's bag, flung it on her back, and shut the doors quietly. She hoped to conceal what she'd done and buy herself some time.

Just as the door clicked closed behind her, a crash sounded from her room.

The man must have kicked open her door.

Sarah had escaped just in time.

But this wasn't over yet. No, Sarah needed to think and act quickly if she wanted to get out of this alive.

Colton's head pounded as he headed down the road from Frank's house.

He'd just spent the past hour and a half talking to police and trying to explain himself. Explaining how he'd found Frank.

He'd told investigators that he'd decided to look into the case himself as a personal favor to a friend who just happened to be their prime suspect. Again he'd been warned that Sarah might not be who he remembered.

He didn't believe that. She was the same Sarah, only a little more broken than before. More than anything, Colton wished he could help put her back together. But it wasn't his place. Not anymore. He'd help her through this situation, and then his life would return to normal. He had no other choice.

But his heart seemed to be telling him otherwise, despite all his logic.

The one piece of good news he'd received was that

the police had talked to John Abram, the man Sarah had worked for who'd accused her of stealing. He'd confessed that she was innocent, and he'd made the story up.

Colton pulled up to the hotel and froze. A black sedan was parked in front of the lobby area.

His breath hitched.

It was the man who'd been following them earlier. The killer.

He'd found them again somehow.

Had he already gotten Sarah and Buzz?

Colton sped toward his room and threw his truck into Park. Just as he drew his gun, he saw the curtain move in the room beside theirs.

A familiar face peeked out.

That was Sarah.

She saw him and threw the door open.

The next instant, she and Buzz darted across the sidewalk and dove into his truck.

"Go!" Sarah yelled. "Go!"

Colton didn't ask any questions. He pressed the accelerator and his engine revved as they raced toward the road. Just as they reached the blacktop, Colton looked back.

A man wearing a black leather coat stepped from his room and stared after them.

They should be a safe enough distance away to lose him.

But Colton had to be certain. He couldn't take a chance on Sarah's life.

He took a sharp right turn and headed back into the city. He needed to disappear among the traffic there.

He glanced in his rearview mirror again.

He didn't see the sedan.

Thank goodness. Maybe they'd gotten enough of a head start.

"What happened back there?" Colton asked.

Sarah shook her head, her cheeks flushed and her chest rising and falling too rapidly. "I don't know. I saw the man pull up and panicked. I knew I had to do something. Buzz went right to the door between the two rooms, and I knew that was my only option. I managed to get the door open. It's a good thing you pulled up when you did, though…"

"Yeah, it is." Colton had come close to losing her, and he could barely stomach the thought.

Right now, he wanted nothing more than to pull Sarah into his arms and hold her. To tell her that everything would be okay. To whisk her off somewhere she'd be safe.

But none of those things were options. No, he had to stay focused here. Stay logical. And to forget about their past and all the old feelings that wanted to bubble to the surface.

Instead, Colton glanced behind him again. He still didn't see the sedan. Maybe they'd finally caught a break.

"I don't know how this guy is finding us, but he is," Colton said.

"I know. I don't like it. Not at all."

Colton's thoughts raced. Where else could this guy have left a tracker or found a means of trailing them?

As he glanced at Buzz, an idea hit him. "What's that thing on Buzz's collar?"

Sarah reached for the collar and touched the tag

there. But she felt something behind it. "What is that, boy?"

She slipped the collar off and pulled it toward her for examination. Then she let out a gasp. "It's a tracker, the kind you can put on your keys so you won't lose them. It should be linked to a phone."

"This guy must have known about it." Colton shook his head. "That's how he's been tracking us. He has Loretta's phone, after all."

"What do we do?"

"Throw it out the window."

Sarah glanced at him, making sure she'd understood correctly. "Really?"

"Yes, really. We'll get Buzz a new one."

She rolled down the window and tossed it into the woods. A moment of silence fell between them, and Sarah shivered. Finally, she asked, "Did you find out anything at Frank's?"

"Not a lot. But I got confirmation that Randolph Stephens's car was stolen about a week ago."

Sarah's shoulders sagged. "So the vehicle that was following us wasn't him?"

"No, it wasn't."

"What about Frank?"

"The police are wondering if he shot Loretta and then killed himself," Colton told her.

"I don't know what to say. I would love not to be their prime suspect, but I can't imagine that Frank did this either. I mean, we went there to find out if he had any idea of who might have a reason to kill Loretta. We didn't go there because we thought he was guilty of it."

"I agree."

"What explanation did you tell the police about why you were there at Frank's house?"

"I was honest. I told them that I knew you. I told them that I couldn't believe you would do something like this, and I wanted to check things out myself, on my own dime."

"What did they say?"

"Not much. As long as I stay out of their way, what can they say?"

Sarah frowned. "Colton, can I see your phone?"

"Sure. Why?" He pulled it from his pocket and handed it to her.

"I remembered an email Loretta sent me. She liked to send a lot of emails, reminding me about various things. Normally, they drove me crazy. But while I was at the art show that night, she sent me one that I didn't even read. I told myself I would do it later, but then everything happened."

"And you wonder if she said something?"

"Yes, I do."

"See what you can find out."

She tapped several things into the phone before leaning back. "Here it is."

"What exactly did she say?"

"Sarah, I need you to take Buzz away for me for the weekend. I've left some money out for you. Please come home soon. I'll be waiting up." Sarah glanced at him. "She knew, Colton. Loretta had known something was wrong, and she was trying to protect us. But why?"

"If I had that answer, all of this would be over right now."

"You're right." Sarah frowned again. "Colton, there's something else. I know it's not as important, but—"

His back muscles tensed at the worry in her voice. "What is it, Sarah?"

"I went out to use the computer at the hotel. It's the only reason I saw that guy coming. So maybe it was stupid or maybe it saved my life."

Colton would reserve his judgment on that. All he'd asked Sarah to do was to remain in the room. Yet he couldn't argue with the point that Sarah may not have seen the man if she hadn't gone out. It didn't matter now.

"Okay…" he started.

"I got an email from the storage facility where I keep my things. It flooded and everything might be ruined."

"I'm sorry, Sarah."

"My…my paintings are all there, Colton. I know it's minor in comparison to what's going on now. But…"

"You want to go check them out?"

"Only if we can."

"I know your paintings are important to you."

"They're my life's work. I know I haven't made it big yet—maybe I never will, but—"

"You have a lot of talent, Sarah."

Her cheeks reddened. "Thank you."

"I mean it. You've always been talented. You'll have your big break one day." Colton had seen her talent from the moment he'd looked at her first painting. She had a knack for picking up on the beauty in life. For sensing things that others didn't. She was truly gifted.

"I appreciate that. I've always appreciated how much you believe in me."

"I never stopped believing in you."

At his words, he glanced at Sarah and saw her cheeks redden. He didn't want his statement to be true. He wanted to put his relationship with Sarah behind him. But he couldn't do that until he knew she was safe.

Twenty minutes later, Colton pulled up to the storage area. He hadn't been followed. But the man in the sedan had figured out a way to track them somehow earlier. Colton needed to make sure there were no other surprises.

He paused only for a moment to glance at the facility. It had interior doors, but the business was located in a bad section of town. No doubt, things had been cheaper here.

Sarah had definitely gone through some financial struggles. His heart went out to her.

Hopefully they could get some answers now, and she'd feel better.

"Let's go check it out. And then we need to hit the road again and figure out our next step, okay?"

Sarah nodded. "Okay. Let's do this."

Sarah typed in a code outside the main doors, and they hurried inside an unmanned lobby. Wasting no time, they turned left. Colton followed her down a dim hallway, pausing as she stopped by a door labeled 138.

She typed in another code on a keypad above the handle, heard a click and shoved the door open. After flipping on the lights, they stepped inside.

Several storage rolls where her canvases were stored rested on the floor. A few mounted paintings leaned against a wall. A couple miscellaneous boxes sat in the center of the room.

"Funny, it doesn't look flooded, does it?" Sarah put her hands on her hips and glanced around, a wrinkle forming between her eyes.

Colton eyed the space, looking for any signs of moisture. Smelling for the scent of mildew. Looking for any indications there had been an incident here at the facility.

There was nothing.

"No, it doesn't look flooded," he finally said. "Unless the water has already dried up. Check your paintings. See if they're damaged."

Sarah reached down and pulled a painting from one of the lower shelves there. A picture of a waterfall stared back at them.

A flawless picture.

With no water damage.

A bright smile crossed Sarah's face. "It wasn't as bad as I thought. Maybe this area was spared."

"That would be great. Good news, right?" Colton said.

"Fantastic news."

Colton reached on top of a box and pulled something off. He seemed to operate on autopilot, not meaning to be nosy. But he couldn't stop himself.

"Is this the blanket I gave you?" he asked.

Her cheeks flushed. "Yes, it is. It's a great blanket."

Colton smiled. "Yeah, it is."

He'd had it made for her out of T-shirts they'd purchased at various state parks they'd visited. Sarah had loved it when Colton had given it to her on her twenty-fifth birthday.

But he'd just assumed Sarah had gotten rid of everything when they'd broken up.

She looked up, something strange in her gaze, like she wanted to explain herself but couldn't bring herself to do so.

Colton was just about to say something—he wasn't

sure what—when he heard something slam behind him. He rushed to the door and pushed on it.

It was locked or jammed somehow.

Colton rattled it again, but nothing happened. His internal alarms began to sound.

"What?" Sarah joined him by the door and pressed on it.

It was no use. Whoever had locked them in had blocked the door too.

Buzz gave out a bark to let them know he wasn't happy.

"What's going on, Colton?" Sarah's frightened eyes met his.

"I have a feeling we were lured here." Colton hadn't wanted to say the words aloud, but it was the only thing that made sense. This had all been a trap.

Colton should have seen through it. He'd chide himself for it later.

Before he could think about his mistake anymore, he froze.

A strange smell teased his senses.

Then he realized what it was.

Gas. Someone was feeding some type of gas through a line at the bottom of the door. Gas that would most likely make them pass out soon.

"Sarah, we've got to find a way out of here," Colton said, his gaze locking with hers. "Now."

FOURTEEN

Sarah rammed her shoulder into the door. Logically, she knew if Colton couldn't break through, she couldn't either. But she didn't care right now. Panic surged through her as survival instinct took over.

That same man who'd killed Loretta was now trying to kill her, Colton and Buzz also.

She pounded on the door, desperation taking over. "Help!"

"Save your breath and stay low." After stuffing a blanket under the door, Colton took Sarah's elbow and swiftly led her to the other side of the room. "Actually, put your shirt over your mouth. I don't know what this is, but don't breathe it."

What were they going to do? There was nowhere else to go. But if they stayed in here, then they had only seconds to remain lucid.

Buzz began barking at them.

"What is it, Buzz?" Sarah asked, her head starting to swim. "I know. We're in trouble."

The dog kept barking, the sound becoming more frantic.

"I think he's trying to tell us something." Colton rushed toward Buzz. "What is it?"

The husky nuzzled his way between some boxes and continued barking at something in the corner. Colton pushed boxes aside and followed behind him.

"Sarah, it's a vent," Colton muttered.

She knelt beside him, her eyes widening when she saw the larger-than-average opening. "Look at that! Can we get through it?"

"We don't have any other choice but to try." He pulled out a pocketknife and began to work the edges of the grate. Finally, the top released and Colton pulled the metal cover off.

Sarah knelt down lower on the ground, coughing with every other breath. The gas was getting thicker, becoming harder to avoid.

If they didn't get out soon, they wouldn't leave here alive. She felt certain.

Colton tossed the vent cover behind him and stuck his head into the space. "It's narrow, but if you head right and then follow it, we should be able to escape. I'm going to let Buzz go first then you. You can do this, okay?"

Sarah nodded, even though she felt anything but confident. What other choice did they have? None.

Buzz barked once more before climbing in through the fifteen by fifteen opening and leading the way. Saying a quick prayer, Sarah climbed in behind him.

The gas had started to fill this area, as well. She pulled her shirt up higher over her mouth and nose, trying to protect her lungs for as long as possible.

"You're doing great," Colton said behind her.

She didn't feel great. She felt claustrophobic. The

space was so dark, and her limbs were getting heavy. The sound of Buzz's claws on metal made her skin crawl.

The dog seemed to instinctively know where they were going. As quickly as she could, Sarah followed behind him. Her knees ached from moving in the cramped space. Her palms were sore. But she kept moving.

They reached the end of the tunnel, and another surge of panic went through her.

What now? Where would they go? Had they come this far just to perish?

Buzz pawed at something.

"Is that another vent?" Colton murmured.

She tried to peer around Buzz. "It's another vent cover."

"Can you push it out?" Colton asked.

"Let me see." She squeezed her arm around Buzz and shoved the cover.

Nothing.

Shoved it harder.

Still nothing.

Giving it one last burst of energy, she pushed against it one last time.

Finally, the metal cover clattered to the ground. Buzz jumped out onto the vinyl floor below.

Sarah pushed herself to make it the last few feet. She climbed from the opening and nearly collapsed on the floor.

But she didn't have time to gather herself. Instead, she glanced around. They were in a stairwell, she realized.

Colton climbed out behind Sarah and took her hand. "Come on. We've got to get out of here."

Sarah didn't have time to think. To breathe.

They left the building, sprinted back to his truck and jumped inside before whomever it was who'd lured them here caught them.

As darkness fell around them, Colton stared at the lonely mountain road. A stretch of blacktop snaked across the mountainside, barely visible except for where his headlights shone. The area was still, as was the conversation inside his truck.

Both of them seemed to be lost in their own thoughts.

The effects of the gas had worn off as soon as they'd stopped breathing it in.

Gas.

That man hadn't wanted to kill them. He'd wanted to knock them out, hadn't he? Why was that? What was the man's endgame?

Colton couldn't figure it out. He only knew that had been incredibly close, and this situation could have turned out so much differently.

His phone buzzed. As he pulled to a stop, he glanced at the screen and sucked in a breath.

"What is it?" Sarah asked.

He hesitated a moment before showing her the screen. "I'm sorry, Sarah."

The pictures showed Sarah's paintings from the storage area. They'd been ripped apart.

She let out a gasp. "No…"

"We must have ticked this guy off when we escaped. I'm so sorry."

"And now he must know who you are," Sarah said. "He texted these pictures to you."

"He probably traced my license plates or something."

Beside him, Sarah said nothing. She only stared out the window, appearing shell-shocked and in mourning.

Yet again.

So many losses and tragedies, and now her paintings.

Colton's heart went out to her. He knew Sarah had lost years of work, and he couldn't imagine how that might feel.

But right now, they didn't talk. Colton knew Sarah well enough to know that she needed time to process— and that's what she was doing right now. There would be time to talk later.

Thirty minutes after that, he pulled to a stop in front of an old log cabin on the edge of the Idaho line. The windows were dark, and snow covered the roof of the tiny nine-hundred-square-foot place. Colton hadn't been here in years.

"Where are we?" Sarah asked, a knot forming between her eyes as she stared at the dark house.

"It's a cabin an old friend of mine owns," he told her. "He said I could use it whenever I want. Turns out, I need it now."

Sarah nodded slowly before reaching down to grab her purse. "Perfect."

Colton's boots hit the ground. He walked around to the other side of the truck and helped Sarah out. Buzz followed behind them.

The snow crunched beneath their feet as they tromped to the front door. Colton reached below a rock on the steps and retrieved the key.

A moment later, they were inside. The place smelled dusty, like it had been closed up too long. But it was safe.

For now.

As Sarah stood there shivering in the middle of the room, Colton walked to the fireplace. Wood had been left there.

He quickly grabbed some logs and put them in the brick enclosure. In a basket on the hearth, he found a lighter and began to work on getting some flames started.

"Listen, can you check the kitchen?" Colton asked Sarah over his shoulder. "See if there's anything to eat. Maybe some canned soup that's not expired or something. My friend usually leaves the electric on here so the pipes won't freeze. Winter is his favorite time to come here normally, but I happen to know he's in Wyoming on a hunting trip right now."

"Of course I'll check." Sarah walked into the kitchen and began opening cabinets.

It would be good for her to have something to do, to keep her mind occupied.

A few minutes later, soup simmered on the stove, and a fire blazed. Colton had apparently turned up the heat, as well, because the whole place felt warmer.

Sarah ladled the beef stew into coffee mugs for her and Colton and put some dog food in a bowl for Buzz. They then sat on the hearth to eat. The heat warmed their skin and began thawing them out.

Colton watched the dog eat for a moment, marveling at how well behaved he was. "What happens to Buzz after this?"

Sarah put her spoon back into her mug. "I don't know. There's no one else to take him. But if I'm in jail…"

"You won't be." Colton paused. "I'm sorry about your paintings, Sarah. I would have saved them if I could."

She nodded slowly, her lips pulling down in a slight frown and a new sadness filling her gaze. "I know you would have. Do you think they're all destroyed?"

Colton didn't know what to say. Instead, he shrugged and put his spoon back into his mug. "I want to tell you no, but I… I can't do that. Who knows what this guy is up to?"

"This is all a disaster, Colton. Everything. My life. I guess it's following a pattern."

"Your life hasn't been a disaster, Sarah."

"Yes, it has been. From my dad leaving, my mom going to prison and then dying, going into foster care. Every time I make plans, they don't work out. Maybe that's why it's better if I don't make plans."

Was that one of the reasons she'd left him? Colton wasn't sure, but he would guess the answer to be yes.

"Life doesn't work out the way we want it to. But sometimes, life can be beautiful. You have to take the good with the bad. Be willing to be flexible. Accept that there's beauty with pain."

She looked at him, a new emotion glimmering in her eyes. "I'm glad you're doing better, Colton."

He set his empty mug on the table. "I went through a hard time after I shot that man, Sarah."

"A hard time? You changed your whole life. Instead of wanting to stay in Seattle, you decided to move to the mountains of Idaho and give up your job."

Colton shrugged. "Maybe it had been coming for a while. Everything had been building up. I'm not sure I ever intended on staying in Seattle long-term."

"What do you mean?"

"I don't know. I've never enjoyed the pressure of the city. The busyness of the rat race. The tension of always feeling pressure to perform. I just didn't want to spend my entire future like that. Especially not if I had kids. I wanted them to feel like they could breathe and explore and be content with the quiet."

Curiosity sparked in her gaze. "You didn't feel like you could breathe?"

"No, I felt like I was suffocating." He glanced up at her. "I hoped you could see the possibilities in moving also. In fact, I thought you would love the idea, that we'd be on the same page."

"It's hard to have a career in art when you're hundreds of miles from everything."

"Or it could have been inspiration." Colton stopped himself and shook his head. "It doesn't matter now, does it?"

Sarah frowned. "No, it doesn't."

Colton stood. "Look, maybe we should get some rest. Tomorrow we need to keep looking for answers. We're going to need our energy if we do that."

Sarah nodded again, but she opened her mouth, like she wanted to talk more.

"We'll be safe here—for the night, at least," Colton continued. He stood and handed her a blanket from the back of the couch. "Besides, Buzz will keep an eye on things for us. He saved us today."

Sarah reached over and patted the dog's head. "He sure did. Twice."

As she bedded down on the couch, Buzz lay on the floor beneath her, the ever-vigilant guard dog.

That was good—because they needed all the protection they could get right now. Not just physically.

Sarah reminded herself to protect her heart, as well.

FIFTEEN

Sarah swallowed a scream as she pulled her eyes open.

The masked man. Where was he?

Her heart pounded out of control as her gaze swung around the room.

"Sarah, it's just a dream."

A tremble raked through her. It really had been a dream. A nightmare.

The masked man wasn't here. No, Colton was here, and he was watching over her, as was Buzz.

She let out a moan as the memories hit her.

This wasn't all a bad dream. No, she was in a desperate situation that she might never recover from.

She blinked. The fire blazed behind her, adding warmth to the room. Buzz lay on the floor beside her place on the couch, looking rather content considering the situation.

Colton came into view. He sat beside her, staring at her with concern in his gaze.

"You okay?" he asked. "That must have been some dream."

"Yeah, it really was." She ran a hand through her hair, trying to gain control of her racing heart.

She'd slept surprisingly hard and needed to gather her wits. But as she saw Colton's phone appear, she noticed that he was staring at it, a concerned expression on his face.

"What's going on?" Sarah pulled the blanket up higher, trying to ward away the cold chill in the air. Based on the wet footprints on the floor, Colton had taken Buzz outside. Opening the door must have added a burst of cold to the room.

Colton said nothing for a minute, almost as if he didn't want to say anything. Instead, he stood, grabbed a coffee mug, and poured some warm liquid into the cup.

He walked over and handed it to her. "Sorry, no cream."

"That's okay." She let the heat from the ceramic mug warm her fingers, feeling incredibly grateful for Colton's kindness. "Thank you."

"No problem." He stiffly sat across from her.

Something was up. What wasn't he telling her? Sarah knew him better than the average person and could tell when he had something on his mind.

"What's going on, Colton?" she asked again.

After a moment of hesitation, he picked up his phone and showed her his screen. "There's security footage of you going into the storage facility yesterday."

"What?" Alarm stiffened her muscles.

He nodded. "The police think you were trying to destroy evidence that might implicate you in Loretta's murder."

"I would never…"

His level gaze met hers. "I know that, Sarah. But, on paper—or film, I should say—it looks bad."

Another thought hit Sarah and sent a fresh round of

worry through her system. "What about you? Did the security camera pick you up also?"

"You can see me, but you can't make out my features."

Well, that was good...maybe. "What about the parking lot? Did they get your license plate?"

"If they have, they haven't released that information."

"This is bad, Colton." She pulled the blanket up higher around her, finding tactile comfort in the action.

He nodded. "I know."

"I didn't mean to pull you into this." She couldn't say that enough.

"Someone is trying their best to implicate you, Sarah. This isn't your fault."

"I know. But your career..." He'd worked so hard at his job—a job where reputation was everything. He couldn't lose it all because of her.

"There are things more important than a career."

Colton's words sent a wave of warmth through her. He meant that, didn't he? Sarah had been running scared, so afraid of getting close to someone, only to be hurt again. But what if that wasn't the case when it came to Colton?

She'd have to think about that later, when there weren't so many other pressing concerns around her.

"What about Frank?" she asked, pulling her legs beneath her. "Any updates?"

"Unfortunately, a neighbor said he saw you at Frank's house yesterday." Colton frowned as he said the words, like he didn't want to say them but had no other choice.

Despair tried to bite deep. "I just can't catch a break. It's like everything's working against me."

Colton moved until he was beside her on the couch, close enough that she could feel the warmth of his body heat as their legs touched.

She brushed off the rush of electricity she felt.

"The police have their blinders on," Colton said.

"What am I going to do?"

"I want to have a conversation with Loretta's lawyer," Colton said. "I want to get his thoughts on the situation. Did he work for her company or for Loretta personally?"

"My impression is that Alfred Jennings worked for Loretta, doing more personal things like wills and things of that nature." Sarah shifted. "What about Yvonne—the head of the other company that's competition? We could talk to her."

"She's on my list also, but she's been out of the country. She still is—at least according to social media. She's been posting pictures of herself in Africa. I checked this morning."

Sarah frowned and leaned back. "So what do we do?"

"We need more information if we're going to find answers. I believe someone not only wants something from you, but also views you as a threat. We need to figure out why."

"I'll do whatever it takes."

Colton stood. "Great. Why don't you get cleaned up? We're going back into town to pay a visit to Alfred Jennings. I want to know what he knows. But we're going to have to be very, very careful."

Sarah swallowed hard, unsure if she was ready for this or not. Because careful might not keep her alive. But finding answers was going to require risk. She couldn't ask Colton to put his life on the line while she sought safety.

But she'd never been so scared in her life.

Sarah's lungs became tighter and tighter with every minute they got closer to the law offices of Jennings,

Morrow and Smith. As they pulled to a stop in front of the large building located on the outskirts of town, she felt beside herself and could hardly breathe.

She'd gotten Colton into this mess, and she couldn't let him take the fall for her. No, she wanted to be there when he talked to Alfred Jennings. She couldn't send Colton onto the battlefield alone. It wasn't right.

"I need to talk to Jennings, Colton," Sarah announced, resolve solidifying inside her.

Colton glanced at her. "I don't think that's a good idea. Your face is all over the news."

She knew what the consequences would be—for both of them. And if the police came after Colton, she fully intended on telling them this was all her doing and that she'd coerced him in some way to participate.

"This is my mess," she told him. "I want to be a part of this."

"Sarah, Jennings could call the police. This could be like walking into the police station and it will undoubtedly get you arrested."

Sarah's stomach squeezed at hearing the words out loud. But she couldn't back down. "I know. But I don't want to sit in the car with Buzz. I'm no safer being away from you while you're doing these investigations than I am being with you."

Colton's jaw tensed, and he said nothing for a minute. Finally, he shrugged. "It's your choice. I advise against it, but I can't stop you."

Sarah released her breath. "Thanks. I'm going."

Colton glanced into the backseat. "What about Buzz?"

"I was thinking he could wait in the truck."

"While we go into the office building?"

"Actually, Loretta told me that Jennings has a hot dog every day for lunch from his favorite stand outside the building. Regardless of the weather, his health, anything. He's a creature of habit." She glanced at her watch. "We should be able to catch him there. If we park close enough, we can keep an eye on Buzz also."

"It sounds like a plan."

As Colton looked for a parking space, Sarah borrowed his phone and looked up Alfred Jennings's picture. She found it easily and studied the image of the man. He appeared to be in his late sixties. He had reddish-brown hair, ruddy skin, and he looked about twenty pounds overweight.

Colton parallel parked in front of the building. "You stay here, boy. Okay?"

Buzz whined.

Colton cracked his window and glanced at Sarah. "You sure you're good with this? It's not too late to change your mind."

"Yeah, I'm sure." She wasn't positive where her courage came from. But she was determined to be an active part of this investigation. Colton wasn't going to be out here alone anymore. She nodded toward the distance. "There he is."

Colton followed her gaze until it stopped on Alfred Jennings. Just as Loretta had said, the man stood beside a hot dog stand and pulled some money from his wallet before being handed his lunch, wrapped in aluminum foil.

He took his food and walked toward a park bench in front of the office building. The space contained various benches with a statue at the center. Several people, despite the bitter cold, were outside there, getting some fresh air.

The good news was that Sarah hadn't seen anyone following them yet. Maybe now that they'd gotten rid of Buzz's collar, they'd lost the man on their trail. She hoped the man pursuing them didn't have any other tricks up his sleeve—but she wouldn't put it past him, either.

"I say now is as good a time as any to talk to him," Colton said. "Keep your hat and sunglasses on. It will buy us some time."

"Whatever you say."

They climbed from Colton's truck and hurried across the sidewalk. Jennings sat with his back toward them, unaware of their presence. He looked like the picture Sarah had seen, except right now he wore a rimmed black hat, a heavy wool coat and a thick plaid scarf.

The garb seemed appropriate for such a gray, bleak day. If Sarah had to guess, they would get more snow later. The sky looked full and ready to burst with icy goodness.

Colton motioned for Sarah to stay behind him as he slid onto the bench next to Alfred. "Mr. Jennings, I was hoping you might answer some questions for me."

Jennings's eyes widened, and he stopped with his hot dog raised in the air. "Who are you?"

"I'm an investigator who's looking into Loretta Blanchard's murder."

"Do you have an ID?"

"I'm working as a consultant, but I was a detective in Seattle before coming here."

Jennings's gaze narrowed, making it clear he was still on guard. "What do you need to know?"

"I'm trying to figure out who might have killed her."

"The police have already named a suspect." He took another bite of his hot dog, not appearing shaken by Colton's questions and showing that he was a seasoned lawyer.

As they spoke, Sarah remained a safe distance away, her back toward them. Hopefully, she looked like someone who was lingering close. But she remained far enough away that Jennings might not notice her.

She glanced around, looking again for any sign of trouble or danger. The sidewalks were busy with people, but no one who stood out to her. Everyone seemed to be minding their own business. Buzz remained in the truck, the top of his head revealed through the cracked window.

Normal.

Everything appeared normal, and her danger radar indicated they were safe—for now.

Even better, Jennings didn't seem to notice that Sarah was there. Instead, he mostly focused on his hot dog and Colton.

Good. That bought them some time. At present.

Just as Colton was about to ask another question, Jennings continued.

"I don't know what I can tell you," Jennings said. "Loretta was a good woman. She didn't deserve to die like that. But I have no idea who might have done it other than that new assistant of hers."

His words hit Sarah. She was the scapegoat here—and an easy one, at that.

How would she ever convince anyone that she hadn't done this?

SIXTEEN

"You think her assistant did this?" Colton glanced back at Sarah as she lingered a few steps away, but close enough to listen. This couldn't be easy for her to hear.

Jennings's expression softened. "I don't want to believe it."

"Why not?"

"Loretta really liked that girl. Said she saw some of herself in her."

"But her assistant was an artist, not a scientist." Colton had no choice but to act like the bad guy for a moment.

Jennings shrugged. "I think it was the passion for her work that she related to. Loretta said Sarah was a wonderful artist and that she wanted to help her out. Honestly, I think she saw the same loneliness in Sarah that she felt herself. Loretta was pretty much all by herself in this world. Just like Sarah."

Colton's heart thudded in his chest at the thought of it. "Is that right?"

"I honestly don't believe the girl did it. I don't know what happened, but I don't believe Loretta's assistant is the culprit. I've never met her before, but Loretta had a good instinct about her."

That was a great first step to having this conversation. "The drug business is cutthroat. Was there anyone Loretta had problems with?"

Jennings sighed and discarded the rest of his hot dog into a nearby trash can. "I don't know. I can say that Loretta wasn't acting like herself the few days before she died. I thought maybe it was her ALS. But she didn't tell me anything."

"And you don't have any theories?" Colton continued, feeling like the man might still know more than he let on.

Jennings frowned and looked up at Colton. "This is the only thing I can think to tell you. Loretta was on the verge of creating a drug that would help people with ALS. That has been her goal for the past several years."

Colton sucked in a breath. Could it be the lead they'd been looking for? "Did she tell many people about it?"

"No. Loretta was working on it on her own. She had a lab there at the company where she could work privately. It was one of the perks of starting her own business, I suppose. She didn't want to tell anyone more than necessary. She did have some control groups, but they'd signed confidentiality clauses so they couldn't tell others."

Colton crossed his arms, trying to think that through. "Is that even legal?"

"I drew up the contract myself. I made sure she was covered. The people involved had seen significant results."

"All of them?" Colton asked, his interest piqued. Because, if not, they might have a new pool of suspects.

"Yes," Jennings said. "From what I understood, they'd all had good results. I can't imagine any of them wanting to hurt her."

"Was there anyone who wanted to get into the program but couldn't? That would be a reason to have a grudge against her."

Jennings shrugged. "Again, because of the confidentiality of it all, I can't see that happening."

"Last question—was there anyone helping her with this? Anyone on her staff who knew what she was doing?"

"From what she told me, no. She only told me because she had to. Otherwise, she kept quiet. She learned her lesson when she split with her friend Yvonne, and Yvonne started her own company. She vowed she wouldn't make that mistake again."

"So it sounds like Yvonne was an enemy." Colton scanned the crowds one more time but didn't see anyone who grabbed his attention. Good. But he still couldn't let down his guard.

"They had a professional competitiveness about them, but I do believe that Loretta ultimately respected the woman's work."

Just then, Colton did a double take. Buzz had somehow managed to jump out of the truck window. The dog bounded toward them, looking like he was on a mission.

Colton looked back at Sarah and saw her eyes widen, as well.

Jennings looked twice when he spotted Buzz. "Wait...is that...?"

Colton looked back at Sarah once more, just in time to see a man appear from nowhere and sprint toward her.

"No!" he yelled.

Colton lunged toward Sarah. But the man reached her before Colton did.

The man grabbed her arm, tackling her to the ground.

Around them, people began to scatter. A few screamed. Several stopped to stare.

Colton glanced over as a streak of fur went past him. Buzz.

The dog darted past Colton, his teeth bared.

He growled before springing on the man. He knocked him off-balance, but the man quickly pulled himself to his feet.

The next instant, the attacker turned on his heel and took off.

Sarah lay on the ground, rubbing her elbow and looking shaken.

Buzz stood guard beside her.

Colton knelt beside Sarah. "Are you okay?"

She looked up, dazed. "Yeah, but we need to get out of here."

"Yes, we do." Colton helped her to her feet.

As he did, he glanced back at Jennings. Concern stretched across the man's face, along with the realization that Sarah was here…and in trouble.

"Good luck," the man muttered, a flash of compassion in his eyes. "Figure out who did this."

Colton wasted no more time. They had to leave this place. Now.

With Sarah's hand in his, they ran toward his truck and climbed inside with Buzz. As soon as the keys were in the ignition, they took off, trying to get as far away from the scene as possible.

"What just happened?" Sarah asked, holding on to the door handle, her breaths coming rapidly.

"I'm still not sure. What was in your purse?"

She shrugged. "Nothing. I mean, nothing of value."

"Nothing from Loretta?" Colton asked, trying to put the pieces together. He headed out of town, going fast—but not fast enough to be noticed.

"No, nothing. There was ChapStick and my wallet. Nothing else."

Colton frowned and wove into the left lane. As he stared straight ahead at the road, the first snowflakes began hitting his windshield.

"That man wants something badly, Sarah," he said. "He'll do anything to get it. He took a big risk by doing that out in public."

"Exactly. But why would he do that?" She took her hat off and raked a hand through her hair. "It just doesn't make sense."

"I have no idea." Colton didn't like any of this. He could feel danger squeezing tighter.

Sarah stared straight ahead, the snow seeming to transfix her for a moment. Then she leaned back, crossed her arms and let out a long breath. "What are we doing now?"

"We need to get far away from here before the police come."

"They'll be looking for your truck."

"You're probably right. But we're going to have to take that chance right now. We don't have any time to waste."

Sarah glanced at Colton, curiosity—and maybe fear—entering her voice. "What are you thinking?"

"I'm thinking that I want to take a look at Loretta's house."

Sarah sucked in a breath. "Why in the world would you want to do that? The police probably have eyes on the place."

"Actually, I doubt they do. They probably don't think you'll come back—not with your face all over the news."

"But why chance it?"

Colton swallowed hard, the plan solidifying in his mind. "Because I need to see it. I need to see if there's anything the police missed. I need to know if anything at the house is different now than when you left."

"What if we're caught?"

"We'll be careful."

She slunk down lower in the seat. "I don't know if I like this, Colton."

He frowned, totally understanding where she was coming from and empathizing. "I don't either. But we don't have any other choice right now. But first, before we go there, maybe we should grab a bite to eat. How does that sound?"

"Great."

Good. He needed to collect his thoughts. Because this mystery was feeling more and more complicated—and dangerous—by the moment.

Sarah breathed easier as they pulled out of town and onto some back roads. She had so much to think about. To process. To attempt to comprehend.

Colton pulled up to a gas station with a fast-food restaurant inside. He chose a spot to the side of the building, out of sight to anyone driving past, and put his truck into Park.

"How about if I run inside and grab some food?" he asked. "I can bring it out to the truck to eat, we'll get gas, walk Buzz and give him some water. It will be a nice breather for all of us."

"Sounds like a plan. If they have a grilled chicken sandwich, that would be perfect. Maybe with a side of salad or fruit."

"That's what I was going to guess." As Colton climbed out, he offered a smile that sent flutters through Sarah.

"And grab a new collar for Buzz if you could," she called.

"Of course."

It had only been two years since they were together, so it probably shouldn't be surprising that he remembered so much. Yet a small part of her still felt delight in knowing he hadn't forgotten what she liked.

Did he think about her as much as Sarah thought about him?

It wasn't important. It was all water under the bridge. There were trust issues between them—issues she wasn't sure they could get past. Sometimes desire wasn't enough to change the facts, and it definitely wasn't enough to change history.

She glanced around, looking for any signs of trouble. She saw nothing but trucks full of people headed out for outdoor adventures. No one looked their way, and Sarah hoped it would stay like that.

As a moment of silence fell, Sarah reflected on Loretta's words. The woman really had liked her. More than liked her. She must have thought of her as a daughter almost.

How could Sarah not have known that?

Despite the hurt and pang of loss, a surge of satisfaction welled up in her. Loretta really had seen something in Sarah. The news caused a warm delight to spread through her.

Several minutes later, Colton climbed back inside with two bags of food, two cups of coffee and a large cup of water. He handed Sarah one of the sacks.

She opened her bag, and her stomach grumbled at the scent of grilled chicken. She hadn't realized how hungry she was.

"They had chicken," Colton said.

"Perfect."

He opened the cup of water and put it in the backseat for Buzz. The dog gulped it up, obviously thirsty from their adventures today.

As they all settled back with their food, Colton cleared his throat. "So, how did you know where to find me? I didn't realize you knew where my cabin was."

Sarah shrugged, picked a pickle from her sandwich before it fell off and popped it in her mouth. "Your mom told me."

"My mom?" Colton's eyes widened as he glanced at her, as if he hadn't heard correctly.

Sarah smiled at his shock. She'd wondered if he knew about those letters and had assumed that he didn't. "She liked to write me letters. You didn't know?"

"I had no idea." He wiped his mouth with a napkin.

"Yes, she kept me updated. Told me where you'd moved. Even sent me your address in case I ever wanted to visit. I kept some of those letters in my glove compartment, so I was able to find your address when I left with Buzz that night. I drove around for hours, unsure where to go or what to do. And then… I did the only thing that made sense."

"You came to my place."

Sarah nodded. "I went to your place."

He didn't say anything for a moment until finally shaking his head. "My mom… I can't believe she did that. I don't even know what to say."

"She sent me letters more often right after we broke up. Told me how much she missed me. Asked me to change my mind and come back."

Colton lowered his burger and let out a long puff of air. "I'm so sorry, Sarah. She's a meddler for sure, but I didn't know…"

"It's okay. Actually, you know how much I loved your family. It was nice to stay connected. And she was always kind to me—even in the letters. She didn't push me as much as she let me know how much I was missed. It's good to feel missed."

A moment of silence stretched between them. "Did she tell you that she and my father are down in Arizona during the winter?"

"She did. She sounds like she likes it in that area." Mama Hawk, as she was called, had told Sarah all about her adventures in retirement. The art of letter writing was becoming lost, but Colton's mom had perfected it. Sarah loved those letters.

"Yeah, I think she does."

Sarah finished her sandwich and turned to Colton, still sensing he was uneasy about his mom's involvement in Sarah's life over the past two years. "You know, Colton, you're really blessed to have parents like you do."

A sad smile crossed his face. "I know I am. I don't always agree with my mom's methods, but she's always been there for me and I know she loves me. She took our breakup really hard. Maybe even harder than I realized."

"Bringing someone into your family and then losing them...it's hard." The words caught in her throat. Sarah had been through so many foster families after her mom had gone to jail. The hardest part was feeling a connection with someone who would take her in, only to have that family send her away for various reasons. It had always felt like her fault, even when it wasn't.

And then there was the fact that she and her sister had been separated. Though they both still kept in touch, something had changed between them during their time apart. Their relationship had never been the same.

"I guess you know all about that." Colton's soft voice indicated that he understood, that he felt compassion.

Sarah glanced at her hands. "Yeah, unfortunately, I do."

"Do you ever wonder what our lives would be like now if we hadn't broken up?"

Every day. Sarah swallowed the words, though. "It doesn't matter, does it? We can't change the past."

"No, we can't." Colton's words sounded as strained as her heart felt.

But it was true. The past was behind them—all their mistakes. And sometimes, you couldn't fix things. You just had to move forward.

Even though this highly charged situation might make Sarah feel like the two of them had a chance together, she had to remember that facing danger together wasn't the same as being in a relationship.

Right now, she just had to concentrate on staying alive.

SEVENTEEN

Sarah could hardly breathe as they pulled up to Loretta's house an hour later. Just seeing the huge, six-thousand-square-foot house brought a rush of memories. It was a grand house, framed out in brick with no expense spared.

The lots in this neighborhood were large—about three or four acres each. Woods came up to the back of the property, along with a stunning skyline.

Flashes of seeing that man standing over Loretta filled her mind. Of Buzz knocking the killer off Loretta. Of running for her life.

A tremble raked through her body.

Buzz nuzzled her face, seeming to sense her thoughts—or maybe the dog was feeling the same way. Canines grieved also. Certainly Buzz missed Loretta right now.

As Colton drove around to the back of the secluded residence, Sarah didn't spot any other cars there. Good. At least this part of the plan was going smoothly. Colton parked behind the garage.

Before opening his door, Colton turned toward Sarah, concern in his gaze. The way he still respected her despite their history touched Sarah and made her crave the happy times of their past.

Back then, Colton would have done anything for her, just like he was doing now.

She'd forgotten how good it felt to have someone like that in her life. A jolt of sadness sliced through the tension she felt inside.

"Are you ready for this, Sarah?" Colton asked, his gaze searching hers—probably looking for the truth despite her bravado.

She shrugged, knowing there was no need to deny reality. "As ready as I'll ever be, I guess."

With one last glance at her, Colton nodded and looked toward the stately house in the distance. "Okay. Let's go inside. But be careful. I don't want to draw any attention or compromise the scene. Okay?"

She nodded. "Okay."

Buzz followed behind them as they darted toward the back door. He trotted, a new bounce in his step. Did he expect to see Loretta?

More sadness pressed on Sarah.

"You still have your key?" Colton asked, his arm brushing Sarah's and sending a shiver through her.

Something about his voice sent another jolt of awareness through her. He was using that tone with her—a personal one. Earlier, he'd only sounded professional and aloof, merely acquainted. She wasn't sure what had changed, but she felt something unseen connecting them at the moment.

Sarah snapped back to reality and pulled the keys from her purse. With shaky hands, she unlocked the back door, memories flashing through her mind of the last time she'd done that—when she'd returned here absolutely clueless about what she would find inside. About Buzz being in her closet. A man being in Loretta's room.

She hesitated before stepping inside, staring at the interior as bad memories flooded her mind.

"I'll go first," Colton said softly. He paused in front of her for long enough to swirl a strand of her hair and brush it between his fingers.

Their gazes caught for a moment, and Sarah's heart fluttered out of control.

She wanted nothing more than to reach up and plant a kiss on his lips. To relive old times.

But that would be a mistake. She had to keep reminding herself of that. Reminding herself that everyone she'd ever loved had left her. Her heart couldn't face that again. One more loss like that might crush her for good.

Colton leaned toward her and gently pressed a kiss on her forehead before whispering, "I've got your back. Always."

The moment ended as quickly as it had started. Colton brushed past Sarah and scanned the area before motioning for her to follow. Buzz waited behind her, silently insisting on bringing up the rear.

Sarah followed behind Colton.

It was obvious the police had been here. Smears of black fingerprint dust stained various surfaces. Drawers were open, as if they'd been searched.

Had the cops found anything?

"Where is Loretta's room?" Colton asked.

"This way." Sarah remembered the brief moment they'd shared, and her cheeks heated. But she quickly pushed those feelings aside and pointed down the first level of the west wing.

She directed Colton all the way there but paused before peering inside Loretta's room herself. She knew what she'd see in that room, and Sarah wasn't sure she was prepared to relive those moments.

Buzz remained in the hallway with her, sniffing the floor like a dog on a mission.

A moment later, Colton stepped out. "We need to figure out if anything is different here, Sarah. You're the best one to do that."

"What do you mean by anything?"

"It can be even the smallest change." He reached down and squeezed her hand. "I know it's going to be hard, but could you take a look?"

She drew in a deep, shaky breath and nodded. "Okay."

Colton didn't let go of her hand as they stepped inside—and she didn't pull away. No, she needed someone to lean on if she was going to face this crime scene again.

She paused in the room, her throat tightening as memories bombarded her. She could so clearly see Loretta sitting by the window just thinking. She did that a lot and said that's how she came up with her best ideas.

That was how Sarah often found her inspiration also.

Maybe she and Loretta weren't that different after all.

"Anything?" Colton asked.

Sarah forced herself to scan the room. Loretta's dresser looked the same. The pictures on top were still there.

The bed and sheets also looked the same.

Everything appeared just as it had been, except for the bloodstain on the floor and a missing rug that must have also had some evidence on it.

"There's nothing—" Sarah started.

But she stopped herself and pointed.

"What?" Colton asked.

"Except that." She stepped across the room toward a painting of mountains and a waterfall.

"That's one of your pieces of artwork," Colton muttered.

Sarah nodded. "It is. It's the painting Loretta bought when we met. The thing is, it used to only be a canvas. There was no frame. Now there is."

"Let's see if we can figure out why."

Colton pulled the sleeves of his Henley down over his fingers before reaching for the picture.

The painting really was gorgeous. The colors that Sarah had chosen were vibrant and pulled the viewer into the scene, making them want to dive into the picture and live there for a minute. He could see why Loretta had chosen it.

But it was strange that in the days before Loretta had died, she'd had this framed without mentioning anything to Sarah.

"You didn't notice this on the night Loretta died?" Colton asked, carefully grasping the edges of the painting.

"I didn't… I mean, I didn't look. But I was in here earlier that day, in the morning, and I think I would have noticed that." Nervous energy emanated off Sarah as she hovered beside him.

He understood—they both understood—the significance of this moment.

The painting released from the wall and Colton carefully carried it to the bed. He pulled a knife from his pocket and pried the backing away. His heart raced with anticipation.

Did this mean anything? Colton didn't know. But he definitely wanted to find out.

Sarah stepped closer to him, and her sweet smell reminded him of better times. Made him miss those moments.

This wasn't the time to think about that. No, this life-or-death situation had to take priority.

The back popped off, and Colton pulled it away. He didn't know what he expected to find. But he thought it was strange that Loretta had gone through this trouble and not mentioned anything to Sarah.

"Colton, what's that?" Sarah whispered.

Using his knife, he slid an envelope from the back of the painting. It had been taped there.

His breath hitched.

This was it, he realized.

This was the clue they'd been looking for. He felt sure of it.

The police wouldn't have noticed a painting like this. Wouldn't have thought to check behind it.

Only Sarah would have.

Which was what made it the perfect place to leave an envelope like this.

"You want to open this?" Colton asked.

Sarah's eyes were wide as she stared at it. Finally, she nodded. "Yeah, I do."

"You want to be alone?"

She shook her head. "No, would you stay with me?"

He reached down and squeezed her hand. "Of course."

Drawing in a shaky breath, Sarah took the envelope from him and carefully opened the seal. Colton braced himself for whatever they were about to learn.

Sarah could hardly see the words scrawled on the note that she slipped from the envelope. But she definitely recognized Loretta's beautiful scrawl with all of its loops and magnificence. As an artist, Sarah knew how to appreciate the simple things—even something like handwriting.

"I… I can't read it," Sarah said. "My hands are shaking too much."

"Would you like me to read it for you?" Colton asked, stepping up beside her—close enough that they touched. That she could smell his leathery scent. That she could feel the electricity between them.

"If you don't mind."

He took the paper from her and cleared his throat. "'Sarah, if you found this, it probably means something has happened to me. I know we've only known each other a short while, but I saw something in you instantly—some of the same qualities I saw in myself. Determination. Passion. And even loneliness.'"

Tears rushed to Sarah's eyes. Had it been that obvious?

"'I know my death will probably come as a shock to you and to most people. But I've felt for a while that someone was after me. I probably should have said something, but I feared it could be my disease acting up and messing with my mind.'" Colton glanced up at her. "Sarah, this note might clear you."

Her heart raced with anticipation. Maybe he was right. "Go on. Please."

"'When you're rich, you never know if people like you for who you are or for your money. But when I met you in the park, I knew you loved Buzz without ever having a clue about me or my wealth. And, if you could do that, I knew you were a good person. We need more good people in the world.'" Colton used his thumb to wipe away the moisture beneath Sarah's eye. "You are a good person, Sarah."

"How could you say that after everything we went through? I can't believe you don't hate me."

"You're not the kind of person a guy can hate. You're too kind."

His words sucked the air from her lungs. Did that mean he still cared for her? That maybe they could even like each other again and be friends?

The thought shouldn't bring her so much joy, but it did.

Colton turned back to the letter. "'When I was first starting out in this business, someone believed in me and gave me money to help get my business started. I would never be where I'm at today without that person. Sarah, I know you struggle with trying to make it in the art world. I don't have many regrets in life, but one of them is that I never married and had children. Toward the end of life, you realize how utterly alone you are in the world. It was just me and Buzz for the longest time.'"

Sarah reached down and rubbed Buzz's head. The dog leaned into her touch as he sat there beside them, acting like he understood every word Colton spoke.

"'As I've been thinking about the end of my life and

the legacy I want to leave, I've decided several things. Upon my death, I want half of my money to go to the charities outlined in my will. But I want the rest to go to you, Sarah.'"

Sarah gasped. "What?"

"You had no idea she was leaving her money to you?" Colton studied her face.

"No, no idea. I've only known her a few months." Why would someone leave that much money to a virtual stranger?

"It sounds like she really believed in you."

"I had no idea."

Sarah wiped the tears that had begun to stream down her face. Loretta's words had touched her more than she'd imagined. She was still having trouble comprehending all of this.

"This could also make you even more of a suspect, Sarah." Colton's soft words felt like a lightning strike in the room.

"What?"

"It gives you a motive, Sarah."

"But she said she felt like someone was after her."

"Yeah, in the days since you moved into the house. The police will turn this around and think that you're that person."

She hung her head. "We really do need to find the person responsible, don't we?"

"Yeah, we really do."

"What do we do with the letter in the meantime?" She looked at the words that Loretta had so carefully crafted. Words that brought her both comfort and distress.

"I'm going to hold on to it—for now. We'll return

things the way we left them. We'll figure out the best course of action later."

Sarah nodded. "Okay."

As Colton put the painting back together, Sarah walked to the window. She peered out and spotted Loretta's neighbor Mr. Everett walk into the garage behind his house.

How could Sarah have forgotten about him? The man was always watching this house. Watching Loretta. It had been so strange... Sarah had thought about asking Loretta about it, but she hadn't had the chance.

But maybe today was the day she could find out some answers.

EIGHTEEN

Colton looked over at Sarah, noting the change in her demeanor just now as she looked out the window. What had she seen? Trouble? The police?

"What is it, Sarah?"

"Mr. Everett next door," Sarah said quickly, glancing back at Colton. "He was always watching everything. What if he saw something on the night of the murder?"

"It's a possibility, I suppose. I'm sure the police have already talked to him, though."

Her words rushed together as excitement lit in her eyes. "But we don't know what he told them. And his son is a cop. Maybe that's why Loretta said not to trust the police. Maybe Mr. Everett is somehow involved in this and his son is connected also."

Colton chewed on her words for a moment. She could have a point. He still found it strange that Loretta had told Sarah not to trust law enforcement. Her words had to be significant, but why?

"You sure you want to take the risk of talking to him?" Colton asked. "He could call and report you. I'm not sure the payoff will be worth it."

She grabbed his arm, her gaze filled with emotion.

"I know what you're saying, but I'm desperate, Colton. I want answers. Mr. Everett could have those answers. If we catch him by surprise, we can get away before he calls the police."

Heat rushed through him as he felt her touch. Sarah had always had that effect on him, and their time apart had done nothing to change that.

He wasn't sure why he'd kissed her forehead earlier. There was just something about her vulnerability that captured his heart, that made him want to connect with her.

It was probably a mistake.

Finally, he nodded. "Then let's go see what Mr. Everett has to say."

"Thank you."

Just as carefully as they'd come into Loretta's house, they exited. Except this time, instead of heading back to the truck, they skirted around the side of the house toward the snowy hedges separating the two residences.

Colton knew this was risky, but Sarah was right. They needed answers right now.

Colton could hear classic rock blaring from a radio. Mr. Everett had his garage door open, despite the chilly weather, and he heard the sound of tools clanking inside.

"He likes to restore classic cars," Sarah whispered. "It became his new hobby after he retired as a stockbroker."

"Good to know." Colton nodded to the other side of the man's garage. "I think you and Buzz should stay out of sight. Close enough to listen, but not close enough to clue him in that you're here. Okay?"

Sarah nodded and took a step back, nudging Buzz to follow her. "Okay."

Sarah and Buzz remained behind some greenery, unable to be seen by Mr. Everett.

"Excuse me, sir," Colton started.

The man paused from examining the engine of a classic Mustang and turned down his music. "Yes?"

Colton examined the man a minute. He looked like a retired businessman with his neat white hair—still full—and lean build. His skin was relatively unwrinkled and even his work clothes looked expensive. "I'm investigating what happened to Loretta Blanchard, and I was hoping you might be able to help."

"I've already talked to the police." His voice held a sharp edge, but he didn't sound angry. No, he sounded grief stricken and cautious.

"I'm just trying to find out more information on what happened."

Mr. Everett still stared, traces of doubt in his gaze. "My son is a cop. I know how these things work."

"What department does your son work for?" Colton asked, trying to both build some comradery and find out more information.

"He's out in California now. Moved there four years ago, wanting more excitement than policing around here lent itself to."

"Everyone's looking for a little something different. I was a detective in Seattle before, and I wanted something slower paced."

"I think you're smarter than my son." Mr. Everett let out a chuckle. "Then again, I told him he should go into finance like me. My advice obviously means nothing."

"You might be surprised."

He shrugged and wiped the grease from his hands onto an old rag. "What do you want to know?"

"Did you see anything suspicious here on the night Loretta died?" Colton shifted as he waited for his answer.

"Yeah, I saw that assistant of hers and the dog run from the house like they were afraid of being caught." Mr. Everett frowned and shook his head, his shoulders slumping slightly. "It's a shame because Loretta really liked that girl. Don't want to believe she would do something like this."

Colton blanched at his incriminating words. "What about after that? Did you stick around long enough to see if anyone else came?"

"No, I called the police. I'd seen everything I needed to see."

"So you went inside to do that?"

Mr. Everett picked up his thermos and took a sip. "That's right. I didn't have my cell phone on me."

"Had you talked to Loretta's assistant before that?"

"No, but I'd seen her. She seemed nice enough. But looks can be deceiving."

The case against Sarah continued to build. And bringing her here had been the wrong choice. Colton had no doubt about that. He needed to get her out of here before Mr. Everett saw her.

But, before he could, a motorcycle heading down the road sounded in the distance. Mr. Everett stepped out to see what the commotion was.

Colton glanced at Sarah as she quickly stepped behind the building.

But it was too late.

Mr. Everett looked down and saw the dog prints in the snow.

"Who else is with you?" Mr. Everett asked, accusation flashing in his gaze. "What's your real reason for being here?"

Colton braced himself for whatever would happen next.

But he maintained his position that coming here had been a bad, bad idea.

And now all his fears might become a reality.

Sarah knew she had to step in and do something. Mr. Everett knew someone else was here. Give him a few more minutes, and he'd probably realize it was her and Buzz.

Praying she didn't regret it, she stepped out with hands raised. "It's me. Sarah Peterson and Buzz. I'm not trying to start trouble."

Mr. Everett's eyebrows shot up, and he took a step back.

"What are *you* doing here?" he gasped. "The police are looking for you. You're a murder suspect."

"I didn't kill Loretta," Sarah said. "I'm trying to find answers."

"Are you not really a cop?" Mr. Everett's gaze swerved to Colton.

"I was a detective in Seattle for eight years, but I'm on a break right now. Mr. Everett, Sarah didn't kill Loretta."

"I'll let a court decide that." Mr. Everett took another step back, like he might take off in a run to get his phone.

"Mr. Everett, please," Sarah pleaded. "Just hear me out for a moment. I'm trying to figure out what happened to Loretta. I saw a man in her room attack her before she died. Buzz jumped on him. I need to figure out who that was."

His eyes still held doubt, but he didn't look ready to do anything stupid—not for the moment, at least. Instead, he reached toward Buzz, who'd sauntered over to him, tail wagging.

"You miss her, don't you, boy?" Mr. Everett murmured. "She always said you were a special dog."

Sarah's heart warmed at the sight of Mr. Everett with Buzz. A certain amount of loss saturated his words, bent his body. If this situation was different at the moment, their grief might have bonded them all.

"How do I know you're not making all of this up?" Mr. Everett finally asked, straightening and putting his hands on his hips.

Sarah stepped closer. "Because I cared about Loretta. Because I'm living a nightmare right now. Because I'm putting everything on the line to find answers." Sarah's voice cracked with emotion as she looked at Mr. Everett.

The man continued to stare.

"Anything you might know will help," Colton said. "Did you see anything else that night?"

"The only thing I saw was you running." Mr. Everett's gaze fell back on Sarah.

Another thought continued to nudge her. Sarah knew she was taking a risk by saying this aloud, but she had no choice. "Mr. Everett, I saw you watching Loretta on more than one occasion. Why did you always keep an eye on her?"

His face paled. "What? You don't know what you're talking about."

"I do, though," Sarah continued. "I saw you on more

than one occasion. What aren't you telling us? Are *you* behind all of this?"

He gasped, his eyes turning beady. "I would never, ever hurt Loretta. Never."

"Then why were you watching her?" Colton asked.

Mr. Everett raised his chin, but there was a quiver there. "You were seeing things."

"But I wasn't," Sarah continued. "Were you memorizing her schedule?"

"No!" His voice nearly came out as a yell. Then his shoulders fell, and he squeezed the skin between his eyes. "I loved her."

Silence feel around them. Had Sarah just heard that correctly?

"You what?" Sarah asked.

"I loved her." Mr. Everett shook his head, grief seeming to overtake him. "I wanted to tell her how I felt, but I was always too chicken to do so."

"And that's why you were watching her?" Sarah repeated, disbelief stretching through her voice. Could he actually be telling the truth?

"Yes. Why would I kill her? I have everything I could want. I made millions in the stock market. I have a big house, but no one to share it with. I'm retired. I just wanted a companion." Tears rimmed his eyes. "I would never, ever hurt Loretta. Never. In fact, I'll miss our talks. Loretta was spirited and passionate. I haven't met many women like her."

Reality settled on Sarah. This man was telling the truth. Mr. Everett wouldn't hurt Loretta, and he hadn't seen anything else at the house that evening.

Disappointment bit at her.

"I'm sorry to have upset you," Sarah said, taking a step back. "And I'm sorry for your loss."

Mr. Everett looked away and said nothing.

"Did your son know Loretta?" Colton asked.

Mr. Everett's eyebrows shot up. "My son? What does he have to do with this?"

"I'm just asking a question."

"No, he's never even met her. I just moved here three years ago. He was already in California, and he hasn't been back to visit since then."

"I'm…sorry," Sarah said, her voice soft. "Are you going to call the police on us?"

Mr. Everett remained silent a moment, a frown tugging at the sides of his mouth. "I don't have much choice. It's my duty as a citizen. Why don't you let the justice system prove your innocence?"

"I might have to eventually. But, until then, I need to find answers. Loretta asked for my help. She asked me to take care of Buzz. And I don't want to let her down."

"I suppose that's admirable."

Colton took Sarah's elbow, seeming ready to usher her away from this area.

But Sarah looked back at Mr. Everett one more time. "At least give us a head start. Because I didn't kill Loretta. I cared about her also. I'm just trying to figure out who's responsible."

After a moment of thought, Mr. Everett nodded. "You've got five minutes until I call the police and tell them what happened when they arrive. And find her killer for me. Please. Because Loretta deserves justice."

Just as he said the words, sirens sounded in the distance.

Colton grabbed Sarah's hand. "Come on. We've gotta get out of here. Now."

Sarah swallowed back her panic.

She wasn't sure which she feared more: the police or the bad guy catching her.

Either way, she'd be a goner.

And that thought only made her move faster.

NINETEEN

Colton knew he, Sarah and Buzz were on borrowed time. If he didn't move now, it might be too late.

"There's a lane behind my house that leads to the highway," Mr. Everett said, pointing in the distance. "Take that. It will give you a little bit of a head start, at least."

Colton hoped the man was telling the truth and not setting them up. "Thank you," he muttered, giving him a final nod.

Then Colton grabbed Sarah's hand and they darted to his truck, climbed inside and quickly tugged on their seat belts.

He was going to have to ditch this vehicle soon, he realized. It was too easily recognizable by now. But Colton would have to think about that later—he didn't want to add car theft to his list of offenses.

Colton knew, deep down inside, that he might not even have a career in law enforcement when all this was done. As far as police were concerned, he was harboring a fugitive. He could be charged as an accessory to a crime.

Casting those thoughts aside, he pressed the accelerator and took off toward the back of the property. He prayed that he didn't regret this. There was no time to think—only to react. Colton just had to move if he wanted all of them to get out of this in one piece.

"You okay?" He glanced at Sarah and saw her holding on to the armrest, her eyes wide and her skin pale.

"I... I guess." She didn't sound convinced.

They'd have to talk more about it later.

Colton reached the end of the lane and held his breath. Finally, he spotted the road that Mr. Everett had told him about. Thank goodness.

It was probably used by hunters who wanted to access the woods at the back of the property during the season.

Colton turned onto it. He hoped to loop around and avoid the police. Most of all, he prayed this wasn't a trap—a dead-end road where they wouldn't be able to get away.

"How'd they find us?" Sarah asked, sounding breathless as she stared straight ahead, looking dazed.

Buzz lay down on the seat behind them and let out a little whine. The canine obviously didn't like this. Neither did Colton.

"I don't know," Colton said. "I'm sure there's an all-points bulletin for my truck. Did Loretta's house have some kind of alarm system maybe?"

"Yes, but it was disabled when we went inside. That shouldn't have triggered anything."

"I don't know. It doesn't matter right now. All that matters is that we get away."

A few minutes of silence passed as the landscape blurred past—lots of trees covered in snow, and occasional glimpses of a river in the distance. Any other day, this drive would be beautiful—the landscape was untouched.

But not right now.

"Colton, I know I've said this before, but I'm really sorry I pulled you into this." Sarah crossed her arms over her chest, her voice wispy with emotion.

Colton hated to see her looking so guilty, so burdened. She blamed herself for too much—for her dad leaving, for her mom being put in jail, for her sister being sent to a different foster home. She just seemed so alone.

"It's okay, Sarah," he told her. "I'm a grown man. I don't do anything I don't want to do."

As he saw three police cars drive past, Colton pulled onto the highway, going in the opposite direction.

He released a breath.

They were clear—for the moment. But Colton knew it wouldn't last long.

"Where are you going now?" Sarah asked, glancing around as if trying to gather her wits. This area had a few little shops and restaurants dotting the streets. Colton didn't know the streets well, but he needed to figure it out quickly.

"We don't have any choice but to hide until this situation clears. We've got to figure out another plan, and I need a new vehicle to drive. We're not safe in this one anymore."

Sarah's jaw clenched as she stared out the window. She was scared.

And she needed to be. When a person felt fear, their survival instincts kicked in. Those instincts could keep people alive as they chose either fight or flight.

Sarah had chosen fight.

Much like Buzz. The dog had great intuition. Without Buzz, they might not be alive right now. He'd alerted them to the man in the park, essentially saving Sarah's life. He'd tried to protect Loretta. He'd won the trust of Mr. Everett.

Buzz was more than a pet or even just an emotional support dog. He was a protector—and that was just the kind of dog Colton could admire.

"What do you think about that letter Loretta left you?" Colton asked, interested in getting her feedback now that the letter had time to sink in.

Loretta's words had touched Colton. The woman had seen the real Sarah—the one who was kind and artistic. Sarah wasn't the killer people were making her out to be. Thank goodness Loretta had seen all the potential in her.

Sarah shook her head. "I really don't know. I had no idea she felt that way about me. Honestly, she was always fussing. I didn't think she liked me at all."

"Your love for Buzz made an impression on her."

Sarah shook her head. "It makes me so sad to realize how, even with all of her success, she felt so lonely in her last days."

"She had you."

"She did, but I was hired help. I… I guess I don't know how I feel yet."

Colton took a quick right onto another road as he saw another police car ahead. He held his breath, waiting to see flashing police lights. Waiting for a chase.

There was none.

The cop car turned the opposite direction.

Colton wasn't sure they were going to get out of

this without being caught. But he was going to try to do everything in his power to make it happen.

Sarah closed her eyes and said prayer after prayer.

She didn't want to be caught. Didn't want to go to prison.

But she really didn't want to ruin Colton's life either. Maybe she cared about him more than she'd ever realized. Because the thought of turning his life upside down broke her heart in two.

Colton didn't deserve this. He hadn't done anything. No, she'd pulled him into this crazy situation, and now Sarah needed to figure out a way to get him out.

Sarah stared out the window at the darkening landscape. They were driving deeper into the heart of the mountains, deeper into the countryside and away from Spokane. Was this how she'd spend the rest of her life? She'd either be arrested and potentially go to jail for a crime she didn't commit—or she would have to go into hiding.

Neither option was appealing.

As Colton took another sharp turn, she grabbed the bar above the door and held on. She trusted Colton as a driver. He was always calm, always in control. He always made her feel safe.

But this whole situation had her on edge.

Crime wasn't her world. Art was. She liked to create beautiful things.

But somehow everything had been turned upside down.

Sarah said more prayers and glanced behind her.

She didn't see any police cars headed their way.

Maybe they'd lost them.

For a while.

Colton also glanced into the rearview mirror. As he did, his shoulders seemed to relax and lower—just slightly. If circumstances were different, she might reach over and try to ease some of the tautness from his back.

But those times were past. Not even his sweet kiss on the forehead would change that.

Sarah looked in the backseat at Buzz. The dog was sleeping—finally. He seemed to be working security detail constantly, never letting down his guard. It would be good that everyone was breathing easier, if only for a minute.

"Are we going back to your friend's cabin?" Sarah asked.

"That's the plan. For now. It's the only safe place I can think of. At least we can regroup there."

The idea of being safe had never felt so tempting. All she wanted was to relax. To pretend like nothing was happening.

What she wouldn't do to turn back time. And just how far would she go if she could?

Maybe she would go back two years. Maybe she should have never broken up with Colton. If Sarah hadn't broken up with Colton, she wouldn't be in this mess right now. No, she'd probably have a safe home to return to. Someone to watch her back. The life she'd always wanted. But she'd sabotaged herself.

That was it, wasn't it? She'd been so afraid of getting hurt that she'd jumped the gun and tried to end their relationship before her worst-case scenarios were played out.

But she couldn't forget the issues they'd faced. It

hadn't been all sunshine and roses, no matter how much Sarah might want to paint the past like that.

It was too easy to forget how withdrawn Colton had become during his crisis. Too easy to forget their problems. The warning flags that had been raised in her mind.

"What are you thinking about?" Colton asked, his voice soft and prodding.

Sarah swallowed hard. Should she tell him?

No, she decided. Her thoughts were too vulnerable. Colton would laugh at her. He'd obviously moved on. Bought a house. Started a new job. Dealt with the emotional blow that had happened when he was a Seattle detective.

"Just…everything," she finally said, glancing down at her hands in her lap.

"That's a lot."

She managed a wry smile. "Yes, it is. I miss the days of worrying about whether or not I would sell a painting."

"Life has a tendency to put things in perspective sometimes."

"Aren't you worried about your career, Colton?"

He remained quiet a moment before offering a half shrug. "Maybe a little."

She appreciated his honesty.

"But we're going to prove you didn't do this, Sarah," he continued. "Then we'll both be cleared."

Just as he said the words, his phone rang.

He glanced at the screen and frowned.

"Who is it?" Sarah asked, already expecting the worst.

"It's one of my contacts with Spokane Police Department."

She sucked in a deep breath at his words. That couldn't be a good sign. No way. "Are you going to answer?"

He frowned again and raked a hand through his hair before nodding. "Yeah, I better. I can only avoid the truth for so long."

TWENTY

"Hey, Manning," Colton said. "What's going on?"

Manning's voice came through the truck's Bluetooth. Any other time, Colton might have pulled over to talk, but he couldn't afford to lose momentum. They needed to keep moving right now.

"Colton, I just got an all-points bulletin for a truck. The license plate indicates the vehicle is registered to you."

He sucked in a breath. That was the last thing he wanted to hear, yet he wasn't surprised. It had only been a matter of time. He didn't want to own up to anything. Not yet. He wanted more answers first.

"I'm sorry to hear that," Colton said, trying to choose his words carefully.

"Should I be concerned?" Manning continued.

Colton's jaw tightened as he stared at the road, apprehension building in his chest. "Manning, you guys are looking at the wrong person. Sarah Peterson didn't have anything to do with Loretta Blanchard's death."

"Then why is she running? It's usually the first sign of guilt."

"Maybe because she doesn't want to take the fall for

a crime she didn't commit. Loretta warned her not to trust the cops."

"Why would she say that?"

"Maybe because a dirty cop was involved in her death."

Manning paused. "And just so we're straight, you're helping her?"

Colton hesitated again. "I'm looking for answers."

"Colton, I've got to tell you that the evidence is pretty clear that she's behind this. Her prints were on the murder weapon. She was seen leaving the scene. She took money with her."

"That doesn't mean she's guilty. She saw a man in Loretta's room. She was set up."

"Why don't you bring her in and let her tell us her side of the story?"

Colton glanced at Sarah. She stared at him, looking like she was barely breathing.

"That's her choice," he finally said.

"You must have feelings for this woman."

Feelings? Did Colton still have feelings for Sarah? "My feelings don't matter right now."

"Just a little advice—don't throw your career away for a woman. You willing to go to jail for this woman?"

Colton squeezed the steering wheel tighter, desperately wishing Sarah wasn't here to overhear this conversation. "If that's what has to happen."

"I wish you hadn't said that."

"You'll see, Manning. She's innocent."

Manning's voice dipped, and he sounded almost apologetic. "Until then, as far as I'm concerned, you're both guilty. And my guys are going to find you."

"How about, instead, you try to find out who the cop is who's involved?"

Before Manning could respond, Colton ended the call and felt the burden of the whole situation press on him. Beside him, Sarah stared out the window, not saying a word—which was worse than her giving him an earful.

Tension stretched between the two of them—tension that he could feel with every pulse of his heart.

Colton didn't want to admit it, but he knew the truth. He'd never stopped caring about Sarah. And he probably never would.

Thankfully, the road leading to the cabin came into view. He turned down the gravel lane and headed up the mountain into an even darker darkness.

He paused at the top, just within eyesight of the cabin.

From here, the house looked clear.

But Colton would need to check it out before he exposed Sarah and Buzz to whatever might be waiting out of sight.

No one should have found this location. But he was better safe than sorry. Loretta's killer seemed to find them at every turn—first through the phone, then the dog's collar. Who knew what other tricks he had up his sleeve, so to speak?

He put the truck in Park and turned to Sarah. "Wait here."

Then he drew his gun and hopped out. He had to make sure everything was clear.

And then he needed to come up with a plan of action. Because what they were doing right now didn't seem to be working.

* * *

Sarah reached back to rub Buzz's head as she waited for Colton to return.

Colton thought someone might be hiding out inside, just waiting to grab them or arrest them or kill them for that matter. The thought wasn't comforting.

Nor was that phone call. It was just like Sarah had suspected. Colton was in serious trouble for helping her. She should have never pulled him into this. But now it was too late. He was in too deep.

"What are we going to do, Buzz?" she murmured.

The dog nuzzled her hand in response, seeming to sense her distress.

A moment later, Colton stepped onto the porch and motioned that it was safe for them to come inside.

Sarah climbed from his truck, waiting as Buzz hopped out beside her. Though Colton had indicated it was safe, that didn't stop her from moving quickly. Her body felt programmed to expect danger. As soon as she was inside, a wave of relief filled her.

For a moment—and just a moment—she felt safe. And she'd never realized just how much she valued that feeling until now.

"We should have grabbed something to eat while we were out," Colton said. "It looks like it will be canned soup again."

"I'm grateful just to have food," she said. And she meant it. If she was doing this on her own…she'd probably be dead right now. Or starving. Or cold.

So many things.

Colton smiled, a nostalgic look drifting through his gaze. "You always were content with the simple things."

"I guess when you've lived with absolutely nothing, you learn to be." The words caught in her throat.

She didn't like to talk about her past. She didn't want people to feel sorry for her. But her past contained so many answers about why she was the way she was today. All of those heartaches had shaped her. Then God's grace had smoothed some of the rough edges. That grace was still smoothing rough edges.

Colton's smile faded. "Yeah, I guess so. So what will it be? Chicken noodle or vegetable beef?"

"Vegetable beef sounds great."

"I'll cook then."

Sarah went over to the fireplace and added logs. It had been a long time since she'd actually started a fire. After finding the lighter, she managed to successfully start the flames. Once they were sufficiently fanned and the logs were burning, she stepped back, satisfied with her work.

She lowered herself near the fire and pulled a blanket over her legs to ward away the cold. The scent of the soup filled the cabin and created a lovely atmosphere, despite their circumstances.

There had always been something about log cabins that she loved, that made her feel warm and cozy inside. In fact, living in a place like this—or even in a cabin like Colton's—would be so perfect.

As long as she had her art supplies, of course.

Why had she ever thought anything otherwise? She'd had everything she wanted and needed right in front of her. She'd been such a fool. And now it was too late to ever make things right, wasn't it?

"You were brave today, Sarah," Colton said across the room.

She felt the heat rise on her cheeks. "I don't know about brave. Maybe just determined."

"No, you were brave. A lot of people would be crushed by now, but not you."

"Thank you," she finally said, unsure of what else to say.

Colton paused from stirring the soup. "You look beautiful, Sarah."

Sarah blinked. Had she heard him correctly? Certainly not, because Colton had told her when they broke up that if she left, they were done for good. And Colton was always a man of his word.

So why in the world had he said those words just now?

Either way, it would be better if Sarah forgot them, along with all the feelings that had begun stirring inside her chest.

Besides, she needed to focus on clearing her name and finding Loretta's killer. Nothing could distract her from that.

Not even Colton.

Especially not Colton.

Colton clamped his mouth shut as he continued to stir the soup. Why had he said that?

He wasn't even sure where the words came from. They'd just left his lips before he had a chance to stop them—and that was something that never happened. Colton was always one to choose his words carefully.

But something changed in him when he was around Sarah.

And looking at her just now with the plaid blanket around her, with Buzz at her feet, with the fireplace bathing her skin in hues of orange and yellow...it made his dreams come alive again.

For better or worse.

A flustered look crossed Sarah's face, and she looked like she tried to smile but failed. Instead, she stood and went to the fireplace to stoke the logs again—probably desperate to avoid his gaze.

He couldn't blame her.

A few minutes later, they were seated in front of the fire with soup in hand. Colton had made some rice and gravy for Buzz also, and he happily ate from a bowl in the kitchen.

For a moment—and just a moment—things felt normal. He and Sarah sitting here and eating together felt normal, like old times.

His heart raced when he realized it was anything but.

"Do you miss police work?" Sarah asked.

Colton nodded slowly. "Yeah, I actually do. Sometimes. But the break has been good for me."

Sarah stole a glance at him, her gaze softening. "I know that last investigation was really hard on you."

He ate another bite of his soup and took his time swallowing, chewing on his response for a moment. "Yeah, it was. But I've been through counseling, and I'm doing better."

"I'm glad."

Colton would have been doing even better if Sarah had stuck with him. She'd given up on their relationship so easily. Given up on him.

They could have had such a great life together. Sarah had brought something out in him that made him feel alive. That made Colton want to explore the unknown. To relax instead of working all the time. To seek out the beauty in life. And Colton liked to think that he'd offered Sarah security and protection and love.

But maybe that hadn't been enough.

She glanced at her hands. "You know, after seeing Loretta…die…and then seeing Frank…it makes me understand what you went through a little more. It's not easy seeing someone lose his or her life…and I can't imagine being in the position you were in."

Colton cleared this throat, touched by her words. "It's not easy. In fact, it can be crippling."

"I'm sorry I wasn't there for you."

His heart pounded in his ears at her soft words. Just that one sentence seemed to unleash something in him. But he still held back, still waited.

"What's next for you, Sarah?" he asked. "When all of this is over?"

"Assuming this ends well?"

"Assuming life goes back to some semblance of normal."

Colton studied Sarah as he waited for her answer. She looked adorable as she sat there. She'd pulled her hair back into a ponytail, making her seem even more youthful than her twenty-seven years.

This was the Sarah he missed.

She paused with her spoon halfway to her mouth. "It's hard to say. I'll no longer have a job. I probably won't be able to find one in Spokane now that my name has been dragged through the mud."

"So you'll move?" He had to keep talking to her like this would end well. He had to keep hope alive. But he knew deep down inside that this whole situation might not have the closure they both longed for.

Sarah shrugged. "Maybe. I haven't even thought

about it. There have been several times I've thought about going back to waitressing. It's not a lot of money, but at least it's a paycheck."

The thought of Sarah throwing her dreams away twisted his insides. "I don't want to sound like a broken record, but you have a lot of talent, Sarah. You should pursue it."

She shrugged. "Why does it really matter anymore? All my work is gone. I've been trying so hard, and nothing has come from it except heartache. Maybe I should take that as a sign. In fact, maybe the writing has been on the wall for a long time."

"Sarah…"

"It's true. Besides, you and I both know that all of this is going to change everything. Who knows if we'll even get out of this situation alive…"

"I'm going to do everything I can to protect you, Sarah."

A sad smile tugged at her lips. "Thank you."

"Further, you'll have some of Loretta's money at the end of this. That's probably several million dollars."

"I don't want her money." Sarah shook her head, moisture flooding her eyes as she remembered all the events leading up to that realization.

"Really?" Not many people would turn down that amount of money.

"Really. I don't… I don't know. I don't deserve it."

"Why would you say that?"

She swiped a stray hair behind her ear. "I didn't know Loretta that well, for starters. And money usually comes with strings attached, you know?"

Colton wondered if Sarah was thinking about the job she'd moved to Spokane for. The one where her boss had expected more than she'd promised. The thought of it still made anger burn in him. "What if there aren't any strings attached?"

She put her mug down, pulled her knees to her chest and shrugged. "I don't really know. I really just wish Loretta was back. I'd rather have people in my life than money."

"I know you would, Sarah."

"I've missed you, Colton." Suddenly Sarah's cheeks flushed and she looked away, a hand going to her forehead like she tried to cover her embarrassment. "I'm sorry. I don't know where that came from."

"I've missed you too, Sarah." His heart panged with longing that he'd tried to bury for so long.

Without thinking—or overthinking—he reached over and put his arm around Sarah, pulling her toward him until her head hit his chest. He hated thinking about her being all alone. He couldn't stop thinking about Loretta's words in that letter—about how they'd shared being all alone in the world. No one should have to say that.

To his surprise, Sarah nestled into him, nearly melting in his embrace.

It felt so good to have her close. To breathe in her honeysuckle scent. To feel her silky hair beneath his chin.

"Colton?"

His breath caught. "Yes?"

Sarah raised her head. "I just thought you should know that letting you go was one of the biggest mistakes I've ever made."

Her words washed over him, causing his heart to thump out of control. Her affirmation was all he needed to confirm that they both still had feelings for each other…feelings that might be worth exploring again.

Colton reached up, his hand brushing her jaw. Her neck. Her cheek.

Sarah was so beautiful. And so perfect for him.

His lips met hers, and all the feelings they'd once shared for each other seemed to explode in one sweet moment.

This was Sarah. His Sarah. The only person he'd ever wanted to be with.

Except she wasn't his.

The thought nearly made Colton's muscles freeze.

He couldn't go through another heartache like the one he'd experienced when they broke up. He couldn't.

Colton pulled away and looked down at the floor. "I'm sorry. I shouldn't have done that."

His words seemed to startle Sarah, and she drew back, her eyes fluttering again with embarrassment. "You're right. Of course not. I don't know what we were thinking."

As the words left her mouth, she stood and grabbed their mugs. "I should clean up."

And then Sarah was gone.

Colton bit down. He'd messed that up. Or had he? He knew he needed to keep his distance, as hard as it might be. When he saw Sarah, there was nothing more that he wanted to do than step back in time. He wanted to pretend that nothing had changed. That they were still together.

But that wasn't the case. She'd broken his heart, and he'd be wise to remember that.

Then why was Colton's heart telling him otherwise?

His jaw tightened.

None of this was supposed to happen. When Sarah walked away, he'd figured she was gone for good. Now they'd been thrown together in these fantastical circumstances.

Colton just needed to concentrate on the goal right now—keeping Sarah alive. That was all that was important. And the task was becoming harder with every day that passed. It had become obvious that the person behind Loretta's murder would stop at nothing to reach Sarah.

And as the noose tightened, Colton needed every bit of his focus to be on this investigation. Their lives depended on it.

TWENTY-ONE

Sarah put the mugs in the sink and began to furiously clean them.

What had she been thinking? Why had she ever even let herself dream that they might have a second chance?

She knew Colton better than that. Knew that once he said they were done, they were done. Yet foolishly she'd allowed herself to think about another future with him. His momentary look of desire had quickly been replaced with a look of hurt.

The thing was that she couldn't even blame him for not giving her a second chance. She was the one who'd messed up things between them, and she'd be a fool to ever think otherwise.

"You know, I'm going to take a shower since we still have water," she said once the dishes were done.

"Okay then. I'll keep watch out here and maybe let Buzz out."

"That sounds perfect." Really, she would take any excuse she could find to get away from the man.

As she stepped toward the bathroom door, Colton called her name.

She paused and glanced at him.

He opened his mouth, as if there were things he wanted to say. Then he shut it again.

"It's okay, Colton," Sarah said. "You don't have to say anything. Really."

Before he could try to force any more conversation, Sarah stepped into the bathroom. As soon as the door closed, she leaned against it, feeling the effects of humiliation and regret.

If she even managed to get out of this situation without jail time, her future seemed so bleak.

Colton nearly kicked himself for messing that up.

But maybe it had been the right thing. Usually these issues were so much clearer to him.

Why did everything feel like it was upside down now that Sarah had come back into his life?

He called Buzz. "Let's go outside, boy."

Colton would let the dog stretch while also keeping an eye on the place. Maybe cooling off was the best thing he could do right now.

After slipping his boots back on and tugging on a coat, he stepped into the frigid winter wonderland outside his door. The blackness around him—even though he should be used to it—still felt unnerving after everything that had happened.

He hadn't really had the chance to explore this property, though he did know that his friend owned about thirty acres. The two went way back. In fact, Jack had dated Colton's sister at one time, and he and Jack had remained friends. However, the connection was so distant that Colton didn't think the police would find him here.

But Colton didn't know how long they'd be safe at this location. He needed to keep thinking of other ideas.

Because he was fully invested in this now. Despite what had just happened between him and Sarah, Colton wouldn't turn his back on her.

He saw a barn in the distance and decided to check out that area, just in case they ever needed it.

Buzz trotted along beside him as he tromped through the snow.

With one last glance back at the house, Colton pulled the barn door open and stepped inside.

A truck was parked there.

Colton went to it and tugged the driver's side door. To his surprise, it opened.

His friend must store this here for off-roading. It didn't surprise Colton.

He climbed into the driver's seat. After reaching under the front seat, Colton found the keys.

Country living at its finest. People out here didn't give a second thought to leaving their keys hidden.

He placed them back under the seat and stepped back out into the barn.

"We should probably get back inside now, huh, boy?" he asked the dog.

Buzz wagged his tail in response.

Colton stepped outside, closing the barn door beside him. He glanced around as he walked back toward the cabin, but he saw nothing unusual. Heard nothing unusual.

He had a hard time thinking that someone could track them down here. They just needed a safe place to stay until they could collect their thoughts.

A safe place…

That was all Sarah said she wanted.

And if she didn't feel safe, she fled, didn't she?

He could hardly blame her considering how she'd grown up.

He stepped inside and heard that the water was off in the bathroom. While he had a free moment, he did a quick online search for Yvonne, Loretta's biggest competitor, and then sent a few emails, including one to Detective Simmons, letting him know what was going on.

A moment later, the door opened, followed by a cloud of steam. Sarah stepped out with her wet hair falling around her face and her skin looking clean and refreshed.

She offered a shy smile.

Colton's heart thudded out of control.

If he was smart, he would grab on to her and never let her go. He would fight for another chance at a relationship with everything inside him.

Was it his pride that stood in the way?

Before he could examine the question any further, Buzz's hair stood on end, and he growled at the front of the cabin.

Colton and Sarah exchanged a look.

Buzz knew something they didn't.

Buzz knew someone else was here.

TWENTY-TWO

Sarah watched as Colton's eyes widened.

Something was wrong.

He grabbed some water and doused out the fire, leaving them in almost complete blackness.

"Put your shoes and jacket on," he whispered.

She did as he instructed, too scared to argue.

"Stay down," Colton said.

Sarah dropped down behind the couch, her skin crawling with fear.

What was going on? What had Buzz heard?

The dog was smart enough to only alert if there was real danger.

There must be someone outside.

And if that man had the chance, he'd kill them. This could be the opportunity when nothing stopped him.

Colton glanced out the window. "He's here."

"What's he doing?"

"I don't know," Colton said. "I don't see him right now. I only see that he parked his sedan behind the truck."

"He blocked us in," Sarah muttered.

"That's what it looks like."

Sarah sniffed, a new scent filling the air. She gasped. "Colton, is that—"

"Gasoline," he finished. "He's going to set this place on fire."

Colton burst from his position near the window and darted toward her. He took her hand and pulled her toward the back door. She barely had time to grab her purse and Buzz's bag before he threw the back door open.

As he did, a ball of flames exploded around them. They leaped over the fire just as it started around them, before landing in the snow.

They didn't have time to stop. Colton pulled Sarah to her feet and called for Buzz to follow.

He grabbed a branch from an evergreen tree near the deck and broke it off. Using the needles there, he covered the tracks behind them as they ran into the barn and climbed into a truck there.

"What's this doing here?" Sarah asked, stopping for a minute to stare in awe.

"I don't know, but I found it earlier."

"What's our plan?" she continued.

"That man will probably check the house."

"Is he trying to kill us?"

"Or smoke us out. Either way, we to need to get out of here soon."

"I can't believe this is happening." A tremble claimed her voice.

"Hold tight," Colton said. "Because once we leave, we're getting out of here and not looking back. I'm not going to give this guy time to find us."

She pulled on her seat belt. "Whatever you say."

But she had her doubts they were going to be able to

pull this off. The stakes were too high. This guy was too relentless.

She lifted a prayer that Colton's plan would work. If it didn't, she had no idea what else to do.

Colton climbed from the truck and peered out a crack in the barn door.

In the distance, he saw his friend's cabin going up in flames.

He was going to have a lot of explaining to do. Colton had never intended on this happening. But that man had found them—again.

What were they missing?

It didn't matter right now. All that mattered was getting out of here.

Movement caught his eye.

It was the man.

He was checking out his work by walking around the house.

Colton wasn't sure if his footprint cover-up had worked. Maybe he'd bought them a little time, at least.

Just as the thought entered his mind, the man paused.

He saw the tracks, Colton realized.

And the man was following them to the barn.

Colton waited until the man was halfway there. Too soon, and he'd allow the man too much time. Too late, and they'd be sitting ducks.

Now he just had to pray that the truck started.

He rushed back to it and climbed inside.

Lifting a prayer, he put the key in the ignition.

The truck started.

Thank You, Jesus.

Wasting no more time, he put the truck in Drive and pressed the accelerator.

"What are you doing?" Sarah asked, again holding on for dear life.

"Sorry—but brace yourself." The truck burst through the barn doors.

As it did, the man froze just outside the structure before diving out of the way.

Colton didn't slow down. He charged forward, moving as quickly as he could.

Soon, the tires hit the gravel lane leading to the cabin. Then the tires hit the road.

He glanced in his rearview mirror.

Headlights lit the dark.

The man was going to follow them.

But Colton had a head start. He needed to utilize it as much as he could.

Their lives depended on it.

TWENTY-THREE

Sarah closed her eyes and prayed. Prayed hard. Prayed harder than she could remember doing in recent years—which said a lot because she'd had many pressing concerns to lift up over...well, over her entire life.

But these back roads were so slick and dark and curvy.

She didn't see how she, Colton and Buzz were going to survive this.

The cabin fire had made it clear that this man was out to kill, and nothing would stop him from getting what he wanted.

As Colton followed the curve of the road, Buzz fell onto her, momentum shifting his body weight.

Sarah leaned into the dog and got a whiff of the piney scent of his shampoo. The scent immediately brought her comfort. This dog had been such a trouper. Sarah felt the need to protect him whatever the cost. Buzz was special to her—and he'd also been so special to Loretta.

Sarah couldn't let her boss down. Taking care of Buzz was nonnegotiable.

"Watch out," Colton muttered.

He made another sharp turn to the left. As the truck

righted itself, its tires left the asphalt and churned on gravel instead. They climbed a steep incline, and the road narrowed in front of them as they snaked up higher and higher.

"Where are we?" Sarah asked, looking around, her heart pounding.

"This is an old logging road."

"What if it's a dead end? What if we're trapped?"

"Let's pray that's not the case." Colton kept moving forward, the tires crunching the rocks beneath them as they sped out of sight and into further isolation.

Sarah looked back, expecting to see headlights.

She saw nothing but darkness.

Had they lost the man? Could she even hope?

She wouldn't breathe easier for a while. No, there was too much at stake.

The road seemed so treacherous, and blackness surrounded them. At any moment, the path in front of them could end at a cliff, undetectable in their vision.

Even if the man didn't directly kill them, there were still so many other dangers.

Please, Lord, help us now! I beg You. We're out of options.

"You have no idea where this road leads?" Sarah muttered, still trying to find hope in this situation as alarms sounded in her head.

"No idea. Probably a field or clearing."

That wasn't what she wanted to hear. "Does it cut through to another road?"

"Also no idea."

Sarah's anxiety continued to rise at the great unknown before them. "Maybe I can check your phone.

Maybe a map feature will show us where we are and where we're going."

"There's no service out here."

"Colton…" Her voice came out as a wispy gasp. There was no need to try to conceal her fear any longer. Her life was flashing before her eyes.

"We're going to be okay."

Colton kept saying that. But did he really believe it? Because nothing in her life had been okay. Nothing. She had nothing and no one. Not even her paintings. Not even the woman who'd let her live in her house.

When this was over, Sarah had nowhere to go and nothing to do to earn money.

She swallowed the despair that wanted to consume her.

Colton muttered something under his breath before swerving to the left.

Ice slid beneath the wheels, and they careened into the darkness.

As Colton tapped the brakes, the truck glided toward the blackness.

Toward what was a cliff at the edge of the road.

She closed her eyes, certain they were going to die.

Colton pressed the brakes, holding his breath as the unthinkable began to play out.

The truck began to slide on the icy ground beneath them.

No! They hadn't come this far for this. No way. He couldn't let it happen.

Dear God, I need Your assistance right now. Desperately. Unequivocally.

Gently, he turned the wheel, trying to veer them

away from the edge of the cliff that would mean certain death.

They inched closer and closer, moving as if in slow motion.

No, Lord...please, help us!

The truck was out of his control and at the mercy of the ice…and God.

Sarah reached over and grabbed his hand, squeezing it as if her life was depending on it.

They both seemed to hold their breath as they watched and waited.

Only a few inches shy of the drop-off, the truck stopped.

Stopped.

It didn't fall.

The vehicle stood still, completely upright and safe.

Colton released the air from his lungs and felt his shoulders sag with relief. They were okay. They were really okay.

That had been close.

Too close.

He glanced over at Sarah and Buzz, checking to see how they were doing. Sarah looked pale but otherwise okay.

Buzz let out a little bark, as if telling Colton he wasn't happy with him right now.

But they were safe, and that was all that mattered.

Colton raked a hand through his hair.

"I thought we were going to die," Sarah finally muttered, her head dropping against the seat behind her.

"But we didn't."

She turned toward him, her eyes full of questions. "What now?"

Survival instincts pounded with each pulse of his heart, and adrenaline rushed through him. "We're going to keep heading down this road—at a slower pace. We're going to see where it leads, and then we'll probably just have to park somewhere for the night and conceal the truck."

"And then?"

He desperately wanted to tell Sarah they were going to get through this unscathed. But he couldn't do that because the closer danger pressed, the more he realized how precarious this situation was.

"And then we figure out what we can do in the morning."

"What if that man finds us here?"

Colton had thought about that. The man was smart. He was no doubt looking for them now. The good news was that there were a lot of logging roads like this in the area.

"I do know that in this area, there are no cell phone signals. It's pretty remote. There's a good chance that if he's tracking us using technology, which is what I suspect he's doing, he won't be able to get a read on our location."

"Most likely?"

He shrugged. "I wish I could offer more, but I don't want to lie to you."

"I appreciate that." Sarah crossed her arms and looked out the window. "I guess we should get going then."

Good. Sarah was staying strong and trying not to panic. Those two traits would go a long way.

TWENTY-FOUR

It took several minutes for Sarah's heart to stop pounding out of control. But Colton had slowed down, and the road right now wasn't nestled up to the edge of a cliff. She could breathe a little easier.

Silence fell in the truck. Buzz lay between them, his head in Sarah's lap. Since the dog was relaxing, it seemed a good sign that Sarah should be able to relax also. No cars followed them. There didn't appear to be any more patches of ice. Just a quiet nighttime drive through the countryside.

In different circumstances, this would seem like an adventure. A chance to see the crystal clear sky above and the stars nestled there. To listen to the sounds of the forest at night. The payoffs would include a campfire and moments of heart-to-heart talks and dreaming about the future.

Those things had changed when she and Colton had split. She hadn't realized how much she missed those times.

Ten minutes later, Colton hit the brakes again and backed into a small clearing between some trees.

"Seems as good a place as any to set up camp for the night."

"If you say so."

Without saying anything more, Colton hopped out, found some branches and covered the front of the truck. He then climbed back in and took Buzz out for a bathroom break.

Sarah listened in silence for a moment.

And that's what it was around here—quiet. There was nothing to hear except for Colton and Buzz walking. A few minutes later, they were back, and Colton turned toward her.

"We should be safe here for a little while," Colton said. His breath already caused a frosty puff to form in front of his face. "We should try to get some rest because who knows what tomorrow holds."

As a brisk wind swept in with the open door, it brought Colton's leathery scent. For a moment, Sarah craved his closeness. His warmth.

Too bad what she craved could never be hers.

"I suppose none of us know what tomorrow holds," she finally said. "Isn't that what the Bible says?"

He nodded slowly, looking weary for the first time since all of this began. "Yes, it is. And then the Bible goes on to tell us that we shouldn't worry."

Sarah crossed her arms, longing for a blanket and a warm drink. She wished for her Bible so she could read it, and maybe even a good devotional book to remind her of what to do when she got off track.

"It feels impossible not to worry in a situation like this one," she said. "I'm trying to cast all my cares upon the Lord, but it's so hard sometimes."

"God knows the path set before us," Colton said. "It's

hard to keep that in mind sometimes, though. I've lost sight of it many times."

"Yes, it is hard to remember." Her faith in God had been all that had gotten her through many difficult seasons. But she felt like she was floundering right now, uncertain about everything.

A few seconds ticked by. Tension stretched between them. Unspoken conversations battled to surface. The desire to relive the past warred inside them both.

Sarah longed to feel the warmth Colton offered. To share sweet kisses and promises of tomorrow. But the reality was that she and Colton were better off keeping their walls up.

"Sarah, about earlier—"

She had to stop Colton before it went any further. The last thing she needed was a clumsy explanation or an awkward conversation. "You don't have to explain. You really don't."

That last case—it was the one that had changed everything. That had turned their relationship upside down. That had driven an invisible wedge between them that neither had conquered.

"I know…it's just that after that last case…" Colton started, his voice taking on a new kind of exhaustion.

"Every officer told you they would have done exactly what you did given the situation."

Colton glanced down at his hands, calloused from hard work. "I know. But I killed a man in front of his wife and kids."

She could hear how haunted his voice still sounded. "You tried to stop him. He was about to kill all of you. Besides, I know you tried every method possible to stop him. Shooting him was a last resort. He had his gun drawn on his wife."

His jaw tightened. "She was just so angry afterward, even though she would have died otherwise. She attacked me, yelling. Furious at what I'd done."

"The human mind is complex. You know that."

He nodded. "I do."

"And you just became so distant after that," Sarah continued. "I didn't think you'd ever snap out of it."

"You didn't give me a chance to. You left." His voice sounded hoarse with emotion.

She glanced at her lap. "I probably shouldn't have. But I got scared. I saw what tragedy did to my father. He lost his job, panicked that he couldn't support his family and he became a different person. He left, and the rest of us never recovered. Since I was a kid, I've learned to put up walls to stay safe and not get hurt. When I saw you changing into a different person right in front of me…"

Colton grabbed her hand, his gaze locking with hers. "I wasn't changing. I was just dealing."

"My experiences don't tell me that. My experiences tell me that I should end things before I get hurt. I've already had enough hurt to last a lifetime."

"Sarah…"

Sarah shrugged. "I don't know what else to say. I regret it. There. Are you happy? I miss you. I cried for days, wishing things were different."

"And they could have been." Colton's voice came out soft, full of regret.

She glanced at him. "But I guess it doesn't matter anymore, does it?"

He frowned. "No, I guess it doesn't. What's done is done."

"Or like you always say, it is what it is."

His jaw tightened again, and he turned away. "I guess you and I should both get some sleep."

"We should." She shifted until her back was toward him. "Good night."

"Good night."

Colton had hardly slept the whole night. No, he'd stayed awake, listening and looking for any sign of trouble around them in the carefully hidden truck.

All he saw was darkness.

Colton could only assume that the person following them had some type of electronic device that he used to keep tabs on them. At first it was Sarah's phone. Then it was Buzz's collar.

What was this guy using now?

Colton would need to go through Sarah's purse when she woke up and make sure there were no tracking devices there. This guy continually had the upper hand, and that wasn't okay.

As the nighttime began to fade to gray, his mind wandered to his friend's cabin. Had firefighters come? Had they put the blaze out? It was only a matter of time before the cops realized Colton had been there.

His truck had been parked outside the cabin. The bloody clothes that Sarah had worn on the night of Loretta's murder were inside. No doubt they would look guilty when the cops found that bag—if it hadn't burned up in the flames. It was hard to know exactly how devastating the fire had been.

He glanced at Sarah as she cuddled against the seat

with Buzz's head on her lap. She looked like such an angel when she slept, as her blond hair fell in her face and her lips were slightly parted.

He'd give anything to wake up to this sight every morning. If only he could forget about the way she'd hurt him.

He had kissed her…and it had felt wonderful. Too wonderful. He'd been swept back in time to better days. Days that he longed for. Maybe it had even sparked some hope in him.

But should he even let himself go there again?

Logically, Colton knew he shouldn't. But emotionally, he wanted to give them another chance. He wanted to believe they had a future together.

He needed to sort out just how much he was willing to risk. The last thing he wanted was to have his heart broken again.

Absently, he reached over and rubbed Buzz's back. The dog was sleeping right now, but Colton had no doubt he would be instantly alert if danger came close.

Finally, the sunlight began to peek over the horizon, and the sky turned a misty gray color. Today was supposed to be sunny, and the snowstorms were supposed to have passed—for now.

Colton had to figure out a plan of action here, but he was drawing a blank as to where to go next. There were no clear options. Not in his mind, at least.

Sarah began to stir. Beautiful, sweet Sarah.

It was too bad there was just so much history between them. That the divide was too vast. His heart ached at the thought.

"Morning," he said.

She sat up straight and smoothed out her shirt as

she blinked and glanced around. "Morning. I guess we survived."

"We survived."

She yawned and stretched as she tried to wake up. "You didn't see anyone?"

"Not a soul."

Instinctively, it seemed, Sarah reached over and patted Buzz's head. The dog mimicked Sarah by yawning and stretching also. "That's good news, at least."

"I agree."

She turned toward him. "What now?"

"Now I think we should head back to Spokane." He'd been giving it some thought as he'd watched the night pass.

"Really?" Sarah's eyebrows shot up. "What are we going to do there?"

"Last night before the fire, while you were in the shower, I checked online, and it looks like Yvonne is back in town."

She was the next logical person to question. However, the woman could be connected with Loretta's death. If Yvonne was the killer, then she could try to silence Colton and Sarah. If she wasn't the killer, she might call the cops.

It was a risk. Then again, everything about this had been risky. They weren't going to find any answers unless they did things outside their comfort zone.

"You think she'll talk to us?" Sarah asked.

"I think there's only one way we can find out."

Sarah turned toward him, her gaze unwavering. "I'm game then. Let's go."

Colton nodded, glad she was willing. But he also prayed this decision was wise and he wasn't putting them in unnecessary danger. It was one thing if he put himself at risk. But putting Sarah in the line of fire was an entirely different story.

Please, Lord. Keep Sarah safe. Help us find answers. And end this nightmare sooner rather than later.

TWENTY-FIVE

Sarah couldn't stop thinking about the conversation she had with Colton yesterday. So much of what needed to be said had finally been spoken aloud. She was grateful for those conversations, even if they opened up reminders that she'd rather forget.

Reminders about what a good thing they'd had. Reminders about how imperfect they both were. Reminders that there were some obstacles too hard to overcome.

Because she might be trying to convince herself of that, but her heart said otherwise. Her heart told her there was no one else in this world she'd rather be with.

They pulled back onto the road leading to Spokane. She glanced around the mountainy road, getting a better glimpse of it right now in the daylight.

"This area really is so beautiful."

"I love it out here."

"Where you live is nice also."

"I like it. It's quiet, but I'm close enough that I can get places if I need to."

Sarah wondered what it would be like to live up there. Now that she'd seen it with her own eyes, she realized there was a tranquility to the area.

"Sarah, I need you to look through your purse and see if there's anything there this guy could be tracking us with," Colton said.

"You think that's how he's finding us now?"

"I just know he's resourceful. I want to check all our bases here."

"Of course." She rummaged through everything there but found nothing that looked like a tracking device. She had her wallet, ChapStick, some powder in a compact, a few mints. "There's really nothing."

He let out a grunt. "It just doesn't make sense."

Just as he said the words, a car pulled onto the road right in front of them.

Colton threw on his brakes to stop in time.

Sarah gasped, bracing herself for impact.

The truck halted just in time.

But before they could even catch their breath, Sarah saw that it was a police car.

"Colton…" she muttered.

"Is this a cop who's chasing us down…or the killer?"

A man in uniform stepped out of the driver's seat. With a gun. Pointed at them.

Sarah saw his face, his build and instinctively knew this man was the killer.

He'd finally caught them. And they had nowhere to go.

"Stay behind me," Colton said, eyeing the cop with the gun.

Colton knew he couldn't reach for his own weapon in time. No, the man would shoot all of them before Colton could reach into his waistband and pull it out.

"Get out!" the man yelled.

Colton glanced at Sarah, concerned for her safety.

There was no one out here on this road. Earlier, that had seemed like a great idea. Right now, it seemed like they'd driven right into a trap.

Above them was a tall mountain loaded with snow. On the other side was a cliff.

"I'm scared," Sarah muttered.

"Like I said, just stay behind me," Colton told her.

Slowly, he climbed from the truck, his hands raised. Buzz jumped out behind him and let out a low growl. Colton didn't bother to tell the dog to back off.

Sarah climbed out also, walked around the back of the truck and stood behind Colton, just as he'd directed.

"What do you want?" Colton asked.

The man chuckled. "You still don't know? Really?"

"We have no idea."

"Oh, isn't this smart. You guys were harder to get to than I thought. Kudos for that."

Colton studied the man. He carried himself like a law enforcement officer.

Was this man a cop? It would explain how he'd tracked them so easily. It would also explain why Loretta had said not to trust cops.

But what was this man's connection with Loretta? He had no idea what the man could be after.

Maybe it was the money Sarah was going to inherit from Loretta? It was the only thing that made sense.

"You should have never gone to work for Loretta," the man said, looking at Sarah.

"Why not?" Sarah asked. "What was so bad about working for her?"

"You got yourself in this mess, didn't you?"

"I didn't do anything. I was just taking care of Buzz."

The man chuckled again. "Well, I'm sorry you have to be a part of this, if it's any consolation."

"It's not," Sarah responded. "What are you going to do with us?"

"I have no reason to keep you alive. This isn't the way I wanted to do it, though."

"You should just let us go. Tell us what you want, and we'll be out of your life," Sarah continued.

"It's not that easy."

"Sure it is," Colton said. "We don't want to be a part of this any more than you want us to be a part of it."

"I just need the formula."

Colton and Sarah both froze and glanced at each other.

"What formula?" Colton asked, trying to buy time.

"For the new drug Loretta was developing."

"I don't have the formula," Sarah muttered.

The man scowled. "Yes, you do. We overheard Loretta talking. That's what she said."

"Who was she talking with?" Sarah asked, looking as confused as Colton felt.

"It doesn't matter. What matters is that you have something I want." Patience—if there had been any—disappeared from the man's voice.

"If I do, I don't know where it is." Sarah's voice trembled.

"Come on. Don't make me do this the hard way."

"Why are you trying to kill me?" Sarah asked. "How will you find this information out if I'm dead?"

It was a great question. Colton tried to put the pieces together.

"At least you'd be out of my way. But I haven't been

able to find this information anywhere, so it must be on you somewhere."

"Where?" Sarah raised her hands. "I have nothing."

"It's somewhere. Tell me where."

"I don't know," Sarah said.

"Tell me!" The man raised his gun in the air, anger flashing in his gaze.

As the man pulled the trigger, Colton dove over Sarah, protecting her from the shot.

But as soon as they hit the ground, a rumble sounded above them.

Colton looked up just in time to see the start of an avalanche.

TWENTY-SIX

Colton grabbed Sarah's hand and pulled her toward the truck. Buzz remained at their heels.

The terrible rumbling that Sarah heard got her blood racing.

She wasn't sure they were going to make it.

They dove into the truck and Colton threw it into Reverse. Carefully—but quickly—he backed the truck down the curvy mountain road.

Sarah wanted to close her eyes. She didn't want to see—what was in front of her or behind.

Yet she couldn't look away.

The road in front of them already had chunks of snow falling on it—chunks big enough to squash someone.

Her eyes searched for the cop who'd been ready to kill them.

His police car was still on the side of the road. He had just climbed inside.

But the snow had already covered half of it.

She said a prayer.

That man might be evil, but she didn't want to see anyone die.

Swiveling her head again, Sarah glanced behind her and sucked in a deep breath.

Another snow clump, the size of a boulder, hit the side of the cop car. Colton threw the truck into Drive and did a three-point turn. Then he quickly dodged around the snow. Another mass hit the top of the vehicle.

This time Sarah did close her eyes.

This could be the end. She had no doubt about that.

Please, Lord. Help us. I know I keep asking that but I'm at the end of my rope.

More boulder-like pieces of snow and ice hit the road. The truck swerved and slid on the ice, nearly skating across the street.

Sarah grabbed the front of the dashboard, trying to steady herself. Her heart flipped and leaped inside her.

They'd left one danger behind, only to face this.

She drew in some deep breaths, trying to calm down.

A few seconds later, the truck was no longer sliding or swerving.

She dared to open her eyes and glance at Colton. His hands were white-knuckled on the steering wheel. Determination tightened his jaw.

But the road in front of them was clear.

She looked back once more and saw the cloud of snow and ice on the road.

The avalanche had destroyed the windy mountain lane.

But she, Colton and Buzz were okay.

She let out a breath, her thoughts swirling. They were really okay.

"You did it," she told Colton. "You got away."

"Only by the grace of God." Colton glanced behind him. "I'm not sure that guy did."

"No, I can't imagine that's the case." Sarah turned back to him, her voice catching. "Colton, a cop is involved with this. That's why Loretta warned me. This appears to be tied in with Loretta's drug company after all." Sarah shook her head in disbelief.

"Are you wearing any jewelry Loretta gave you? Do you have a credit card? Anything?"

"No, just that money that was in the backpack I took with me when I left Loretta's house with Buzz."

"Somehow, someway, this guy thought you had the formula. That's why he's been chasing us. The man also used the word *we*. That means he's working with someone."

Sarah stared out the window. "I just have no idea who that would be."

Colton handed her his phone. "Why don't you see if there's any new information in the news today? It might be our best source at this point."

She typed in Loretta's name and waited for the search results to populate. Several articles filled the screen. Mostly they were about the snow this winter, about an avalanche not far from here, and then there were more articles about Loretta.

"I guess they're having a funeral for Loretta in two days," she muttered. "They're expecting it to be big."

"As to be expected," Colton said. "Who's planning it?"

She skimmed the article, her eyes widening. "It looks like Yvonne is."

"Interesting. I guess that's why she came back into town early."

Sarah's gaze stopped at a quote from the story. "Colton, Yvonne is calling me out here in the article as Loretta's killer."

"What did she say?"

"That I should come forward. That Loretta trusted me, and I should be ashamed of myself for what I did. That it's my fault there's such a great loss to the medical community."

"You know none of that is true, right?"

Sarah nodded, knowing logically that Colton was right. But emotionally, the words felt like a stab to her heart. Even if she survived, how would she recover from this? Everyone thought she was a killer.

Maybe she had nothing to lose at this point. She needed to find answers now more than ever.

Colton wished he could snap his fingers and things would automatically right themselves. But he knew that couldn't happen. Though they'd made progress on this case, they still had so far to go.

Who had that man worked for? How was he involved in this? Colton still had so many questions that he wanted answers.

Behind him, Buzz let out a low whine and licked his paw.

"Sarah…?"

She leaned toward the dog. "What is it, boy?"

Buzz let out another whine when she touched his leg.

"Colton, there's a cut on his paw." Her voice tightened with worry. "It must have happened when we ran for the truck before the avalanche."

"How deep does it look?"

She cringed as she peered at the injury. "It looks pretty deep."

"See if there's anything in the glove compartment. Maybe we can wrap it."

She opened the door and pulled out a handkerchief. "This will work."

Carefully, she wrapped it around Buzz's paw. Within seconds, the cloth had turned red, though.

"We're going to have to take him to the vet, Sarah," Colton said.

"I agree," Sarah said. She couldn't stand the thought of the dog being in pain. "But Buzz is so identifiable. People will know who he is. They'll know who we are. How are we going to deal with that?"

"I'm not sure. But we don't have any other choice."

Sarah nodded. "I guess we'll just have to take that chance. He's risked his life for us more than once. Now it's our turn to help him."

TWENTY-SEVEN

Apprehension grew in Colton as they headed down the road. The man in the police car might be out of the picture right now, but someone else had been calling the shots. Whoever that person was, they were still faceless—and still a danger.

The man had mentioned a formula, which made Colton assume this had to do with the drug business. His thoughts immediately went to Yvonne.

It made sense for someone at a competing company to want to steal information. And Yvonne had the financial means to hire someone to help her get this proprietary formula. Maybe Yvonne had even planned for everything to happen while she was out of the country so she could have the perfect alibi.

Colton didn't know, but those things seemed like a good possibility.

"Sarah, I know this is going to sound crazy," Colton started, his mind snapping back to the present. "But I think we should take Buzz to his regular vet."

Her eyes widened before she quickly shook her head in disbelief. "Why would we do that?"

"Because it's another connection to Loretta. Maybe she talked to him."

"Loretta did love to talk about Buzz. And I did hear her mention the vet a few times. But it's so risky."

"At this point, everything is risky. I'm sure every cop within sixty miles of here is looking for us. It's only a matter of time, Sarah."

She frowned, a far-off look in her eyes. "If you really think that's what we should do, then let's do it. I trust you."

Instinctively, Sarah seemed to reach out and run her hand down Buzz's back. Fluffy pieces of hair floated in the air, but she didn't seem to notice.

Sarah's words did something to Colton's heart. *I trust you.* The two of them had come a long way over the past couple of days, Colton mused. Being thrown together in these circumstances had caused them to reevaluate everything, he supposed.

"What do you think of this, Buzz?" Sarah murmured.

The dog offered one affirmative bark.

"You like the idea?" she continued.

He barked again.

"I guess it's settled then." Sarah shrugged. "If Buzz is okay with it, then so am I."

Colton held back a smile. If only circumstances were different, this would be a memory to always hold close. "I guess so. You remember the vet's name?"

"It's Devon Kellogg. I even know where his office his. I went there once. Nice man."

"Great. Let's go."

Sarah directed him on how to get to the office. As Colton traveled, he kept his guard up, looking for anyone who might follow them.

He saw nothing.

But he couldn't relax yet. If any law enforcement saw them, they'd be done.

Colton wasn't ready to face that. No, they needed more answers first. Because whoever was behind this had resources. He had no doubt this person would do everything within his or her power to frame Sarah for Loretta's murder.

He couldn't stomach the thought of Sarah being behind bars, and he would risk everything to stop that from happening.

Fifteen minutes later, they pulled up to a little brick office building that sat on the corner of a secondary road. Behind the vet's office was a gas station and then a grocery store stretched at the back of the lot. At least it was partially secluded here. He was thankful for that.

"What now?" Sarah asked, turning toward him in the truck.

Colton glanced at his watch. "It's lunchtime now. Do you think they close for lunch?"

She studied the area around them and shrugged. "I don't know. There aren't that many cars in the parking lot right now. Maybe that's a good sign."

As if on cue, a woman in scrubs stepped from a back door and climbed in her car.

"Any idea how many office workers he has?" Colton asked, trying to get a feel for the office.

"It's a small practice. Loretta liked it that way. When I came here with her once, the only people I remember are the receptionist and the doctor. I can't say for sure that's accurate, though."

"I think I should go inside with Buzz first," Colton said. "I'll be less recognizable with the dog."

"What about me?"

"Give it a few minutes and then come in. Keep your hat and sunglasses on. Make sure you wear the coat. It covers up some of your frame."

Sarah nodded, but the action made her look nervous. "Okay. Got it."

Colton took Buzz's leash, hoping this risk paid off. "Let's do this, boy."

Carefully, he helped the dog out, and he prayed for the best.

Sarah couldn't stop reliving the images of the avalanche covering that man's car. Though he'd tried to kill them, it still startled her to think about dying in that manner.

It also startled her to think about the fact that she, Colton and Buzz could have easily died that way also. If it hadn't been for Colton's quick thinking, none of them would be here right now.

Sarah always felt so safe when Colton was around. She deeply appreciated his involvement right now. She literally wouldn't have survived without him.

But as she stared at the door leading into the vet's office, a tingle of worry crept in.

A bad feeling lingered in her gut. Certainly Dr. Kellogg would recognize Buzz. He'd probably feel inclined to call the cops, whether he believed their story or not.

And then what would they do?

Sarah had no idea. But she wasn't ready to go to jail yet. She had to make something of her life first. Redeem her mistakes. End the pattern of sorrow her parents had laid out. It couldn't be too late for that.

Please, God...

She waited for five minutes before climbing from the truck. Tugging her hat down lower, she glanced around. She didn't see any cops or people watching her. That was a good sign. Maybe that meant that things were going smoothly inside so far. She hoped they would continue.

Sarah pulled the front door open and paused. Colton sat in the waiting area with Buzz lying at his feet. No one else was around.

She slipped into the seat beside him and whispered, "What's going on?"

"The vet just stuck his head out and said he'd be a minute," Colton whispered back. "That's all."

Anxiety continued to build. Dr. Kellogg hadn't seen Buzz yet. It was the calm before the storm.

Just then, Dr. Kellogg stepped out from the hallway, a big smile on his face. The man was probably in his fifties, but his hair was already white and matched his full mustache. The doctor was tall and thin and friendly.

"I'm afraid we're closed for lunch right now," he said pausing in front of them, his hands pressed together. He glanced at Buzz who wagged his tail at the sight of the doctor. "What's going on?"

Colton cleared his throat. "Our dog cut his foot. He's bleeding."

The doctor's eyes narrowed as he gazed at Buzz. He squatted down in front of the canine and picked up his paw. "Yes, you did hurt your foot, didn't you?"

"We're just worried that it won't heal correctly," Colton said.

"I understand." He rose. "You know what? I'll squeeze you guys in. Let me just get the room ready." He stepped back down the hallway.

But Sarah's warning bells were going off. He'd recognized Buzz, hadn't he? The doctor wasn't getting the room ready. No, he was probably calling the cops.

Before she could second-guess herself, Sarah stepped down the hallway and nudged the door open an inch or two. Sure enough, the doctor had his phone in his hand and had begun dialing.

"Wait," she said, stepping into the room. "Please, don't."

Dr. Kellogg's eyes widened, and he lowered the phone. Realization washed over his features. "I almost didn't recognize you, Sarah."

"That's me."

His grim frown was all the answer she needed.

"A lot of people are looking for you right now," he said.

"I know. And I know why they're looking for me. But I would have never hurt Loretta. In fact, I'm trying to protect Buzz and figure out who did this."

"Protect Buzz?"

Sarah nodded. "The real killer has been chasing us. He thinks we have something that used to belong to Loretta. But I don't. But he's willing to hurt us to get what he wants. That's how Buzz was injured."

Dr. Kellogg observed her for a minute before nodding slowly. "Loretta always spoke highly of you, you know."

"That's what I heard. I was…surprised." There was no need to skirt around the truth.

"She liked for people to be scared of her initially. After time, she would get softer." He smiled.

"I guess we didn't have enough time then."

"No, you didn't." His grin faded. "I was really sorry to hear what happened to her."

She swallowed hard. "Me too. Look, I know it's weird that I came here. But I'm desperate for answers, and Buzz truly does need help. I thought you might have talked to Loretta. That you might know something that could help us find her killer."

"What are you looking for?" He crossed his arms, phone still in hand, but then shook his head. "You know what? Bring Buzz in here. Let me look at him. And we can talk while I do that."

Sarah stepped into the hallway and motioned for Colton and Buzz to join her. A minute later, they all squeezed into the examination room, and Dr. Kellogg checked out Buzz's paw.

"I don't know what to tell you about Loretta," Dr. Kellogg started. "She didn't tell me anything too personal. Most of our conversations were about Buzz."

"When was the last time you saw her?" Colton asked. "I know Sarah said she brought Buzz in once. I'm talking before that."

"She came in about two months ago. Brought someone with her. I guess she hadn't hired you yet back then."

Sarah's breath caught. "Do you remember who she brought with her to help? She had trouble going out with Buzz in her wheelchair alone."

His lips twisted in thought. "I believe she said it was her landscaper."

Sarah and Colton exchanged a look.

"Frank?" Sarah asked. "Frank Mills?"

The doctor nodded, his eyes lighting up with recognition. "Yes, that sounds right."

Was that the connection they'd been looking for? Had Frank known more than they ever suspected?

"Why did Loretta come in?" Sarah asked. "For a normal checkup?"

"No, she actually wanted to update Buzz's microchip."

Everything began falling in place in Sarah's mind, but she still needed confirmation. "A new one? Was something wrong with the old one?"

"She said she'd developed a new, more effective one herself. She asked me if I'd mind helping her with it. Normally, I'd say no to something like that. But this was Loretta, and I knew she was on the genius level as far as IQ. Since it was her request, I did it for her."

"Did she say why this one was more effective?" Colton asked.

"No, she didn't. But I trusted her."

Sarah rubbed Buzz's head. "Is that all she said?"

"It is. I didn't ask too many questions." He bandaged Buzz's foot and then stood. "He should be all better now."

"Thank you for your help," Sarah said.

He turned apologetic. "I'll pretend you weren't here. I'm headed out to lunch. But be gone when I get back. And find Loretta's killer, okay?"

"We will," Sarah said.

He smiled down at the dog. "Buzz is a great dog."

Dr. Kellogg slipped out the back door. Sarah and Colton waited a couple minutes before stepping into the lobby.

Colton turned toward her, excitement dancing in his eyes. "The formula. It's on the microchip. It all makes sense now."

"You're right. It does."

Just then, a shadow darted out from behind the front desk.

A shadow holding a gun.

Sarah looked up. It was Debbie Wilcox, the CFO of Loretta's company.

Based on the lasers shooting from her eyes, she was here on a mission.

TWENTY-EIGHT

Colton stepped in front of Sarah and Buzz.

"What are you doing here, Debbie?" he asked, more puzzle pieces clicking together in his mind.

Yvonne was never behind this, was she? No, it had been Debbie this whole time.

Gone was the placid woman in mourning from the office. In her place was someone with vengeance and greed in her eyes. Right now, her business suit looked disheveled, as did her hair, as she stood in front of them.

"I tried to call Tad." Debbie sounded breathless. "He didn't answer. That's when I heard about the avalanche."

"Tad?" Colton asked. "Was he your boyfriend?"

Tears welled in Debbie's eyes. "Yes, that's right. We were in this together. You…you killed him."

"That's not true," Colton said. "He fired his gun, which started the avalanche."

"If you hadn't made things so difficult…" she sneered.

"How have you been following us, Debbie?" Sarah asked. "Were you tracking us via Buzz's microchip?"

She let out a haughty laugh. "No, there's no GPS in the microchip. My life couldn't possibly be that easy."

"Then how?" Sarah asked.

"Well, at first it was your phone, then it was Buzz's collar. But you two were smarter than I'd assumed. Finally, we started to track Colton's phone."

"But my phone is untraceable. You might have been able to get a radius from the signal triangulation, but you shouldn't have been able to track my exact location."

She smiled again. "Everything is traceable when you have the right resources."

"But you didn't know the formula information was on the microchip until today, did you?" Colton asked.

"I had no idea until I just heard you saying that. I only knew that Loretta had given the formula to you, Sarah. If we could get to you, we could get the information we needed."

Sarah's eyes widened with surprise. "How did you know that she'd given it to me? I didn't even know that."

"I heard her say she had the utmost confidence that you would protect it with your life."

Sarah let out a soft laugh. "She was right. I would protect Buzz with my life."

Debbie sneered again. "It wasn't supposed to end this way."

"It doesn't have to end this way," Colton said, his voice placid.

Debbie sniffled and then straightened. "Actually, it does. It just took me a while to realize it. Give me the dog."

"No way," Sarah muttered.

Debbie smiled again. "Of course you're not going to do this the easy way. That dog was the perfect place for Loretta to hide the formula for that new drug she was working on."

Colton frowned. "That dog has a formula in his microchip that will make you a lot of money, in other words."

"Exactly." Debbie's nostrils flared. "I should have been helping her. Loretta asked me some questions about this drug, but she never told me exactly what she was working on. So I sneaked into her lab one day and found out."

"And then you wanted to steal it from her?" Colton's stomach churned at the thought of the lengths people would go to for wealth and notoriety.

"I deserved this. I helped her with so much. And then she decides to give half her money to her." She snarled at Sarah.

"How'd you know?" Sarah asked, holding on to Buzz's leash like a lifeline.

"I overheard Loretta on the phone talking about it. After I figured out that she was up to something, I decided to get creative and planted a few bugs here and there. With the help of Tad, of course." The satisfaction in her voice tapered into sadness.

"I don't care about the money," Sarah said. "It was never about that."

"Must be nice to live in that kind of world," Debbie said.

"What about Frank? Why did you kill him?" Colton asked, even though he thought he knew the answer.

"I tried to get information from him. I figured he knew. But he wouldn't talk. He knew what I'd done. I had no other choice."

"You're a heartless, cruel woman," Sarah said, a look of pure disgust on her face.

"I just want what rightfully should be mine."

"You won't get away with this." Sarah pulled Buzz back.

"We'll see about that. I just need to get the microchip from Buzz, and I'll be out of your way." Debbie patted her leg. "Come here, boy."

Buzz growled.

Debbie's scowl grew. "I said come here. Don't make me do this the hard way."

Sarah stepped in front of Buzz. "Over my dead body."

"Okay, if we have to do it that way." Debbie raised her gun again.

"No!" Colton shouted, panic racing through him. "It doesn't have to be like this."

Debbie sneered. "Oh, honey. I've thought of every way possible. Yes, it does. Nothing is going to stand in my way."

"Try Buzz one more time," Sarah said.

What was Sarah doing? Certainly she had a plan here. No way would she say something like that without a good reason.

Colton hoped.

Debbie eyed her a moment before tapping her leg, a touch of hesitation to her actions. "Come here, boy."

Just as Sarah released the leash, she clucked her tongue. It was some kind of signal, wasn't it?

When she did, Buzz hurled toward Debbie, teeth bared.

Debbie's eyes widened with fear. She raised her gun. Pulled the trigger.

But the gun misfired. Nothing happened.

Instead, Debbie raised her hands to protect herself and let out a scream.

Buzz pounced on her, pinning her to the ground.

Colton grabbed her gun. Buzz continued to hold her down, growling on top of her, as the doors flew open. Police flooded inside.

As Detective Manning from the Spokane Police Department stepped inside, he gave a nod to Colton. "Someone from the gas station spotted you both in the truck that was taken from the cabin fire. They called in the tip."

"I figured we were on borrowed time," Colton said.

Manning frowned. "I got the email you sent, explaining what was going on."

"As you'll find out, Sarah wasn't behind any of this. Debbie Wilcox was." Colton glanced at Sarah, who practically crumpled on a bench there in the waiting room. He wanted nothing more than to go and be with her right now.

Soon enough. First, he needed to wrap up some loose ends.

"We're going to have a lot of questions," Manning said.

"Of course," Colton said. "Listen, I need a minute with Sarah before all the craziness starts. Is that okay?"

"Take five."

Colton walked toward Sarah and touched her shoulder, trying to get her attention and pull her out of her daze. Her head snapped toward him and she darted to her feet. As soon as their gazes connected, she folded herself into Colton's arms.

"I'm so glad you're okay," Colton murmured, drinking in her scent and the softness of her skin.

"Me too."

Colton stepped back, everything suddenly abundantly clear. "Sarah, I'm sorry."

She blinked up at him, her eyes warm and full of love. "For what?"

"For letting you walk away." He wiped a hair off of her face, realizing what a fool he'd been not to go after her.

"You didn't let me. I just did it on my own and—"

Colton shook his head, desperate to stop Sarah before she put too much blame on herself. "No, I should have come after you. You were right—I was so wrapped up in my own problems and issues that I was only thinking about myself."

She rested her hands on his chest, and her lips tugged down in a frown. "You had every right to do so. I didn't realize that until now. Until I experienced what it was like to see someone die. To feel…responsible."

"Loretta's death wasn't your fault." He stroked her arms, trying to reassure her. It would take a while for both of them to process everything that had just happened.

"I know." Her voice cracked. "But it felt like it was. It will feel like that for a while."

"I can help you through that, and maybe you can help me also."

Sarah smiled. "I would like that."

"But you were wrong about one thing." Colton pulled her even closer, never wanting to let go. He'd been such an idiot to wait this long to connect with Sarah again.

"What's that?" Sarah gazed up at him.

"I should have never turned my back on you. Your dad left and then your mom went to jail…all you needed was stability."

"It's definitely hard to trust people, to think they're going to want to stick around. My mind automatically wants to go to the worst places."

"I know." Colton cupped Sarah's face with his hands. "I'm so sorry. I would have done things differently if I knew then what I know now. I would have listened to you more. I would have tried harder."

"I should have dealt with my past so I wouldn't have had that knee-jerk reaction. I'm the one who should be apologizing."

"Oh, Sarah." Without saying anything else, Colton's lips met hers. This time, there wasn't any hesitation. It was just the joyous reunion of two people who'd loved and lost…and who'd found each other again.

Before their kiss ended, someone nuzzled between them.

Colton paused and looked down. It was Buzz.

He pulled away and laughed.

"Good job back there, boy." He patted the dog's head.

Buzz seemed to soak up the attention, a new light entering the dog's eyes. He knew this was over too, didn't he? Maybe the canine even knew that he'd saved the day.

Because Buzz *had* saved the day. They wouldn't be alive right now without him. And they would make sure he was treated like a king for the rest of his life.

TWENTY-NINE

A month after Loretta's killer had confessed to everything, including Tad's involvement, Sarah stood in front of Colton at a little church not far from Colton's cabin in North Idaho. The building was quaint, with stained glass windows, a white steeple and glossy wooden pews.

There weren't a lot of people here at the wedding, as per Sarah's wishes. But Colton's family had come in, as well as Sarah's sister and her family. Alfred Jennings and Yvonne were also in attendance. In recent weeks, the two had become friends.

Sarah hadn't wanted a big ceremony, no bridesmaids or groomsmen. But Buzz did sit on stage beside them, their wedding rings tucked into a holder on his collar.

Yes, Buzz had officially become a part of Sarah's family, as per Loretta's last wishes.

Shortly after Debbie Wilcox had been arrested, Sarah and Colton had met with Alfred Jennings, and he'd told them about the changes to Loretta's will, as well as how Loretta had felt strongly toward Sarah. Loretta truly had left that money to Sarah and said she viewed her almost like a daughter. He theorized that Loretta had left the cash in Buzz's bag because she'd feared someone would try to kill her. She wanted to make sure Buzz was taken care of.

The microchip had been obtained from Buzz. On it there were instructions from Loretta. Yvonne was to be given the proprietary formula for the new ALS drug she'd been working on. She'd known the formula would be in high demand. The new drug had apparently had great results in Loretta, and those closest to her had seen the changes.

She'd hidden the formula in the one safe place she could think of. Only Alfred Jennings knew the truth, but he hadn't been able to reveal the information until a month after her death. She wanted her will to be sorted out first.

Though Sarah had initially wondered if Yvonne was guilty in all of this, once she'd met the woman, she'd really liked her. She truly had been a friend to Loretta. Despite her tough words in that newspaper article concerning Sarah, she realized Yvonne had just acted out of loyalty to her friend.

Everything seemed to be falling in place.

Finally.

Because it had been a hard-fought battle to get to where she was today.

Sarah was going to continue with her art, working from a studio Colton had set up for her in his barn. He'd even added a heater for those cold winter days. A gallery in Coeur d'Alene had asked for several pieces of her work, and one of the potential buyers from the last art show she'd been to—right before Loretta died—had purchased one of Sarah's paintings.

As for the money Loretta left her...though Sarah had

initially been tempted to give it back or refuse it, Colton had convinced her not to do that. Instead, she invested it in several nonprofits. One was for foster children. Another was for incarcerated women with children. The third was for a husky rescue group.

The rest…well, Sarah was considering starting her own gallery one day.

But for now, she just wanted to stay here with Colton and to explore how great life could be together. Colton had taken that job with the Idaho State Police after all. His healing had come full circle.

"Do you take this man to be your husband, to have and to hold, from this day forward?" the pastor asked.

Sarah smiled up at Colton, realizing she'd never loved someone as much as she loved him. Having him come back into her life was an answer to a prayer she hadn't realized she'd prayed.

"I do," she said, her voice unwavering.

"And do you take this woman to be your lawfully wedded wife?"

"I do." The same smile stretched across Colton's face, and love radiated from his gaze.

A few minutes later, Colton kissed the bride, and the two became man and wife.

Despite everything that had happened, good had finally come from it all. Sarah was forever grateful to have Colton by her side and to have found her safe place in his arms.

* * * * *

An eternal optimist, **Hope White** was born and raised in the Midwest. She and her college sweetheart have been married for thirty years and are blessed with two wonderful sons, two feisty cats and a bossy border collie. When not dreaming up inspirational tales, Hope enjoys hiking, sipping tea with friends and going to the movies. She loves to hear from readers, who can contact her at hopewhiteauthor@gmail.com.

Books by Hope White

Love Inspired Suspense

Hidden in Shadows
Witness on the Run
Christmas Haven
Small Town Protector
Safe Harbor
Baby on the Run
Nanny Witness
Mountain Hostage

Echo Mountain

Mountain Rescue
Covert Christmas
Payback
Christmas Undercover
Witness Pursuit
Mountain Ambush

Visit the Author Profile page
at Harlequin.com for more titles.

MOUNTAIN HOSTAGE

Hope White

Now the God of hope fill you with all joy and peace
in believing, that ye may abound in hope,
through the power of the Holy Ghost.
—*Romans* 15:13

To the volunteers of
King County Search Dogs, State of Washington,
for their commitment to saving lives.

ONE

Zoe Pratt lost her footing on the icy trail and gasped. Stabbing her hiking stick into the snow for balance, she peered over the steep drop below into the vast, white blur of nothingness. A shudder ran down her spine.

Maybe a winter hike hadn't been the best idea.

"Shannon, slow down!" Zoe called, recentering herself to keep up with her friend.

"I can't," Shannon said. "Wait till you see the view from Prairie's Peak!"

"Do we have to risk our lives getting there?"

"You know I'd never let anything happen to you."

Zoe adjusted her red scarf to cover her mouth and nose. It was cold in the Cascade Mountains, and Zoe wasn't an experienced hiker. She'd come to the charming town of Mt. Stevens, Washington, to hang out with Shannon, her childhood best friend. Zoe thought they'd spend time relaxing, catching up on their lives, maybe even laughing a little. She eyed the steep drop to her right. Nothing to laugh about there. One wrong step and—

"Pick it up, pokey!" Shannon teased.

Zoe glanced at the gray sky. Light snow began to fall. "You sure it's safe out here?"

"What, you're not afraid of a grizzly, are ya?"

"A grizzly as in a bear?"

"They're probably more afraid of you than you are of them." Shannon continued her enthusiastic pace and Zoe struggled to keep up.

Shannon had always been the one to challenge Zoe out of her funk when things seemed desperate. Well, things weren't exactly desperate, but Zoe did need a break, both from her challenging job as a social worker for adolescents and teens, and from her dismal personal life. She still couldn't believe how badly she'd misjudged things with her ex-boyfriend, Tim.

Shove it aside, Zoe. This was supposed to be a rejuvenating getaway, not a depressing one.

Zoe inhaled the fresh mountain air and let it clear her lungs, her thoughts. She felt grounded and at peace in the mountains. She could see why Shannon loved it so much and why she thought it the perfect place to bring Zoe.

She caught up to her friend, who hesitated at a small outlook, gazing out across the Cascade mountain range.

Shannon eyed Zoe's jacket. "You warm enough?"

"Sure, I'm okay."

"Yeah, you should've worn my spare, matching jacket."

"And look like a pumpkin?" Zoe eyed Shannon up and down.

Shannon smiled, then redirected her attention to the horizon.

Zoe noticed a tower in the distance. "What's that?"

"Portage Fire Lookout. It's ridiculously easy to get to from the Frontage trailhead. You can really see the vastness of God's beauty from that spot." She glanced at Zoe. "It helps to get perspective on things."

Zoe smiled. "This is exactly what I needed to get my mind off my love life."

"Yeah, tell me about it."

"Are you having problems with Randy?"

"Who knows."

Zoe had noticed a photo of Randy and Shannon tucked in a kitchen drawer as if it had been recently put away, out of sight. The couple looked happy, both with wide grins, although Randy's was partially hidden by a full beard.

"Shannon?" Zoe prompted.

"He's been acting weird lately and I haven't heard from him since he left a few days ago to visit family in Denver."

"I'm sorry."

"No." She touched Zoe's shoulder. "We're not going to let guy trouble spoil our fun. Come on."

"How much farther?" Zoe asked.

"Depends how slow you hike." Shannon winked. "Race ya?"

"Ah, come on, Shan. What are you trying to do, prove how out of shape I am?"

"You'll thank me later when you sleep like a baby." Shannon picked up her pace. "I packed snickerdoodles for our snack. That should motivate you."

"With red and green sprinkles?"

"Of course!"

Before Zoe could open her mouth to demand a snickerdoodle for sustenance, Shan had reached a sharp turn up ahead and was out of sight.

It made sense that Shan could outhike Zoe, considering Shan's job at the Mt. Stevens Resort was mostly physical, whereas Zoe's job required hours of sitting and listening.

A woman's scream echoed across the mountain.

"Shannon!" Zoe called.

Adrenaline coursing through her body, she rushed to get to her friend. She must have twisted an ankle or injured herself somehow. "Shannon, answer me!"

Nearly losing her footing, she took a deep breath. *Slow me down, Lord. Keep me safe.* If Zoe injured herself as well, she'd be no help to Shannon.

As Zoe reached the turn, Shannon darted around the corner and slammed into her. "Run, Zoe, run!" She pushed her for encouragement.

A bear, it had to be a bear, right? There was no way they could outrun a bear. Zoe had seen her share of National Geographic specials on wildlife. Would he try to eat them or—

"Stop!" a male voice said.

That didn't sound a like a bear.

"Don't stop, Zoe!" Shannon said.

Zoe focused on bending her knees to give her balance as she scrambled down the trail. Her pepper spray, why had she left it back at the house? *Because you didn't expect to need it out here*, she told herself. She thought hikers were nice sorts of people, nature lovers, tree huggers and—Shannon slammed into Zoe from behind. Zoe slid and prayed. *Please, Lord, not now, I'm not ready to end my work on earth!*

With a thunk, she hit a boulder meant to guard hikers at the outlook from the steep drop below. She glanced up...

In time to see a man the size of a pro wrestler grab Shannon from behind.

"No! Let go of me!" Shannon cried, trying to pull away from him.

The guy, wearing a brown snow jacket and maroon ski mask, started dragging her away.

"Zoe, run!"

Instead, Zoe scrambled to her feet and went after them. *Pay attention, Zoe. Pay attention to every detail.* They were going to survive this assault and she would have to testify against this creep.

She grabbed Shannon's arm and swung at the guy with her hiking stick. With a frustrated grunt, he threw Shannon aside and yanked on Zoe's stick, pulling her within inches of his face.

Those eyes. She'd never forget his practically black eyes, glaring at her from behind the knit mask.

"This is not your fight," he said in a low, threatening voice.

"She's my best friend!" Zoe struggled to pull free.

"Then you'll die with her."

"Leave her alone!" Shannon charged and hit the guy shoulder to midsection. A linebacker couldn't defend himself against her velocity, a skill Shan had learned from her two football-playing brothers.

The attacker loosened his grip and Zoe wrenched free from his hold.

"Run, Zoe!"

The man grabbed Shannon again, and she struggled against him. He started to hoist her over his shoulder, but she managed to rip off his ski mask.

His long, angular face, flushed bright red with anger, etched itself in Zoe's brain. He was in his midthirties with a scar above his left eye.

"Let me go!" Shannon cried.

Zoe charged, more out of instinct than intellect, and in one swift motion, the giant backhanded her.

Zoe's head snapped to the side and she stumbled back over the edge…

…into the white abyss below.

The text came in at 1:21 p.m.

Search-and-rescue volunteer Jack Monroe subtly flashed the alert on his phone to his second-in-command, Heather Bond, and excused himself from the business meeting with Brighton International. This was why he'd hired Heather: to manage his IT security business so he'd have the flexibility to leave Seattle and join a search when necessary. Depending on the mission he could be gone for days, taking up temporary residence close to the action.

At 3:02 p.m., Jack pulled up at the command center in the Cascade Mountains with Romeo, his border collie–Bernese mix, and was given instructions by the command chief.

By 3:15 p.m., Jack and Romeo had joined a team and were hiking up Mt. Stevens. Their assignment: find a fallen and suspected injured hiker, called in by a pair of hikers who had heard a woman scream and seen someone in a royal blue jacket fall down the mountainside. They weren't sure where she'd landed.

Fresh snow covered the trails and the wind was picking up.

"Amateur hikers should never go out in this kind of weather," Beatrice Spears said under her breath. Bea's Lab mix, Cooper, continued his search for scent.

"It was supposed to be mild in the mountains today," Leslie Vonn said. Her dog hadn't been qualified yet, but it was good to have the extra person to offer praise when the dogs found the lost hiker.

When. Because *if* was not an option in Jack's mind.

"Did you hear about the hiker who disappeared at Crystal Mountain last weekend?" Bea asked.

"Got buried in an avalanche?" Leslie recalled.

"The dogs found her in less than twenty minutes. Fast."

Jack listened. He wasn't much for small talk, didn't know how to execute it effectively or, for that matter, what the purpose was. Another reason he'd hired Heather.

"I think Cooper's got something," Bea said.

The three humans watched Cooper zigzag up ahead. Something sparked in Jack's chest, a familiar pang whenever one of the dogs caught scent and went into a hyperfocused state.

Maybe this would be an easy rescue, unlike...

Hope dissolved into frustration as the memory surfaced. He shoved it aside. There was no added value in remembering his failure.

Romeo raced ahead of Cooper and stopped, nose in the air, tail up, intently focused. The team caught up to Romeo on the snow-covered trail, where the dog stood over a red scarf. Jack praised him for the find, then Romeo sat, awaiting further instruction.

"Think it belongs to the victim?" Bea said.

"It's possible." Leslie reported their finding to Command. "Let's continue up the trail."

"If the victim was seen falling from the Prairie's Peak area, how would her scarf end up here?" Bea said.

"Maybe it's not hers," Leslie said.

"Or she was coming down the trail when she fell," Jack finally said.

The women glanced at him, as if they'd forgotten he was there. Jack liked it that way, dissolving into the background, watching, listening, so he could better understand people.

Another twenty-one minutes passed as they continued their ascent. The snow had let up a bit. Jack naturally hiked ahead of the women due to his tall stature and long gait.

They had gone silent, probably not wanting to interrupt the dogs' focus, especially now that they knew they were on the right track. Another reason Jack liked being part of this group was the singular concentration required by the work. The ability to multitask mystified him as much as small talk. When he directed his attention to something, it became his sole focus.

Like today's mission.

"It'll be dark soon," Leslie said.

Her words hung in the cold air between them. Although the team was skilled at making camp overnight, the woman who'd fallen and was potentially injured would be ill-prepared for the drop in temperature.

Romeo started a zigzag pattern, then abruptly stopped. His ears pricked.

Jack took a deep breath. Suspected what was coming.

Romeo took off into a full sprint, and Jack followed, frigid air filling his lungs. It was senseless to tell Romeo to slow down. Once the dog caught scent, nothing would stop him. It made him an excellent search-and-rescue dog, but sometimes his enthusiasm made Jack nervous. He feared the hardworking dog might lose his footing and slide off the edge.

Jack pushed harder to catch up to Romeo. The dog

was trained to return to Jack's side and pull on his toggle if he found something. Back and forth, back and forth, until Romeo united his handler with the missing hiker. Instead of exhibiting his trained indication, Romeo frantically paced at the edge of the trail up ahead. Jack interpreted this as him being in scent, but unable to make physical contact with the subject. Cooper ran up to Romeo and exhibited similar behavior.

Jack approached the dogs and glanced at what sparked their excitement.

A person in a royal blue jacket lay on a plateau.

"Good boy, good." Jack played a quick game of tug-of-war with Romeo as his reward as he radioed Command. "I think we found her, over."

"Status?"

He peered over the edge, sensing Bea and Leslie come up on either side of him. "Miss?" Jack called down to the prone hiker. "We're with Mt. Stevens Search and Rescue!"

Silence.

"Unresponsive, over," he said into his radio.

"Location?"

Jack opened his tracker app, took a screenshot and texted it to Command.

"We'll send a medical team," the command chief responded.

"Roger, out."

The search-and-rescue K9 team hovered on the trail in stoic silence.

"You think she's alive?" Bea asked.

Leslie glanced up at the mountain. "Depends on how

far she fell. If she hit anything…" she hesitated "…
critical."

More silence.

"I'm thinking this is a recovery, not a rescue," Bea
said.

"Miss? Miss, can you hear me?" Jack shouted, not
liking the direction of the conversation.

Romeo barked as if he was also trying to get her attention.

Jack hated this, hated feeling…out of control of a
situation.

Romeo must have felt the same way, because his
barking grew more insistent as if he were saying, *Open
your eyes already!*

"Romeo, stop," Jack commanded. The dog quieted
and flopped down beside him.

Jack glanced at the horizon, realizing they had less
than ninety minutes before they lost natural light. Rescuing the woman in the dark would present its own set
of challenges.

"Wait, I think she's moving," Leslie said.

He snapped his gaze to the plateau. The victim
started to get up.

Jack whipped out his binoculars. Peered below. He
had to try to get a read on her expression even though
that wasn't his particular strength.

A bruise formed across her right cheek and blood
seeped from her lip. Her eyes rounded with fear as if she
suddenly realized she was in a vulnerable, dangerous spot.

"Don't move!" he called. "I'm with Mt. Stevens
Search and Rescue!"

She acted as if she didn't hear him, as if she were
disoriented beyond rational thought, which meant she
could accidentally fall even farther…

To her death.

"Medics are on the way!" he tried.

Ignoring him, she dropped to her knees and glanced over the edge of the plateau. What on earth was she doing? It seemed like she was trying to figure out how to climb down. A decision that was both unrealistic and potentially deadly.

Then again, she could be dazed from a concussion and not know what she was doing.

"I'm going down," Jack said.

"Wait, shouldn't you—"

"He's right," Leslie interrupted Bea's protest. "Who knows what she'll do? Besides, Jack's done this before."

He had done it before, although not with favorable results.

Pulling rope off his pack, he anchored it to a nearby tree root jutting out from the mountain. Romeo shot him a look, like, *Don't go without me.*

"Stay," Jack said, in case the dog got any crazy ideas. He shouldered his pack, gripped the rope with gloved hands and let himself drift so he'd land gently on the plateau, about a hundred feet down.

He wouldn't be too late this time, wouldn't let any harm come to the woman in the blue ski jacket.

A few moments later he landed on the small ledge. Her back was to him and she acted as if she hadn't heard his landing. "Miss?"

Startled, she turned quickly, her eyes wide with fear. "Don't touch me!" She stepped back, precariously close to the edge.

He instinctively reached out to grab her arm.

"No, don't—" She stumbled backward over the edge of the cliff.

TWO

Jack dove and caught the woman's arm. It wasn't too hard, considering she waved both of them like a helicopter trying to take off, or in her case, a woman trying to stop the momentum that would catapult her down a mountainside.

He landed on his chest, and air rushed from his lungs, but he didn't let go. He grabbed her arm with his other hand, as well. Considering his size versus the petite victim's, he calculated a more than 50 percent chance of hoisting her safely up.

"Don't! Don't hurt me!" she cried, thrashing about.

If she kept squirming, his chances dropped way below 50 percent. "Stop moving or I won't be able to pull you up."

"Why, so you can kill me?"

Kill her? At this point he had to assume she'd hit her head and was suffering from delirium. At the very least she was irrational, which meant she was unpredictable and potentially dangerous. Especially if she kept shifting and broke free of Jack's grip, or even pulled him over the edge with her.

Jack scanned his brain for information on overly

excited people and how to manage them. Something he'd read in a psychology book surfaced: *An irrational person's meaning of a situation is different than ours.*

For some reason the woman in the blue jacket thought Jack wanted to harm her. She was stuck in that reality and he needed to yank her out of it. He decided to go completely random.

"My dog needs me!" he shouted.

She stopped squirming and looked up. Her wide brown eyes sparkled with unshed tears of fear. "What?" she said.

"My dog needs me."

"Your dog?"

"If you fall, chances are I'll go with you, because I won't let go of your arm. Then I'll die, or at the very least I'll be injured, and Romeo will be all alone."

"Romeo?" she repeated.

Make a personal connection and/or connect the irrational person back to reality.

"Romeo Albert Garrett Monroe," Jack said.

She frowned, as if trying to figure out what he was talking about.

"I know," he said. "I've been told that's a lot of names for a dog. I'm Jack Monroe. Just two names."

She blinked and was no longer squirming.

"I'm going to pull you up now."

He didn't wait for a response, didn't want to take the chance she'd drift back into hysteria. In one swift motion he yanked her up and her lithe body slid across his and landed on the other side of him.

Flat on his back, an uncomfortable position considering his backpack, he took a deep, relieved breath. Snow started falling again, a little more insistent than today's earlier dusting of flurries.

The woman sat up and scooted away from him. "Who are you?"

He'd just told her his name. Had she forgotten already?

"I'm Jack Monroe," he said. "I'm a volunteer with Mt. Stevens Search and Rescue, K9 unit."

Romeo barked from above, frustrated that he wasn't a part of the action.

She glanced up.

"That's Romeo," he said. "You know my name and his name. What's yours?"

"Zoe. Zoe Pratt."

"Is she okay?" Leslie called down.

"Yes!" Jack responded, although he suspected she wasn't totally okay. He wasn't sure how serious her injuries were.

"Did you find Shannon?" Zoe asked.

"Who is Shannon?"

"My friend."

"Did she fall, too?"

"No, she was…" Zoe hesitated and hugged herself "…taken."

"Taken, you mean…?"

"A big guy attacked us and grabbed her and…" Her voice hitched.

Jack was supposed to do something here, something that would make her feel better. But what?

"They're sending a team to treat your injuries and bring you safely down the mountain," he offered.

She pinned him with intense brown eyes. "No, I'm not leaving without Shannon."

He searched his mind for a logical response. There was none, since staying out here, injured and cold, wasn't sensible. He didn't want to upset her, so he tried something he'd heard before. "I understand."

Although he didn't. This woman might be helpful in the search for her friend, but delaying treatment of her injuries could make her condition worse. At least, her physical condition. He had no idea how to assess her mental condition.

"Because of Romeo?" she said.

"Excuse me?"

"You understand because you love your dog, Romeo?"

"Sure."

He'd initially said he understood her desire not to leave the mountain because that was the appropriate response. Now that she connected her situation to his dog, it actually made some sense.

He didn't like the fact that this irrational and highly emotional woman was making sense to him.

He took off his gloves and pack, and dug for the first aid kit. "You have a cut on your cheek." He tore open an antiseptic wipe and reached out to treat her wound.

"Don't." She jerked away and started shivering. Not from the cold.

Although he wasn't an expert at reading emotion, he knew fear when he saw it. His gut clenched. "I won't hurt you," he said.

She glanced at him with those expressive eyes, hugging her knees to her chest. Her body still trembled.

Although he'd talked her out of her hysterical response to falling, she might still be processing that trauma, or the trauma of seeing her friend kidnapped, or the trauma of... Oh. Something clicked in his brain.

"The man who took your friend," he started, "did he hurt you, too?"

She pinched her eyes shut and nodded.

"Did he push you off the trail?"

"Yes," she said softly.

"Zoe?"

She opened her eyes.

"He's not here now. He can't hurt you."

"He's got Shannon. Please call someone, the police, and tell them what happened."

Jack wouldn't be able to tend to her injuries unless he did as she requested. He clicked on the radio. "Command, this is Jack Monroe."

"Go ahead, Jack."

"The victim says her friend was taken by a stranger, the same man responsible for the victim's fall, over."

"Taken, as in kidnapped?"

"Affirmative."

"I'll notify the sheriff's office. Which way are they headed?"

Jack glanced at Zoe.

"Up toward Prairie's Peak," she said.

He shared the information with base.

"Sheriff's office might radio back for details," Command responded. "This changes things. Be careful."

"Roger, out." Jack hooked the radio to his belt. Unfortunately, making the call didn't seem to ease Zoe's anxiety. "They'll do their best to find her," he said, but stopped before giving her the statistics on such a rescue. Given the criminal element of the situation, combined with weather reports calling for heavy snowfall… They wouldn't be encouraging.

She reached up and fumbled for where her scarf would be.

"We found your red scarf on the trail. Leslie has it above," Jack said. "You can use mine."

"My necklace, where is my necklace?" She unzipped her blue jacket and searched her neck with trembling fingers. "It's a silver dove. It represents the Holy Spirit. I need to hold it, to pray and…and… Shannon's mom gave it to me when I was thirteen." She shifted around, as if it had fallen off and was lying beside her.

She was growing more agitated. He had to calm her down. "'Have I not commanded you? Be strong and of good courage. Do not be afraid, nor be dismayed, for the Lord your God is with you wherever you go,'" Jack said.

Zoe's fingers froze, and she slowly lowered them. "'… The Lord your God is with you wherever you go,'" she repeated. "You know the Bible?"

"I read everything in my aunt Margaret's house growing up, including the Bible."

She sniffed, a tear trailing down her cheek. Jack needed to do more.

"I will find your necklace," he said, unsure how he was going to make good on that promise. Yet his words seemed to calm her. "I'd like to treat the cut on your head so it doesn't become infected. It might take medics a few hours to get here."

She nodded, hugging her knees tighter to her chest.

He tentatively reached out with one hand and brushed dark hair off her cheek. She closed her eyes as if he was hurting her, although he knew he wasn't. Maybe she didn't like to be touched, especially after everything that had happened today.

Lightly pressing the wipe against her skin, he said, "Did you have a hat?"

"Yes."

She must have lost it when she fell.

Her wound wasn't deep, which was good. It would be a shame if she ended up with a scar on her perfect skin, a reminder of the trauma she'd endured today. Yet she'd survived the fall and apparent kidnapping in fairly decent condition. At least from what he could see.

He took off his own knit hat and placed it on her head to keep her warm. "How about other injuries? Legs, arms, does anything else hurt?"

"My heart."

That concerned him. Was she having breathing issues relating to a collapsed lung? "A pinching feeling or dull ache or...?"

"All of the above." She pinned him with those soulful brown eyes. "I may never see Shannon again."

He exhaled a sigh of relief. "Oh, okay. I thought you'd sustained a serious injury like a punctured lung or cracked ribs."

"What I'm feeling is very serious."

As he studied her expression, an image flashed across his mind.

His parents driving away from Aunt Margaret's house, Jack standing on the porch holding his Lego lunch pail, a peanut butter and honey sandwich with chips tucked inside.

He didn't want to drift back there, didn't want to remember how he'd felt when his parents had abandoned him. He'd spent the last twenty-plus years shoving that persistent ache down where it couldn't hurt him anymore.

Yet here it was.

"I apologize," he said. "What you're feeling *is* serious, but it's not what I was referring to."

She broke eye contact and glanced up at the sky. "Will they keep searching for Shannon at night?"

"The sheriff's office will make that decision based on weather conditions."

She frowned as a few flurries landed on her dark eyelashes. "You mean snow?"

"Snow and wind and available law enforcement personnel to accompany the teams."

"Won't they have a better chance of finding her tonight than if they wait until tomorrow?"

"The decision to proceed with a rescue is determined by both recovery of the subject, and safety of the team. If team members are hurt, that adds to the burden of the rescue. Not to mention this rescue is more complicated because of the kidnapping element."

At the mention of the kidnapping, she hugged her knees even tighter.

Wanting to pull her out of her fearful state, he decided to make an attempt at small talk. "Are you from the area?" he asked.

She shook her head. "No. City girl."

"Which city?"

"Portland."

"And your friend, Shannon?"

"She lives in Mt. Stevens and works at the resort."

"Is she an experienced hiker?"

"Yes. She's the activities director at the resort and

part of her job involves taking guests on hiking adventures."

"And she chose to take an inexperienced hiker like yourself out on a winter hike?"

She shot him a look. He must have overstepped.

"You probably want to save details of today's incident for the authorities," he said.

"I, well… It sounded like you were being critical."

There was truth to her assessment. Jack had little tolerance for people who didn't use their good sense, and he was ill equipped to mask his judgment. Another reason why he'd struggled to make and keep friends: his brutal honesty. *It comes with your brilliance, Jackie boy*, his aunt used to say.

Some days, being smart was overrated. As he sat with Zoe Pratt, waiting for help to arrive, he wished he had less smarts and more compassion or understanding or some other characteristic that would ease that tense frown off her face.

Instead, he only had facts.

"Since your friend is an experienced hiker, she will have an advantage over her kidnapper. Unless she's injured," he offered.

Zoe's eyes widened. Perhaps he should have left out the part about her friend being injured.

"Did she have a personal locator beacon?" he asked, trying to recover from his mistake.

"Yes."

"Then her priority will be to activate it." Now he was making stuff up. "Experienced hikers know how to make a fire and stay warm throughout the night."

"Unless she's unable to get away from that jerk." She paused. "Or she's hurt."

Once again, Jack had done more harm than good. He thought it best to keep his thoughts to himself during the remainder of his mission. One thing he knew for sure, the sooner he distanced himself from Zoe Pratt, the better off they'd both be.

Now she knew how her teenage clients felt when they claimed no one was listening to them.

Zoe told rescue workers she wanted to stay in the mountains until her friend was found.

Search and Rescue had denied her request. Their job was to rescue Zoe and bring her to the hospital. If she denied their assistance, she'd be putting the SAR volunteers at risk.

After being checked out by medics at the scene, she'd been assisted down the mountain. *God, please take care of Shannon.*

As she waited in the ER to be officially released, a police officer in his forties joined her in the examining area.

"I'm Sergeant Peterson with the sheriff's office," he introduced. "Are you up to answering some questions?"

"Sure." She shifted into a better position and winced.

"How do you know Shannon Banks?"

"She's my best friend from childhood."

"And you two were up in the mountains because…?"

"A winter hike, to clear our minds."

"Was she upset or concerned about anything in particular?"

"I think she and her boyfriend were having trouble."

"What kind of trouble?"

"She didn't go into detail."

"Where were you headed?"

"Prairie's Peak Overlook."

"Could you identify the kidnapper if you saw him again?"

"Absolutely."

His nodded and checked his phone. "Excuse me, I have to take this."

Zoe leaned back, still trying to wrap her head around it all. This was not how she'd planned to spend her time in Mt. Stevens: Shannon kidnapped by a stranger; Zoe bruised, terrified, and rescued by an enigmatic man named Jack.

He was an odd sort of fellow, asking random questions, then going completely silent as they waited on the plateau for help. Yet when she'd inquire about his work as a search-and-rescue volunteer—how a dog is trained, how many hours of training it takes for a person to be qualified as a handler—to distract herself from her worry, Jack Monroe was Mr. Chatterbox. It seemed like he was more comfortable talking about facts, figures and percentages of lost hikers rescued in the Cascade Mountains than dealing with Zoe's panic about Shannon.

Once she had come down from her emotional spin, she surmised that Jack was highly intelligent and socially challenged, perhaps even on the spectrum. He and his dog with the four names had stayed close to her when SAR helped her down the trail.

Away from Shannon.

Would she ever see her again?

"Hello?" a voice said from the other side of the curtain.

"Yes?"

Jack stepped into the examining area and stood at the foot of her bed.

"Shouldn't you be out looking for Shannon?" she said. Then a horrible thought seized her. "Unless…"

"We've cleared the section of trail up to Prairie's Peak," Jack answered.

"And you haven't found her?"

"No."

"So that's it? You're giving up?" She realized she was being awfully hard on the man who'd saved her life.

"They've temporarily called off the mission due to weather," he said. "If there was any way to continue the search, I would be out there."

"Of course." Zoe sighed. "I wish I knew why this was happening to us."

"Maybe your friend got involved with the wrong people."

She snapped her attention to him. "Excuse me?"

"Your friend got involved—"

"I heard you the first time. Why would you even think that?"

He shrugged.

"Well, it's not true."

"People aren't usually randomly kidnapped without cause."

"How dare you malign Shannon. You haven't even met her."

He just looked at her.

"Well, say something," she said.

"Like what?"

"Like you're sorry for starters."

"You posed the question, so I assumed you wanted—"

"It was a rhetorical question, thank you very much."

A puzzled frown creased his forehead. His suggestion bothered her more than it should, which meant... she sensed potential validity to his comment.

"I'm feeling exceptionally vulnerable and I need people around me that I can trust," she said. She was a jumble of emotions and feared she might completely lose it in front of this stranger. She wanted privacy. She wanted counsel with God.

She needed her friend back.

A man in a dark suit joined them. "Miss Pratt, I'm Detective Perry." He narrowed his eyes at Jack. "What are you doing here?"

"Checking on Zoe."

Zoe felt anxious and confused, both by Jack's accusation and her own visceral response.

"I need to question Miss Pratt," Detective Perry said.

With a slight nod, Jack left her alone with the detective.

"Any news about Shannon?" she asked.

"No, ma'am. I'd like to ask you a few questions about what happened."

"Oh, okay." She wondered how many police officers she'd have to repeat her story to.

"Why were you out hiking today?"

"To clear our minds of stress. Prairie's Peak is a favorite spot of Shannon's and she wanted to share her special place with me, you know, to cheer me up."

The detective waited for more.

"I broke up with my boyfriend a few months ago," she explained.

He nodded, wrote something down in a small notebook. "Can you describe the assailant?"

"A large man, over six feet tall, with an angular face

and dark eyes. He was in his thirties with a scar above his left eye."

"You think you could identify him?"

"Yes."

"I'll have you get with a forensic artist. What did the assailant say, exactly? Did he seem to know your friend or call her by name?"

"No," Zoe said. "He didn't say much only…" She reflected back on the moment she decided to catalog every detail about the man. "When he got close, I smelled cigarettes on his breath. I tried to help Shannon and he said, 'This is not your fight.'"

"So, he was specifically targeting Shannon."

"I don't know. I guess it seems that way."

"Then what happened?"

"When I wouldn't let go of Shannon, he said…" the memory resurfaced in a flash "…that I would die with her." She eyed the detective. "You've got to find her."

"We'll do our best. Specialized training is needed to go after a violent criminal in the mountains. We're putting together a few teams, including police officers, that will be on standby for when the weather breaks. We can't let search-and-rescue teams of civilians head up there without police officer escort. It's too dangerous."

She didn't like his answer, but she understood it.

Zoe spent the next fifteen minutes answering the detective's questions about Shannon. It was only then, when Zoe didn't have the details that he seemed to be looking for, that she realized she didn't know as much about the adult Shannon as she should.

Why hadn't Zoe asked questions of her friend? Why hadn't she found out more about what happened between Shannon and Randy, about her job, her social life? She felt helpless and utterly alone.

An hour later Zoe was officially discharged and for some reason she wished Jack would have returned. How silly.

"You are a fortunate woman," the nurse said, then explained how to wrap her bruised ribs and manage the concussion. "Your injuries could've been much worse."

Zoe didn't feel fortunate. Her friend was still out there, cold, vulnerable and probably hurt.

Hopefully still alive.

God, grant me the serenity to accept the things I cannot change… She recited the prayer silently.

Shannon had been violently kidnapped. Zoe couldn't change that fact, but she wasn't powerless. She could pray for her friend's safety. Zoe didn't believe Shan had gotten involved with the wrong people; she might find clues at Shannon's house to assist with the investigation into her kidnapping.

As she waited outside the hospital for a ride to take her back to Shannon's modest home, she considered her next move. Yeah, like what move? Hike up a mountain in the dark with a concussion and bruised ribs to find her friend?

For half a second, she wondered if the concussion was, in fact, affecting her good sense.

A squad car pulled up and a deputy got out. "Are you Zoe Pratt?"

"Yes."

"I'm Deputy Ortman. Sergeant Peterson asked me to give you a ride."

Once inside the cruiser, she decided to press Deputy

Ortman for news about her friend. "What's the status of the search?" she asked.

"Three search teams are ready to deploy once the storm passes."

Well, three was better than one. Still…

"How is Shannon going to survive?" she said softly.

"If the kidnapper wants something from her or her family, it's in his best interest to keep her safe."

She kept circling back to the same question: Why Shannon? And who was going to get the ransom call? Her parents were stable financially, but not wealthy.

She wished she had a sounding board, someone to process it all with.

An image of Jack standing at the foot of her hospital bed flooded her thoughts. The unique man who'd saved her life. She had either been brusque with him, or an emotional tornado. She assumed he'd feel safest keeping his distance.

But who could blame her for being an emotional basket case in her situation?

She wondered if Jack was on one of the search teams standing by to look for Shannon.

They had to find her. Zoe wouldn't accept the alternative. Few people other than Shannon knew the real Zoe, understood and loved her, faults and all.

The deputy turned into Shannon's snow-dusted driveway leading to the charming, two-bedroom house. The snow hadn't accumulated nearly as much down here as it had up on the mountain.

Zoe spotted a lone figure standing on the front porch. From this vantage point, it could almost be… Shannon. Hope flared in Zoe's chest.

The deputy parked the cruiser and Zoe thanked him

for the ride. As she approached the house, she said, "Shannon?"

The woman pulled the scarf off her face.

"Oh, sorry," Zoe said. "I thought you were Shannon."

The visitor extended her hand. "I'm Kelly Washburn, Shannon's friend. We work together."

"Zoe Pratt."

"No offense, but I was hoping it was Shannon in the back of the squad car," Kelly said. "I heard what happened and had to come over. I don't know why. I had to do something."

"I know the feeling."

"I even brought sloppy burgers, her favorite, from the resort's restaurant."

"That was thoughtful, thanks." Someone with a positive attitude. Zoe liked that. She scanned the porch. "I wonder where she keeps the spare key?"

"It's probably unlocked," Kelly said. "People out here rarely lock their doors. If not, she keeps the spare under the mat."

Zoe twisted the door handle and it opened. Small towns were so different than urban areas. She would never leave her apartment door unlocked. They entered the modest home and Kelly proceeded to turn on some lamps.

Shannon had decorated the open floor plan with simple, comfortable furniture, plenty of throw blankets and insulated drapes. Each of the two bedrooms had its own heater and thermostat, as did the main living area, although Shannon said she relied on the fireplace to warm that space.

Zoe glanced at the fireplace. She and Shannon had stayed up until 1:00 a.m. the first night she'd arrived, reconnecting, talking about their careers, sharing accomplishments and disappointments. They weren't done. They had so much more to discuss. Would Zoe get the chance?

She felt Kelly's hand touch her shoulder. "We need to remain positive."

Zoe nodded, grateful for the kind words. Although she was starting to feel the drain of the day's trauma on her body and mind, she didn't want to be rude. "So, you and Shannon met at work?" she asked.

"Yes, we bonded over our love of hiking, volunteer work and snickerdoodles." Kelly placed the take-out bag on the table.

Zoe sat at the kitchen table but didn't reach for the bag right away.

"Guess this was a bad idea," Kelly said. "I mean, it's not like either of us is hungry at a time like this."

Zoe thought about the colorful snickerdoodles Shannon had packed for their hike. "I should probably eat something since my last meal was breakfast."

"I'll get us something to drink," Kelly said.

"There's juice and soda in the fridge. I'm good with water."

Kelly went to the kitchen and pulled glasses out of the oak cabinet. "How did Shannon seem today?"

"Pretty good. Happy to be going on a hike. Why?"

"I don't know. She'd been distant lately."

"She said she was having boyfriend problems," Zoe offered.

"Couples always have minor bumps," Kelly said.

"Or major ones," Zoe muttered.

"Uh-oh. Recent breakup?"

"Yeah. It's done. I've moved on."

Kelly placed a glass of water in front of Zoe and joined her at the table. "If it was meant to be, it will work out, right?"

"How about you? Do you have a steady boyfriend?"

"Semi-steady."

"I've never heard that term before."

Kelly opened the bag of food and shrugged. "It's still too new to define."

"Ah."

Zoe appreciated the distraction of sitting here chatting about life and guys, almost pretending as if there weren't some larger crisis taking place outside these four walls.

Shannon was gone. Kidnapped by a brutal man.

"What, you don't like the burgers?" Kelly asked.

"Sorry, kind of distracted."

"Hey, give me your phone and I'll put my number in the contacts," Kelly said. "That way you can call me anytime and vice versa."

"Good idea." Zoe handed her the phone. "Tell me more about Shannon's behavior lately."

"She'd been a little withdrawn. I figured that was because of Randy."

Zoe nodded.

Kelly handed Zoe's phone back. "Call me anytime. I mean it."

"Thanks." She opened the bag and pulled out a burger.

A tinkling sound chimed from Kelly's phone. She glanced at it. "The boss." She stood. "I'm sorry, I have to leave."

"No worries. Thanks for coming by and bringing food." Zoe walked Kelly to the door.

Kelly hesitated. "Call or text if you hear anything."

"Absolutely."

Zoe shut the door behind Kelly and sighed. It was nice to have someone to talk to about all this, someone who knew Shannon. It was also good to know that Shannon had friends in town, people who cared about her.

Zoe put the bag of burgers in the fridge. She decided to lie down, rest her sore body and eat later.

"Let go and let God," she whispered. She grabbed her purse off the sofa and opened it. She found the tin of tummy-soothing herbal lozenges and took one, then spotted her canister of pepper spray. If only she'd had it earlier...

She sighed. It did no good to blame herself for what had happened, even if it felt like it was somehow her fault. She headed toward the guest bedroom, gripping the pepper spray as if she could somehow rewrite history. *"If only" is a diversion from grace*, a minister had once said. How true.

Stepping inside the darkened guest room, she reached for the light switch.

A firm arm wrapped around her neck from behind.

"Where is she?"

THREE

The mission was on indefinite hold. Although three teams were ready to go, the weather had taken a turn for the worse. They wouldn't be going out tonight to search for Shannon Banks.

Instead of heading back to his rented hotel room, Jack sat in his SUV eyeing the small house in the distance. When he'd left the hospital earlier, he'd gotten a call from Leslie that she'd found the silver dove necklace belonging to Zoe Pratt. He'd gone to retrieve it in the hopes it might comfort Zoe, yet now he hesitated to knock on the front door of her friend's house where she was staying. Why?

The woman's fragile emotional state made him uncomfortable. He didn't want to say the wrong thing, didn't want to upset her again. After all, she was still angry with him for speculating about her friend's association with questionable persons.

He eyed the silver dove in his palm. There was no downside in giving her the beloved trinket. Then again, his very presence would remind her that the search had been suspended.

He was overthinking things. Nothing new.

A low growl emanated from the back seat. Romeo sensed something outside.

Jack opened his door. Listened.

He decided it was an owl discussing evening plans.

Romeo barked repeatedly. Maybe he needed a bathroom break. Jack let him out of the truck and the dog bolted past him, sniffing the ground intently. It wouldn't be the worst idea to bring the canine along when Jack encountered Zoe again. Romeo's presence might take the edge off their human interaction.

Romeo bolted up the stairs to the front porch.

Jack started to have second thoughts. What if Zoe thought he was bringing news about her friend? She'd be sorely disappointed and possibly more upset. Yet he wanted to offer her comfort in the form of her necklace. It also wouldn't hurt to recalibrate their relationship with a positive interaction. Assuaging things between them could help Jack become more familiar with her missing friend. If Shannon Banks had been able to escape her captor, Jack understanding her thinking process could potentially expedite the rescue.

He knocked firmly on the front door. Waited. Had Zoe already gone to bed?

He tried again.

Romeo's ears pricked.

Jack studied him. This made no sense. They weren't in the field, weren't tracking scent.

Romeo bolted around the side of the house. Jack followed and found the dog barking furiously at a side window. Jack peered through a crack in the curtains but couldn't see much as the room was pitch-black.

"Come on, before we get arrested for peeping."

Jack commanded his dog to accompany him to the front door.

He knocked again.

Romeo anxiously paced back and forth.

Dogs know things humans don't. Words spoken by Jack's mentor and dog trainer, Riley Cooper.

A crash echoed from inside the house.

Jack twisted the door handle. Locked.

He shouldered the door once, twice. Decided not to dislocate his shoulder.

Another crash and a woman's scream pierced through the window.

He scanned the porch for potential spots to hide a key.

Under a planter. No.

Behind the rocking chair. No.

Aunt Margaret hid hers beneath the...

He flipped over the colorful, braided welcome mat and grabbed the key.

"Romeo, wait," he ordered, not wanting the dog to be harmed.

Jack unlocked and flung open the door. A large man charged Jack, slamming the door shut and pinning Jack against the wall. Romeo barked from the front porch.

The man slugged Jack in the gut, then spun him around and applied some kind of choke hold. Jack shoved the assailant back against the kitchen counter, hoping the pain of making contact would weaken him. Instead the guy clung tight to Jack's neck, putting pressure on his windpipe. Swinging Jack to the right, he smashed Jack's head against the refrigerator.

Jack was not a rag doll to be tossed around at will.

He had the strength necessary to free himself. He was not that weak kid anymore.

He jerked his elbow into the guy's stomach once, twice. On the third jab, the attacker's grip loosened enough for Jack to slip out of the hold and stumble away. Sucking in air, he fought to clear the stars from his vision. He had to think, strategize.

The assailant turned, his face red with anger. He had black hair, dark eyes and an angry expression. The guy was about to charge again. Jack scanned his immediate surroundings for a weapon.

"Not happening, dirtbag!" Zoe cried.

The guy turned toward her.

Jack charged him and put a hold of his own on the attacker.

Zoe had other plans. She was aiming what looked like a canister of pepper spray at the guy. "Get down, Jack!"

He pushed off the man and hit the floor. A hissing sound was followed by the guy's howl of pain. From his position on the floor, Jack watched the assailant stumble across the room toward the back door.

"You'd *better* get out of here!" Zoe shouted. She opened the front door and let Romeo inside. The dog took off after the assailant but the screen door slammed shut before the dog could follow him outside. Romeo kept barking and jumping at the back door, wanting to go after him.

"Romeo, stop," Jack said, then glanced at Zoe. "Call 911." He leaned against the wall, finally able to catch his breath.

She knelt beside him. "Are you okay?"

"911," he repeated, not wanting her to waste time

worrying about him when police could be in pursuit of the attacker.

She pulled her cell phone out of her pocket and sat beside him on the floor. As she made the call, she scrutinized Jack's forehead and cheeks for signs of injury. The attention made him uncomfortable.

Romeo plopped down, laying his chin on Jack's thigh. With soulful eyes, he looked up, and Jack stroked the dog's head. "It's okay, buddy."

Zoe finished giving a description to the 911 operator and ended the call. Jack glanced at her worried expression. An expression that reminded him of his failures. An expression that made him feel ashamed.

"I'm fine," he said, starting to get up.

Zoe pressed her hand against his shoulder. "Can we wait for paramedics to confirm that?"

"I don't need paramedics."

"You were violently assaulted."

It wasn't the first time, Jack thought.

But it was the second time in one day that Zoe had been brutally attacked.

"Did he…hurt you?" Jack asked, his gut twisting into a knot in anticipation of her answer.

"Scared me mostly."

He nodded, relieved.

"You saved me again," she said.

He shrugged, not knowing if her remark required a response.

"Why did you come back?" she asked.

"To give you this." He pulled the silver dove necklace out of his pocket.

Her face brightened as she took it from him. "Oh, thank you."

"And to apologize," he said.

"For what, being honest?"

"You were angry with me for being honest."

"Actually, I think I was angry with myself."

"I don't understand, but then I don't understand a lot of things when it comes to human interaction."

"I should have done more to help Shannon, for one. Plus, you had a valid point. But if she were in trouble, you'd think she would have told me."

"You live five hours away. Why would she tell you?"

"Distance shouldn't matter. Friends confide in each other."

"Okay."

"What, don't you have any friends?"

Riley came to mind, but no one else. Volunteers he'd met through SAR weren't close friends; they were teammates, work associates.

"You shouldn't have to think about it," Zoe said. The left corner of her mouth turned up slightly.

"You're making fun of me," he said.

"No," she said, touching his shoulder. "I'm teasing, joking around."

When he didn't respond, she continued, "You know, making light of something?"

He knew what she meant, yet in his experience teasing someone made them feel small and foolish. Zoe's comment didn't make him feel that way. This felt… different.

"I didn't mean to offend you," she offered.

He shrugged. "Like I said, I don't always understand people."

"I've been there, too." She reached out to pet Romeo. Jack noticed her hand was trembling.

Although still shaken, she was down on the floor trying to console Jack. He didn't need consoling. He wasn't traumatized by the assault as much as disappointed in himself that he hadn't restrained the guy for police.

"I'm going to get up now," he said.

"Okay, sure." She straightened and extended her hand.

Jack ignored it and stood on his own, wanting to let her know he wasn't seriously injured, and she didn't have to worry about him. From her wistful expression, he wondered if he'd made a mistake.

They sat at the kitchen table and Romeo trotted up to Jack, waiting for direction. Jack pointed at Zoe. "Go help."

Romeo went to Zoe's side and waited expectantly.

"Pet him," Jack encouraged. It always made Jack feel better when his fingers touched Romeo's soft, Bernese–border collie fur.

A few minutes later the tension in Zoe's features softened. Good, it was working.

"Did you recognize the man who broke in?" Jack asked.

"No."

"Did he steal anything?"

"I don't think he was a burglar."

"Why do you say that?"

"Because..." she hesitated "...he said, 'Where is she?'"

"She? As in... Shannon?"

"I guess? This whole thing is so—"

"Puzzling," he said.

"And scary. I mean, one guy kidnaps Shannon and

another is trying to find her?" As she kept stroking Romeo's fur, Zoe's expression grew contemplative.

"Would you like me to make you some tea?" he offered.

His question elicited a slight smile. "Tea?"

"Tea calms the soul." He repeated the phrase he'd learned from Aunt Margaret. Whenever he'd get tied up into knots about kids taunting him, or he felt like an idiot because he didn't know how to interact properly, Aunt Margaret would brew two cups of tea and sit with him at the kitchen table.

"You're an interesting guy," Zoe said.

"So, yes? You'd like tea?"

"Yes, that would be nice."

Good. It gave him something to do, a way to make her feel better. A challenge, since his skill set did not include nurturing.

"I'm sorry about before," Zoe said.

"Before?" He flipped the gas burner on beneath the stainless teakettle.

"Being rude when you said Shannon could have gotten involved with the wrong people."

"I wasn't trying to be malicious."

"I know."

"I'll try to be less insolent next time."

"Interesting choice of words."

A word that his grandmother once claimed defined Jack.

"Why 'insolent'?" Zoe asked.

He pulled two mugs out of the cabinet and formulated an answer, not sure how much he wanted to share.

"Sorry, I didn't mean to pry," she said.

"You apologized for being rude earlier, yet I come

off as rude more often than not," Jack said. "It's the way I am. Rude, insolent, impertinent."

"Whoa, which adult used those words against you?"

He turned to her. How could she possibly know?

Sirens echoed in the distance. "Police will be here soon," he said. Excellent timing. He didn't like talking about himself, his childhood.

"You should consider relocating," he said.

"I feel close to Shannon in her home. Besides I want to be here when they bring her back."

Zoe would risk her own safety to be here for her friend *if* authorities found her? It didn't seem like a wise choice to Jack.

"Is there anyone who can stay with you?" he said.

"No, I don't know anyone in town other than Shannon, her friend Kelly and…" she hesitated "…you."

Unfortunate. More people in the house would discourage the attacker from returning. But not just anyone. That gave Jack an idea.

"What is it?" she said.

"Excuse me?"

"You got…" she motioned to her face "…a look, like the gears were spinning in your head."

Wait, she recognized a change in Jack's features when an idea was forming? How could she read him better than most of his closest associates?

"What do you do for a living?" he asked.

"I'm a counselor for adolescents and teens, why?"

That explained why she was able to read him so easily. Counselors were trained to identify feelings buried beneath the surface. He'd have to be more careful with Zoe. He didn't want a repeat of his ex-fiancée,

who used her intimate knowledge of Jack against him
in the worst way.

"I expect you're good at your job," he said.

"Some days better than others. How about you? What
do you do when you're not rescuing damsels in distress
from a mountain?"

"IT security. I own my own business."

"I'm guessing that's lucrative."

"Privacy is priceless." He wondered if she caught on
to the double meaning.

"That sounds like an ad campaign."

He glanced at her.

"Teasing again, sorry," she said.

"Don't apologize for my shortcomings."

"I don't see it as a shortcoming. Making light of
things is simply not something you do. That's okay.
So, IT security, rewarding work, is it?"

He suspected she was making conversation to distance herself from tonight's attack. "Rewarding enough,
for now."

"And what happens after now? I mean, you seem like
the type of guy who would have a plan."

Of course, it wouldn't take long for a woman in her
profession to assess his personality and figure out his
type.

"My plan is to sell my business and travel the world."

"Sounds lovely," she said.

Her tone belied her words. He wondered why she
disapproved.

"You won't miss people when you move away?" she
asked. When he didn't answer right away, she said, "You
have to have some friends, Jack. Or family?"

"Between the business and SAR, I don't have time for a social life."

Now she was the one to look confused.

Someone knocked on the front door. Romeo charged across the room, and Jack ordered him back to his side.

"It's Detective Perry," a voice called.

Good timing. Jack was growing more uncomfortable by the minute. Sharing intimate details about his life, his future plans, was not something that came easily to him.

Zoe stood and went to let the detective in, giving Jack the breathing space he needed to process their conversation. Regardless of feeling exposed to her in a way he hadn't felt in years, Jack had an intense need to protect her, a woman who touched things in his psyche he'd thought lost or damaged or...nonexistent.

Detective Perry entered with another officer Jack recognized as Sergeant Peterson. Jack was relieved to see the sergeant, considering Perry's obvious dislike of Jack.

"Jack," Sergeant Peterson greeted.

"You again," Detective Perry said to Jack.

"I was returning something to Zoe."

"Something that could be used as evidence in this case?" Perry pressed.

"He brought me my dove necklace." Zoe held it out between her forefinger and thumb. "It represents the Holy Spirit and Jack knew how important it was to me."

"Your timing was convenient." Detective Perry looked at Jack.

"Yes, wasn't it?" Zoe said. "I don't know what would have happened if Jack wasn't here. And Romeo." She reached out and stroked the dog's head. She motioned the two officers to the kitchen table, and they sat down. Jack remained standing. "Jack and Romeo saved me, again." She shot Jack an appreciative smile.

He looked away. This was dangerous, something beyond his understanding. Jack didn't like things he couldn't make sense of or control.

Detective Perry took their statements, including a description of the intruder.

"Midforties, about my height wearing a leather jacket," Jack said.

"He spoke with a raspy voice and had a birthmark on his neck below his jawline." Zoe pointed to her own neck.

"Good thing you had pepper spray," Perry said.

"Too bad I didn't have it with me earlier on the hike."

As they discussed the attack, Jack texted the SAR command chief and asked him to contact certain team members to put Jack's plan into motion. The people he had in mind were perfect for his goal of protecting Zoe.

"So, he was looking for Shannon." Detective Perry's comment was a statement, not a question.

"It's possible, yes," Zoe answered. "Which means she escaped her kidnapper. That's a good thing, right?"

"It could be," Perry said.

"But?"

"There are too many unanswered questions."

"At the very least, the kidnapping and tonight's break-in are related, right?"

"We'd be speculating," Perry said.

"Then speculate," Zoe pushed.

Jack had considered her fragile a few minutes ago, but not right now. Right now she was challenging authorities.

Jack's phone vibrated with a text message. Good, his plan was coming together.

"It would expedite the investigation if we had more detailed information about Miss Banks," Sergeant Peterson said.

Detective Perry shot him a look, then redirected his attention to Zoe.

She continued to pet Romeo, who seemed to be offering comfort. *Good dog.*

"How about problems at work or more specifics about her boyfriend?" Perry said.

"She hadn't heard from him since he went to visit family in Colorado. She didn't talk much about work."

The officers shared another look.

"What?" Zoe said.

"We suspect she was involved in criminal activity, which is the motivation behind her kidnapping," Detective Perry said.

"No, that can't be right," Zoe said, glancing at Jack.

He looked away, uncomfortable at seeing the pained expression on her face.

"What…what kind of criminal activity?" she asked.

"Drugs," Jack guessed.

"Why would you say that?" Perry countered.

"It's logical."

"Is it? I don't think so. I think you know something and you're holding back."

"Detective," Sergeant Peterson intervened. "Jack's been with Search and Rescue for four years. He's solid."

"Everyone's solid until they're not. How's it logical, Einstein?" Perry said.

"Stop!" Zoe put out her hand like she was breaking

up a fight between middle school kids. "Why do you think Shannon was involved in drugs?"

"We can't discuss an open investigation," Perry said.

"Fine, then we're done." Zoe stood and planted her hands on her hips.

The men hesitated before standing. "Sergeant Peterson is going to move you to a different location," Perry said.

"No, thank you."

"Ma'am, not only is it not safe for you here, but we need to send a forensic team to dust for prints."

"Pointless," Jack said. "He wore gloves."

Detective Perry glared at him.

"You may leave now," Zoe said, polite yet firm. "I'm capable of taking care of myself."

"Considering what happened tonight, I would have to disagree," Perry said.

"Well, Detective, the assailant is not here, and wherever he is, he's in a world of hurt from my pepper spray. I am unharmed and have more spray in my possession."

"Ma'am, I must insist—"

"Thank you for coming tonight." She crossed the room and opened the door.

The detective hesitated as he passed her. "I can't protect you if you make unwise choices."

"I understand. Good night."

Detective Perry left.

Sergeant Peterson paused by the door and handed her a business card. "My cell number. Call anytime. I can see about having an off-duty deputy watch the house, but I can't make any promises."

"I've got tonight covered," Jack said.

The sergeant and Zoe both looked at him.

"A few SAR members will spend the night until we're called out again tomorrow morning."

"Wait, when did this happen?" Zoe asked.

"You shouldn't put civilians at risk," Sergeant Peterson said.

"Sally Frick and George Connelly are part of the group. They've been informed of the situation. Should be here shortly."

"Ah," Peterson said.

"Ah?" Zoe questioned.

"Frick and Connelly are former military," Peterson explained. "No one's getting in the house if they're here."

"We'll take turns keeping watch," Jack said. "Zoe will be safe."

Zoe will be safe.

Jack's words gave Zoe enough comfort to allow her to get some sleep. That was, until a nightmare abruptly woke her the next morning.

She struggled to calm her breathing. Glanced around the room. The six-foot-tall armoire had been moved to block the window, probably to prevent the intruder from gaining access to the room.

Low murmurs drifted through the wood door from the living room. She washed up and dressed in jeans and a sweatshirt. She opened the bedroom door to a four strangers with backpacks and bedrolls. She'd been so exhausted last night that she hadn't heard the team members show up and lay out their sleeping bags on the floor.

"Good morning," she said, searching the room for Jack, but didn't see him.

A woman in her fifties greeted her. "Hi, Zoe, I'm Sally Frick." They shook hands. "Sorry if we woke you."

"You didn't. So, you're the heroes who stayed over to protect me last night?"

"Hero, I like that," said a man in his thirties.

An older man gave him a playful shove. "Who says she was talking about you? Come on, let's move."

"Weather conditions have changed," Sally said to Zoe. "We're meeting law enforcement personnel and heading back up Mt. Stevens to search for your friend."

"Where's Jack?"

"He got an early start with the first team. Sergeant Peterson posted a deputy outside to keep watch of the house, although I think Peterson would prefer you to find another place to stay temporarily given what happened last night. We may not be back for a few days. Weather is looking good."

"Oh, okay. Be careful."

"Thanks, we will," Sally said.

The group of two men, two women and three dogs headed out. Zoe watched them through the window, wishing she could have seen Jack this morning to thank him.

For coming back last night and saving her.

For going out this morning to find Shannon.

For being a grounding presence in her life.

Whoa, back up. The trauma of the last eighteen hours and possibly the concussion must be messing with her cognitive ability. It wasn't like her to rely on a man for stability, especially a man with such opposite views on life.

Jack Monroe was an IT genius who planned to sell

his business and travel the world. Where was the stability in that? She had endured too much instability growing up and had made herself a promise never to feel unsettled again. Wasn't that why she and Tim had ultimately broken up? Because his obsession with climbing the corporate ladder and constant, last-minute canceling of their plans left her feeling untethered? She wanted to be able to count on something, someone. Tim wasn't the guy.

And neither was a man like Jack Monroe.

This was definitely her concussion talking. She barely knew the man and had no business thinking of him in those terms.

She turned toward the kitchen a little too quickly, her body aching from the fall yesterday. Well, that and perhaps being yanked around by the creep in the leather jacket last night.

Frustration burned in her gut, as if she'd ingested a handful of chili peppers. While teams were out searching for Shannon, Zoe was stuck in the house doing absolutely nothing.

A familiar feeling of helplessness spread through her chest.

"Oh no, I'm stepping off that one," she said, referring to an expression called the *victim triangle* that her counseling mentor had taught her years ago.

Deciding to be proactive, not reactive, Zoe fixed herself peanut butter on toast for sustenance. As she ate, a plan formed in her mind. She'd search the house for clues, insights into Shannon's state of mind, and maybe even prove that police were way off base suspecting Shan of being involved with drugs. The nerve.

Opening a small, cherrywood nightstand beside

Shan's bed, Zoe spotted a pale blue journal. She turned to the first page, her gaze settling on her friend's fluid handwriting.

She quickly snapped it shut. This felt wrong, like she was violating her friend's trust.

But if it was the only way to gain insight into Shan's life…

"I'm sorry, Shannon." Zoe opened it again and began reading, first the usual stuff—frustration at work, pressure from her parents to move back home—then stories from Shannon's work as a volunteer counselor at a local youth center.

Zoe flipped another page and landed on an entry titled "Randy and Kelly."

I can't believe what's happening. I trusted them with my heart and they betrayed me. Isn't there anyone who loves me and will protect my heart?

"Me, I'll protect your heart," Zoe whispered. She flipped the page.

And saw her own name.

Zoe is coming to visit. I don't know if I have enough energy for her, if I have the strength to comfort her when my own heart is breaking.

Was that how she felt about Zoe? That she was an energy-sucking friend who needed comforting, a friend who sapped Shannon's emotional strength?

"I can't think about that now." Zoe found renewed strength in her determination for answers, especially about Randy and Kelly.

She decided to call Kelly, be pleasant and set up a meeting where Zoe could confront her face-to-face about what she'd read.

"Hello?" Kelly answered.

"Hi, it's Zoe. I need to talk to you."

"I'm actually at the SAR command center prepping food for the team. Why don't you come by and help?"

"Okay."

Kelly gave her the location. "See you soon."

"Thanks."

Zoe left the house and spotted a police officer parked out front. She thanked him for being there, and told him where she was going.

As she drove off, she tamped down her anger so she'd be rational when she questioned Kelly. She considered the possibilities in her mind and landed on the most obvious: Kelly and Randy had a relationship behind Shannon's back.

How could they betray her like that?

She punched the address Kelly had given for the command center into her phone and pulled her compact car onto the main road. She planned what she'd say, intent on being calm, not accusatory. She'd never get answers that way.

Thirty minutes later Zoe pulled up to the command center and approached the food tent. Kelly spotted her and smiled. "Hi, Zoe."

Zoe couldn't bring herself to smile back. As she was about to question Kelly about the journal entry, a middle-aged man with jet-black hair stepped up beside Kelly. Zoe did not want an audience.

"Zoe?" the man said. "As in Shannon's friend?"

"Yes," Zoe said.

"I'm Curt Underwood, Shannon's boss at Mt. Stevens Resort." He extended his hand. "I'm sick about all this. She's one of my best employees. Please, if there's anything I can do while you're in town. How about I comp a room for you at the resort?"

"Thanks, but I'm staying at Shannon's place."

Curt pulled out a business card and handed it to her. "Call anytime, if you need anything."

"Thank you." Zoe turned to Kelly. "Could I talk to you?"

"Sure." Kelly motioned to Curt. "Can you take over packing the sandwiches for a minute?"

"Of course."

Zoe led Kelly away from the group.

"What's wrong?" Kelly said.

Once they were out of earshot, Zoe turned. "I know about you and Randy."

"Me and Randy?"

Someone touched Zoe's arm. She glanced over her shoulder at Jack. "Jack? I thought you were up searching for Shannon."

"I was." He broke eye contact.

Dread filled her chest. "You mean…?"

She glanced behind him at two men carrying a body bag.

FOUR

Buzzing echoed in Zoe's ears. It was so incredibly loud that she wanted to cry out in pain but couldn't find her voice. Her legs buckled and she went down.

"I've got her," a deep voice said.

And then she was floating, drifting. Unable to hear anything clearly but the rumblings of low voices, her name interspersed between unintelligible words.

It was as if she were having an out-of-body experience, like in a dream when you're watching the situation unfold from the corner of the room, but you're also an active participant in the action.

She blinked against a bright white light glaring directly at her. No, she knew it wasn't her time to meet the Lord. The light faded, and she could see more clearly—she'd been carried under a tent, worried faces of strangers hovered above.

Jack's face. His eyes, usually warm blue, were dark and cold. He looked…angry. Why would he be angry?

Then the muted sounds grew crisp and clear, as if someone had cranked up the volume on the radio.

"Please step back," a man on her left said to Jack. "I need to examine her."

"Go ahead and examine her." Jack didn't move. Dark blue eyes pinned her in place.

A woman stepped up beside him. "Give him space, Jack."

Zoe squeezed his hand tighter. Wouldn't let go. "Jack," she said in a small, strained voice.

"Hi," he responded. "You just fainted."

"Zoe, I'd like to examine you."

She glanced to her left. A man in his sixties with a graying beard and warm smile looked down at her.

"I just fainted," she repeated Jack's words.

"That's probably true, but I'd like to be sure it's not more serious."

She started to feel Jack loosen his grip and she clung tighter. "Jack…stay."

The doctor nodded that it was okay. He took her pulse and watched her breathing, then listened to her heartbeat with his stethoscope.

"Look straight ahead for me."

"She's suffering from a concussion," Jack offered.

"Then it's a good thing you caught her." The doctor checked her eyes with a penlight. "We need to protect that head of yours." He clicked off the light. "Have you had anything to eat or drink today?"

"Peanut butter on toast. Nothing to drink."

"Water," he ordered someone out of view. A minute later she was presented with a bottle of water and the doctor helped her sit up.

"Stay hydrated," he said. "I think you're okay."

"Thanks."

The doctor left her and Jack alone. Jack's dark eyes had warmed slightly.

"The body bag," she started, "was it…?"

"We haven't identified the body yet."

"Surely you could tell from her clothes?"

He glanced down at his hand, still holding hers.

"She had no clothes?"

"She was wearing clothes, but she'd stripped off her outerwear."

"If she was cold, why would she—"

"In the last stages of hypothermia, something called paradoxical undressing can occur. You think you're hot when in fact you're losing the feeling in your limbs."

She nodded, trying to make sense of what he'd said. "The body you found, it was a woman?"

Jack nodded.

Zoe closed her eyes and said a silent prayer.

"It could be someone else," he said. "Not your friend."

She opened her eyes and sighed. "Have there been other missing hikers reported in the last twenty-four hours?"

He didn't answer, which meant no. Yet he was trying to keep Zoe's hope alive. It was a kind thing to do.

"Thanks," she said.

"Why are you thanking me?"

She shrugged. "For catching me when I fainted, for being a friend."

His brow furrowed slightly, and she guessed he was processing her use of the word *friend* in this scenario.

"Why are you here this morning?" he said.

"I found something in Shannon's diary that disturbed me."

"Her diary?"

She nodded. "I know, diaries are private, and I shouldn't have gone snooping, but I needed to figure out what is going on."

"What did you find?"

"She felt betrayed by her boyfriend, Randy, and her friend Kelly. They did something that hurt Shan deeply."

"Something, like…?"

"I don't know. That's why I wanted to meet with Kelly, to question her."

"You still want to do that?"

"You don't think I should?" Zoe snapped.

His eyebrows furrowed again, as if puzzled by her reaction.

"Sorry," she said. "I'm a little raw right now. I can't believe Shannon is gone."

"The body hasn't been identified yet."

"I… I should be the one to do that."

"You may not want to see her like that, bruised from the fall."

She clenched her jaw against another possible fainting episode. She would not be a wimp about this. "I don't have to identify her by her face, only her right wrist."

"How?"

Zoe hiked her jacket sleeve up to expose the tattoo she and Shannon shared of a cross with a heart. "We figured our parents couldn't be too upset with us for getting tattoos symbolizing our love of God and our eternal friendship. We started with matching bracelets, but you can lose a bracelet, we rationalized. I think Shan still wears hers. Anyway, we got the tattoos."

"Are you sure you're up to this?"

"Yes." Well, she was 50 percent sure anyway. "Is the body…?" She glanced past Jack.

"They've already transported it to the medical examiner's office."

"Then let's go."

* * *

Zoe Pratt was more puzzling than trying to figure out a sophisticated DDoS attack, Jack thought as he pulled into the medical center parking lot. One minute she fainted at the thought of her best friend being dead, the next she was intent on identifying the body.

How could someone so fragile be concurrently strong? Or maybe her strength was a pretense to cover her grief.

He parked and got out to open the door for Zoe. Romeo paced in the back seat. "We won't be long," Jack said to the dog, cracking the back windows.

It would only take seconds to examine the victim's wrist and confirm her identity as Zoe's friend.

And Jack would be ready to catch her again.

As Zoe and Jack headed for the building, Romeo let Jack know he wasn't pleased about being left behind. Jack pointed a finger at the truck. "Quiet." Romeo complied.

"Romeo seems a little bossy today," Zoe said.

"That's the border collie part of him."

"And the other part?"

Jack wondered if she made small talk as a distraction from what was about to happen. "Bernese mountain dogs are gentle giants," he said. "All about love and affection."

"Which mellows out the bossy border collie part?"

"Border collies aren't bossy, they're intelligent. If intelligence is not channeled properly it can be..." he hesitated "...troublesome."

"Not just in dogs."

Was she referring to Jack? There was no way she could know him that well, could she?

"Some of my most challenging clients are teenagers

who are off-the-charts smart," she said. "I think intelligence, or even creativity for that matter, can turn sour inside of a person if they don't express it."

"Is it interesting work, being a counselor?" he said.

"Some days. Other days it's…sad."

They paused at the front door to the medical building and he looked at her, about to ask if she really wanted to do this.

"I'm sure," she said, without even hearing the question.

With a nod, he opened the door.

A young receptionist with copper-streaked hair greeted them. She called into the back where they examined bodies and did autopsies. "We have someone here to identify the body found by Search and Rescue… Okay, sure." She hung up the phone and addressed Jack. "They need a few minutes. You can wait over there." She pointed to a small waiting area.

"Thank you," Zoe said, pretending to be sure of herself, pretending to be strong.

Thankfully Jack played along with her mindless conversation, actually asking a question or two, which must have been hard for him. She needed to keep her mind off the dread threatening to consume her. If she looked at the woman's wrist and saw the beloved tattoo…she would be devastated.

Struggling to remain strong, she kept talking as Jack led her to a waiting area with green chairs.

"If you wouldn't mind, I'd like to exchange phone numbers," Jack said. "In case we need to communicate."

"Sure." She handed him her phone.

"I also thought we could activate location services.

That way you can track me when I'm on a mission if the reception is good."

And Jack would know where Zoe was, in case trouble found her again.

"Oh, great, thanks," she said.

He added his number to her phone and vice versa, then handed her phone back.

"How hard was it to train Romeo?" she asked.

"Not hard. He has a high play drive and more energy than a toddler. Not that I've been around many toddlers, but I've heard things."

"And why Romeo?"

"You mean the name?"

She nodded.

"Chick magnet."

She almost smiled. "Excuse me?"

"When I first got him, I couldn't decide on a name right away. The vet recommended exposing him to as many people as possible as a puppy and it became clear rather quickly that he was a charming sort of guy. My friend referred to him as a chick magnet, so I named him Romeo."

"Cute."

"You don't like it."

"No, it makes sense. He certainly has won my heart. What about all his other names?"

"Albert is for Albert Einstein and Garrett is for Garrett Morgan, a famous inventor who invented the smoke hood."

"Mr. Monroe?" the receptionist called. "You both may go back now. Down that hall and the first door on the right."

Zoe hesitated before getting up.

"Have you changed your mind?" Jack said.

"No." She glanced toward the hallway, her legs still locked in place, unable to support her.

"You won't need to see her face, just her wrist," Jack reminded her.

With a nod, Zoe stood and took a deep, fortifying breath. Putting it off wasn't going to change the outcome and the sooner she knew the truth, the sooner she could either start the grieving process or continue investigating her friend's disappearance.

The walk down the hall was oddly quiet, her senses attuned to her surroundings: the pale, yellow walls, speckled vinyl floor, and plastic trim around the edges.

Please, God, don't let it be Shannon.

"Should someone else be here?"

Jack's question jarred her out of her desperate thoughts. She glanced at him.

"Other friends or family?" he asked. "We can wait for them."

"Why would I want to wait?"

"For…" he hesitated "…emotional support."

"You're going in with me, right?" she said, sounding a little too needy considering she hadn't even known the man twenty-four hours.

"Yes, I'll be with you."

Silence rang in her ears as they approached the large white door. She could do this. She could be strong for her friend.

Jack paused and looked at her.

"God give me strength," she whispered. Then she nodded and Jack pushed open the door.

A tall man in scrubs stood up from a desk and greeted them. "I'm Dr. Gonzales. You're here to identify the body?"

"Yes," Zoe said.

"She needs to see the right wrist," Jack said.

Zoe shot a quick glance at the glass window, covered on the other side by a curtain. Her heart pounded in her chest.

"One moment." Dr. Gonzales went into the other room.

Zoe took a deep breath and prayed for strength.

The curtain opened to reveal a body beneath a sheet on a table. The doctor went to the body and blocked their view, she assumed to adjust the sheet so only the arm would be exposed.

She could use a boost of strength right now. Without looking at him, she gripped Jack's hand. He didn't resist the connection.

I can do all things through Christ who strengthens me.

The doctor stepped aside, exposing the victim's bare arm.

No tattoo. No cross and heart.

It wasn't Shannon.

Zoe let out a sigh, not realizing she'd been holding her breath.

"Are you going to faint again?" Jack asked.

She glanced at his worried expression. His blue eyes warmed with concern.

"No, I'm okay."

She didn't seem okay, Jack thought as he drove her back to the command center. Gazing out the window at the towering pine trees on either side of the road, she was taciturn at best, and her pensive expression hadn't changed since they'd left the medical examiner's office.

Although Jack preferred the quiet to nonstop chatter of some people, he found himself missing the verboseness of Zoe Pratt who'd asked him questions about his dog and actually smiled when he'd called Romeo a chick magnet.

Wait, this was no time to be smiling. Then again, she knew her friend wasn't dead, so she shouldn't be too upset, right?

"The victim wasn't your friend. Aren't you…?" He wasn't sure what word he was looking for.

"Happy?"

"No, that's not the word."

"Relieved?"

"Yes, relieved," he said, turning onto the access road.

"I'm very relieved and thankful, but I don't want to get my hopes up too much." She eyed the mountain range bordering them. "Shan's still out there somewhere." She snapped her attention to Jack. "Did you—"

"Notify Command that it wasn't Shannon? Yes."

"How did you know what I was going to ask?"

"It seemed like a logical question. They've sent two more teams up the north side of Mt. Stevens. They're focusing on an old bunker off Trail 415 and Portage Fire Lookout. Sometimes hikers will leave behind food or water bottles for the next person. It's possible Shannon escaped and found shelter and sustenance at the lookout last night."

"If she escaped," she whispered.

"It's a good possibility, considering someone's looking for her now."

She nodded, but it didn't seem like his explanation satisfied her.

"They're doing everything they can," he said.

"I know." She glanced at him. "Sorry about the whole hand-holding thing back there. It was automatic, to reach out for support. I mean, I sense you're not a touchy-feely type of guy and I didn't mean to make you uncomfortable."

"You don't have to apologize."

"You must think I'm a fragile ditz or something. I mean, I'm always leaning on you or fainting on you or holding your hand." She shook her head.

"You're upset about your friend. It's understandable."

This time he meant it. He actually understood. Even though he had little appreciation for emotions, he'd experienced his share of hurt and remorse when he was a child and young adult. It was after his twenty-first birthday that he'd decided to focus all his efforts on shutting down the emotional part of himself and locking it away where it wouldn't be used against him ever again.

They pulled into the command center parking lot. Jack let Romeo out for exercise. Jack wasn't sure if he needed to head back up the mountain at this point, since teams had already been assembled and dispersed. Although he might be able to catch up, something held him back.

Zoe.

He didn't like the idea of her being on her own with the threat still out there.

"I'd better talk to Kelly," Zoe said.

As she headed toward the food truck, Jack walked alongside her.

"Aren't you going back up?" she said.

"I'd like to hear your conversation if possible." He didn't want to get into a discussion about his motivations and why he planned to stay close.

They approached the food tent and found Kelly unloading equipment from the back of a flatbed truck. She saw Zoe and her eyes lit up.

"I heard it's not Shannon." Kelly rushed toward Zoe as if to give her a hug, but Zoe stepped back. "What's wrong?" Kelly said.

Zoe motioned her out of earshot of the rest of the volunteers.

"What was going on between you and Randy?" Zoe asked.

"What do you mean?"

"Shannon thinks you betrayed her, you and Randy together. What's that about?"

Kelly sighed and crossed her arms over her chest. "Oh, so you know about the intervention."

"What intervention?"

"Randy was worried about her and came to me for advice. She seemed...depressed. He kept asking her what was wrong, but she blew him off, said she was fine."

"But?"

"Something felt off. Randy asked Pastor Mike for advice. He suggested we have a meeting, me, Randy, Shannon and Pastor Mike. It backfired. Shannon felt ganged up on."

"When did this happen?"

"A few months ago, around the time one of the kids from Angie's Youth Club was hospitalized for an overdose. I sensed maybe Shannon felt responsible."

"Why?" Zoe pressed.

"I guess because she didn't realize the girl was using and out of control."

"She never told me."

"That came a few months after another teen from the youth club died in the mountains."

"Was she close to these girls?"

"Very. After our intervention, she slowed things down

with Randy and could barely fit me in for coffee. She withdrew from both of us and took extra shifts at work."

Jack watched Zoe's reaction to Kelly's story. Zoe seemed to believe her, but Jack couldn't be sure. Perhaps she was being polite.

"I'd like to speak with Randy," Zoe said.

"I can text you his number, but I don't know when he's coming back. He took it pretty hard when she shut him out."

"Hey, Jack," Sally Frick said, approaching them. "They're putting together another team. You with us?"

He hesitated before answering and glanced at Zoe. Although he wanted to stay and make sure she was safe, he read desperation in her eyes, desperation to find her friend.

"Go on," Zoe said. "Thanks for everything today."

With a nod, Jack turned and joined the team. He had the urge to look back, to make eye contact with Zoe, but wasn't sure why. Instead, he remained focused on the group assembling by the trailhead. He had to concentrate on finding Shannon Banks.

And giving Zoe peace.

As Jack walked away, a chill fell across Zoe's shoulders.

Kelly reached out and touched her arm. "Hey, they're doing everything they can to find her."

Zoe nodded. "I know."

Sergeant Peterson pulled up in a police car. He got out and approached Zoe and Kelly. "Ladies."

"Sergeant," Zoe said. She shot another glance in Jack's direction but couldn't see his dark green jacket among the other team members. He must be leading the charge up the mountain, putting his life at risk to find Shannon.

"I need a moment with Miss Pratt," Sergeant Peterson said.

"Sure." Kelly left them alone and Zoe eyed the sergeant. She suspected he had bad news.

"Although the body they recovered wasn't your friend, we found Shannon's name and phone number written on a piece of paper in the woman's pocket," he said.

"I don't understand. Why would a stranger have Shan's information?"

"We'll know more after we identify the body. We also found drugs on the victim."

"Shannon is not involved in anything criminal, Sergeant."

He glanced down, uncomfortable. She was speaking from a place of faith; the sergeant was trained to consider only facts.

"I can't offer you 24/7 police protection, but I'll do what I can."

"I understand."

"Be careful. Don't go anywhere alone. I'd strongly suggest you not remain at Shannon Banks's house. There are plenty of lodging options here in Mt. Stevens."

"Thank you. I'll look into it." She wondered if he was concerned more about her assisting with the investigation than her personal safety. Okay, now she was growing paranoid. Frankly, she only trusted one person and he'd gone up the mountain to find her friend.

"Ma'am?" Sergeant Peterson said, interrupting her thoughts.

She glanced at him.

"You have my number. Call if you need anything."

* * *

Wanting to stay busy, Zoe stuck around to help pack meals for more SAR teams. She found the work both distracting and rewarding. It gave her a reprieve from worrying about Shannon and Jack. Even though law enforcement had gone up with the SAR teams, she was still concerned about the potential danger waiting for them.

Then she received a text from Jack stating they hadn't found anything of significance. A storm front was brewing up above and the teams were heading back down. She was relieved that he was okay, yet disappointed that they were postponing the search. Again.

The conflicting emotions were taking their toll, so she decided to be proactive and made a reservation at a local bed-and-breakfast. The sergeant was right, she'd be safer in a new location.

She reserved a room at the Ashford Inn, but needed to get her things from Shannon's place before checking in. The thought of going back to the house alone sparked anxiety so she called the sergeant and asked if he could have a deputy meet her there as a safety precaution. He assured her he would.

"Good work today," Kelly said as she passed Zoe.

"Thanks."

Kelly caught up to a group of women and turned back to Zoe. "You have dinner plans?"

"No, why?"

"Some friends are meeting at the Cardinal Café and you're welcome to join us."

"Okay, thanks. I have to check into a bed-and-breakfast first."

"Sounds good."

The camaraderie of being with a group of women would be beneficial, plus Zoe could ask more about her friend's state of mind.

Shannon, why didn't you confide in me? The thought that Shannon considered Zoe the needy one in their relationship disturbed her.

She glanced at the trailhead, but the search teams still hadn't returned. She hoped the weather wasn't making things hard for them. She prayed Shannon had somehow escaped her captor and found refuge.

Zoe walked over to the command chief, Lou Treadwell. "Excuse me, how long before the teams return?"

"Estimated arrival time, forty minutes," Lou said.

"Thank you."

If they were only a few minutes away, she might have waited for Jack.

Really, Zoe? Why? So you can lean on him some more?

This wasn't good. And it certainly wasn't like her. She'd been independent her entire life, starting when her younger brother, Ryan, got sick and she had to pretty much take over running the Pratt household.

Although she could use support during this crisis, she certainly didn't need to depend on a stranger like Jack Monroe to cope with her situation.

Her situation. Shannon had been taken more than twenty-four hours ago.

Glancing one last time at the mountain, she got in her car and headed for Shannon's place. Although she was an independent woman, she felt more than a little lost. Understandable, she counseled herself.

A car honked and she glanced in the rearview mirror at a sedan flashing its lights. She slowed down, assuming he wanted to pass. She surely didn't want to get into an accident on top of everything else.

She rolled down her window and waved him past.

Instead he dropped back.

A car passed by in the oncoming lane. She figured that's why the car behind her hadn't passed. She approached a sharp turn and slowed down. Glanced in the rearview mirror.

And couldn't even see the sedan's headlights, it was so close.

The car slammed into her back bumper.

She started to skid, turned the wheel into the spin, and lost control, veering off into a forested area bordering the road. Her car smashed into a tree and came to an abrupt stop. The force caused the airbag to burst open in her face.

Her head ached with the pressure, and her mind spun with fear. She fumbled in her pocket for her phone. Couldn't get her hands around it.

The door swung open.

"Is she okay?" a voice yelled from the distance.

"Yeah," a raspy voice called back.

"I'll call 911!" the distant voice shouted.

"Already did," the raspy voice answered. "I got this!"

The airbag was pushed aside and the creep who'd broken into the house last night was staring down at her. "Miss me?"

FIVE

Disappointed. That's how Jack felt when he came down the mountain.

He was disappointed that they hadn't been able to find anything, any clue as to Shannon Banks's whereabouts. He was disappointed that the weather had turned on them.

And disappointed that Zoe wasn't at the command center when he returned. He found himself worrying about her when she wasn't around, and worry was a distraction.

Worry is a waste of creative energy.

He'd said that in a lecture to University of Washington students last year, encouraging them to be bold and think out of the box, even if it meant risking failure. Worry only served to derail a person from achieving their goal.

In this case, finding Shannon Banks.

Jack couldn't control the weather and decided to take his own advice, not worry about Shannon, and perhaps check on Zoe. Sally Frick approached as he packed gear in his car.

"See you tomorrow, then?" she said.

"Or maybe sooner." Jack gazed across the mountain. The weather was so calm down here compared to the intensity of the storm up above.

"I heard it's not supposed to break until tomorrow midday."

"Weather reports can be inconsistent with reality," he said.

"True. Do you need us to bunk at the cottage with Zoe again?"

"No, she's moving to another location. Thanks."

"Anytime."

SAR members packed up and headed out to various locations, either their homes or temporary housing. Their mission wasn't over yet, not until they found Shannon Banks.

As he got into his truck, he wondered how long Shannon could survive up there, either in captivity or on her own. If she managed to escape, she'd still have to navigate the elements.

He'd do an analysis back at his motel room. Right now, he needed to make sure Zoe was safely checked into the Ashford Inn. He called her number but it went to voice mail. He wondered if this was inappropriate, if he cared too much for the stranger with the expressive brown eyes.

He wasn't sure, but he hoped if she felt uncomfortable with his attention that she'd say so. He suspected she would. She didn't seem like, how did she refer to herself, *a fragile ditz*?

On the contrary, there was nothing fragile about Zoe Pratt. She knew her own mind and made no apologies for her decisions. Even if they wouldn't be Jack's decisions, like staying at Shannon's house last night. He was able to acquire protection for her, but what if he hadn't?

When he'd received her text about moving to the Ashford Inn, he'd been relieved indeed. He was glad she told Sergeant Peterson so he could assign patrols to regularly cruise by the inn. Maybe she registered under a different name. That would protect her identity and location. Yet he suspected Zoe wasn't one to misrepresent herself.

He knew little about the Ashford Inn, but after reading the reviews, he thought it a good choice for her, at least for tonight. Unfortunately it didn't accept canine guests, so Jack couldn't stay there, as well.

Would she consider it pushy if he wanted to stay on the same property?

You're thinking too much.

One step at a time. Next step: make sure Zoe was safely settled in.

He directed his phone's virtual assistant to call the Ashford Inn.

"Ashford Inn, Ruthie speaking."

"I'm calling to confirm my friend, Zoe Pratt, has checked in."

"I'm sorry, sir, I cannot share that information."

Irritation quickly dissolved into appreciation.

"Of course, thank you." He ended the call. He'd cruise by the property to see if her car was parked out front.

A few minutes later he spotted flashing lights of two patrol cars near a car that had gone off the road. It wasn't raining so he wondered why the driver had lost control. He shot a quick glance toward the scene.

And spotted Zoe's car.

His fingers clenched the steering wheel. He pulled over to investigate. As he approached her car, he could tell the airbag had deployed and the front end of the car was smashed against a tree. Since he didn't see an ambulance, he wondered if they'd already transported Zoe to the hospital.

A deputy blocked Jack from getting too close. "Stay back, sir."

"Zoe Pratt," was all he could say.

Sergeant Peterson turned. "Hey, Jack." He motioned the deputy to allow Jack access.

"What happened?" Jack said. "Is Zoe okay?"

"We don't know."

"What?"

"We found the car like this, abandoned with no one inside."

Jack thought about that for a minute. "She wouldn't have wandered off, unless she went back to the road and caught a ride."

"Maybe."

"Or maybe what?"

"We received a report from a motorist who saw the accident. He said another motorist stopped to assist. The second motorist said the first one had called 911, but when we arrived, Zoe and the other motorist were gone."

"Did you get a description of the Good Samaritan?"

"The second person who stopped only saw him from behind, but they said he was about six feet tall, had dark hair and wore a leather jacket."

"The guy from last night," Jack blurted out.

"We don't know that for sure."

Jack turned and walked away.

"Jack!" Sergeant Peterson called. "Stay out of it!"

Not possible. Jack wasn't going to sit by and do nothing while Zoe was being tormented. He shouldn't have left her.

No, she wasn't his responsibility.

Trauma flooded to the surface.

Zoe was an adult, capable of taking care of herself. She wasn't a lost and injured teenager. Not his fault. Jack had done everything humanly possible to help her, save her.

The trauma he'd managed to keep locked away suddenly burst free. He got into his truck and slammed the door. Pounded closed fists against the steering wheel, his heart racing.

Romeo whined from the back seat.

"We've got to find her, Romeo."

The dog barked as if he'd understood Jack's words.

Jack thought he'd successfully put that tragic incident behind him. He'd cataloged all the evidence from other SAR members, from the elements, from the Lost Person Behavior resource guide. He and his team had done everything according to proper procedure.

They were still unable to save her. Bottom line.

It didn't seem like other team members, including Sally Frick, were unduly affected by their failure. It happened. Part of the job.

People died.

Zoe's bright, expressive eyes filled his mind. He would not lose Zoe.

He ripped out his phone and did a cursory search. Grabbing his laptop, he opened his locator app to track Zoe's phone. It was more powerful than similar apps and would give him an exact location in real time. Wherever her phone was, he'd find it.

He hoped she still had it in her possession.

A ding indicated the location. The bright red spot on his screen was…

Not far from him. In the middle of the surrounding forest.

Zoe raced through the woods like a woman with her hair on fire. That's how she felt: like her head had been lit up with firecrackers. But she shelved the pain and focused on getting away from the creep.

Good thing she remembered the special karate move Shannon's brother had taught her, the one that never failed to neutralize a male attacker when he was coming at her head-on. It was enough to stun him so she could flee, although she hadn't a clue where she was going.

She still couldn't believe the goon who'd broken into the cottage last night thought she'd surrender without a fight.

She glanced over her shoulder. Didn't see or hear anything. Her attacker must have given up. After all, it wouldn't take long for someone to see her car tangled with a tree and call the police. If the guy didn't want to be identified or caught, he'd have to flee the scene.

Zoe crouched low beside a tree to catch her breath. She had no idea which way to go. She'd been swerving so much she couldn't tell north from south or east from west.

She was lost. It was pitch-black. And she was running out of phone battery. Maybe she had time to make one more—

Then she saw it. The blink of a flashlight.

Had the creep found her?

She dialed 911 in the hopes the little bit of battery she had would enable her to make the call. "It's Zoe Pratt," she whispered as soon as the operator answered. "I'm in the woods. He's coming for me."

The phone went black.

She searched the ground for a fallen branch, anything she could use as a weapon.

The sound of boots crunching on twigs pierced the night. The guy was coming closer.

She grabbed a branch off the ground, the rough bark pricking her skin as she clenched it tight. She pushed up, leaning against the tree for cover and waited.

Snap. Crunch. Snap.

He was only a few feet away.

What if she missed?

Heartbeat pounding in her ears, she rested the branch on her shoulder. She grew dizzy, unsure if it was the concussion or the car crash or both.

Snap.

She pushed away from the tree and swung. Missing her mark, she stumbled forward and nearly fell to the ground.

"Miss Pratt, stop!" a voice said.

A young voice. She spun around.

And was looking at Trevor Willis, one of her teenage clients, wearing goggles on his face. Okay, she was losing it. She'd passed out and was dreaming up this scenario.

"Sorry," Trevor said, removing the goggles. "Didn't mean to scare you."

"What's happening?" was all she could say.

Someone sprang out of nowhere and tackled Trevor to the ground.

"No, stop!" she cried. After all, in this dream sequence, someone was hurting her client. "Leave him alone!" she cried. She swung the branch and it connected with the attacker's back.

In one swift motion he jumped up and ripped it out of her hands. She squinted and covered her face with her arms, expecting the branch to be used on her.

"Zoe."

Her name. Yes, her name was Zoe. But who was—

"Zoe, it's Jack."

She slowly peeked through her arms. A lantern clicked on, illuminating his face. She glanced from Jack to Trevor, who lay on the ground, eyes wide, terrified.

"Why did you attack Trevor?" she asked Jack.

"Who's Trevor?"

She knelt beside the young man, who sat up.

"Isn't this the guy—" Jack began.

"No," she interrupted. "Trevor is one of my clients from Portland. Wait, is this really happening?"

"The pain in my back would suggest it is," Jack said.

"Right, sorry." She turned to Trevor. "What are you doing here, buddy?"

"I was worried about you."

"But how did you—"

"Helen and Dirk are responsible."

"Your foster parents?" Zoe said. "They're responsible for Shannon's kidnapping? But—"

"Who's Shannon? No, I came because I heard Dirk say he was going to put an end to the counselor's meddling."

* * *

"We should go," Jack said, scanning their surroundings. "We can discuss this when we're safe."

"You think he's still out there?" Zoe said with a tremble in her voice.

"I'd rather not take a chance."

Zoe helped Trevor stand.

"Hang on." And he grabbed something off the ground.

"What are those?" Zoe asked.

"Night vision goggles," Jack and Trevor said at the same time.

Jack motioned the pair to follow him, then texted his location to Sergeant Peterson.

"Be alert," Jack said to Zoe and the teen, not knowing if the threat was still in the area.

Although Jack was focused on his surroundings, he couldn't avoid hearing the conversation taking place behind him.

"You and your foster parents... It's getting worse?" Zoe asked.

"Yeah."

"Trevor?" she pressed.

"No, he hasn't done that again."

Jack wondered what the teenager meant.

"It's difficult when the people who are supposed to love you don't act loving," Zoe said.

Love. Jack found himself picking up his pace, as if to distance himself from the four-letter word.

"How did you find me? How did you get here?" Zoe asked.

"I tracked your phone."

"Trevor, you're not supposed to use your talents for things like that. It's inappropriate."

"I'm sorry."

"How did you get here?"

"I borrowed Gran's car. I needed to warn you so you'd know to be careful, but then I saw the accident and the guy pull you out of the car and then you nailed him and escaped into the woods. That was rad."

"You should have called the police," Zoe said.

"Then Helen and Dirk would have come for me."

"They don't know you're here?" Zoe asked. "Does your grandmother?"

"No, I didn't want to worry her. I was hoping to come out and warn you, then get back home before everyone figured out I was gone."

"Still, there are better ways to warn someone of trouble."

"You could have called," Jack said.

"Who's this guy?" Trevor asked.

"A friend," Zoe said. "He's good."

"I did call her, but it went to voice mail and I didn't want to leave a message, okay?"

"Trevor, you know how we talk about privacy in regards to what you share with me in session?"

"Yeah?"

"The same goes for me. I deserve my privacy, right?"

"Yeah." The kid sounded disheartened that Zoe was upset with him.

"Jack!" Sergeant Peterson called out.

"Over here!" Jack responded.

"Who's that?" Trevor said.

"Sergeant Peterson."

"Aw, man, not the cops."

"There's more going on here than your paranoia about your foster parents wanting to hurt Zoe," Jack said.

"It's not paranoia, dude."

"It's okay, Trevor," Zoe said. "And thank you for caring so much that you'd drive all this way to find me."

An hour later, back at the sheriff's office, Zoe described the accident and her near kidnapping. Since it was the same guy who broke into the house looking for Shannon last night, authorities surmised this was still about the Shannon Banks case, not a conspiracy Trevor had dreamed up about his foster parents being out to get Zoe.

Detective Perry turned his focus on Jack. "You knew where Miss Pratt was and didn't contact the police?"

"It's fine, he found me. It's all good," Zoe said.

"Ma'am, it's not fine. It's our job to protect you."

"Then where were you when her car was run off the road?" Jack let slip.

Trevor snickered. Zoe shook her head that Jack's reaction was inappropriate. Jack seriously needed to keep his thoughts to himself.

So many things seemed inappropriate lately, beginning with the accusations leveled against him. He wasn't exactly sure what the detective's purpose was. Jack had found and rescued Zoe. Wasn't that everyone's goal?

"Jack," Sergeant Peterson said. "This is a police matter."

Jack was being shamed, in front of Zoe, her teenage client and Detective Perry. "I did what I thought was best for Zoe."

"And I'm okay," Zoe said. "Shouldn't we be focused on getting Trevor home?"

"We left a message for his foster parents," Detective Perry said.

"Great," Trevor muttered.

"Kid, this is serious stuff," Perry said. "You insinuated yourself into a police investigation."

"He was trying to protect me," Zoe defended.

"Do you have any idea what your dad meant, what he had planned in regard to Miss Pratt?" Detective Perry asked Trevor.

"No, but I think he'd do anything to keep her out of court."

Detective Perry glanced at Zoe.

"I'm scheduled to go before a judge in two weeks to discuss custody issues," Zoe said. "Trevor's grandmother is filing for custody."

"There must be pretty serious abuse if you're recommending he be removed from his foster parents' house," Detective Perry said.

Zoe didn't respond. Jack figured it was part of the counselor's code of ethics to keep things confidential.

"Dirk beat me and locked me in the shed for two days." Trevor glanced down, as if he felt somehow responsible for his foster father's behavior. As if he deserved it.

"Sorry," Detective Perry said.

"Why don't you call his grandmother and see if she can come get him?" Zoe suggested.

Detective Perry had Trevor write down his grandmother's number. "I'll be right back."

Perry and Sergeant Peterson left the conference room.

"It'll be okay, Trevor," Zoe said. "I truly appreciate your concern."

"But I shouldn't have come," he said softly.

"You were brave," Jack blurted out.

Zoe and Trevor both looked at him.

"Going against your foster parents' wishes, wanting to rescue someone, even though you knew it could get you into trouble," he continued. He didn't know where the words were coming from.

Jack finally sat at the table with them. He fingered the night vision goggles. "Homemade?"

"Yeah."

"Rad," he said, repeating the kid's word.

Trevor's frown eased a bit.

Jack wasn't sure how, but he was successfully engaging with the young man, who was both bright and caring. An intriguing combination.

"Jack?"

He glanced at Zoe.

"How did you find me?"

"Tracked your phone."

"Hey, that's not fair," Trevor said.

"Trevor," she started. "You're my client. Jack is my friend. There's a difference."

She just referred to Jack as her friend. Did she mean it, or was she trying to illustrate a point for the teenager?

The door opened and Sergeant Peterson poked his head into the room. "We've reached Trevor's grandmother and she's on her way to get him."

"How? I've got her car," Trevor said.

"A friend is driving her."

"Any word from his foster parents?" Zoe asked.

"None."

"Let's hope Gran gets here first," Trevor said.

"Jack, can I have a word?"

Jack stood and went out into the hall with Sergeant Peterson.

"Perry is steaming mad and considering bringing charges against you," Peterson said.

"For what?"

"Interfering with an open investigation."

"Because I wanted to help Zoe?"

"Because you didn't keep us in the loop."

"I was in a hurry."

"Look, I told him you meant well, but you have to keep your distance."

"Someone needs to help Zoe if you can't offer 24/7 protection."

"True, but you can't help her if you're in jail." Peterson hesitated. "I've got an idea. Since we don't know what Miss Pratt's role is in all this—"

"Meaning you think she's involved in drug smuggling?"

"Let me finish. I could tell Perry that by keeping an eye on her, you can get us valuable intel—"

"No."

"Jack—"

"I won't spy for you."

"You can't protect her from lockup either."

"He has no cause to arrest me."

"That won't stop him. Look, I'm on your side. This way everyone wins. You stay out of jail and protect Miss Pratt, she'll be safe, and we get information—" Peterson put his hand up to stop Jack's protest "—if you deem it important to share. Okay? Tell me what you discover. You won't have to deal with Perry. Just think about it?"

Jack didn't need to think about it. He had no intention of betraying Zoe's trust. But still, he appreciated the sergeant's efforts.

"I'll think about it," he said, and went back into the conference room.

It was nearly midnight when Trevor's grandmother arrived to pick him up. Zoe was exhausted both physically and emotionally. Jack offered to drive her to Shannon's place to retrieve her things, and then to the Ashford Inn.

A combination of things had zapped her energy: the constant threat lurking in the shadows; concern about Shannon; and worry about Trevor once he got home. She felt like a robot going through the motions to get her from point A to point B.

So much had happened today and she hadn't had enough time or space to process it all.

"He'll be okay," Jack said.

She glanced at him across the front seat.

"Trevor," Jack clarified.

"Why do you say that?"

"He's a strong kid."

She nodded. "Is there any update on the search for Shannon?"

"They'll head out again after the weather breaks, probably tomorrow afternoon."

"They? What about you?"

"Once I'm convinced you're safe, I will rejoin a search team."

"You shouldn't stay back on my account."

"You need protection."

Crossing her arms over her chest, she felt a slow burn

creep up her cheeks. "I think I've done pretty well on my own."

"I agree."

"Then why are you—"

"I don't like to leave things unfinished. I like to see them through to the end."

"O-kay." So this was about his process. It had nothing to do with how he felt about Zoe.

You've known him twenty-four hours, Zoe, not long enough for him to develop genuine concern for you.

"Plus I don't want to see you hurt again," he added.

On the other hand, that was an awfully intimate confession from a man like Jack.

"Thanks." She glanced out the window. "It's nice to know someone's looking out for me. I'm usually the one looking out for everyone else."

"Like your clients?"

"Yes."

"You can't fix them. You know that, right?"

"I knew that when I pursued this profession." *But it still doesn't stop me from trying.* Ugh. Old habits died hard, didn't they? She didn't like that Jack could read her so well. "You know about not being able to fix people from personal experience, do you?" she asked.

"Not exactly, but I read a lot. How long will it take you to gather your things?"

"Ten minutes should do it."

"It might be too late to check into the inn," Jack said. "Some bed-and-breakfasts have check-in rules so you don't disturb the other guests."

"Makes sense. Where will I find a room at this time of night?"

"I booked you a room at the hotel where I'm staying." He glanced at her before she could protest. "As a backup. Just for tonight."

"You didn't have to do that."

"I know."

Zoe felt she was being rude again, ungrateful that Jack had thought ahead and planned for her, taken care of her. She wasn't used to it. "Thanks."

"You're welcome." He pulled onto Shannon's street and narrowed his eyes as he focused on the house in the distance.

"I'm not usually this ungrateful," Zoe said. "I'm sorry."

"Don't apologize."

"But—"

"Did you leave lights on?"

"I don't remember, although Shannon might have timers because she works late shifts." A light glowed from the main living area.

He parked about a hundred feet away, not in front of the house.

"Stay here," he said. "Lock the doors."

"Wait, you think—"

He slammed the car door on her question.

"So bossy," she muttered.

Romeo whined from the back seat.

"You think so, too, huh?" She reached back and petted his soft fur, keeping her eyes trained to the house in the distance.

She didn't like this, didn't like the adrenaline flooding her body, or the pitch-black surrounding the truck. She could, however, make out Jack's form as he approached the front door.

Then she saw a flash of something else: a person racing from the house.

Wearing a bright orange jacket.

"Shannon?" Zoe flung open the door and got out. "Jack!" she called, but he'd already gone inside. She started toward the house, wanting to tell him what she'd seen. The front door swung open.

"Get back!" Jack shouted.

Registering alarm on his face, she turned and ran, terrified to her core. She sprinted faster than she thought possible across the snow-covered lawn. Romeo barked furiously from inside the truck.

An explosion reverberated behind her and she instinctively hit the ground.

SIX

Ringing echoed in her ears. It took Zoe a few seconds to regain the breath that had been ripped from her lungs.

Take your time. Advice she'd offered her clients many times.

The sound of burning wood crackled behind her.

Had someone blown up Shannon's house? And what about Shannon? Was that her racing away? Did that mean she could be responsible for—

No, Zoe wouldn't go there.

She scrambled to her feet and saw flames consuming the house. She pulled out her phone and called 911. "An explosion," she said, and gave the address.

Then a horrible thought seized her. Where was Jack?

She scanned the surrounding property but didn't see his green jacket against the white snow.

"Jack," she said. Panic took hold despite her calming efforts. She rushed toward the house, trying to find a safe way to see inside and make sure he wasn't there.

And if he was…

"No!" She stopped short of the house as the heat of the flames warmed her cheeks. There was no way to help Jack if he was inside, no way to save him.

Yet he'd saved her many times in the few days they'd known each other.

She paced back and forth in front of the burning house, trying to make sense of it all.

"Get back!" A firm hand gripped her arm.

She looked up into Jack's rich blue eyes.

"What are you doing?" he said. "It's not safe here."

Still holding her arm, he led her away from the blazing flame, the heat making her eyes water.

Or was something else making them water?

They approached his truck and Zoe leaned against the front grille.

Jack examined her. "Are you okay?"

She shrugged, indicating she wasn't sure what she was. His eyes darted from left to right, then up and down, as if his brain was calculating something and trying to come up with the correct answer.

Then he looked straight at her. She felt a warm tear trickle down her cheek. She nodded, as if she knew what he was considering.

He pulled her into a hug.

Yep, that was what she needed. The knot in her gut eased and she sighed, welcoming this nurturing moment. It wouldn't last long; it shouldn't last long because it would obviously make Jack uncomfortable.

Plus, she didn't want him to think her weak.

"Thanks," she said, and pushed away.

"Why were you trying to get into the house? Were you trying to get your things?"

"No, I thought you were inside."

He frowned, probably thinking she didn't stand a chance of helping him even if she'd gained access to the house, so why put herself in that kind of danger?

She couldn't analyze her motivations, not now, not with her emotions in a tangled mess. Instead, she changed the subject.

"I think I saw Shannon." She wasn't sure if she should tell Jack or the authorities, but she knew at the very least she wanted him to know.

"Where?"

"Running away from the house."

Jack shot a puzzled look toward the burning home. "Are you sure it was her?"

"No, but the person was wearing her orange jacket and they were the right height."

"Hair color?"

"Wore a ski cap."

They both gazed at the flames consuming the small structure.

"Why destroy the house?" Zoe asked.

"To destroy evidence."

"Shannon is not a criminal."

"We don't know for sure the person fleeing the scene was Shannon."

The sound of sirens grew louder. It was a blessing that Shannon's house sat on half an acre, not too close to another home.

He studied her face intently.

"I'm okay," she said, sensing he thought she needed another hug. She didn't want to keep making him uncomfortable just because she needed compassion.

"Get in the car with Romeo," he said, motioning her to the back of the truck.

"Oh, okay." She didn't argue. She sensed he was trying to protect her, or make her feel better, or a little of both.

He opened the door and she slid in beside Romeo. The dog automatically nudged her shoulder, and Jack shut the door. Although it was comforting to have the dog as her companion, she also liked having Jack close. She wondered what he was going to do now. Manage questions from neighbors? Answer questions from police who were sure to arrive any minute?

The opposite door opened, and Jack got into the back seat with Zoe and Romeo.

"I've notified authorities that we're waiting to give our statements when they arrive," he said.

"Thank you." A few seconds passed. "I guess I'll have to go shopping tomorrow."

Jack illuminated the car with a phone app and looked at her.

"What?" she said.

"I'm trying to determine if you were joking or being serious."

"Yeah, I guess that was a strange thing to say, especially when you consider we both could have been inside when…" She made an exploding sound with her mouth. "Uh, I'm so tired I'm not making sense."

"Studies have proven that people who are overly tired can have difficulty processing thoughts and suffer from an inability to concentrate. Long-term effects increase the risk of heart disease, high blood pressure, depression and a weakened immune system."

"Wow, I'm glad my sleep deprivation is only temporary, due to stress because my best friend was kidnapped, someone assaulted me, tried to kidnap me, and then set fire to Shannon's house."

He narrowed his eyes.

"Yes, I was being sarcastic," she explained. "Sorry, I think it's a coping mechanism."

"You need to sleep."

"That would be nice."

"You need to feel safe in order to sleep."

"True."

"Which is why I will stay with you tonight."

"Look, I appreciate everything—"

"Police have arrived. Wait here."

Before she could open her mouth to protest, Jack was gone again, managing the situation, her situation. She sighed and petted the dog, unable to gather the strength to chase after Jack and argue his decision to play bodyguard.

She didn't need that kind of help, did she? Had someone torched Shannon's house to destroy evidence of wrongdoing? Or were they hoping Zoe was in the house?

The thought spiked her adrenaline. She didn't want to be inside Jack's truck waiting for the next thing to happen. She was a fighter and continued to fight even when the battle seemed hopeless.

Even when specialists had told her family that her little brother probably wouldn't live to see his tenth birthday.

When her parents failed to pursue any and all options, Zoe had taken over. She did the research, investigated new studies into treatments for Ryan's rare disease. Sure, she had eventually surrendered; if God needed Ryan in heaven, then Zoe would have accepted that outcome.

But He hadn't, because Ryan was alive and well,

married and raising two adopted children with his wife, Adele. Because Zoe hadn't given up on his situation.

She wouldn't give up on Shannon either, no matter what evidence presented itself.

But in this moment, she'd relax and pet the dog. She'd pray for God to fill her heart with love, not fear, and prepare herself for questioning from the detective.

"She's exhausted and needs sleep," Jack said to Detective Perry.

"She needs to come to the station and answer questions about what happened here tonight."

"I'll answer your questions."

"Are you covering for her?"

"There's nothing to cover. Her friend was kidnapped, Zoe was nearly kidnapped herself, and now the house has been destroyed. She's a victim, not a perpetrator."

"Sergeant Peterson said you'd get information from her, correct?"

Jack's answer could land him in jail on obstruction charges where he wouldn't be able to protect Zoe.

"Yes, I said I'd share pertinent information with him, should it come to my attention."

"Is there anything pertinent about tonight?" Perry said, with an edge to his voice.

"I went inside the house and smelled gas. It was strong. I fled the house and it burst into flames."

"And where was Miss Pratt?"

"I told her to wait in the car."

"Why?"

"I wanted to make sure the house was safe before she entered."

"Then what?"

"I saw her walking toward the house and shouted for her to get away. I hit the ground when I heard the explosion."

"Did you see anyone or notice anything?"

He'd seen Zoe racing toward the burning building. He couldn't figure out why.

I thought you were inside.

Zoe's words puzzled him.

"You saw something?" Detective Perry interrupted Jack's analysis of Zoe's actions.

"No, but Zoe said she saw a person run from the house, wearing Shannon's jacket."

"I need to speak with Miss Pratt. Now."

Might as well get this over with. Jack led the detective to his car and opened the door.

Zoe's eyes were closed. She looked peaceful, content. Romeo lay across her lap.

"Miss Pratt?" Detective Perry said.

Jack wished he'd wait until tomorrow. "Zoe?" Jack tried.

She awoke with a start and gasped. Romeo sat up, watching her. "Shannon?" she said, glancing at Detective Perry. "Did you find her?"

"No, ma'am. I'd like to ask you about what happened tonight."

"Tonight," she repeated, obviously still trying to process whatever dream she'd been wrenched out of. "We came to get my things. Jack told me to wait in the car. Then I saw…" she hesitated "…a person who I thought might be Shannon running from the house. I went to tell Jack." She caught Jack's gaze and he had to look away. "He told me to run. I heard an explosion. The house was, is, on fire."

She looked beyond the detective at firefighters working to put out the blaze.

"Why did you think it was Shannon running from the house?" Detective Perry said.

"The person was wearing Shannon's orange pumpkin coat."

"Pumpkin coat?"

"I teased Shannon that the jacket made her look like a pumpkin. It's pretty bright."

"Any other descriptive details?"

"Black knit cap. That's it, sorry."

"I'll put out an alert. Where will you be staying?"

She glanced at Jack. Detective Perry glared at him.

"We're staying at the Blue Cedar Motor Lodge," Jack said.

"We?" Perry said.

"Yes," Jack said. "Are you finished asking us questions?"

"For now."

Jack nodded at Zoe and shut her door. As he went around to his side of the car, Detective Perry shadowed him.

"I don't trust you," Perry said.

"That is your prerogative."

"Listen." Perry stepped in front of him. "I could have held you for obstruction, but I didn't because Peterson said you'd help us out. All you need to do is earn her trust and relay important information to me."

"And if she doesn't have any important information?"

"We'll decide what's important."

"Understood." What Jack understood was that Perry was another version of the bullies he'd dealt with his entire life. Only Jack wasn't about to cave to this one. He was putting Zoe's best interest before that of a detective who, for some reason, seemed to think she was involved in the kidnapping case.

Detective Perry still blocked him, staring him down, trying to intimidate him.

Jack didn't respond, didn't clench his jaw or narrow his eyes. He knew any reaction would fuel the man's aggressive nature.

"Houses don't randomly explode. We have to assume this was intentional."

"I concur."

"Don't try to be a hero," Perry said. "It didn't work before, and it won't work this time."

Although the mention of Jack's failure at being unable to save the young woman last year would have normally twisted his gut into knots, he considered the source of the barb. Detective Perry was trying to manipulate and control him.

Jack stepped around the detective and got into his SUV.

The next morning Jack paced outside the bedroom door in the suite he'd rented for Zoe, having canceled his original reservation. Romeo had spent the night in the bedroom with Zoe, while Jack stretched out on the sofa in the main living area. He got maybe five hours of sleep, which would be enough to sustain him through the day.

He still hadn't received a call from Search and Rescue. A part of him was relieved. He didn't want to leave Zoe until he knew she was safe.

He needed to let Romeo out to do his business, but

didn't want to awaken Zoe. He tapped softly on the bedroom door. Romeo offered a yelp in response. Jack cracked open the door and Romeo skirted out.

Jack cast a quick glance in the room. Zoe was still asleep, buried beneath layers of bedding.

Jack took Romeo outside, across the parking lot to a small patch of grass where he could keep an eye on the door to his suite. His and Zoe's suite. She had made it clear last night of her intention to pay half the rental fee. Jack was starting to understand that Zoe was a woman who relied on herself first and foremost, that she didn't like asking for or accepting help from others.

Jack sensed most people liked having support from others. At least he'd seen that with his SAR friends, how they gave each other rides, shared snacks and supported one another when field-testing their dogs.

Being a loner himself, Jack could relate to Zoe's need for distance, yet it seemed out of character for a woman like her to shun support and friendship. She seemed to enjoy Shannon's friendship, so maybe she needed to deeply trust a person before she would allow herself to rely on them.

Yes, that had to be it. She didn't know Jack well enough to trust him fully, although she seemed to accept his quirks more than most new acquaintances in his life.

Because that was what she was, an acquaintance. Not a friend. Jack didn't have true friends, nor girlfriends. No, his ex-fiancée had been enough for him. The Mari experience had taught him never to open up again, that even if he wanted to be like other men, he couldn't change who he was—a man with missing pieces.

You'll never able to satisfy a healthy woman emotionally, she'd said, then enlightened him about love, explaining that if he cared about her, he wouldn't imprison her to an emotionless marriage.

To Mari, being with Jack felt like being in prison.

He shook his head to snap out of it. Apparently lack of sleep caused the dark memories to surface, reigniting the pain as if it had happened yesterday.

Then again, maybe it was the lack of sleep coupled with something else triggering his analysis. The way he felt about Zoe Pratt. Concerned. Protective. And something he couldn't quite articulate.

No reason to analyze things beyond his understanding. They had a full day ahead of them, and neither of them knew what would come next.

He grabbed dog food from the truck and went back into the suite.

"Hey," Zoe said from the kitchenette.

"Did we wake you?" He shut and double locked the door.

"No, I had a nightmare."

"I'm sorry."

She looked at him and smiled slightly.

"What's wrong?" he said, dumping kibble in a bowl and placing it on the floor.

"I just… Never mind."

"It makes me uncomfortable when I can't interpret facial expressions. I thought you smiled."

"I guess I did." She poured herself a cup of coffee. "Thanks for making coffee."

"So why did you smile?"

She sat down at the kitchen table. "You held space for me. That's unusual for someone like you."

"Someone like me," he repeated, pouring himself coffee. "You mean…?" All the names he'd been called since childhood started spinning in his head: *Brainiac, freak, dork.*

"Brilliant, gifted, astute," she said.

He stepped around the table to read her expression, wanting to assess if she was being ironic or not.

"This is my authentic, honest face," she clarified. Again, with a smile. "Why do you look so bewildered?"

"Brilliant, gifted and astute aren't usually the first words that come to mind when a person is describing me."

"Ah, you mean people usually focus on the socially awkward aspects of your personality."

He sat across the table from her. "That is correct."

She waved her hand in dismissal. "People get offended if you don't respond the way they think you should. I'll admit I was at first, until I got to know you better. Whatever happened to giving someone another chance or turning the other cheek?"

"The book of Matthew," Jack said.

"You're a man of faith?"

"Not exactly, but I've read the Bible front to back."

"Oh," she said.

He thought he heard disappointment in her voice.

"Thanks again for letting me stay here, but I'll move to the inn later today." She paused. "After I get some clothes and a toothbrush and comb and everything else that burned up in the fire. Which still has me mystified."

"I spoke with Sergeant Peterson. Initial reports indicate the fire was intentional."

She shuddered.

"I'm sorry, I shouldn't have told you that," he said.

"No." She reached out and touched his arm. "Tell me

the truth, always. Even if you think it will upset me. Do they have any idea who set off the explosion?"

He hesitated.

"Go on," she prompted.

"If you saw Shannon fleeing the scene—"

"I didn't say it was Shannon."

"But a woman fitting her description was seen leaving the scene. They suspect she set the fire to destroy evidence."

She leaned back, breaking contact with him. "I won't accept that. Ever." She stood and went into the bedroom.

Jack continued to process their conversation about understanding, or rather others' lack of understanding of how his mind worked. He also puzzled over her directive to be completely honest with her. In his experience people didn't always appreciate honesty.

Zoe rejoined him in the kitchen and placed a light blue journal on the table. "They didn't get Shannon's journal. I'm going to use it to figure out what's going on and why she was kidnapped."

"No," Jack said.

"Excuse me?"

"You shouldn't involve yourself in the investigation. Let the police do their jobs and find Shannon."

"The police think she's involved with drugs."

"They will uncover the truth."

"Wait, you agree with them?"

"I didn't say that."

"It sounded like it."

"I have no evidence either way, so I have no opinion."

"Well, she's my friend and she's in trouble, so I *do* have an opinion. She's innocent of any wrongdoing and shouldn't be blamed for her own kidnapping." Zoe's voice raised in pitch.

He wasn't sure what he'd done to cause her to be upset.

"They should be focused on saving Shannon, not tying her to a drug operation," she said.

"That's not what they're trying to do."

"It sure sounds like it to me."

"Because you're being overly emotional."

She stood so quickly her chair tipped over. Romeo barked as he dodged out of the way of the falling chair.

"Oh no, Romeo, I didn't hurt you, did I?" she said, kneeling beside him.

As she stroked the dog's fur, Jack realized he'd crossed the line again. He'd been too blunt even for Zoe Pratt, who claimed to understand and wanted complete honesty.

"What I meant was—" Jack started.

"It's okay. You're right. I'm being overly emotional." She glanced up at Jack. "I still need to help Shan, at least by finding answers to prove she isn't involved. Can't you understand that?"

He wasn't sure he did, but he wanted to try. "Sure, okay."

"I won't do anything dangerous. I'll make some calls, talk to some of her friends and coworkers. Get to know my best friend," she said, a sadness in her voice.

"I'd like to help." Jack found Zoe intriguing and amiable. He didn't want anything bad to happen to her, and not because he feared failing again. This felt different. She was pleasant and respectful of him.

Whether she wanted to admit it or not, she needed his support.

"Don't you need to go up with SAR to search for Shannon?" she said.

"They haven't sent out an alert yet. As long as I'm not on the mountain, I'll be with you."

Zoe and Jack made a trip to a local retail store that sold everything from fresh produce to clothes. Jack had even managed to find a new canister of pepper spray, in case she'd used up her original. She picked up essentials, plus a couple of pairs of jeans and some tops.

Then Zoe spent the rest of the morning going through Shannon's journal and coming up with a list of people to talk to. She didn't let Jack read the journal per se, because even she felt guilty about peeking into her friend's most private thoughts. But making the list was a good start, and made her feel like she wasn't so helpless.

A part of her wondered if Jack was humoring her, if he thought the journal could reveal answers. Sometimes even she couldn't figure out what was going on in that mind of his. Which was okay. Zoe appreciated that she wasn't doing this alone, and she sensed he didn't have a malicious bone in his body. Instinct told her his motivations were honorable.

Jack focused on work, creating a proposal for a prospective client, and developing code for another. The most Zoe understood about computers was how to turn one on and use her word programs to create assessments, plus how to check email, although she mostly did that on her phone. She received an email from Trevor stating he was staying with his grandmother for a while. Zoe sighed with relief and shared the news with Jack.

A while later, a forensic artist stopped by to work with Zoe on her descriptions of the kidnapper and home intruder. After the artist left, Jack made them both tea and continued to work on his laptop.

"I'm sorry, I forgot you have a life outside of all this," Zoe said.

"Why are you sorry?" He turned to her and leaned against the counter.

She was momentarily distracted by his good looks. Boy, did she need a full night's sleep. "I'm sorry because I'm taking you away from your work."

"It will still be there later. Tomorrow. Next week."

"Do you like your work?"

"I like the challenge, yes. Plus, I like helping clients keep important information secure."

"You're quite a giving kind of guy."

He shot her that cute frown that indicated he didn't know how she'd come to that conclusion.

"Well, you help protect your clients, you help find missing hikers. How did you get involved in Search and Rescue?"

"Romeo needed a job." He glanced at the dog. "Turns out I like the physical challenge, as well."

"When you sell your company and travel, won't you miss Search and Rescue?"

He shrugged. "I'm ready to start today's investigation. Where to first?"

She found it interesting that he wouldn't answer her question. "I thought we'd start with the community center. Shannon volunteered there with the teen program."

"Very good."

Jack left Romeo at the motel and swung by a burger place for lunch. The community center didn't open until 1:00 p.m. so they had time. Sharing a quiet lunch, Zoe realized she was too tired to make mindless conversation, and Jack probably appreciated the stillness.

They occasionally made eye contact, but it wasn't awkward. The silence seemed to satisfy them both. It gave her time to think about what she'd ask employees at the community center. It also gave her time to reflect.

As long as I'm not on the mountain, I'll be with you.

She considered Jack's words from last night. His promise both calmed and worried her. She liked the idea of having personal protection, but she also suspected he was one of the best search-and-rescue volunteers available. He should be out there looking for Shannon, not babysitting Zoe.

"Still no text from SAR," he said. "The weather must be dangerous up there."

The timing of his comment was incredible.

"Well, let's see how much we can get done together before you're called out again," she said. "I should probably contact someone about having my car fixed."

"I believe the sheriff's office took it to process for fingerprints."

She nodded. "Don't suppose you know where I can rent a car?"

"Move that off the list."

"The list?"

"The list of things you need to do. You have me to drive you around, so move that off your list for now."

"Yes, but you won't be around for long."

"You worry a lot."

"Can you blame me?" Zoe asked, incredulous.

"I've upset you again."

"No, yes, maybe. It's this feeling of helplessness that's got me tied into knots."

"What can you do right now?"

"Figure out who to talk to at the community center."

"Finish your burger. That's what you can do."

"Jack—"

"Staying present and grounding yourself is a tool that can manage anxiety."

She leaned back in the plastic booth. "That's what I tell my clients. Yet I totally forget to take my own advice."

"We rarely listen to ourselves."

"You should be the counselor," she said.

"I'm too blunt."

"Sometimes that's what's needed."

"But mostly kids need to be listened to. I'm not a good listener."

She started to disagree but held her tongue. It was interesting how Jack saw himself versus how Zoe saw him.

"Do you need more ketchup?" he asked.

"No, I'm good." She finished her burger and sipped her lemonade.

A few minutes later they were in his truck headed for the community center. She noticed how he continually scanned his rearview and side mirrors, as if expecting trouble.

She made a plan in her mind about who she'd talk to and what she'd say.

How has Shannon been acting lately?

Did she seem upset or worried?

She'd start there and see if those questions opened any doors.

They entered the front of the center and checked in with the receptionist. Zoe noted that the building was previously a school that had been freshened up with a coat of paint and colorful posters on the walls.

A few minutes later a woman in her sixties joined them. She was dressed professionally in dark slacks and a burgundy sweater.

"Hello," she greeted. "I'm Wendy Yost, director of the community center."

"Nice to meet you." Zoe shook her hand. "I'm Zoe Pratt and this is Jack Monroe."

Wendy eyed Jack. "Jack Monroe from Search and Rescue?"

"Yes," Jack said.

"Oh, it's very good to meet you. We all appreciate everything you've done."

"You're welcome," he said, his voice flat.

"As I explained on the phone, I'm good friends with Shannon Banks," Zoe said.

"Shannon was such a wonderful young woman," Wendy said.

"She still is," Zoe blurted out.

"We're still searching for her," Jack added. "She has not been found."

"Oh, that *is* good news."

"Anyway, I was hoping you could answer some questions about Shannon?" Zoe said.

"Of course. Let's go to my office."

They headed down the hall and Wendy motioned to various rooms as they passed, explaining what they were used for: an exercise room, a mom and tots room, a club room where everyone from knitters to water color artists gathered.

"We serve residents of Skagit County, from children to retirees. Shannon mostly worked with kids on Tuesdays and Fridays from 6:00 to 9:00 p.m."

"You mean Angie's Youth Club?" Zoe asked.

"Yes, renamed after teenager Angie Adams." Wendy glanced at Jack.

"She died," Jack added.

Zoe sensed the subject disturbed him, so she redirected the conversation. "What types of things did Shannon do for Angie's Youth Club?"

"She created the program by developing activities and field trips to local businesses. She even worked with Sergeant Peterson to coordinate a few ride-alongs."

"I'll bet the kids loved that," Zoe said.

"They did. Shannon also taught kids how to set goals in her life skills workshop, and had a friend assist with a computer workshop."

"I have a right to be here!" a young voice echoed from around the corner.

Wendy picked up her pace, a worried expression creasing her brow.

"I'm sorry but you need to leave," an older, male voice said.

Wendy, Zoe and Jack turned the corner and saw an elderly gentleman trying to escort a teenager out of a classroom. The teenage girl had jet-black hair with streaks of dark red, and wore a torn denim jacket. Her face was flushed pink.

"I want to see Shannon!" the teen shouted.

"Hey, I'm Shannon's friend," Zoe said. "Can I help?"

Wendy motioned for the elderly man to step back.

"I have to talk to Shannon," the girl said.

"Well," Zoe began cautiously, "we don't know where Shannon is right now. We're all worried about her. I'm sure she'd want me to help. You seem very upset."

"She thinks I'm a loser, but I'm not!" the girl shouted.

"I doubt Shannon would think that you're a loser," Zoe tried.

"She kicked me out of Angie's Club. She hates me."

"She asked you to take a break and return when you could control your disrespectful attitude," Wendy offered.

"No, she kicked me out, I'll never be allowed back," the girl said.

"I'm sure we can figure this out," Zoe went on, trying to de-escalate the situation.

"I miss my friends." The teen's voice hitched.

"I would, too. I'm Zoe. What's your name?"

"Jeanie." She eyed Jack. "Who's he? A cop? Are you here to arrest me, cop?"

"He's my friend Jack."

"Your friend." Jeanie clenched her jaw as if she didn't believe Zoe.

"Yes. We sincerely want to help, Jeanie," Zoe promised.

"Then take this." Jeanie extended her arm, a piece of paper clutched between her fingers.

The elderly man took a step toward her.

"No, not you." She nodded at Jack. "The cop."

"I'm not a cop."

"Whatever." She waved the piece of paper.

Something felt off.

"This is proof I belong here," Jeanie said.

Jack took a few steps toward her.

"Jack, wait," Zoe said.

He froze, his back to Zoe, and raised his hands.

"Jack?" Zoe said.

He turned around with a defeated look on his face. Jeanie stepped slightly to her left so Zoe could see her clutching a gun.

SEVEN

Jack took a slow, deep breath. Calculated his options. The possibility of Zoe being shot outweighed any benefit of trying to disarm the teenager. He was stuck, because he hadn't read a signal, hadn't seen the signs that the girl intended violence.

Zoe must have because she told him to wait at the very moment the teen pulled the gun. She'd known something was about to happen.

"I'm going to sit down." Zoe went to a nearby table, her hands also up and visible.

"Get out of here, Zoe." The words escaped his lips before he even realized he'd spoken.

"No, I want her to stay. But they can go." Jeanie nodded at Wendy and the older man. They backed out of the room.

"Put the gun down," Jack tried.

"Shut up, cop."

There was no reasoning with this kid. She'd decided Jack was a police officer, the enemy, and only wanted to do her harm. If he tried to disarm her, the slightest miscalculation could end up in disaster.

"Come on, sit down," Zoe said, motioning to a nearby table.

The girl pressed the gun barrel into Jack's back. "You first."

Jack slowly sat at the table, unable to make eye contact with Zoe. Instead he focused on a poster across the room. It showed a mountain range and the words imprinted across the top read, Faith Can Move Mountains.

Faith. Too bad Jack didn't know how to access faith in a higher power. He could use some divine assistance right about now.

He noticed the girl had yet to sit down at the table, but Zoe and Jack were both seated, which put Jeanie in a position of control.

This was even worse than when Jack had stood as a barrier between the gun and Zoe. There had to be a safe solution. He considered everything from the position of the chairs around him to using the table as cover.

"You seem incredibly frustrated, Jeanie," Zoe said. "How can I help?"

What an odd question, Jack thought.

Jeanie didn't answer. Out of the corner of his eye, Jack saw her step closer to Zoe.

"Talk to me." Zoe touched the table beside her.

No, he didn't want the girl getting too close to Zoe.

As he was about to stand up and block Jeanie's aim toward Zoe, the girl started to back away toward the door. Good. He hoped she'd flee the scene and no one would get hurt.

"Come on, Jeanie. I seriously want to help," Zoe pushed.

"Then find Shannon," Jeanie said.

"We're trying, believe me," Zoe said. "But the

weather is preventing Search and Rescue from going up into the mountains to look for her."

"You have to find her. She's the only one who can get me back into Angie's Club."

"You've got bigger problems than your social life."

"Jack," Zoe admonished.

Shame coursed through him as he shot a glance at Zoe. He'd never seen that look before. He snapped his attention to the Faith poster.

"Jeanie, please excuse my friend," Zoe said.

"What a jerk."

"He doesn't mean to be. Talk to me about the situation with Shannon."

"She cut me off and turned me away. This was the only place where people accepted me. It was bad enough when she stopped giving me the stuff for my dad, but then she said I couldn't come back because I was a danger to other kids. I'm the danger when she's dealing drugs?"

Jack snapped his attention from the poster to Zoe. No visible reaction. Then he saw her eyes blink three times rapidly. Blink, blink, blink. Pause. Blink, blink, blink. He wished he knew what she was thinking.

"I didn't know she was dealing drugs," Zoe said.

"Guess you weren't that great of friends, then," Jeanie said.

Zoe sighed. "Please know, I am sorry for your pain."

"Dad's the one in pain. That's why he needed the drugs. On Fridays I'd leave cash beneath the bear statue out back and she'd put drugs in my backpack. Then one Friday, nothing. We paid her and everything. When I asked her about it, she acted like she didn't know what

I was talking about. We got into this huge argument and she kicked me out of the club."

"You didn't exchange money for drugs in person?" Zoe asked.

"We're not stupid, duh."

"Then how do you know it was Shannon?"

"She left a note with the first bottle of pills. It said she's got something for my dad, but it's not free."

Sirens echoed through the window.

"Oh no, they called police. I'm outta here."

"Jeanie—"

"Forget it." She turned and ran down the hall.

Jack stood to follow her and glanced at Zoe, though he wasn't sure why.

"Go," she said. "Don't get shot."

Jack cautiously followed the teenager. He spotted her at the end of the hall by an exit door. She paused, put the gun in a garbage can and took off outside. Why dump the gun?

Jack went after her, hesitating at the door in case she was waiting for him with another weapon. He wouldn't be caught unawares again.

He cracked the door open and leaned back, out of range. Nothing.

He peered around the corner into the recreation area. Didn't see anyone. Jeanie had essentially disappeared.

Something was incredibly wrong. As Zoe waited for Jack to return, she tried making sense of what the teenager had said.

Shannon was a drug dealer.

Nope, did not make sense. Not even a little bit. Zoe wouldn't accept it.

Wendy poked her head into the room. "Police should arrive any minute."

"Great, thanks. How did you know it was safe to come back here?"

Wendy pointed to a camera in the room. "Some have cameras, some don't. I saw her leave."

Zoe nodded. "Did you hear what she said, too?"

"No, why?"

"She claims Shannon's been dealing drugs."

"I'll never believe that. Jeanie's trouble and Shannon knew it. She wanted her to get help and not be a bad influence on the other kids."

Zoe stood from the table, suddenly needing to feel taller, in control. The truth was, she felt totally out of control, like she'd been sucked into a tornado barreling across the countryside.

Jack returned with a strange look on his face.

"What?" she asked.

"She dumped the gun in the garbage can, then disappeared."

"Okay, good."

"Why is that good?"

"I didn't want to see her hurt during a shoot-out."

"She tried to kill me—you—us," Jack said. His tone sounded nothing short of judgmental.

"Did she?" Zoe said. "I think she was scared, angry and utterly frustrated."

"You've been scared and frustrated and haven't threatened to kill anyone," he said.

"I'll go greet deputies when they arrive." Wendy excused herself, probably wanting to get away from the tension bouncing back and forth between Jack and Zoe.

"You knew, didn't you, that she planned to do us harm?" Jack asked.

"I sensed something, yes. But the more I spoke with her, the more I realized it was about her pain, not her wanting to inflict pain on others."

"I don't understand how you came to that conclusion."

"No, you wouldn't." She glanced at him, realizing she needed to clarify her statement or else he'd take it the wrong way. "I have a master's degree in counseling, plus five years' experience with this age group, remember?"

"I'm sorry about your friend."

"Whoa, signal before you change lanes next time."

"Okay. I'll try."

She would've chuckled at the fact he was playing along with the banter, but she was too distraught about Shannon to find anything funny.

Especially because Jeanie had accused Shan of dealing drugs.

"That's wrong," Jack said.

"What?"

"I said that wrong. I meant, I'm sorry you had to find out that way, about your friend dealing drugs."

"I'm not accepting it yet, so let's drop the subject."

"The sheriff's office will ask us what Jeanie said."

"I know."

"We'll have to tell them the truth."

"Yes, we will. That still doesn't make Shannon a drug dealer."

Jack headed back to the suite where Zoe would pick up what she'd purchased this morning, and then he'd take her to the Ashford Inn.

So much for proving Shannon's innocence, Zoe thought. Her statement to Detective Perry seemed to solidify his suspicion that Shannon was a criminal.

Zoe wished she could speak with Jeanie again, but it seemed that she had run away. Detective Perry sent a deputy to Jeanie's house, but she had not returned.

Detective Perry. Zoe could hardly look at him when she'd repeated what the girl had said: *I'm the danger when she's dealing drugs?*

No, Zoe wouldn't believe it. There had to be another explanation.

"They issued a BOLO for Jeanie, so they'll find her," Jack said.

Again, it amazed Zoe how he sensed what she was thinking about. "Let's hope they're kind to her when they do."

"You'll have to explain that to me some time," he said.

"Explain what?"

"How you can be so forgiving to someone who threatened you and accused your friend of being a drug dealer."

She glanced out the window. "It's called giving someone grace."

"It's foreign to me."

"You're not alone." She remembered the last argument she and Tim had before their breakup. Their challenges weren't solely caused by his need to climb the corporate ladder. No, Tim had lacked the ability or at least the interest to learn to offer grace. The implosion of their relationship taught her it would be easier if she found someone who shared her values, including her faith. It also taught her how blind she could be when she loved someone, blind enough to look past their faults.

Like she had with Shannon?

Was that what was happening with her best friend?

This was different. She knew Shannon, her family, her upbringing. Zoe would not accept that Shannon had changed so much in the past ten years.

Then again, Tim seemed to change in the fourteen months they'd dated, from generous dating partner to self-absorbed jerk, and Zoe hadn't even seen it happen.

"You need to love Jesus to do that, right? To give grace?" Jack said.

His comment snapped her out of her analysis.

"I don't even know Jesus," he said.

"Well, you're more like Him than you think."

"Why do you say that?"

"You volunteer to save people's lives. That's pretty selfless."

His eyebrows furrowed, like before when he was processing something.

"Can I ask you a question?" she said.

He nodded.

"Angie Adams…?"

His grip tightened on the steering wheel.

"I'm sorry," Zoe backtracked. "Never mind."

"She died."

"I know."

"She didn't have to die."

"That's…sad. How did—"

"She made a foolish choice to go into the mountains during a snowstorm with her friends."

Zoe waited, thinking he had more to say.

"Those weren't friends. Friends would have stayed with her after she fell."

"And they didn't?"

"No, they were worried about getting into trouble. Only after they came down off the mountain did they call Emergency, made up a story about Angie going up there alone. By the time we found her…" His voice trailed off as he pulled into the motel parking lot.

"She was gone?"

Jack didn't look at her, just stared straight ahead at their motel room door. "Not quite. But she did eventually die." He pinned her with dark blue eyes. "Because I couldn't save her."

Zoe opened her mouth to correct him, to say it wasn't his fault, that he wasn't a doctor, nor did he make the unwise decision to hike in a snowstorm or choose friends who would abandon him.

But she recognized the look on his face: a look of self-defeat and guilt that couldn't be eased with platitudes from a stranger. And in his eyes, Zoe was still a stranger he'd known only a couple of days, a stranger who had no right to tell him how he should feel.

Zoe didn't have any right to insinuate herself in his feelings, his life.

"You're not talking," Jack said.

"No, I'm holding space."

He looked at her hands.

"It's another term for compassionate listening."

"The purpose of which is…?"

"To support you, to sit with your pain."

"That's pointless." He opened his door.

She grabbed his arm. He froze and looked at her.

"I'm sorry you weren't able to save Angie."

"I need to check on Romeo."

She released him and watched as he walked to the motel room and opened the door. The dog practically jumped into his arms, easing the strained expression pinching at the corners of Jack's eyes. He didn't know how to deal with emotions like guilt, and she didn't want to "shrink" him, an expression used by some of her friends when she offered advice. In this case she had no advice or wisdom to give a man who obviously held himself accountable for a young woman's death.

He was brave indeed to feel such guilt, yet still search for lost or injured hikers. For some, the loss of one life would be enough to walk away.

She grabbed her shoulder bag, got out of his truck and went into their room at the lodge. Romeo greeted her with a perfect sit.

"Good boy," Jack said, then looked at Zoe. "I got a text from SAR. There's a break in the weather and Command wants to send teams up."

"Go, go," she said.

"You'll stay here?"

"I'll call a cab to take me to the inn."

"No, I'll take you."

"I don't want you to waste time."

"It's on the way."

Zoe quickly gathered her shopping bags and they were back in the truck within minutes, headed for the Ashford Inn.

"You didn't tell anyone where you'd be staying, correct?" he said.

"Other than police and you? No."

"Good."

"You still think I'm in danger?"

"You're vulnerable if you're alone. At least at the inn you'll be with other people. The innkeeper seems strict about not giving out information regarding her guests."

"You know her?"

"No, I tried to find out if you'd checked in yesterday and she wouldn't confirm or deny."

"So that's good."

"Yes. You should be safe there. I did a background check on the owners. They are solid people."

"Wow, thanks."

"I can call the sheriff's office and see if Sergeant Peterson can park a patrol car out front or at least check on you tonight. I'm not sure how long I'm going to be gone. It could be hours, or if the weather holds, days."

"No problem. I've really appreciated your support." And she did, but she realized she was growing more dependent on him than she should. This man had a life and, at present, a critical mission.

She needed him to find Shannon.

Two hours later Jack and his team approached the location where a ranger said he'd spotted a woman in an orange ski jacket running through the snow shouting. The ranger wasn't close enough to assist, so he'd called it in. Jack hadn't told Zoe the part about the woman shouting for help because he didn't want to upset her.

If the woman was Shannon, that meant she had escaped her captors, which would explain why the man who'd broken into her home the other night and assaulted Zoe asked where "she" was.

The kidnapper had lost his hostage.

Yet Shannon had been unable to find her way to safety or call for assistance. That puzzled Jack. Perhaps she didn't want to return home, fearing the repercussions of her drug dealing activity?

He'd never forget the look on Zoe's face when Jeanie dropped that bomb. It was like Zoe hadn't understood what the girl was saying, that the prospect of Shannon dealing drugs was completely nonsensical.

A lot of things seemed nonsensical to Jack these past forty-eight hours, the least of which were Zoe's inconsistent reactions.

A young woman threatens her; she forgives her.

Jack confesses his worst failure; she "holds space" for him.

And then there was her question about Jack missing SAR once he sold his company and went traveling.

His plan had always been to conquer one goal and move on to the next. Develop a successful company and sell it. Go traveling and explore places he'd never been. It seemed like a worthwhile plan.

Zoe's comment about missing SAR bothered him. He hadn't considered the human element in his plans. He never had to consider anyone else but himself. So why did her comment set his mind spinning like a hard drive gone bad?

He embraced order and sense, something not often found in relationships. He puzzled over his new acquaintance, Zoe Pratt, especially the fact that he liked being around her. Perhaps a good reason to distance himself. Being fascinated by something he didn't understand didn't mean he had to embrace it.

Overthinking again.

"I think I see tracks up ahead," Sally said.

Command had assembled two teams. Jack had been paired with Sally and her dog, Butch, plus Deputies

Hauf and Ortman, who had hiking and even climbing experience. The second team was approaching from the north end of the red zone, as they'd named it.

Hauf and Ortman scanned their surroundings for anything suspicious, while Sally, Jack and their dogs focused on tracking the missing woman.

Romeo stopped and stuck his nose in the air. At least this area was relatively flat, and Jack wouldn't have to worry about Romeo sliding over the edge of a cliff.

His dog took off, and Butch joined in, the dogs racing up ahead and out of sight.

"Where'd they go?" Deputy Hauf said.

"They'll be back."

Jack picked up his pace, but Romeo didn't return to pull at the toggle at Jack's belt. Neither did Butch. Jack and Sally shared a look, not sure what to make of the unusual behavior.

"What?" Deputy Hauf said.

"Something's not—"

The crack of a gunshot echoed across the canyon.

EIGHT

The deputies and Sally hit the ground.

Jack took off, the only thought in his head that he had get to Romeo. The dog had been a stabilizing force in his life, a good friend. A searing pain slashed through his chest to think Romeo had been hurt by a coward with a gun.

"Get down!" one of the deputies called after him.

Jack's leg muscles burned as he raced through the snow in almost slow motion, fighting the heaviness as it collected on his boots. He reached a sharp turn and didn't even hesitate to forge ahead around the blind corner.

Another shot rang out. Was it close? Far away? There was no way to know due to the vastness of the mountains and their echoes. Jack choose to ignore the threat.

A third shot. This one hit a boulder not twenty feet from Jack's position.

He had to get to—

Romeo sprang from the nearby forest and dove at Jack. Jack caught him and went down, scrambling behind the boulder for cover.

"You okay, buddy?"

The dog whined and released a few yelps. Jack ripped off his gloves with his teeth and ran his hands over the dog's fur. No blood. He breathed a sigh of relief.

Barking echoed in the distance. Butch was still out there, and knowing that Lab's attitude, Butch was probably trying to disarm the shooter. This was one instance when Jack was appreciative of the Bernese blood running through Romeo's veins. Like his name, Romeo was a lover, not a fighter. Butch, on the other hand…

"Hey!" Sally said, coming around the back of the boulder.

The deputies were close behind. "I told you to stay back," Deputy Hauf said to both Jack and Sally.

"Our dogs are like an appendage, so save the lecture," Sally said, then looked at Jack. "Butch?"

"I hear him, but haven't seen him."

"He never knows when to back down, stupid dog," Sally said.

Jack sensed she used the word *stupid* because she was hurting for her dog, worried about his well-being.

"Try the whistle," Jack said.

With a nod, Sally pulled out the specialized whistle that only a dog could hear. She blew, and Romeo immediately started barking.

It took less than ten seconds and Butch came racing through the white snow toward the group. He rushed up to Sally and she hugged him.

"You stinker, stop picking fights." She looked at Jack and nodded her thanks.

"They found something that disturbed them," Jack said.

"Yeah, but we can't get to it," Sally said.

"Base, do you copy, over?" Deputy Hauf said into his radio.

"Go ahead, over."

"This is Deputy Hauf. We're taking fire, over."

"Can you retreat, over?"

"Questionable, over."

"We can assemble a backup team, but it might take a while to get to you, over."

"Roger that," Hauf said.

"We may not have a while," Deputy Ortman muttered, clutching his gun in his hand.

"They're awfully bold to be shooting at police," Hauf said.

"The kidnapper wants to get her back before we find her," Jack said.

"You think the dogs found her?" Ortman said.

"Doubtful, or they would have returned to us and pulled on the toggles," Jack said.

"What do you think?" Deputy Ortman said.

"We wait for backup," Hauf ordered.

Twenty-seven minutes later they got a call from base that they were sending backup, but it would take at least an hour.

The shooter had been quiet in those twenty-seven minutes, which made Jack wonder if he was still present.

"What should we do?" Ortman asked Deputy Hauf.

"Cover me."

"Wait, what—"

"Return fire if he shoots." Hauf got into a position and Ortman knelt beside him.

Hauf ran up the trail, dodging behind trees and snow-drifts to stay out of range.

No shots were fired.

It was a good assumption that the shooter had left the scene. He'd probably fled to avoid getting caught by police. But had he found Shannon Banks?

Hauf went higher, then disappeared out of sight. Deputy Ortman was still aiming his gun at the ridge above.

The buzz of silence was deafening.

Jack pulled out his binoculars and scrutinized the area where Deputy Hauf had disappeared. Had the shooter been quietly waiting for one of them to come looking for him?

Ortman's radio crackled with the sound of Hauf's voice.

"All clear. Get up here."

Jack spotted Deputy Hauf wave from the top of the ridge.

"You stay back," Ortman said to Jack and Sally.

As he climbed up the trail to join his partner, Sally and Jack looked at each other. They shook their heads and followed the deputy. The dogs anticipated the plan and ran ahead of them, straight back to what had intrigued them before. Sally and Jack got to the top of the ridge and found the deputies standing over an odd site: an orange jacket stretched across a stick, almost like a scarecrow.

"What on earth is that?" Sally said.

"Perhaps Shannon's pumpkin coat," Jack offered.

The deputies looked at him.

"Apparently she owns a jacket that color."

"What is this, some kind of game?" Deputy Hauf said.

"Looks like," Ortman said. "But why draw us out here?"

"It's a distraction," Jack said. It was the most logical explanation.

"And shooting at us?" Ortman said.

"To keep us engaged." The reality of what was happening flooded Jack's chest with dread.

"Because they didn't want us to find Shannon?" Sally asked.

"He went to a lot of trouble to bring us out here, why?" Deputy Ortman said.

"To keep us occupied because…" Jack hesitated. "Zoe." He motioned for Romeo and headed back to the trail.

"Where are you going?" Sally asked.

"Back to town. They're after Zoe Pratt."

Jack never should have left her alone.

Zoe spent a few hours at the inn reading Shannon's journal and making notes. She had a pretty good idea about what to do next, who to talk to. She'd continue speaking with work associates, then people from church.

She flopped back on the bed and sighed. *Please, Lord, let them find Shannon.*

As she lay there praying, trying to relax and get out of fight-or-flight mode, something Jeanie said popped into the forefront of her mind: *On Fridays I'd leave cash beneath the bear statue out back and she'd put drugs in my backpack.*

They'd made the exchange anonymously. Anyone could have been selling Jeanie drugs and claiming to be Shannon.

"I still don't believe it." Zoe sat up, determined. She needed to do something besides hide out in this room and pray.

But she didn't have her car, or know anyone who could drive her. Her driver was otherwise indisposed by his real work: finding Shannon.

Glancing at the clock, she realized it was nearly six. Marsha, the innkeeper, said she and her husband would put out light refreshments from four to six. Hopefully they hadn't been cleared away.

Zoe brushed her hair in the private bathroom, put on a fleece in case it was chilly downstairs and went in search of food.

A crackling fire warmed the main living area. Beside the fireplace was a serving table with a pot of coffee, tea and snacks. She approached the table and her mouth watered at the sight of a cheese and fruit plate, scones and butter cookies.

"Hello?" she said, wanting to share her thanks. No one responded. She seemed to be completely alone.

When Zoe checked in, Marsha had said she might go out for supplies, but Zoe had hoped she'd be available for an afternoon chat. Zoe wouldn't mind the distraction of light conversation, otherwise she'd keep worrying about Jack, Shannon and the mission.

She poured tea into a purple-and-pink-floral china cup, put grapes and strawberries on a plate and plucked a scone from the serving tray.

As she took a bite of the scone, the lights went out, plunging her into darkness. She stifled a gasp.

They'd found her.

Instinct drove her to crouch behind a Queen Anne chair for cover, although it wouldn't take a rocket scientist to find her back there. Staying out of sight, she quietly set her plate and cup on the floor. She wished she had something with which to defend herself, but how could she have known going for snacks would put her in danger?

Then again, she should assume she was always in danger until they found Shannon.

The click of a door echoed from the kitchen.

She held her breath. *Don't make a sound.*

She carefully slipped off her shoes. Waited.

Floorboards creaked, announcing someone's presence. If it was one of the innkeepers, or even a guest, they'd speak out, right?

Creak, creak.

The sound moved from the back of the house to the front, toward the stairs.

She could hear soft footsteps climbing the stairs to the second floor. She glanced up at the ceiling.

The intruder was upstairs.

This was her chance.

She grabbed her shoes and tiptoed toward the back of the house, through the kitchen and out the door. She wished she had her jacket, but there was no time for that now. Slipping on her shoes, she eyed the surrounding property, looking for a spot to hide and call 911.

Thankfully the sidewalk out back had been cleared of snow. She rushed toward the garage and darted behind it, then peeked up at the house.

And saw a man in a black jacket pass by the window as he searched her room.

The journal. She'd left it upstairs.

She'd tucked it beneath the pillow, but if the guy tried hard enough, he'd find it.

The same man who'd kidnapped Shannon? But if Shan had escaped and search teams went to find her, why was this creep down below when he should be up in the mountains looking for her?

Because he was after Zoe.

He stepped into view as he passed by the window. Hugging herself against the chill, she squinted to see if it was the same guy who'd kidnapped Shan.

It wasn't.

It was the man who'd broken into Shannon's house that first night.

He peered out the window and she darted out of view. Had he seen her?

She turned and tore off, racing down the partially shoveled sidewalks toward a house with lights on. Surely someone would let her in. Then she considered how she appeared right now, terrified, without a jacket and probably wild-eyed. She needed to calm down before she knocked on a stranger's door asking for help.

Help. She hadn't called 911 yet. Needed to do that—

The sound of a door slamming shot fear down her spine. He'd seen her and was coming after her.

She ran faster, panic ringing in her ears. She got to the corner and turned, scanning the surrounding homes. Spotted one with Christmas lights still up, more than a month after the holiday.

A car engine started behind her. Was he going to run her down?

She glanced over her shoulder. The beam of headlights made her squint. Instinct drove her to veer right, up a sidewalk to the closest front door. But this house was dark. No one was home.

Heading toward the neighbor's yard, she stumbled through the juniper bushes. She'd make it to the house with the Christmas lights. She'd get help there, she'd—

A tall form stepped into her path up ahead. She spun around and ran back the other direction. There were two of them? Since she didn't have her purse, she didn't have the pepper spray.

She should've called 911. Now she was racing through the neighborhood, and no one knew where she was, no one would know what had happened to her.

"Stop." A hand gripped her shoulder.

She started swinging, fully expecting the assailant to grab her wrists or toss her over his shoulder.

"It's Jack."

She froze. Opened her eyes, and looked up into his handsome face, lit by the ambient glow of a streetlight.

"Come on," he said in a soft, gentle tone.

He took her hand, the contact warm and comforting. Jack led her toward an evergreen tree and they climbed beneath the apron for shelter.

From this vantage point, Zoe had a clear view of the street. An SUV cruised by, a piercing spotlight flickering as it pointed at the houses across the street.

"Shhh," Jack whispered, shielding her from view.

She realized his dark green jacket would blend in with the trees, whereas she was wearing a light-colored fleece. She automatically leaned into him and focused on slow and steady breathing. *Inhale on the count of five, exhale on the count of five.*

As seconds stretched by, she realized Jack was holding her firmly against his chest.

Both she and Jack turned their heads away from view so their faces wouldn't be seen by the driver of the SUV.

Maybe twenty or thirty seconds later Jack glanced up and so did she. The car was gone.

"Did you call 911?" he whispered.

She shook her head.

"Call them." He started to get up, but she couldn't let go of his jacket.

"Good idea. Here." He removed her grip, took off his jacket and placed it around her shoulders. "Got your phone?"

She nodded and pulled it out of her back pocket.

"Call 911."

"Okay."

But it wasn't okay. She didn't want him to leave her alone in the tree.

He started to get up and she gripped his sweater sleeve.

"I'll be right back," he said, and gave her hand a squeeze.

She released him, trusting his word. This was Jack Monroe, a man incapable of lying. A man who was honest to a fault. If he said he'd be back, then he would.

"Call." He nodded at the phone in her hand and climbed out from beneath the cover.

It took every ounce of self-control not to wrap his arms around Zoe again and stay hidden with her. The look of fear and vulnerability on her face struck something deep in his chest, something that argued staying with and protecting her was more important than getting the license plate and description of the SUV that was stalking her.

But in order to put an end to the danger constantly threatening her, Jack had to get more information. He would help authorities identify the assailant that had nearly taken Zoe.

Because Jack hadn't been there to protect her.

He rushed down a driveway to the street in time to see taillights disappear around a corner. Gone. Jack had nothing but a vague description of a tan-colored SUV. He turned to go back to Zoe and found himself facing off with a middle-aged man with a beard.

Pointing a rifle at Jack's chest.

Jack raised his hands, a myriad of thoughts racing through his brain.

Stay hidden, Zoe.

What an idiot to expose myself like this.

Is this guy just going to keep me here while his partner pulls around in the SUV?

"Hands behind your head," the bearded guy ordered.

Jack did as he was told, having calculated the kind of damage a rifle like that could do to a human being. Where were the police? Surely Zoe had called them.

Unless she'd been too traumatized to accurately describe their location.

"Now turn around," the guy demanded.

Not good. The only reason to turn around was to make shooting Jack an easier task.

"What's this about?" Jack said, trying to buy time.

"Where is the woman?"

"I don't know." If he charged the guy, Jack was dead. He needed to buy enough time for the sheriff's deputies to arrive.

"Who are you?" Jack asked.

The guy motioned with the rifle. "On your knees, hotshot."

If there *was* a God, Jack hoped—no, he prayed—that

Zoe was still hidden beneath the evergreen and wasn't watching this.

He slowly lowered himself to his knees, calculating an angle at which he could attack without being shot squarely in the chest.

The sound of muted sirens echoed in the distance. Zoe had made the call. Jack just needed a few seconds. Five, four…

"You sure you want to do this?" Jack said, his knees wet from the snow.

Calculations were done. He knew the correct angle that would cause the least amount of damage.

Three, two…

"You talk a lot."

One.

Jack charged.

The gun went off.

Something smashed against Jack's head.

A woman screamed. Zoe?

Jack went facedown in the snow, his last thought that the guy's accomplice had Zoe.

NINE

"The street behind the Ashford Inn, I don't know the name," Zoe said to the 911 operator. She peered through the tree branches, needles scratching her cheek, to see what was going on out front.

Was that…?

"No," she gasped.

"Ma'am, what is it?" the operator asked.

Jack was on his knees, his hands interlaced behind his head. Facing a man with a long rifle.

Zoe was about to scream, when Jack charged the gunman. They stumbled out of view and a gunshot rang out. Zoe shoved branches aside to get a better look.

Jack was down, motionless in the snow. And the shooter was standing over him.

"He's going to kill Jack."

"Ma'am—"

She bolted out of the cover.

Don't be stupid. Don't sacrifice yourself, because then Jack's death won't count for—

His death? No, she wouldn't let that happen.

She was smart. As a kid, she'd outwitted a rare genetic disease. She could certainly figure out a way to save Jack.

"How close are deputies?" she said into the phone.

"Four, maybe five minutes away."

"I'm going to distract him."

"Ma'am, I have to advise you—"

She pocketed the phone and took off through a backyard, still out of view, screaming at the top of her lungs. She hoped to both lure the shooter away from Jack's defenseless body and get some Neighborhood Watch action going. The more people who came out to see what was going on, the less likely the guy would commit murder on someone's front lawn.

She heard a door open at a neighboring house. Good, people were paying attention. As she crossed through another backyard, she came face-to-face with the shooter. "Don't shoot, please don't shoot!" She put her hands together and prayed.

"I'm not going to shoot you," the man said.

Of course not. He wanted to kidnap her.

She kept praying, prayed that the police would arrive, prayed that Jack would be okay, even if she was taken on his watch.

"Ma'am, are you okay?"

Her eyes popped open.

"Am I okay? What an odd question coming from the guy who's trying to kidnap me and beat up an innocent man."

"That man out front? I don't know how you can call him innocent, considering he was chasing you through the neighborhood. That's why I came out here in the first place. And I certainly have no interest in kidnapping you."

"Oh, right," Zoe said. From an innocent bystander's perspective, Jack had been chasing her, even though he'd been trying to protect and defend her. To this bearded guy, it probably looked like Jack was the perpetrator.

"There's been a misunderstanding," she said, walking toward the front where Jack had been assaulted. "The man out front is actually with Search and Rescue. He protected me from an attacker."

The bearded guy shook his head in frustration. "Why didn't he say so?"

"Well, in his defense, he probably assumed you were the bad guy. But you are...?" she prompted.

"Billy Arndt. I live across the street." He pointed to a brick bungalow where a dog was barking insistently from the window. "My dog, Tank, knew something was up. When I checked the window, I saw you running from that guy and figured I'd assist. I called 911."

"So did I. How badly is my friend hurt?"

"He'll probably have a headache for a few hours. He came at me and I had to defend myself. I'm sorry about that."

"I understand."

"He could have told me who he was."

"Did you identify yourself as a concerned neighbor?"

"No." He glanced at Zoe. "Point taken."

When they reached the front of the house, the sound of sirens grew louder. She went to Jack, who lay on the ground, and she knelt in the snow beside him.

"Jack?" She willed his blue eyes to open. She placed her palm against his cheek in the hopes the connection would bring him back to consciousness. "It's okay," she said. "We're safe."

He blinked his eyes open. She offered an encouraging nod. Then he glanced over her shoulder, and his jaw clenched.

"He's not one of them," she said. "He's a neighbor, Billy Arndt. He was trying to help."

Jack glanced back at Zoe, as if trying to reconcile her words with what had happened to him. "He threatened to kill me."

"I was trying to hold you for police," Billy said. "I didn't know you were friends with the young lady. I'm sorry."

She took off Jack's jacket.

"No," Jack said. "You need it."

"I'm not soaked in snow." She started to lay it across him. Jack sat up, gripping his head.

Two squad cars and a dark sedan pulled up to the curb. Billy laid his rifle on the ground. Detective Perry got out of the sedan and approached Zoe and Jack.

"Did the kidnapper assault him?" Perry asked.

"I assaulted him by accident," Billy said. "I thought he was the bad guy."

Two deputies joined them. A few front doors opened, and neighbors peeked out to get a look.

"What happened?" Detective Perry asked Zoe.

"The lights went out at the Ashford Inn and I feared they'd found me, so I took off."

"I saw her running away and followed," Jack said. "I saw another guy, over six feet tall, in pursuit so I strategized a way to assist without revealing my presence."

"At least not to humans," Billy interjected. Perry glanced at him. "My dog alerted me that something was going on outside and I saw the young woman tearing through the neighborhood like a cougar was on her heels. I got my weapon and went to investigate. That's when I ran into this guy." He nodded at Jack.

"They both mistook the other for the guy who was after me," Zoe said.

"Everything okay, officer?" a woman called from her front porch across the street.

"Yes, ma'am, please go back into your house," one of the deputies said.

"Did you get a look at him?" Detective Perry asked Zoe.

"The man in my room was the intruder from the other night."

"He drove a newer model SUV, tan, with some kind of rack on top," Jack offered.

"Plate number?" Perry asked.

"Too far away. It had a spotlight on the side, like you have on squad cars."

Detective Perry glanced at the deputy on his right. "Question the neighbors. Maybe they saw something." He nodded at the other deputy. "Head back to the Ashford Inn and locate the innkeepers. Radio me when it's safe and we'll take her back to get her things."

"After I go to the urgent care with Jack," Zoe said.

"I don't need urgent care," Jack said.

"To check out your head injury?"

"I'm fine." He stood to prove it and winced only slightly. "Where are you going to move her?"

"Not sure yet," Perry said. "But wherever it is, no one can know the location, not even you."

Of course the detective was leaving Jack out of the loop, because Jack had utterly failed. He could have gotten the plate number, or some other detail about the car that would help authorities find the intruder and unravel this mess, but he hadn't. Instead, Jack ended up in the snow, threatened by a well-meaning neighbor.

Maybe if his social acumen had been more sound, he would have asked the right questions to decipher that Billy wasn't the perpetrator. Instead, he'd missed an opportunity to develop a lead in the case.

And Zoe was still in danger.

Jack and Zoe waited in the back of Deputy Perry's sedan for the all clear to return to the inn and gather her things. Then she'd disappear. Jack would never see her again, at least not while this was an open investigation.

"I won't agree to it, by the way," Zoe said.

"Agree to what?"

"Shutting you out. I don't care what police say, you know details of this case better than anyone and I have confidence you're the one person who can keep me safe." She hesitated. "Unless you need to get back to your business. I would totally understand if you—"

"I didn't keep you safe today."

"Uh, yeah, you did."

"I ended up facedown in the snow."

"You hid me from the guy chasing me."

"The friendly neighbor could have been one of them."

"But he wasn't."

"I shouldn't have gone on the search mission."

"Whoa, you forgot to signal again."

"I can't protect you if I'm not here."

"I appreciate that, but you're not the only one with the goal of protecting me. I have a whole police department on my side, remember?"

"I don't like Detective Perry."

"You don't have to like him. As long as he does his job and solves this case. Anyway, I won't agree to their plan of whisking me off to some secret location without you knowing where I am."

"You may not have a choice."

"We always have a choice. That's the beauty of living."

He studied Zoe, an adorable woman who had been threatened more times in the past two days than most people were in an entire lifetime.

"Is it your faith that makes you so strong?" he said.

"Partially. And life experience."

He waited, hoping she'd share more.

"My little brother was very sick growing up. They told us he may not make it, but I wouldn't accept that. I researched the condition, encouraged my parents to ask the right questions, and basically took over running the household. But there was no one to take care of me. Then Shannon's family treated me like one of their own, including taking me to church with them. Life isn't easy, but it's exciting, that's for sure."

"You were so upset when we were under the tree."

"Me and adrenaline, not a good mix. I kind of fall apart, sorry."

"I liked it, I mean, that I could make you feel safe."

"Me, too." She smiled.

Did his heart skip a beat? That's what it felt like.

"That's one reason I need you around," she said. "The fact you make me feel safe."

"There are other reasons?" He could feel his pulse quicken.

"Shannon is not a drug dealer and I need to prove it. You know how the community center has a video feed?"

"Yes."

"Jeanie said she never got the drugs directly from Shannon, but they mysteriously appeared in her backpack. What if we accessed the center's video feed, went back a few weeks and looked for whoever put the drugs in Jeanie's backpack?"

His heart sank. Zoe wanted his tech skills more than anything else. He sighed.

"What, is accessing the video feed against the law or something?"

"I'm sure if we asked nicely, they'll let us take a look."

"But?"

But I was hoping you wanted me around because you liked me, that you were feeling this intense pull between us, too.

"It's a long shot. They may not keep weeks of video," he said, noting her hopeful expression. "But it's worth a try." He glanced out the opposite window, suddenly needing distance and fresh air to recalibrate his mind. "I'm going to check on the status of things."

As he got out of the car, she touched his arm. "What did I say?"

He glanced back at her concerned face.

"I upset you," she said.

Jack managed to hide his immediate reaction, which was to affirm that she had, in fact, hurt his feelings. What good would it do to admit the truth? She wanted his assistance to find her friend, that was all. There was nothing more going on here, at least on her end.

"I'm worried about your safety," he said.

"Are you sure it's not something else? I mean, besides that?"

Detective Perry stepped up to the car to address them both. "It's safe to go back to the inn and get your things. We located the innkeeper, who was asleep in her suite downstairs. We're considering the possibility someone drugged her tea."

"You mean the tea that was out in the living room?" Zoe asked.

"Yes. Why, did you drink it?"

"I didn't have time. A good thing, I guess."

"How did they know where Zoe was staying?" Jack asked. "I called the inn and they wouldn't confirm or deny her presence."

"Don't have an answer on that yet. Deputy Ortman will drive you to the inn, then we'll move you to a secure location."

"With Jack."

"Excuse me?"

"He needs to be a part of this."

"*He* is a search-and-rescue volunteer, not a police officer."

"He is also a friend and I need his support."

The next morning Zoe awoke with a gasp from a fitful night's sleep. She sat up and scanned her surroundings, remembering where she was and why.

Someone had discovered her location at the inn. Police had whisked her away to a motor lodge outside of town and Perry had reserved a suite under a false name to protect her identity.

She was in a bedroom, under the covers, with her clothes on. Alone.

"Jack," she whispered.

She didn't like the fact that her first thought upon

waking was of him. She should be focused on finding answers to Shannon's crisis.

But Jack was on her mind. Had she thanked him appropriately for saving her last night? For pulling her under the tree for cover and holding her until the threat had passed?

She shared her gratitude with the Lord that she'd been able to convince Detective Perry she needed Jack in her life. Hopefully he was in the next room.

She washed her face and brushed her teeth, thanks to supplies she'd picked up yesterday. She opened the door to the main living area, complete with kitchenette. It was empty.

She wandered to the front window and pushed aside the curtain, spotted a squad car out front, plus Jack's SUV. The front door opened and Romeo raced inside.

"Hey, I missed you." Zoe reached down to pet the dog's fur.

"Got us some breakfast," Jack said, carrying a brown take-out bag to the kitchen table.

Deputy Ortman poked his head into the suite. "Everything good?" he asked Zoe.

"Yes, thank you."

He closed the door and Zoe joined Jack at the kitchen table. "Any news?"

"Yes, actually, some good news."

She held her breath. *Shannon.*

"Sorry, not about your friend."

She sighed.

"They found the suspect, the man they think was after you last night. His vehicle fits the description, including the floodlight. They have him in custody, but he's not speaking until his lawyer arrives. They're doing a background check. Detective Perry wants you to come to the station to identify him."

"Oh, okay. I can go right now." She stood.

"Not yet. Detective Perry will notify us when he needs us. In the meantime, we stay here."

She sat back down. "You never told me about the mission yesterday."

Jack pulled out a foam container and placed it in front of her. "Egg sandwiches."

"Thanks. The search-and-rescue call?"

"A park ranger radioed in that he saw a woman in an orange jacket."

"Shannon?" Zoe said, hope filling her chest. Then again, if anything good had come from the search, Jack would have told her already.

"Maybe Shannon," he said. "We don't know for sure who it was."

"An orange jacket, it had to be her. What was she doing? Did she look okay? Was she hurt?"

He didn't answer right away. Instead, he meticulously opened his breakfast sandwich container. She sensed he didn't want to answer.

"You didn't find her…body, did you?"

He snapped his attention to her. "No, why?"

"You're stalling. That means you don't want to tell me something. As long as you didn't find my friend's dead body, I can handle whatever you've got. Come on, what happened?"

"It doesn't matter, we didn't find her."

"What aren't you telling me?"

He glanced at Romeo, who lay next to him on the floor. "Someone shot at us."

"At the dog?"

"Sounded like it. Romeo was way ahead of us and we heard shots. But he's okay, aren't ya, buddy?" His tone seemed lighter than she'd heard before.

Romeo wagged his tail, excited about Jack's attention.

"I think it was a diversion, a way to keep law enforcement occupied while they came for you again."

"Wow."

"I've contacted the community center and they're fine with us looking through video feed. They keep twenty-one days at a time, so there's a chance we'll see the drug exchange."

"It's not Shannon."

"You should eat your sandwich and raise your blood sugar so we can work."

"Okay, Doctor Jack."

She thought a slight smile curved the corner of his lips, but couldn't be sure.

As they ate, Zoe mused how comfortable it was to share a meal with this unusual man. The silence between them was pleasant, not stressful. She didn't feel silently judged like when her ex would take her to a fancy restaurant and then wrinkle his nose when she chose to order French fries instead of rice as her side dish with salmon. It was like Tim was always worried about impressing people around him, whereas Zoe's priority was feeling at ease and comfortable in her environment.

She'd grown up walking on eggshells, never knowing when an argument would be triggered by financial strain or a medical diagnosis. Her parents and Zoe were stressed out because they loved Ryan so much and didn't want to lose him. But even after he recovered, the family didn't seem to heal. The stress had taken its toll, and her parents had never been the same.

Shannon's family had always been there for her.

"The video feed," Zoe said. "Can we go back to the community center and take a look after we stop by the sheriff's office?"

"We don't have to go to the community center. I received permission to access their server, so we can do that now."

Zoe nodded. She was both anxious to prove her friend's innocence and nervous about the possibility she was a drug dealer.

"Unless you want to wait?" Jack offered.

"No, let's do it." Zoe moved her chair to sit beside him, and he opened his laptop. After a few minutes, he had access to the community center's video. They focused on the hours Shan volunteered for Angie's Youth Club.

"Jeanie said the drugs appeared in her backpack on Fridays," Zoe said.

Jack fast-forwarded to the appropriate date. The first Friday they watched showed nothing, at least nothing featuring Shannon Banks.

"Maybe I'm being unrealistic," Zoe said.

"Hang on, let me see if I can find another camera." Jack tapped at the keyboard. A few seconds later another shot appeared, this one focused on the entry to the building. Teens entered and dropped their backpacks in a room on the right side of the hallway. "This could be promising."

Wendy Yost shut the door.

Jack fast-forwarded the video at the perfect speed

so as not to miss anyone entering the room with the backpacks.

They watched.

They waited.

Tension coiled in Zoe's shoulders.

"Wait," Jack said, slowing the video to normal speed. A blonde woman, about Shannon's height and build, hesitated at the door.

Zoe sat straight. "I can't tell if it's her."

"We'll get a better look once she leaves the office."

A few minutes passed. Zoe reminded herself to breathe.

When the woman finally exited, she had flipped her hood over her head and backed out.

"It's like she knows where the camera is," Jack said softly.

"I don't think it's her."

"Why do you say that?"

"Her hoodie."

"What about it?"

"It's black."

"And…?"

"Shannon does not wear black. Ever. Trust me, I've seen her closet. She's a bright pink, lime green, tangerine kind of girl. Can you back it up?"

They watched the video again, Zoe hoping to discern more evidence proving it wasn't Shan.

"Interesting," Jack said.

"What?"

"That patch on her sleeve." He pointed to the screen, froze the image and zoomed in. "It looks like a bald eagle."

"I've never seen her wear animals on her clothes."

Head lowered, the hood blocking her profile, the woman turned and disappeared down the hall.

"Are there any other cameras?" Zoe said.

"The back parking lot. But let's keep an eye on this camera to see if the woman returns and we can get a better look."

They focused on the screen, but the woman did not reappear. Wendy Yost opened the office to let the kids in and when Jeanie got her backpack, she held it close and peeked inside. With a satisfied nod, she shouldered her pack and left.

"Looks like she got the product," Jack said.

"I'm not convinced it was Shannon who delivered it."

"I can see how you wouldn't be."

"What about you? What do you think?"

"I think we should examine more video."

Someone knocked on the door. "It's Detective Perry," a muffled voice said.

Jack put out his hand for Zoe to remain seated and he went to open the door.

Perry stepped inside. "When you're done with breakfast, I'll take you to identify the man we have in custody," he said to Zoe, ignoring Jack.

"I can finish this on the way." Zoe stood and closed the foam box. "Thanks for breakfast, Jack. You'll be here when I get back?"

"I'm coming with."

"You sure? You can stay here and finish your breakfast."

"I'll follow you."

"Okay."

She sensed the detective's displeasure as she accompanied him to his car. She'd offered Jack a pass by giving him permission to stay back. The man had a life, and since she was in police custody, she would be safe. Jack surely had work commitments to deal with, if not a search-and-rescue mission to join. She glanced at the clear sky.

"The weather's cleared up, so they'll be able to search for Shannon again, right?" she asked Detective Perry.

"Unfortunately the weather can be sunny down here, and completely opposite a thousand feet up. SAR Command decides if it's safe to send out teams."

She and Perry got into his dark sedan and pulled away. She noticed Jack's SUV following them in the side view mirror.

"Although we haven't identified her yet, the victim they recovered from the mountain had drugs in her system and on her person," Detective Perry said. "We suspect she got high, went for a hike and fell, sustaining life threatening injuries."

Zoe shook her head. "Tragic. But why did she have Shannon's number?"

He didn't respond, probably expecting Zoe to fill in the blanks. The most obvious answer? The victim had her number because Shan was her drug supplier. Zoe still wouldn't accept that possibility.

"How do you and Jack Monroe know each other?"

She turned to him. "He's the one who rescued me off Mt. Stevens."

"You didn't know him before that?"

"No, why?"

"It seems like… Never mind."

"What?"

"It seems like you're awfully dependent on him considering you barely know the guy."

I know enough, she wanted to say. She realized how ridiculous that would sound, especially to a man like Detective Perry.

"He's been a good friend in the short time we've known each other."

"If you say so."

"Hey, why the attitude?" she challenged.

"I'm trying to solve a case here, while keeping you safe, and figure out what your friend got herself into."

"Nothing criminal."

He sighed. "I don't know who took her, but now someone's after you, and whoever it is knows where you're going to be before you even get there. Only four people knew you were staying at the inn—me, you, Sergeant Peterson and Jack Monroe."

"Let me understand this. First you accuse my best friend of being a drug dealer, and now you're accusing Jack of being involved in the kidnapping?"

"Being suspicious comes with the job."

"What about gut instinct? Isn't that part of the job?"

"You don't wanna know what my instinct says about Jack Monroe."

"Why, because he comes off as rude and arrogant?"

"He *is* rude and arrogant."

She realized Detective Perry was unable to look past his own perception to see another side of things.

"I don't see him that way," she said.

"Well, you should know his arrogance got Angie Adams killed."

"Hold on a second, you're blaming Jack for—"

"He tried to save her using basic first aid skills when he should have called for a chopper to evac her out of there."

"What about the other members of Jack's team? Couldn't any of them call for help?"

"He was the team leader."

"And he jumped into action to save a girl's life."

"You weren't there."

"But you were?" she snapped.

He clenched his jaw.

She'd pushed back too hard but still, she didn't like the man maligning Jack's character for trying to save a girl's life.

"Okay, let's try again," she said, putting on her counselor's hat. "Angie's death is tragic, especially considering her friends abandoned her."

Perry snapped his attention to Zoe.

"Yes, Jack told me. How about you clue me in about what else is going on here."

"I'm a cop. I'm supposed to protect people, especially my own family members," he paused. "She shouldn't have died."

"Agreed. And Jack did everything he could to save her."

"If Monroe had called for a helicopter, they would have gotten her to the hospital that much sooner, and my niece would be alive today."

His niece? Whoa. Zoe let that one digest for a minute. Okay, it was making sense: why he was so angry at Jack, why Perry wanted to protect Zoe, why he didn't trust Jack.

"Detective, I am so sorry," she said.

"Now you know why you can't trust Jack Monroe."

"I understand why *you* feel you can't trust him. That has nothing to do with my situation."

"Be smart, and distance yourself from the guy."

"I appreciate your concern."

"But mind my own business."

"I didn't say that. The more people I have on my team protecting me, the better. Make no mistake, Jack is and will continue to be a member of that team."

They spent the next fifteen minutes in silence, Zoe considering the detective's words and then saying a prayer for his healing and his guilt. She could feel it oozing off him when he confessed that as a cop, he was committed to protecting his family. It had to be horrible to lose his niece the way he had, especially given the circumstances Jack had shared about the girl being abandoned by her friends.

Detective Perry pulled into the police department's parking lot.

"Sometimes it helps to talk about things," Zoe offered. "With a professional."

"What?" Perry turned off the engine.

"Your grief."

"Talking about it isn't going to change anything. Let's go."

He quickly got out of the car and she felt saddened by the shield of pain encasing the detective's heart. He'd never heal from the loss unless he walked straight into the fire of grief and came out the other side.

Jack joined her and Detective Perry, who led them into the police station. As they walked through the main office, Zoe noticed it was empty. Of course, their personnel were on the street patrolling neighborhoods.

"Wait here," Detective Perry said, motioning Zoe and Jack into a tidy office. "I'll bring you back when the lineup is ready."

Zoe sat in a chair opposite the walnut desk, but Jack remained standing, looking out the window.

Zoe's gaze drifted to a few framed photos of what she assumed were the detective's family. She understood his anger at Jack. Perry had to be angry with someone, and it was an act of self-defense to be upset with someone else, rather than look too closely at one's own guilt. It wasn't the detective's fault any more than it was Jack's.

"We talked about Angie in the car," she said.

Jack snapped around to look at her. "Why?"

"It just came up."

"You shouldn't talk about it, especially with him."

"Why not?"

"You just shouldn't." Jack looked back out the window.

"I don't suppose you've talked about it with anyone else either, have you?"

He didn't answer.

"Jack—"

"Don't involve yourself in this, Zoe. It's none of your business."

Again, someone else might consider his response rude. Zoe simply felt his pain.

"I'm sorry," she said.

He turned again and studied her. "Why? It's not your fault."

"Jack, me saying I'm sorry is me holding space for you, like before."

"Why would you do that?"

"What, hold space?"

He nodded.

"Because I can imagine the kind of pain you felt

when you couldn't save Angie, and I want to be here for you so you won't feel so alone."

He shook his head.

"Still not computing, huh?" she said.

"I don't know."

Which was better than no.

Sudden, loud pops made Zoe shriek and she dove under the desk.

TEN

It was an automatic response on Zoe's part, having trained for the possibility of an active shooter event at school. She'd hoped, she'd prayed she'd never have to use her training.

Jack reached down and took her hand. "Get up. We're leaving."

Just like that. Without an edge of fear or concern or anything resembling the panic that hummed in her body.

She mimicked his affect and did as ordered.

As he guided her into the hallway, a door opened behind them and Detective Perry stumbled down the hall. Blood stained his shirt.

Jack froze and positioned Zoe behind him.

"Get her out of here," Perry said.

"You're wounded," Jack said.

"Out!" Perry ordered.

Jack hesitated a second, as if he didn't want to leave the man behind, but then turned and led Zoe away.

Silence rang in her ears. The shooting had stopped. Her panic hadn't.

They approached the exit and Jack put his hand up to signal they should wait.

He listened.

She wondered what he heard that she didn't, and what was going on in that mind of his.

He looked at Zoe and nodded. He guided them to his SUV, and the doors unlocked with a click.

"Get in the back," he said.

She climbed in beside Romeo and wrapped her arms around the dog for comfort.

Jack got behind the wheel and they pulled away. "Call 911."

"Wouldn't they already know?" Zoe asked.

"Please, call 911," he repeated.

Good. Fine. He obviously had his wits about him, whereas Zoe was about to unravel. Again. Considering she thought herself a strong woman, she was certainly falling apart a lot lately. Of course she was—someone had opened fire in a police station.

Zoe made the call and reported shots fired at the sheriff's office.

"At the Mt. Stevens sheriff's office?" the operator repeated. "And with whom and I speaking?"

"Zoe Pratt. I was there for a lineup and someone opened fire and we escaped."

"Who's we?"

"Me and—"

Jack reached back and touched her knee.

She froze.

"No," Jack said.

"Ma'am?" the operator prompted.

She trusted that Jack knew what he was doing. "Please send help. Call other police departments, send whoever you can." Zoe ended the call. "Why didn't you want me to say I'm with you?"

"I don't want them tracking my car, not right away."

"The police?"

"The shooters might have access to the frequency. I want to make sure you're safe, then I need time to think."

"Where are we going?"

"I don't know yet, maybe back to Portland."

"No, Jack, I need to stay in the area."

"That's not sensible."

"And you need to stay in the area to join the next search."

"There are plenty of other volunteers."

"But I have faith in you. Please, let's not run away from this."

"I do not want to see you hurt."

"Back at ya."

He glanced into the rearview mirror.

"We'll protect each other," she said.

We'll protect each other.

Was she kidding? How could Zoe protect Jack?

Then again, she'd talked both the teenager and the neighbor with the rifle out of shooting Jack. She had also neutralized the home intruder with her handy pepper spray.

Who was protecting whom here?

She didn't want to disappear, yet Jack didn't know any other way to avoid harm.

He'd been good at disappearing growing up when he felt threatened by bullies. He'd hide behind cabinets at school, or dive into a bush to camouflage himself, afterward feeling like a supreme loser.

That must be how Zoe felt when he suggested they leave town.

This was different. Her life was at stake.

He shot a quick glance into the rearview. Her eyes were closed, and she'd interlaced her fingers. Was she praying again?

A few seconds later she opened her eyes and caught him looking at her. He refocused on the road.

"Does praying help?" he asked.

"Absolutely, and it gave me an idea."

"What?"

"The Mt. Stevens Resort. Curt, the manager, offered me a room. I'll tell him, under no uncertain terms, not to let anyone know I'm there."

"I'd rather take you to Bellingham or Seattle."

"One night, okay? Depending on what happened at the police station, we'll make our next move tomorrow morning."

Their next move? Jack didn't think they had any moves left to play at this point. Shots fired at a police station meant both a bold villain and a serious breach of security. Was Detective Perry even still alive? Jack didn't like the man, but he didn't wish him harm. "Do you have the resort manager's number?"

"Yes." She dug into her shoulder bag and pulled out a business card. "Shall I call him?"

"Yes, make the arrangements."

She made the call. "Hi, Mr. Underwood. This is Zoe Pratt, Shannon's friend… No, no word about Shannon. I could use a room at the resort after all, if you can still make that happen… Sure, no problem. I'm on hold," she said to Jack. "Oh, hi again. Actually the isolated, private option would be great. Had kind of a crazy day… Can't go into it."

"Tell him to register under my name," Jack said.

"Also, can you put it under the name Jack Monroe? The fewer people who know where I'm staying the better… Yes, a lot of questions. Right. I could use the peace and quiet… Okay, great. Thanks." She ended the call. "Well, that's all set. They've got a duplex available right now if I want to check in early."

"We have to address a few things before we head over there."

"Like what?"

"Your appearance."

"What's wrong with my appearance?"

"You look like you."

"Wait, what? Ooohhh, you want me to look like someone else, not like Zoe Pratt, who's being stalked because her friend was kidnapped."

"That is correct."

Jack was amazed by the way she boiled down the past few days of nonstop threat and danger into one concise sentence.

"Are you thinking hair dye, wig, what? It's not like I can eat my Wheaties and grow five inches."

"You're being funny or sarcastic?"

"A little of both. Again, it's my defense mechanism because I'm nervous."

He glanced in the rearview, but she was playing with Romeo and he couldn't see her eyes. Although her voice and her tone had a lightness to them, her meaning was very clear: she was, in fact, afraid about her current situation. And yet she was determined to stay in the area.

"To be clear, you want to stay in Mt. Stevens because…?"

"To clear Shannon's name."

"You'll need to keep a low profile."

"I understand that."

"You may not like what you find out…" he hesitated "…about your friend."

"Do you know something I don't?"

"No, but it's been my experience that people can surprise you, and not always in a good way."

"I love Shannon. There's nothing she could have done that would tarnish that love. It's unconditional. Like God's love is unconditional."

"For people who believe in Him."

"For everyone, Jack. We are all God's children."

Unconditional love. Interesting.

An hour and seventeen minutes later they had purchased supplies and Jack waited outside a gas station bathroom for Zoe to exit with her updated look.

She'd decided not to permanently dye her hair, because she said she'd tried that once and it turned out lime green. Instead, she'd bought a temporary spray-on color that her high school kids used. She'd also found a pair of glasses at the drugstore, and he'd managed to find the boots he was looking for at the country co-op store with two-inch heels to adjust her height. That and the monochromatic outfit and matching jacket would throw someone off track at first glance.

The bathroom door opened and she stepped out.

Maybe to anyone else she'd look plain and unremarkable, not worthy of a second glance. But to Jack she deserved a second, third and fourth glance. Beneath the all-black ensemble, gray-tinted hair and thick-rimmed glasses stood the enchanting Zoe Pratt. And she was looking at him.

"Well?" she said.

"Looks good." He hit the key fob to open his truck.

"But not good, right? I mean, I look boring, that was the plan?"

"Correct. That was the plan."

"Well, I think we've achieved that goal."

He motioned her into the truck and shut the door. Zoe Pratt could never look boring.

Jack scanned the surrounding area, including the burger restaurant parking lot next door for anything out of the ordinary, anything to indicate they were being followed or had been found. Although he didn't want Zoe telling Dispatch she was with Jack, he knew it was only a matter of time before authorities pieced it together, especially considering they'd been inseparable for three days.

He climbed into the front seat.

"I don't look that bad, do I, Romeo?" she asked his dog.

As Jack was about to clarify he didn't think she looked bad, just the opposite, his phone rang. He recognized Detective Perry's number. He hit the speaker button.

"Detective."

"I assume you still have Zoe?"

"I do."

"That was good work, getting her out of there unharmed."

"Thank you."

"Are you confident you can keep her safe?"

"I am."

"You do that and I'll focus on the case. Let me know where you end up."

"Are you all right?"

"No, I'm not all right. Someone assaulted my deputy and tried to break the perp out."

"Tried?"

"The perp's dead and his coconspirator fled the scene. Be on the lookout for a white minivan. Washington plates."

"Detective Perry, were you shot?" Zoe asked.

"Yeah, not serious. I'm going to text you a picture of the perp to determine if he was the intruder from the other night. Let me know. And check in periodically."

"Yes, sir," Jack said.

"Graham, you can call me Graham."

"Okay, we'll get back to you on the photo."

"Be safe."

"Thanks." Jack ended the call and passed the phone to Zoe.

"That was cool."

"What?"

"He wants you to call him by his first name."

"I don't understand why."

"It means he respects you, probably because you wanted to help him back at the police station."

"But I didn't help him."

"He sensed you wanted to, but getting me out of there was more important."

Jack puzzled over her comment. It was a natural reaction for him to want to assist the detective, especially since he'd been injured, but Jack had been torn. He needed to protect Zoe more.

He was certainly relieved that the detective didn't demand Jack return with Zoe to the sheriff's office. Not that the perp's coconspirator would make a reappearance, but because it would be traumatic for Zoe to have to reenter the building where gunfire had sent her diving under a desk. It had been a smart move on her part.

Jack felt there had been a shift in the communication channels between him and the detective. A good thing. He would rather have Detective Perry as an ally than an enemy. Jack and Zoe had enough enemies at present, including the weather, which was preventing teams from going back up to search for Shannon.

"We got Detective Perry's text," Zoe said, looking at Jack's phone. "It's the guy who broke into Shannon's place and assaulted you."

"Text the detective and let him know."

She did, then passed the phone back to Jack in the front seat. "So, the man who came for me at the inn wasn't the man who kidnapped Shannon, which means that guy still has her? And how many people are involved in this thing?"

"There's no way to tell."

"That was a rhetorical question."

"It didn't require an answer?"

"Nope, and yours wasn't very comforting," she muttered.

"I'm sorry." He needed to keep his mouth shut, wait for a clear signal that she expected an answer. Only, he wasn't sure he knew the right one to give.

She placed her hand on his shoulder. "It's okay. You're trying to be helpful and I'm overly emotional. Not a good combination."

"I didn't mean to make you feel bad."

"I know." She leaned back and petted Romeo.

Jack wished she was still resting her hand on his shoulder. When she touched him, the world seemed to make a little more sense. He wanted to do the same for her.

"Would it help to talk about the case or talk about something else?" he said.

"Definitely talk about solutions, possibilities, ways to bring this to resolution. Huh, I kinda sounded like you. You're rubbing off on me, Jack Monroe. So, I was able to retrieve the journal from the inn last night when I collected my things. Let's start there."

He heard her digging in her shoulder bag, and considered her words: *He* was rubbing off on *her*? He hoped not. Yet he could use some of her intuition and good nature to soften his edges. He heard the sound of pages flipping.

"Oh, right here she wrote about Randy, her boyfriend, that he was acting weird."

"Define weird."

"Knowing Shannon, that could mean he was withdrawn, quiet. She is quite a lively person and enjoys being around people who are upbeat and energetic, as well. I practically fell off the mountain trying to keep up with her on the trail."

"You did fall off the mountain."

"Not because I was clumsy. That jerk shoved me off."

"Right."

"If it hadn't been so slippery, I could've gotten the advantage."

"The advantage?"

"Kicked his kneecaps or done something to throw him off so we could have escaped."

"I'm sure you could have."

"Wait, are you teasing me? I thought you didn't have a sense of humor."

He shrugged. Maybe she was rubbing off on him after all.

"Shan also wrote about a subordinate who was giving her trouble, said he was skeegy."

"That is not a word."

"Shan made it up when we were kids. It means he was creepy, made her feel uncomfortable. His name is Walter Grosch. Maybe we should talk to him while we're at the resort. That would be easy and under the radar since he's already there, right?"

"Maybe easy, but perhaps not a good move if he's involved in this."

"True."

"I can do a check and see what pops up."

"Sounds good. I'd feel better knowing we're doing something and I'm not sitting around wallowing."

"I would feel better, too." Actually he felt better because she felt better. "We'll start with Walter. Then what?"

"It would be nice to talk to her boyfriend, ex-boyfriend, whatever he is. Who knows if or when he'll return. But he's not high on the suspect list since he's not even in town."

"That doesn't necessarily mean he's not involved."

"You make good arguments, you know that?"

"Is that bad?"

"Not at all. It keeps me sharp."

"There's the resort." He nodded. "Three hundred and twenty-five rooms. Tourists ski in the winter and hike in the summer. I'll pull up to the lobby and check in."

He pulled up and parked on the far end of the parking lot. "I'll be right back."

"He's coming right back, Romeo," Zoe said, petting the dog. Jack would return, they'd check her into the duplex, and she'd be safe.

For the time being. What would happen when he was called out on a mission? He couldn't be here 24/7, and he wouldn't have to be if they made progress on figuring out who kidnapped Shannon and why.

She thought about what he'd said, about the possibility she may not like what she found regarding Shannon. Fine, she would brace herself for the worst, but she still didn't believe it.

"'I can do all things through Christ who strengthens me,'" she said softly. And she could. She could stand up to the anonymous threat hounding her, and she could accept whatever truths they'd uncover about Shan.

A sudden tapping on the window made her jump. Kelly stood outside, waving. Zoe opened the door.

"I recognized Jack's car and was hoping you were inside," Kelly said. "You're not going to believe what happened."

"What?"

"Move over." Kelly climbed into the back seat and shut the door. "This." She held out her cell phone for Zoe to read.

Zoe was looking at a text…from Shannon.

"Whoa, I don't believe it."

"I didn't either, but it's her, and she's okay. Read it."

Zoe read the text: Got away from goon. In trouble. Don't tell police.

"Don't tell police?" Zoe looked at Kelly. "Why not?"

Kelly shrugged. "Have no idea. Did she text you?"

Zoe checked her phone. Nothing. "No. What are you going to do?"

"Not tell police, that's for sure."

"Hang on, shouldn't they know so they can send more search teams out? Maybe they can triangulate the location where the text came from or something. Jack would know about that stuff."

"She's my best friend and she asked me not to tell police, so I won't. I'm so glad she's okay."

"I wish we knew where she was and what's going on."

Kelly's phone beeped with another message.

"Is it Shannon?"

"No, my boss. Gotta run." Kelly leaned forward to give Zoe a hug, then left.

Zoe watched as Kelly crossed the parking lot and passed Jack. Kelly nodded her greeting, but didn't stop to chat, so Zoe figured she didn't share the news about Shannon.

Should Zoe? Yes, she should definitely tell Jack, no question. She trusted him implicitly. But how much should she share?

"Everything. He needs to know it all." Even if Zoe wasn't pleased about the *in trouble* part of the text. She needed to practice what she preached, and that meant unconditional love no matter what kind of trouble Shannon had gotten herself into.

She sighed, anxious for him to return, and considered the text. It seemed odd that Shannon referred to the kidnapper as a "goon." That didn't seem like a word Shan would have used. Even more odd that she'd texted Kelly instead of Zoe.

Jack slid into the front seat. "He reserved half a duplex in the northeast corner."

"Kelly got a text from Shannon."

Jack turned and looked at Zoe.

"Shan's text said she escaped the guy, but she's in trouble and not to tell police about the text."

Jack blinked his warm blue eyes, but didn't say anything.

"I'm ready. I can handle it." And she could. She waited for Jack to tell her they needed to call the police. Immediately.

"What do you want to do?"

"You're asking me?"

"Yes."

"Let's get settled. Then I'll call Detective Perry."

"Okay." He put the car in gear. "She could be in trouble because she got all turned around up there and can't find her way back. Did she mention any landmarks?"

"I didn't even think of it that way. No, she didn't mention landmarks. I'll text Kelly and ask her to reach out and see if Shan will respond."

"Why did you assume the mention of trouble was nefarious in meaning?"

"Because she said not to tell police, plus Shan didn't text me, she texted Kelly."

"And…?"

"I mean, I was with her up there when she was taken. I was shoved off a mountainside and you'd think she'd wonder if I was okay, and she'd know how upset I'd be about what I'd witnessed and…" Her voice trailed off. "Wow, I sound like a self-centered jerk."

"It's normal to say things out of character when you're upset."

"In other words, I'm not usually a self-centered jerk?"

"That's rhetorical again?"

"I guess."

"Don't do that."

"What?"

"Be hard on yourself. I don't think many friends would have stuck around like you have, considering the danger you're in."

"Yeah, and I am so done with being a target. I want Shannon back and safe."

They pulled up to a duplex and he turned to her. "Then let's focus on finding answers."

Zoe and Jack spent the afternoon going through Shannon's journal and making up a chart to guide their investigation. He realized he'd never been this comfortable working with a partner. He'd been a one-man team, ever since childhood.

Yet Zoe and Jack bounced ideas off each other, which stimulated new ideas, new avenues to explore.

She had shared the information from Shannon's text with Detective Perry hours ago. Jack had hoped that would move the investigation forward, but it was nearly dinnertime and they hadn't heard back from the detective.

He noticed her constantly checking her phone, probably hoping for a text from Shannon. It seemed like the absence of such a text further wounded Zoe each time she looked at her phone.

Jack wanted to distract her but wasn't sure how.

Her phone vibrated and her eyes lit with hope, then quickly dimmed.

"It's Curt. Walter Grosch has arrived for his shift." Zoe looked at Jack. "We should question him."

"Not here. Ask Curt to suggest an alternate location on the property."

She responded. "Need a place to meet. Not our duplex," she said as she texted. She sat down at the kitchen table. Her anxiety was palpable.

"You could stay here and let me talk to him alone," Jack suggested, although truth be told, he didn't want to leave her.

"No, I need to do this." Her phone pinged with a text. "He's sending Walter to meet us at the storage facility on the north end of the property."

"Okay, let's go." They got their coats on and Romeo thought it was time to work. "Romeo, stay."

The dog lay down, but didn't look happy.

Jack asked her to wait for him to exit first, so he could be sure to scan the surrounding area. No one should know where they were, but he didn't want to take any chances. They shouldn't have found Zoe at the inn either, or at the police station, although that incident seemed to be related to breaking out the suspect, not kidnapping Zoe.

They headed north in his SUV.

"I hope Walter is helpful," Zoe said.

"Aren't you worried that he's skeegy?"

"Very funny."

"I wasn't making a joke."

"Oh, sorry. No, I'm not worried because you're with me."

Jack's chest swelled with pride. As he drove to the storage facility, he wondered if he should have called Detective Perry. Too late now. Besides, Walter didn't have a record or even a speeding ticket for that matter. He was a retired schoolteacher. Harmless.

The facility was a tall, gray building with a metal roof and large barn-type doors. Spotlights illuminated the property. One of the barn doors was open about three feet.

"Curt told him to wait inside for us," Zoe said.

When Jack parked, she reached for the door. "Are you sure you don't want to stay in the car?" Jack said.

"No, absolutely not."

He studied her face, wondering if she genuinely meant no, or if she was putting up a brave front. After all, the guy was *skeegy*.

"That's really no, Jack," she said. "I want to go with you."

He nodded, and they exited the SUV. He motioned for her to stay behind him. Apparently the gunfire from this morning had left its mark on Jack's psyche, as well.

He slowly entered the storage facility. Floor-to-ceiling shelves ran down the center of the building and also bordered the outside walls.

He felt Zoe take his hand. Warmth crept up his arm and he gave her hand a squeeze, letting her know everything was going to be okay, although he didn't know that for certain. He didn't have instincts like other people, couldn't always tell when something was amiss, as evidenced by Jeanie's attack with a gun.

"Walter?" Zoe called out. "Walter Grosch?"

Silence answered them. Then a clicking sound echoed from the other end of the building. Jack put his finger to his lips and led her down an aisle. He wasn't letting her go now, not if his life depended on it.

Then Jack reconsidered his direction. The sound could be designed to lure them into a position of vulnerability.

He turned to head back to the SUV, he wasn't sure why.

"You're not going to get me!" a man shouted.

ELEVEN

Jack shoved Zoe aside and ducked, but the two-by-four connected with Jack's shoulder.

"No!" Zoe shouted.

"Get out of here!" Jack ordered.

The board came down a second time across Jack's back. At least it wasn't his head. Jack scrambled to get away from the attacker.

"I'm not taking the fall for you!" the guy shouted. He sounded crazed, out of his mind.

As Jack braced himself for another blow, he saw Zoe pull something out of her bag.

"Get away from him!" she ordered.

"Aaahhh!" the man cried out.

She'd nailed him with the pepper spray.

Jack got to his feet and stood beside Zoe, who pointed the spray at the guy's face. The man, midsixties with graying hair, stumbled backward. But he still clung to the piece of wood.

"My eyes!" he shouted. "You blinded me!"

"It's pepper spray. It's temporary," Zoe said. "Why did you attack us?"

"He warned me you were coming. I'm not going to

jail for you. You can't prove I'm involved." He waved the board in front of him, unable to see his targets, but determined to keep Zoe and Jack away.

"Calm down," Jack said.

"I don't have the drugs!" He turned to run.

"No, wait!" Zoe said, following him.

"Zoe," Jack grabbed her arm to put distance between them and the crazed man. He disappeared around the corner.

A shriek and a grunt echoed through the facility. Jack and Zoe rushed to the end of the aisle.

Kelly stood over the man's still body on the floor. Blood seeped from a head wound. Kelly dropped her weapon, a metal pipe. "Walter," she said. "What have I done?"

So, this was Walter.

"Kelly, call 911," Zoe ordered.

Zoe went to Walter's side, whipped off her scarf and held it against the wound on his head. It seemed like he tried opening his eyes, but they were swollen from the pepper spray.

"Walter, it's okay," Zoe said. "We're calling the paramedics."

"No police. They'll arrest me."

"Why would they arrest you?" she said.

"My back," he said.

"You hurt your back just now?"

"No, that's why I needed the drugs. Got them from her…so I could work."

Zoe wasn't sure if she wanted to ask the next question. "Shannon sold you drugs?"

Walter nodded and closed his eyes.

"Walter?" Zoe placed her ear to his chest. A strong heartbeat.

"He's still alive." She looked at Jack, who was making the 911 call.

Kelly crumbled to her knees beside Zoe, hugging herself. "I didn't know what else to do. I thought he was going to hurt you and I couldn't let him hurt Shannon's best friend."

"Jack, can you take over here?" Zoe said.

As Jack knelt, she noticed him wince slightly.

"How's your back?" she said.

"Take care of Kelly."

He pressed the scarf against Walter's head wound and Zoe turned to Kelly. "It's okay, Walter's going to be okay."

"I didn't...kill him, did I?"

"No, you didn't kill him."

Kelly glanced at Zoe with fear in her eyes. "Are they going to arrest me?"

"No, you didn't do anything wrong."

Zoe spent the next few minutes consoling Kelly as they waited for police to arrive. The young woman was coming apart, traumatized by the violent action she'd taken to defend Zoe and Jack.

I couldn't let him hurt Shannon's best friend.

Speaking of best friends, Zoe wondered if she really knew Shan at all.

A drug dealer? Walter was the second person to claim as much. Even if they were able to prove it wasn't Shan who put the drugs in Jeanie's backpack at the community center, what explanation could there be about Walter's story?

Zoe's phone rang with a call from Curt, the resort

manager. "I need to take this. Are you okay?" she asked Kelly.

"Yes," Kelly said, still staring at Walter.

Zoe stood and answered. "Hi, Curt."

"I saw an ambulance speeding by the main building. Is everyone okay?"

"Walter attacked us." She glanced at his still body.

Kelly leaned close to him. "I'm sorry, Walter. I'm so sorry."

"Attacked you? Why would he—"

"I think he's on drugs." She'd sensed as much from his crazed behavior and dilated pupils. "I'll call you back after police take our statements."

"Police?"

"This might be tied to their investigation into Shannon's disappearance. I've gotta go."

Jack opened the barn doors wide and waved emergency crews into the storage facility.

Detective Perry stormed up to Jack. "You were supposed to keep her safe."

"He did," Zoe said. "I'm fine. Walter isn't."

"Who assaulted him?"

"I got him with pepper spray, then Kelly hit him with a pipe," Zoe said. "She was defending me and Jack. Walter was acting crazed and violent. Kept saying he didn't want to go to jail."

Two paramedics took Walter's vitals. "Anyone know if he's on anything?" the younger of the two asked.

"I suspect so, but don't know what," Zoe offered.

After a few minutes they shifted Walter onto a stretcher. Kelly didn't move from her position on her knees. It was as if she still thought Walter was on the ground in front of her.

"Come on," Zoe said, encouraging her to stand.

Kelly stood, wearing a dazed look on her face.

"Why were you two out here anyway?" Perry said.

Sergeant Peterson entered the storage facility and joined them.

"Shannon mentioned Walter in her journal," Zoe explained. "We wanted to meet him and ask some questions."

"Why, because you think you can do my job better than I can?" Detective Perry directed his question at Jack.

"It was my idea," Zoe said. "And I think you're doing a fine job, but we were already here, and I thought it wouldn't hurt to get a little more information for you, for the case."

Detective Perry slowly turned his gaze to Zoe. "And what did you find out?"

Her heartbeat pounded into her eardrums as she mustered the courage to admit everything they'd learned. She wouldn't look at Jack because she didn't want the detective to think he had undue influence over her.

"Walter claimed that Shannon was selling him drugs."

"We're losing him!" a paramedic shouted as they hesitated in the doorway.

Zoe put her arm around a whimpering Kelly.

"I didn't hit him that hard," Kelly said, turning into Zoe's shoulder to look away from the scene. Zoe felt Jack's arm slide around her. The three of them waited, listening to the sounds of paramedics trying to keep Walter alive.

"Clear!" a man shouted.

Zoe jerked at the sound of paddles shocking a heart back to life.

Long, grueling minutes stretched by as Zoe tried to block out the sound of the paramedics, trying to revive Walter.

"I didn't hit him that hard," Kelly repeated.

"Shhh," Zoe said, patting her back.

"Come on," Jack said, leading Zoe and Kelly to the other side of the storage facility.

Detective Perry and Sergeant Peterson didn't follow, which was good since their presence upset Kelly. She probably thought they'd arrest her for murder if Walter didn't make it.

But why? Why wouldn't he make it? It was true, Kelly didn't hit him that hard, and the pepper spray wouldn't cause cardiac arrest.

"Got a heartbeat. Let's go!"

Zoe sighed and closed her eyes. *Thank you, God.*

She felt Jack squeeze her shoulder and she looked at him. He offered what she interpreted as a subtle and comforting smile as if to say *it's okay.*

But it wasn't okay. It was looking more and more like Shannon was involved in the drug business.

And she was still missing.

Nothing was okay.

Jack led the women back to the opposite side of the storage facility to finish their interview with Detective Perry.

"Jack, you okay?" Sergeant Peterson said.

It was only then that Jack felt the warm trickle of blood seeping down the side of his head. "I'm fine," he said.

Curt entered the facility, but Detective Perry put out his hand. "This is a crime scene. Please stay out."

Jack agreed. The fewer people in here, the better. More people would confuse the situation, maybe even upset the women further.

He sensed how distraught Zoe was by the tension in her shoulders. The more they dug into her friend's life, the more evidence they uncovered that Shannon was a drug dealer. Jack wished he could give Zoe comfort, but he knew he'd fall short in that department. Wasn't that what Mari had said when she broke off their relationship? That Jack was missing the skills necessary to fulfill a woman in the emotions department?

Now why was he going there, he wondered. Head injury, no doubt.

"Am I going to jail?" Kelly asked the detective.

"I'm not arresting you for trying to protect Jack and Zoe," Detective Perry said. "Jack, you're next." He motioned Jack to follow him, away from the women.

Jack didn't like the idea of being even a few feet away from Zoe, but at least he could still see her. He gave Perry an official statement, pretty much repeating what Zoe had said.

"Is there anything else? Anything Zoe didn't mention?"

"I'm not sure I understand your meaning."

He narrowed his eyes. "You're a smart guy, smarter than most. Maybe you picked up on something she didn't because she was blinded by loyalty to her friend."

Jack thought about that for a moment. "Well, the assault seemed personal."

"Personal how?"

"Walter seemed like he had targeted me specifically,

but I never met the man until today. I can't explain it."
And he couldn't because he wasn't a people or behavior expert.

"What gave you that idea, that it was personal?"

"Something he said, that he was warned about us, that I was coming to get him."

"He knew you were coming? Maybe you need to relocate."

"No, he meant here, at the storage facility. He said, 'I'm not going to jail for you. You can't prove I'm involved.'"

"Involved?"

"Drugs? As Zoe told you, Walter admitted he bought drugs from Shannon."

Detective Perry glanced at Zoe, who was still consoling Kelly. "How's Zoe taking it? The confirmation that her friend is a drug dealer?"

"I don't know."

Detective Perry frowned at Jack. "You need to be up front with me, that was the agreement from the beginning—share information about Zoe to help the investigation."

"I'm not keeping anything from you."

"I wish I could believe that."

"I do not lie to the authorities."

"No, but you could be holding back."

"Could be, but I'm not. I haven't had a chance to speak with Zoe alone to find out how she's processing all this. How much longer will we be detained?"

"Almost done."

"What about the text from Shannon to Kelly?" Jack asked.

"I spoke with Kelly earlier. That was the only one

she received. We don't have the tools to track the phone to an exact location, but they're trying to triangulate a general area."

"I could do it."

Perry eyed him.

"If I can't pinpoint the exact location, then it can't be done."

"Yeah, okay, hotshot."

Jack noted the sarcasm. "It's my business. It's what I'm good at."

"I'll think about it."

"Were you able to trace the car that left the scene of the police department shooting?"

Jack must have said the wrong thing because the detective's countenance seemed to harden even more. "The minivan had been reported stolen by Curt Underwood."

"From the resort?"

"No, he'd parked it at the Village Supermarket, and when he came out, it was gone. We found it three miles outside of town. Working on prints now. In the meantime, why don't you head back to your lodging and keep a low profile? I'll post a deputy in an unmarked car on the property. Don't leave the premises for any reason, you got me?"

"I understand the wisdom of your concern, but I cannot dictate what Zoe does or does not do."

"Well, you'd better learn to dictate, Jack. I don't want to lose her, too, because you failed."

The detective, whom Jack would obviously no longer call by his first name, turned abruptly and walked away. Jack stood there, feeling like...like what? He felt like he'd been kicked in the stomach with a steel-tipped boot. Twice.

These past few days his focus had been to keep Zoe safe, yet the detective was calling Jack a failure for not being able to control her decisions, her actions.

No, the detective was doing much worse: he was blaming Jack, to his face, for Angie Adams's death.

Jack knew some people questioned his actions up on the mountain; he even questioned himself from time to time, when his mind drifted, when he wasn't absorbed in one project or another. But his team said he'd made the right call, done his best to administer emergency aid. They'd said it wasn't his fault that the chopper didn't make it in time because it was on another assignment.

"Did you really just say that to him?"

Jack glanced up. Zoe was blocking Detective Perry.

"Excuse me?" Perry said.

"That snarky remark about Jack losing me, too? He wasn't the sole person responsible for Angie's death, Detective, and to suggest as much is utterly cruel. You need to get right with yourself about what happened to your niece before you start casting blame on others."

Jack went to intervene, but Zoe put out her hand, as if she wouldn't allow him to speak on his own behalf.

With fire in her eyes, she glared at the detective. "This is bullying behavior and it's unacceptable. They say bullies are victims, that they've been bullied themselves. I think you've been beating yourself up over your loss, and now you've aimed that frustration and self-loathing at Jack. It needs to stop because it's only causing more friction and confusion when we're trying to find my friend and apparently shut down a drug ring. Isn't that our goal?"

"It is," Perry said.

"Then deal with your grief and leave us out of your misery."

Silence blanketed the storage facility. Sergeant Peterson glanced at his phone and frowned. Another deputy, who was collecting evidence, looked away.

Zoe held the detective's gaze, not backing down. "Are we done?"

"For now."

She glanced at Jack. "Take me back?"

"Of course," Jack said.

Then she turned to Kelly, who was still staring blindly at the spot where Walter had landed after she'd hit him. Her boss, Curt, was patting her shoulder.

"Kelly, do you want to come with us?" Zoe asked.

"I'm going to drop her at her parents' house," Curt said.

"Good, she shouldn't be alone." Zoe gave Kelly a hug. "Thank you for defending us. It will all be okay."

Back at the duplex Zoe's prayers had changed. Well, not changed completely, but they had been amended. Instead of praying solely for Shannon's safe return, Zoe also started praying for strength to deal with the potential reality of her friend being a drug dealer.

"No, I simply won't believe it," she whispered as she gazed out the window of the suite. She stood behind the curtain so no one outside could see her standing there. Along with sunset came more snow, which meant no search teams would be sent into the mountains.

That's when Zoe realized it didn't matter if Shan had gotten involved in something shady. She was still loved, unconditionally, both by Zoe and God.

"Thank you," Jack said.

Zoe glanced at him, but he didn't look up from his laptop. "For what?"

"What you said to Detective Perry."

"You're welcome, although I'm a bit embarrassed about that."

That made him look at her. "Why?"

"I kind of lost it. You don't think I was too harsh?"

"Sometimes harsh is necessary."

"I know, but I do feel sorry for the man. Yet I can't stand watching someone be abused because the abuser hasn't dealt with his own pain." She went to Jack and glanced over his shoulder. "Any luck finding Shan's phone?"

"Not yet." He tapped away at his keyboard, as if not wanting to give up, although she sensed it was a lost cause. Romeo slept contentedly by Jack's feet.

"I know you're doing your best." She placed her hand on his shoulder.

His fingers stopped.

She snatched her hand away. "Sorry, I shouldn't touch you while you're concentrating."

"No, it's okay," he said. He continued to type in code of some kind. "It makes no sense."

"What?" She went to the kitchenette and turned on the stove to warm water.

"Are you making tea?" Jack said.

"Yes, you want some?"

"Please."

"What makes no sense?"

"My program, designed to track a GPS signal, keeps giving me a bounce back."

"Meaning?"

"It's giving me Kelly's phone location, instead of Shannon's. I'm not sure how they're doing that, rerouting the location to the receiving phone."

"So we're dealing with someone who's tech savvy?"

"Yeah, but more tech savvy than me?" he said.

"Ego much?" She winked.

He half frowned.

"Teasing again," she said. "You sounded so surprised, maybe even horrified that someone could be better at this tech stuff than you. It's kinda cute."

His frown deepened at that comment.

"Don't listen to me," she said. "I'm worn out, hungry, confused, maybe a little sad."

"Tea will help."

She felt herself smile slightly at his comment. Jack thought he could assuage her emotional turmoil with the mention of tea. She appreciated his intention.

"And food," he said. "I'll call the restaurant and place an order." He stood and went to the bureau where he pulled out a leather-bound resort directory that included a restaurant menu. "You want a burger, sandwich, fish dinner...?" He glanced up. "What sounds good?"

For half a second, she wasn't a grieving friend, worried about Shannon, sucked into a maelstrom of danger. Zoe was a woman being asked to make a decision about dinner.

Jack studied her, then looked back at the menu. "Or if that doesn't sound good, they serve breakfast all day, even at night."

"Thank you."

He glanced up again. "For what?"

"For making me feel a little normal during all this craziness."

"I'm not sure how I did that."

"Just say 'you're welcome.'"

"You're welcome?" And he shared a curious smile.

"I'll take a turkey sandwich on wheat."

"Okay. I'll place our orders."

"And fries."

"With ranch dressing?"

"Ooohhh, I never through of dipping fries in ranch. Sure, I'll try that."

As Jack called in their order, Zoe found tea bags in a cupboard. The food would do her good. No doubt the drop in her blood sugar was contributing to her morose mood.

Her phone pinged with a text. Kelly was texting for an update. Zoe felt so frustrated. How could she respond that Shannon was a criminal?

She wouldn't, because Zoe wasn't 100 percent convinced of that fact herself. All indications pointed to Shannon's involvement, but Zoe clung to hope that it was a mix-up.

"Okay, thanks." Jack hung up the phone and went to join her in the kitchenette. "It will be here in thirty to forty minutes."

"I'm not satisfied," Zoe said.

"Well, it is the dinner hour so they're pretty busy."

"I'm talking about Shannon. I mean, a nice, Christian woman doesn't suddenly become a drug dealer." She started pacing, thoughts spinning in her brain. Was she onto something here? Or was this the last vestiges of denial?

The kettle whistled, and she went to pour hot water over the tea bags. "What's her motivation? She didn't live extravagantly, and was driving a fifteen-year-old Honda."

"Those cars do last a long time."

"She dressed humbly, didn't take vacations, didn't own expensive jewelry, and the house she rented was modest at best. Where is all the money that she would have made from dealing drugs?"

"I don't have an answer."

"Because there's no evidence of her receiving large sums of money. Someone doesn't become a drug dealer, make a ton of money and not spend it. Can you break into her financial records?"

"Break in?"

"Sorry, access her financial information? Credit cards, stuff like that?"

"I shouldn't."

"Please?"

He glanced down. She touched his arm and he looked at her, his blue eyes brighter than normal.

"I need to help my friend, Jack."

With a nod, he went back to his laptop.

Half an hour later, Jack said he was close to accessing Shan's accounts.

Zoe paced, feeling both hopeful and guilty about what they were doing. If it would somehow support Shan's innocence, it was worth the risk.

"Okay, I'm in," he said.

She rushed across the room and stood beside him.

They scanned her deposits, withdrawals and online payments, checking everything they could think of to find evidence of her friend's extreme spending behavior.

"What do you think?" she said.

"I don't see anything unusual here. We've gone back six months, yet there are no cash deposits."

"That's good, right?"

"Hmm."

"Hmm, what?"

He tapped away, opening screens and closing others. She couldn't make sense of what he was doing.

"It looks like someone else may have accessed her accounts," he said.

There was a knock at the door.

"Dinner," Jack said, still focused on his laptop screen.

"I'll get it." Zoe started for the door.

"No, Zoe—"

The door flew open and three men burst into the suite.

TWELVE

Romeo barked protectively but kept his distance.

"Hands where I can see them, and control that dog," one of the intruders ordered. He was a tall, skinny man wearing dark pants and jacket.

"Romeo, right here," Jack said.

The dog sat beside him, and Jack raised his hands.

"Identify yourselves," Jack said, not that he had any leverage in this situation.

"DEA. Hands behind your head. Now."

Jack did as they ordered, glancing at Zoe who seemed more angry than upset. Good. He hated seeing her upset. "What's this about?" he asked.

One of the other agents, short and stocky, wearing a leather jacket and permanent scowl, zip-tied Jack's wrists and led him to the sofa. Romeo followed and jumped up beside Jack. A low growl rumbled from his throat.

"Romeo, quiet," Jack said.

The stocky agent motioned for Zoe to sit beside Jack. She did and crossed her arms over her chest, denying them the access to restrain her. They most likely didn't force the issue because they didn't consider her a physical threat.

Zoe and Jack were so close that their thighs touched. He hoped the contact would calm her because he didn't want her spouting off at the agents and escalating the situation.

"I'm Agent Trotter," the tall, skinny agent said. "Is that your laptop?"

"Yes, sir," Jack answered.

Agent Trotter motioned for the third agent, the youngest of the group with red hair, to sit at the table. He opened the laptop and tapped on the keyboard. He hesitated and looked at Jack. "Password?"

"Romeo1215_&#." A password he'd quickly change once he got his laptop back.

Agent Trotter motioned for the stocky agent to stand watch by the door, then swung a chair backward, straddled it and studied Zoe and Jack.

"How are you involved with Shannon Banks?" Agent Trotter said.

"Involved?" Jack said.

"In her drug operation."

"She's not involved with drugs," Zoe snapped.

The room fell quiet. Agent Trotter eyed her. "And you are?"

"I'm Shannon's best friend, Zoe. I was with her when she was taken."

Trotter turned to Jack, expectant.

"I'm Jack Monroe with Search and Rescue. I found Zoe last Friday after she fell off the mountain—"

"Was pushed," Zoe interrupted.

"—and was injured," Jack finished.

"You were the one who accessed Miss Banks's personal accounts?"

"I am," Jack said.

"Then you're under arrest."

"He was doing me a favor," Zoe said. "I'm trying to prove Shannon's not a drug-dealing criminal."

"How about it, Red?" Agent Trotter said to the agent working intently on Jack's laptop.

"They didn't move anything around," the agent said. "Just went exploring."

"Ask Detective Perry," Zoe said. "He can tell you we're not involved. I'm trying to help my friend and in the meantime, I've become a target."

"Maybe because you keep doing things like breaking into bank accounts."

"If she's a drug dealer, where's the money?" Zoe said.

"Zoe," Jack said, trying to temper her.

"We couldn't find it," Zoe said. "Could you? No, because she's not involved. You've got the wrong suspect, and she's probably up in the mountains dying a slow, miserable death while we're all down here more focused on a phantom drug ring than saving her life."

Agent Trotter tapped his fingers on the chair. Jack feared they were both going to be arrested.

No, he couldn't let that happen. "It was my idea to access Shannon Banks's accounts. Arrest me." He turned to Zoe. "Take care of Romeo."

"Jack, no," she said in a soft voice, as if she were in pain.

He was trying to protect her, yet only managed to upset her further.

"Where's your cell phone?" Agent Trotter asked Zoe.

"In my bag," she said. "Side pocket."

The stocky agent retrieved her cell phone.

"Is Detective Perry's number in here?" Trotter said.

"Yes," Zoe said.

Trotter motioned for the stocky agent to give her the phone. "Call him. Tell him to come over."

As she made the call, Jack puzzled over why the agent didn't call Detective Perry himself.

It didn't completely surprise Jack that their paths had crossed with the Drug Enforcement Agency. Since this mystery seemed rooted in a drug distribution business, it was only a matter of time before they appeared. Jack sensed they were not working hand in hand with local law enforcement or else the DEA agents would have known whose room they were breaking into tonight.

"Someone's coming," the stocky agent said, peering through the curtains.

"Room service," Jack offered. "Zoe hasn't eaten since eleven this morning." He didn't care if they kept him restrained, but he wanted her to be comfortable.

"What do you want me to do?" asked the agent by the window.

Trotter nodded at Zoe. "Don't let him in. Take the food and close the door."

She stood and went to retrieve her purse.

"What are you doing?" Trotter asked.

"I need to tip him." She grabbed cash out of her wallet, went to the door and waited, seemingly irritated. The stocky agent flanked the other side of the door.

Jack presumed that the DEA didn't want it to be common knowledge they were close to nailing the drug ring, for fear the players might disappear. By tracking

Jack's activity today, they probably thought they had found one of the key suspects in this scheme.

The resort employee knocked, and Zoe opened the door. "Hi, thanks."

"I can set it up for you in the—"

"No, I'm good. I'll take the tray."

A moment later she kicked the door shut and carried a tray over to the kitchen table.

"Can I sit at the table or is being hungry against the law?" she said.

Jack wondered why she thought sarcasm was a good idea in this situation. Then again, she relied on sarcasm when she was anxious.

"You've got quite an attitude for someone who's about to be arrested," Trotter said.

"For what? For loving my friend so much I want to prove her innocence?"

She and the agent stared at each other, and Zoe didn't back down. Jack knew she was strong but didn't know how strong she was until this very moment. She had pushed through the fear of the past few days and had come out the other side a tenacious woman.

"Go ahead and eat," Trotter said.

"Jack needs to eat, too."

"Don't push it."

"Look, I'm a social worker for teens, and Jack's an IT entrepreneur. We're out of our league here, I know that, but we're trying to do the right thing for an innocent woman who was taken against her will."

"Or she disappeared of her free will."

"You weren't there," Zoe said, her voice low. "You didn't see how the man brutalized her…and me."

"You could be covering for her."

"Do a background check on me, go on. And do one on Jack. He's got nothing to hide either."

An interesting assumption on her part, although she was right, Jack had a squeaky-clean background.

Trotter studied her, still assessing.

"We're trying to help you," she said.

"By getting involved in police business?"

"By proving she's not your suspect so you can focus on finding the real criminal."

Agent Trotter narrowed his eyes.

"Are you going to let Jack eat dinner with me?" Zoe asked.

Trotter motioned with his hand.

Jack stood, waiting for someone to remove the cuffs.

"Zip ties stay on," Trotter said.

His ego swelled at the thought that these three men thought Jack could physically overtake them.

"Come on," Zoe said. "I'll feed you."

He hesitated, not wanting to be embarrassed by being spoon-fed.

"Jack, the food will get cold."

She motioned the tech agent to move aside and she sat down, lifting the cover off one of the plates. She pulled out a chair and Jack joined her at the table.

"Haven't you been working with the local police on this case?" she asked Agent Trotter.

"No."

"Why not?" She dipped a French fry in ranch dressing.

"Because they suspect someone in the sheriff's office is involved," Jack guessed.

Trotter sat across the table from him. "Why would you say that?"

"It's the most logical assumption as to why you are keeping your investigation hidden from local authorities."

Zoe held a ranch-dipped fry to Jack's mouth and he ate it, surprised that he wasn't embarrassed at being fed like a child.

"My turn for questions," Trotter said.

"Don't you have to read us our rights first?" Jack said.

"Only if he's going to arrest us, which he hasn't," Zoe said.

"Yet," Trotter said.

Zoe shook her head, then dipped another fry in ranch.

"What's with the shaking of the head?" Trotter said.

"I'm so over all this bullying. Bullying and threats. Which is what I thought I was taking a break from back at work."

"I'm not bullying," Trotter said.

"You were threatening. Same thing. Whatever, ask your questions." She bit into her fry and her expression softened as she looked at Jack. "This is good."

Jack took pride in the fact she liked his food suggestion.

"What makes you think Shannon Banks is innocent?" Agent Trotter said.

"I've known her since we were kids. She's a good person. There's no evidence of a money trail or large purchases, the kinds of things someone who was making illegal money would buy. I'm assuming you already knew that, so what makes her your number one suspect?"

When Trotter didn't answer, Zoe continued, "I've

got a clean record. Jack's got a clean record. We're obviously not involved, but like I said before, we'd like to scratch Shannon off your suspect list."

"I doubt that will happen."

"Why's that?"

"Because one of our agents was with her when she smuggled drugs across the border from Canada."

Zoe's hand, holding a French fry, froze and her face drained of color. She slowly put the fry back on the pile. She looked like she'd lost her best friend which, in a sense, she had.

Jack fisted his hands, wanting the zip ties gone. He wanted to wrap his arms around her and hold her close.

"I don't believe you," she said.

"Excuse me?" Agent Trotter said, indignant.

"Give her a minute," Jack said. "She's processing."

"You're saying you're her best friend, yet you had no idea?" Trotter said.

Zoe shook her head. Jack wondered if she was unable to speak because she was angry or devastated, or a little of both.

"Did the agent see the drugs?" Zoe said.

"Eventually, when they returned to the resort."

"Oh." Zoe sat back and crossed her arms over her chest. "Who was this agent? You trust him?"

"Yes. Randy Green is one of our top guys."

"Randy? Her boyfriend?"

"That was his undercover assignment—to get close to Shannon Banks. And now he's gone, too."

"Gone?"

"Missing. He hasn't checked in for days. We suspect her people took him out."

"You're making it sound like Shannon was a drug lord with a team of hired killers on her payroll."

"This new drug is an incredibly profitable hybrid with intense effects. It's offered in pill form, liquid, or even gummy candy for kids."

"Shannon would never—"

"Maybe she had good intentions, who knows. A little can manage pain, but users can't stop with a little. After a few months they start to need more and more until they can't responsibly dose themselves, leading to irrational behavior and hallucinations. A teenager in Tacoma took too much and jumped off a bridge. We're trying to prevent that from happening again."

"That's tragic, but Shan is not involved. Wait, back up. She loved Randy, and he was…using her?"

"We're trying to keep drugs out of the hands of children."

"Shannon worked as a volunteer *with* children. You think she wants to get them hooked? That makes no sense."

"The only thing that *does* make sense is that she's involved in a drug ring, she knew we were onto her and she faked her own kidnapping and disappearance."

"You weren't there. You didn't see what happened. The kidnapper tried to kill me. Shannon would never let that happen."

"Or, she lost control of the situation."

"Enough. I don't want to hear any more. My friend is still missing."

"So is my agent, and if anything happens to him, we'll be adding kidnapping and murder to the charges against Shannon Banks."

"Someone's here," the third agent said from the window. "Looks like a cop."

"Detective Perry," Trotter said.

The situation was going from bad to worse, Jack thought. He sensed Zoe's emotions were strung tighter than a tennis racket. Adding Perry and his chip-on-the-shoulder attitude to the equation would only exacerbate things.

"Are you going to arrest me?" Jack said.

Zoe glared at Agent Trotter, her jaw clenched.

"Let's see what Detective Perry says."

Zoe shared a look with Jack. Perry was not their champion, which meant Jack might be spending the night in jail.

Perry knocked on the door.

Romeo sat up, ready to charge.

"Romeo, stop," Jack said.

The dog flopped down with a harrumph.

The agent opened the door to Detective Perry.

"Who are you?" Perry said, then stepped into the room. He frowned at the sight of Zoe and Jack sitting at the table with Agent Trotter, Jack's hands secured behind him. "What's going on here?"

Agent Trotter stood and flashed his badge. "Agent Trotter, DEA. Have a seat."

"I'll stand, thanks. Let me guess, you've been investigating Shannon Banks for months, but didn't bother to inform my department."

"That is correct."

"Why?"

"We suspect someone in local law enforcement might be involved."

"Great, that's just great. You keep me in the dark,

then accuse someone on my team of being dirty. What about them? Why are you harassing Jack and Zoe?"

"Our tech agent caught someone accessing Shannon Banks's accounts and we followed the IP address here. Jack Monroe accessed the files at the request of Zoe Pratt, perhaps to move money around."

"We were trying to prove her innocence," Zoe said.

Jack wished she'd remain quiet. They didn't have many friends in the room, make that zero friends, and baiting the agent would only force him to take action against her.

And Jack. He didn't want to spend a night in jail, and be separated from Zoe. He struggled to come up with the right words to reduce the tension, convince the DEA of their honorable intentions.

"How well do you know them, Detective?" Trotter said.

"I met Zoe Pratt for the first time a few days ago after they brought her down off the mountain. Jack Monroe…" he hesitated "…I've known him for a few years."

"He illegally accessed bank accounts," Trotter said.

"That's unfortunate."

"Out of professional courtesy, I'll let this one pass once we clear him through a background check."

Jack sighed. There was no way Perry would burn a favor with the federal agency to free Jack. Instead of making eye contact with the detective, Jack studied Zoe. Her eyes flared as she looked at Detective Perry.

Out of the corner of his eye, Jack saw the detective glance in his direction.

"Let him go," Perry said. "He's one of the best search-and-rescue volunteers in Washington State."

Jack turned his attention to Perry, but he was focused on his phone. "They're sending teams into the mountains first thing tomorrow morning. They've narrowed down a new area of bunkers where someone could survive for days, maybe even weeks. Shannon Banks could have ended up there." He looked at the DEA agent. "You'll increase your odds of finding her if Jack is on the search team."

The next morning, as Zoe watched Jack pack up for the mission, she thanked God for his freedom. *Miracles do happen*, she thought as she remembered Detective Perry standing up for Jack, saying he was one of the best and discouraging the DEA agents from arresting him.

The federal agents ran background checks on both Zoe and Jack, and accepted the fact they were innocents caught up in a complex whirlwind of criminality.

Although the DEA agents had left last night, Zoe assumed they'd assigned an agent to the premises to keep an eye on things in case Shannon reached out to Zoe. She closed her eyes, fighting the image of Shannon being arrested at gunpoint if she were to randomly show up on her own.

Authorities seemed to be completely ignoring the fact Shan might be severely injured in the mountains. Zoe glanced out the window at the surrounding wilderness and sighed. She didn't care if Shan had gotten involved in something illegal, yet she also couldn't bring herself to believe it to be true.

All that mattered was getting her friend back alive.

Jack touched her shoulder. She looked up and was able to read his expression. He was offering comfort and strength.

"Keep praying for us," he said.

"I will."

He leaned forward and kissed her cheek. Her breath caught in her throat. It was a gentle kiss from a fascinating man.

"I will keep in touch via text message," Jack said.

"Thanks."

"You'll stay here, you won't leave the duplex?"

"Not even to get some French fries and ranch?"

He frowned with concern.

"I'm teasing. Don't worry. I'll stay here. If I'm desperate, I'll order room service. How long do you think...? Never mind, you probably have no idea."

"I'll be back as soon as the mission is complete." With a nod, Jack left.

She watched as Romeo jumped into the back seat of his SUV, Jack got behind the wheel and drove away, not looking back.

But she wanted him to look back. She wanted him to acknowledge...what? That he cared about her, too?

Pressing her hand to her cheek, she realized she still felt the warmth of his lips there. How was it possible that during such an intense crisis Zoe had met a man she could very well be falling in love with?

Talk about a complicated situation: feelings amplified by physical danger, emotional worry and even grief. Yes, she was starting to grieve the potential loss of her friend. Even if she did return, Shannon may not be the person Zoe had known all those years ago.

Per Jack's request, Zoe sat at the kitchen table, interlaced her hands and prayed. She prayed for the search team's success, for their safety, for Shannon's return, and...for Jack, that no harm would come to him.

A sudden knock at the door startled her. She crossed the room and looked through the peephole.

Kelly stood on the other side of the door.

Zoe opened it and smiled. "Hi, Kelly."

"My shift starts in an hour. Do you want to grab something to eat at the restaurant?"

"I'm not supposed to leave the duplex. Why don't you come in and we'll order room service?"

"Okay." Kelly glanced over her shoulder.

"You okay?"

"Sure, just paranoid I guess." Kelly joined her inside.

"That makes sense considering everything that happened yesterday."

"Walter fell into a coma last night."

"Oh no."

"Yeah, but not from the head injury. Apparently it was a drug overdose."

"Poor guy."

"Yeah, what a mess. This whole thing."

Trying to brighten Kelly's spirits, Zoe said, "I've got a good feeling about today's search."

"I like your optimism."

"Cheeseburgers okay?"

"Sure." Kelly pushed aside the curtain and peered outside. "There's a police cruiser in the lot."

"Probably keeping an eye on me."

Kelly glanced at her.

"Because I'm a target," Zoe said.

Kelly nodded and looked out the window.

Zoe ordered their meals and went into the kitchen to heat water for tea. *Tea calms the soul.* The memory of Jack's words comforted her.

A beep sounded from Kelly's phone. She glanced at it and spun around. "It's Shannon. She's here."

"What? Where?"

"Near the stables. She wants us to meet her." Kelly looked at Zoe. "She says she needs help."

Zoe grabbed her jacket and purse. She turned and hesitated. *Don't worry. I'll stay here.* She'd promised Jack she wouldn't leave.

"What's wrong?" Kelly said.

Zoe weighed her choices carefully. If she stayed here, she was turning her back on her best friend, ignoring her request for help.

She simply couldn't do it, not after everything that had happened.

She pulled out her phone to text Jack about where she was going.

"We've got to go now," Kelly said. "I saw the deputy walk away from his car, probably to get coffee or something. Hurry, so he won't see us leave."

Zoe pocketed her phone, slung her purse over her shoulder and followed Kelly to the door.

Kelly cracked it open and spied outside. "Let's go."

They left the duplex and Kelly shut the door, guiding Zoe quickly away, down the shoveled path past another duplex, then a quick right, so they'd be out of view of the police cruiser.

"How far is it?" Zoe asked.

"Not far."

"I hope she's okay. I mean, if she texted, then she's okay, right?" Zoe rambled.

A car suddenly pulled up. Zoe turned just as the original kidnapper got out and grabbed her.

"Stop!" she screamed. "Let me go!"

Kelly's eyes widened and she froze.

Before Zoe could *think* pepper spray, the guy applied a neck hold, pressing his arm against her throat and cutting off her ability to breathe or call out.

She struggled against him, swinging her arms. Her eyes watered.

Oh, why had they ditched the police surveillance?

Stars arced across her vision. She had to stay conscious, had to break free.

The pressure against her throat was too strong.

She struggled to breathe.

And lost consciousness.

THIRTEEN

Three teams had been assembled and assigned a specific search area. Jack and his team, consisting of Deputy Hauf and Sally Frick and her dog, Butch, hiked up the trail hoping to find evidence of Shannon Banks along the way. Even better, they hoped to find Shannon, either camped out or taking refuge in a bunker.

The only reason he'd joined this search was because there was a good chance he'd find Zoe's friend. Not only had the weather complied, but Command had gotten word that people had been seen in the area of the bunkers on the northern face of the mountain.

If it had been any other search for any other person, Jack would have stayed back to be with Zoe. However, this time he felt authorities had enough at stake that they wouldn't let her out of their sight. Even if they didn't consider Zoe a suspect, they knew her friendship with Shannon could be crucial in tracking down the missing woman.

Still, he hated leaving Zoe.

An odd turn of phrase. What would happen when this case was solved and they returned to their respective lives? He didn't want to think about that, wasn't sure how to process the thought.

It's not that complicated—you love her.

He stretched his neck and watched Romeo sniff the ground up ahead. No, it wasn't possible to develop intense feelings like love in such a short period of time, was it? It surely wasn't logical.

Then again love wasn't a logical emotion.

Nor was it logical that he was slightly hurt that Zoe hadn't responded to his last text message, sent four minutes ago.

"Everything okay?" Sally asked.

He glanced at her in question.

"You've got this frown like you're trying to understand a foreign language."

"I'm okay, thanks."

"You're welcome." Her dog rushed back to her and tugged on her toggle. "What'd you find, Butch?"

Butch spun around and ran off. The human team members followed the dogs as they continued to lead them farther up the trail. A few minutes later Jack noticed the opening of a bunker. This could be it.

Deputy Hauf called it in and turned to Jack and Sally. "Keep your dogs back, and stay behind me."

Hauf drew his firearm and led the way. Although snow had fallen on and off these past few days, the trail was still manageable, thanks to determined hikers who would come up here regardless of weather conditions. Jack could understand why. Being out in nature tended to put everything into perspective, made problems and challenges seem smaller, more manageable.

He hoped he would have the chance to hike with Zoe once this was over.

Focus, Jack. Pay attention to your surroundings, to your K9 partner.

Romeo trotted in front of Jack. Sally and Butch were ahead of Romeo, and Deputy Hauf led the way. Jack didn't mind Hauf and Sally leading since they were both carrying firearms.

He found himself more concerned with his own welfare than usual.

Because of Zoe and their potential future together.

As they approached the bunker, Deputy Hauf put up his hand and snapped a flashlight off his belt. "Wait for me to give the all clear."

Romeo had other ideas and took off ahead of Deputy Hauf.

"Romeo, back," Jack said.

The dog stopped and turned to look at Jack. Jack tapped his thigh. The dog trotted to Jack's side, visibly frustrated.

Deputy Hauf entered the bunker.

As Jack and Sally waited, he noticed her unzip her jacket and rest her hand at her waist, where he assumed she kept her firearm.

Jack continued to scan the area for signs of anything unusual. Seconds stretched by slowly, as he worried about how he'd tell Zoe if or when they found Shannon's body. He wanted desperately for Zoe's friend to be alive. The thought of grief crushing Zoe's heart…

Pain ripped through him as surely as if he were feeling the potential grief.

He found himself silently praying, an odd, yet comforting feeling.

I'm new at this, God, but I could use Your support.

Whatever we find, please help me find the words to comfort Zoe. Amen.

The pain in his chest seemed to soften a bit.

"Clear!" Deputy Hauf called.

The two K9 teams joined Deputy Hauf in the bunker. Jack was relieved that Shannon's body wasn't inside. The deputy was standing over an extinguished campfire. Jack knelt, took off his glove and touched the burned kindling. "Not warm."

Romeo burst into a round of barks. Deputy Hauf aimed his flashlight at the dog. Romeo was sniffing and pacing. Butch rushed up to him and barked. Jack spotted a scarf on the ground. With a brown stain.

"Blood," Jack said.

Deputy Hauf squatted, pulled a knife off his belt and used the tip to push the scarf aside. "This could belong to anyone."

"There's more over here," Sally said, aiming her flashlight into the corner where it appeared more articles of clothing were strewn on the ground. "More blood stains, like someone was trying to stop bleeding."

Jack pulled out his own flashlight and scanned the small area.

The beam illuminated a sparkle of silver against the dirt floor. "Deputy Hauf?" Jack motioned.

The deputy crossed the bunker and picked up a silver chain with the tip of his knife. A charm dangled from the end.

"It's a heart and a cross," Hauf said.

"It belongs to Shannon Banks," Jack said.

"How do you know?"

"She and Zoe have tattoos, same design."

"I'll call it in," Sally said, stepping out of the bunker.

It seemed that Shannon had been injured, but wasn't here now, which meant she'd hiked out on her own. That seemed hopeful.

"What's this?" Hauf pulled a tarp off a small mound to reveal plastic bags of a powdered substance. "This must be where they store the drugs."

Which meant, authorities would conclude Shannon's involvement in the drug ring since she was here, at the secret storage bunker.

"That doesn't necessarily mean—"

"Jack," Sally cut him off as she reentered the bunker. "They need you back ASAP. Zoe is gone."

The sound of men's voices awakened Zoe. She tentatively opened her eyes. She was on the floor, staring at a gray wall.

"What are we waiting for?"

"Confirmation he's got her."

Her? As in Shannon?

"Then what?"

"We end this thing. Let's go."

A few moments later there was the sound of a door clicking shut. Zoe sat up and looked around. She was in a one-room shed. A small lamp stood on a crate in the corner.

She spotted a man lying on the floor, his back to her. Rubbing her hands together, she realized the shed wasn't heated nor did it have windows.

She was a prisoner. Had they gotten Kelly, too?

The man coughed.

She tentatively crossed the shed. "Hello?"

He rolled over.

"Randy?" she said, recognizing him from the photo at Shan's house.

"I don't know you."

"I'm Zoe Pratt, a friend of Shannon's."

He nodded, but it seemed like he was out of it. The left side of his face was discolored with bruises, his pupils dilated, and he clutched his ribs with his arm.

"You're a DEA agent," she said.

He pinned her with dull green eyes.

"Agent Trotter told us about you, how you were assigned to make Shannon fall in love with you."

A slight chuckle escaped his lips and he winced, closing his eyes. "Funny story... She would have made the better agent."

"What do you mean?"

When he opened his eyes again, Zoe knew instantly what he meant.

"You love her?" Zoe asked.

"Yeah, I fell for a drug dealer."

"I don't believe it."

"It's true. I lost my perspective."

"No, I mean the drug dealer part."

He nodded and closed his eyes.

Great. This guy loved Shannon, yet even he believed she was a drug dealer.

"Why are we here?" Zoe asked.

"Leverage. They've been trying to get Shannon to tell them where the drugs are," he hesitated, breathing slowly. "They think she's been stealing from them. But..."

"But?"

"I saw her...in the mountains."

"Is she okay?"

"Yeah. Acted like she had no idea what they were talking about, what they wanted."

"See, I knew it. She's not involved."

"She escaped." He winced as he shifted position. "Now that they have you, they've got the advantage. They think she'll do anything to save us." He looked at her, a sad smile easing across his lips. "The two people she loves."

"And if she doesn't?"

Randy shook his head and closed his eyes.

Jack returned to town in a state of...disassociation. He couldn't quite define any one feeling surging through him.

Anger? No. Frustration, yes. Panic, definitely.

Disappointment, most definitely.

She'd gone against his wishes and left her safe accommodations.

Jack pulled up to the lodging and the first thing he noticed was the room service tray on the ground by the door. Why would she have ordered room service if she was going to flee?

He approached the duplex and the door swung open. Detective Perry scowled at him. "Okay, you know her better than anyone else in town. Where would she go?"

"Hello, Detective Perry." Jack entered.

"She's gone," Perry said. "Probably met up with Shannon. She's made so much money, she's probably paid for fake ID's and fled the jurisdiction."

"No, that's not Zoe. You don't know her."

"And you do?" Perry said. "Come on, Jack. You've known her for less than a week. I checked, she was having problems at work. They said she'd taken time off to reevaluate things. She comes up here, and she and Shannon cook up this kidnapping ploy, and then Zoe waits for Shannon to give her the green light to meet up."

"You're wrong."

"Great, well, if you know her so well, where'd she go?"

"I don't know."

"She didn't text you or call you? I mean, being that you're such good friends."

"I haven't heard from her." His gaze drifted across the room. He imagined her there, making tea, petting Romeo…smiling.

"You don't seem very upset," Detective Perry said.

"I'm upset."

"You know what this means?" Perry asked.

Jack looked at him.

"It means she's been manipulating you," Perry said.

Jack went to look out the window. *Where are you Zoe? Why did you go against my advice to stay put?*

The betrayal hurt worst of all.

Was it all a lie? Their intimate conversations? Discussions about faith? Her acceptance of his quirks and awkward demeanor? Had she been setting him up all along?

The thought tore through his insides. He hadn't felt this kind of pain when his ex-fiancée ended their relationship.

Detective Perry stepped up beside him. "Jack, I'm sorry."

Jack glanced at him, sensing Perry was apologizing for more than his harsh words.

"You're a smart guy. Help me out," Perry said. "Let's assume she isn't partners with Shannon."

Jack eyed him.

"I'm willing to take a leap of faith. If that's the case, why would she leave?"

"The only thing that would motivate her is the well-being of her best friend."

"Shannon."

"Yes."

"Then we're back to square one."

"Not necessarily. I can track her phone."

Perry quirked an eyebrow.

"I'm not a stalker."

Perry put up his hands. "No judgment."

Jack sat at the table and opened his laptop. "This program is better than the typical phone-tracking app. Give me a few minutes."

As Jack typed in the parameters, Detective Perry paced the living area.

"You're going to give yourself ulcerative colitis," Jack said.

"So I've been told. I hate being blindsided, first by the Feds, then by Zoe Pratt, the supposed victim."

So did Jack. He still wasn't sure what was going on, and the flood of emotional energy was so overpowering he chose numbness over emotion in order to process what was happening.

Zoe had left him.

Intentionally. There had been no sign of a struggle, no reports of a woman screaming. She'd left of her own volition.

Although, the food tray outside still bothered him.

As the program searched for Zoe's phone, Jack stood and went to the door.

"Where are you going?"

Jack opened the door, picked up the tray and brought it inside. "There are two plates here."

"Yeah?"

"She ordered food for two." He lifted the covers to reveal uneaten meals.

A ping rang from his laptop. He went to view it.

"She's not far away." Jack stood. "Are you notifying Agent Trotter?"

"They're in the mountains examining the bunker. I'll call a few of my deputies. Let's go."

Jack hesitated, surprised that the detective was including him in the search-and-retrieval mission.

Perry opened the door and looked at Jack. "Unless you don't want to."

"I'll follow you in my truck."

A key rumbled against a lock and Zoe dashed to her corner. She turned her back to the door and pretended to be asleep. The door shut with a click. She interlaced her fingers and prayed.

Jack, please find me.

That's when she realized if everyone thought Shan was a criminal, they might throw Zoe into that category as well, considering she'd mysteriously disappeared. She had to do something to let Jack know she was in trouble.

"They're both asleep," a man said.

He must be on the phone. But what would he do when the call ended?

She reached for her Holy Spirit charm to calm herself. As her fingers touched the smooth silver dove, the answer became clear.

"It's better if we do it up there anyway. Easier to dispose of the bodies."

The bodies? As in dead bodies? Her heart raced.

A sudden needle prick at the base of her neck made her yelp.

She swung her arm to push the guy away.

"Keep still."

Suddenly he was yanked back. Randy was trying to defend her, get her free. As the men struggled, she scanned the small shed and spotted a footstool.

The kidnapper shoved Randy against the wall.

Zoe swung the footstool at the kidnapper's head. He spun around and grabbed Zoe's wrist. It was the guy who attacked her on the mountain and took Shannon. A shudder ran down her spine.

"Enough," he said. "Or I'll kill you both right here."

He shoved her aside and she stumbled, falling on the dirt floor of the shed. As she looked up, it felt like she was watching a movie, like she wasn't the one in the shed being brutalized.

The drug. It must already be taking effect.

"Now let's go," he said, pulling Randy up. "You, too."

She knew he was talking to her, but her mind felt soggy.

He grabbed her arm.

She wrapped her fingers around her necklace, yanked hard and dropped it by her side.

Find this, Jack. Find my necklace and come save me. One last time.

FOURTEEN

Jack tracked Zoe's phone to a shed on the far perimeter of the resort property. Detective Perry contacted the resort manager, Curt, to notify him they needed access. Curt gladly gave Detective Perry the key.

Two sheriff's deputies, two DEA agents, Detective Perry and Jack surrounded the small shed. Perry led the team. He approached the door. Inserted the key and turned the lock. With a nod to his team, he swung the door open. "Police!"

His deputies followed him inside the shed.

A few long seconds of painstaking silence passed, then—

"Clear!"

Jack hurried into the shed behind DEA agents. And saw a woman on the ground wearing a knit cap. "Zoe?"

He wasn't even sure if he'd said her name aloud. His heart clenched.

Detective Perry put out his hand for everyone to stay back. The two deputies, Ortman and Hauf, made room for Jack. Detective Perry gently rolled the female over.

It was Shannon's friend, Kelly.

Relief warred with panic in Jack's chest. It wasn't Zoe, which was good, but then where was she?

"Ma'am, can you hear me?" Detective Perry asked.

Jack vaguely sensed the other DEA agents searching the shed.

"I…what?" she said.

"Detective?" one of the DEA agents said, as he picked up a cell phone.

Zoe's phone.

"Ma'am, are you okay?" Perry said.

"Her name is Kelly," Jack offered.

"Kelly, can you hear me?" Perry said.

"I…yes."

"What happened?"

"Zoe… Shannon…"

"They were here?"

Kelly nodded. "It's cold." She wrapped her arms around herself and started shivering.

"Find me a blanket," Perry said. One of his deputies rushed out of the shed.

"You saw Shannon Banks?" Perry redirected to Kelly.

"Yes. She and Zoe left."

"Do you know where they went?"

Deputy Hauf returned with a blanket and Perry wrapped it around Kelly's body.

"Thank you," she said.

"Did they say where they were going?"

"Canada."

Perry nodded at the DEA agents. "Notify Trotter so you can intercept them at the border. We need an ambulance."

"On its way," Deputy Hauf said from the doorway.

Detective Perry helped Kelly sit up. He glanced over his shoulder at Jack. "Sorry."

Jack nodded but didn't respond. What could he say? That yes, he was, in fact a complete fool? He shook his head and glanced down.

That's when he saw it. A flash of silver on the floor. He crouched and picked it up.

Zoe's silver dove charm. She never would have left it behind, not intentionally.

"You find something?" Perry said.

Jack glanced sideways and noticed Kelly watching him with an odd expression. Zoe would know what it meant. As Jack struggled to interpret its meaning, the blanket slipped off her shoulder.

Exposing a patch on her black hoodie. Of a bald eagle.

In a flash, things started to click in Jack's head.

If it had been Kelly giving drugs to Jeanie…and perhaps to Walter…

Kelly was the drug dealer, not Shannon.

Anything that came out of Kelly's mouth was a lie; the story about Zoe and Shannon heading to Canada meant as a diversion. But he needed to play along. He didn't want Kelly informing her cohorts that they'd been exposed.

Jack nodded at Detective Perry. "They'll call off the search for Shannon Banks since she's on her way to Canada. Are you done with me?"

Perry studied him with a curious expression. "Sure. Thanks for your help."

"You're welcome." He exited the shed and walked toward his truck.

Curt, the resort manager, pulled up in a company vehicle. "Did you find them?"

"Kelly, yes. But not Zoe or Shannon."

"How is she?"

"She'll be okay," Jack said, assuming as much since she was involved in this criminal activity.

"Will Search and Rescue—"

"They'll most likely call off the search since Miss Banks and Miss Pratt are said to be heading to Canada."

Curt sighed. "So, the threat is over."

Not hardly.

With a nod, Jack got in his truck and considered his options. Time was of the essence. The real criminals, of which Kelly was one, were sending authorities north to Canada, which meant Zoe and Shannon were not heading north.

He took a deep breath and decided to flip the entire hypothesis on its head.

If Shannon was the victim...

If Shannon, as the DEA claimed, was transporting product across the border but didn't know the contents of her transport... But someone else did—Kelly—and she started to skim off the top...

Everything started to make sense.

If the criminals thought Shannon was stealing, they'd demand their product be returned. If she pleaded ignorance, because she had no idea what they were talking about, they'd find another way to pressure her into returning the stolen product, like threatening someone she cared about...

That's why they'd been after Zoe from day one. Not because she could identify the kidnapper, but because they could use Zoe as leverage against Shannon.

Jack and Romeo had to find Zoe, and they had no time to spare. They couldn't do it alone so he sent two text messages, one to Sally Frick and the other to Detective Perry.

"This could be dangerous, buddy," he said to his dog who sat patiently in the back seat.

Jack pulled away to convince anyone who was watching him that he was leaving, giving up.

But he'd never give up on Zoe.

Hiking.

Zoe was hiking again. Up into the mountains.

The last time she went hiking, she'd been with…

"Shannon?" she said, as she put one foot in front of the other.

"She's meeting us up ahead," a man's voice said.

Zoe felt like she was floating, her boots light, her mind cushioned by a purple cloud of happiness. Yes, she was very happy, ecstatic because she was going to see Shannon.

Her friend had been lost for days. Search-and-rescue teams had scoured the mountain.

"Romeo?" she said, looking for Jack's dog. Jack and Romeo must have found Shannon and were waiting for Zoe.

Someone nudged her from behind, she stumbled and nearly fell onto the snowy trail. She giggled, thinking how silly she would have looked falling down like a child.

She glanced over her shoulder and saw a large man wearing a ski mask pulling up another man who had fallen.

"Up!" the big guy shouted.

The man struggling to stand had a kind, furry face and bloodshot eyes. Zoe helped him up. "Upsy-daisy." She looked at the guy with the ski mask. "Why are you being so mean?"

"We've got to get to Shannon before the weather breaks."

"Oh, okay." She turned to the man who'd fallen, and remembered who he was—Shan's boyfriend, Randy. "Didn't you hear him? Shan's waiting for us. Come, come." Zoe encouraged Randy forward.

She hadn't a clue where they were going, but as long as Shannon would be there, it didn't matter.

She wasn't sure how much time had passed when she spotted the fire lookout. Shannon had mentioned seeing God's beauty from there. This had to be the place where she would meet Zoe and Randy. Zoe could hardly contain herself. She'd been so worried about her friend…

…Because why again?

Because she'd gone missing. And then authorities were saying horrible things about Shan, things Zoe refused to believe.

Zoe approached the last rocky bit of trail.

Her ankle turned and she lost her balance, but Randy grabbed her from behind.

"Thank you," she said, stepping onto the porch surrounding the lookout. She went around to an open door.

"Shannon?" She stepped inside.

Shannon, who sat in the corner of the one room structure looked up. "Zoe?"

Zoe rushed to her friend and they embraced. "Randy's here, too."

"Randy?"

"Isn't it great?" Zoe said.

"What's going on?" Shannon said to someone behind Zoe.

Zoe turned and spotted a man she recognized. A police officer.

"Oh, Sergeant Peterson, thank you for finding my friend," Zoe said.

Randy stumbled and fell onto the floor. Shannon went to his side. "Are you okay?"

The big man stepped into the lookout.

Shannon pulled Randy away and clung to him.

"Shannon?" Zoe said.

"Zoe, get out of here!" Shannon cried.

Zoe glanced at the big guy and then at Sergeant Peterson. "It's okay, Shannon. Sergeant Peterson is here. He'll protect us."

The sergeant tapped his fingers against his belt.

"How could I have been so stupid?" Shannon said.

"What do you mean?" Zoe said.

The big guy grabbed Randy's arm to pull him away from Shannon.

"No!" Shannon cried.

"Tell us where it is, or I'll slice him up right here in front of you."

"Stop," Sergeant Peterson said.

Zoe sighed with relief.

"We're waiting on orders," the sergeant said.

"You don't need orders to arrest a bad guy," Zoe offered.

The sergeant looked at her.

"Use your gun, show him your badge." Zoe motioned with her hands.

"Oh, Zoe," Shannon said softly.

"What?"

"He *is* one of the bad guys."

Zoe was confused. She looked at Shannon, then at the sergeant. Zoe couldn't process what it was all about, but she knew one thing for sure. She wished Jack were here.

The sound of footsteps echoed against the wooden platform. Curt, the resort manager, stepped inside.

"Curt?" Shannon said.

"Yes, Shannon, it's me, the man you've been betraying for the past three months."

"I don't know what—"

"Stop!" Curt stepped closer to Shannon. "Did you honestly think you could steal from me and I wouldn't notice? Do I seem that stupid?"

"Steal what? Specialty linens?"

Curt burst out laughing. The other two men stood there, stone-faced. Zoe hugged herself. Something terrible was happening.

"You have my drugs and I want them back," he said.

"I didn't take your drugs. I didn't even know I was transporting drugs."

"Police found a stash in a bunker on the north face of the mountain," Sergeant Peterson said to no one in particular.

"Tell me you didn't store my drugs in a damp bunker," Curt said to Shannon.

"I didn't take and never had your drugs."

"No?" Curt nodded at the big guy.

He crossed the small space toward Zoe and grabbed her arm.

"No, don't!" Shannon charged and he backhanded her.

"You jerk!" Zoe bit the big guy's hand that clung to her arm. He tossed her aside and she hit the floor, hard.

As she lay there, head throbbing, she decided to pray:

for her life, for Shannon's and Randy's life. For Jack to come find her.

The sound of a dog barking gave her hope. Romeo.

"Did you hear that?" Sergeant Peterson said.

To mask the sound of Romeo barking, Zoe started singing "Amazing Grace," rather loudly.

"Where are the drugs!" Curt shouted at Shannon.

"'…to save a wretch like me…'" Zoe sang.

"No! Leave Randy alone!" Shan shouted.

"'… Was blind but now I see…'"

"There's someone out there," the big guy said.

"Check it out," Curt ordered, then turned and started kicking Randy.

"She doesn't care about the boyfriend. She cares about this one." Sergeant Peterson grabbed Zoe.

She yelped and stopped singing.

Romeo's barking echoed across the mountain range.

Sergeant Peterson released Zoe and went to the window.

The barking continued.

He withdrew his firearm from his holster and cracked open a window.

"Nooo!" Zoe charged him.

The gun went off.

The sergeant shoved her aside and aimed his weapon at her.

A gunshot rang out. Zoe automatically dropped to the wood floor and pinched her eyes shut. It didn't hurt. Nothing hurt. How was that possible? She hugged herself and rocked back and forth.

"Freeze!"

She cracked open her eyes…

And saw Sergeant Peterson sprawled on the floor

in front of her. Detective Perry stood in the doorway aiming his weapon.

What just happened?

Perry entered the lookout and someone pushed around him to get to Zoe.

Jack. He rushed to her and pulled her against this chest.

"You found me," she said.

"Romeo found you."

"Is he okay?"

"Romeo, right here!"

The dog darted into the lookout and rushed up to Zoe. "Help her," Jack said.

Romeo nuzzled Zoe's leg and licked her hand.

"Oh, Romeo, you're my hero." She glanced up into Jack's rich blue eyes. "You, too, Jack. I love you both."

FIFTEEN

As they sat in the conference room at the sheriff's office, Zoe wondered why Jack wasn't making eye contact. He'd been acting more aloof than usual since they'd returned to town. Was that it? In his mind, once the case was over, was their relationship over, too?

Or was he embarrassed that she'd professed to love him back at the lookout? She couldn't stop herself. She'd been under the influence of the drugs they'd given her and had completely lost her filter.

The truth was she *did* love Jack or was starting to love him or… Whatever, it didn't matter anyway.

"I made good money transporting supplies for the resort, extra money I donated to the community center youth programs," Shannon said. "I had no idea I was smuggling drugs." She shuddered. "So I was like a mule or something?"

"Yes, ma'am," Agent Trotter said. "Curt Underwood was the leader of this operation, with support from Sergeant Peterson."

Detective Perry clenched his jaw.

"I still can't believe it," Shannon said. "I volunteered

with him at Angie's Youth Club. That's why I called him, why I trusted him above everyone else."

"We all trusted him," Detective Perry said.

"How did he get involved in this?" Zoe said.

"His son is seriously ill and needed treatment at Children's Hospital," Agent Trotter said. "Peterson ran out of money. Curt found out and made him an offer. Peterson felt he had no choice."

"That's so sad," Zoe said. "So that's why Curt's men always knew where I was, because Sergeant Peterson told them?"

"That and because Kelly was tracking your phone. She'd also cloned Shannon's."

"That's how she was able to send text messages that looked like they were coming from Shannon," Jack said, leaning back in his chair.

"Once product started disappearing from your shipments, Curt hired Vic Jones to kidnap you, threaten you and convince you to turn it over," Trotter said to Shannon. "But you didn't, so they came after the people you cared about."

"Randy and Zoe," Shannon said softly.

"I'm okay," Zoe said, glancing at Jack.

"He also had a second man working for him, the one who broke into Shannon's house, and was killed trying to break out of jail. We suspect Curt was the other man at the scene."

"But why blow up my house?" Shannon asked.

"To convince authorities you were involved with a violent drug cartel," Trotter said. "Curt sent Kelly Washburn to cut the gas line and leave a candle burning, which set off the explosion. Kelly was who you saw fleeing the scene wearing a jacket similar to Shannon's.

Everything she did, she did with the intention of making it look like Shannon was a criminal."

Shannon shook her head. "Why would she get involved in this? I mean, she didn't have a sick child or anything."

"Some people don't need a noble motivation. They just like money," Trotter said. "She knew Curt was having you smuggle product against your knowledge and decided the fact you two look similar could work in her favor. She was skimming off your shipments so she looked clean to her boss. Then, pretending to be you, she'd sell product to customers. She made a nice chunk of change."

"That's why Jeanie thought I was selling her drugs. Because Kelly was pretending to be me," Shannon said. "And to think I kicked her out of the club because she kept demanding I get her more stuff. I had no idea what she was talking about and she became hysterical."

"What about Jeanie?" Zoe asked.

"She's home and safe with her father," Detective Perry said. "If you want to press charges—"

"We don't." Zoe glanced at Jack, but he was still avoiding eye contact.

"Not only had Kelly been selling to kids at the community center, but she also took the lead on throwing us off course during the investigation," Agent Trotter said, addressing Shannon. "She left the bloodstained clothes in the bunker to convince us you were too injured to survive, and she left drugs there as evidence against you."

"What about the woman who died in the mountains?" Zoe asked.

"A customer of Kelly's," Trotter said. "The young woman had Shannon's name written on a piece of paper, but it had the number for a burner phone probably belonging to Kelly."

"Kelly Washburn did everything in her power to convince authorities you were the mastermind of this drug operation," Perry said to Shannon.

Shan looked at Zoe. "Did you think…?"

"She didn't," Jack said.

Everyone in the room turned to him.

"Not for one minute did she believe you could be capable of smuggling or dealing drugs," Jack reiterated. "She used your journal to try to prove your innocence. That's how much she believed in you."

Zoe offered a smile. He still wouldn't look at her.

"Shannon, why didn't you notify police sooner when you found out what was going on?" Agent Trotter said.

"I didn't find out until after I'd been kidnapped. The kidnapper kept demanding to know where _it_ was. I had no idea what he was talking about. Even after Randy told me not to trust anyone, I called the one person I thought was solid, Sergeant Peterson. That blew up in my face."

"You couldn't have known, honey," Zoe said.

"No, but I should have," Detective Perry said. "My apologies, Shannon."

"Thank you. I'm glad everyone's okay." She glanced around the table.

Zoe noticed Randy wouldn't make eye contact with Shannon either.

"I'm still amazed you survived out there for so long," Zoe said.

"Me, too. I actually escaped that first day, but he caught me again and kept me hidden in a bunker on the east side of the mountain. Then Randy found me and helped me escape the second time. Randy?"

He finally looked up.

"Thank you."

He nodded, and lowered his gaze.

Shannon turned to Zoe. "I'm sorry you got dragged into all of this."

"Hey, it's not your fault. Besides, I met some exceptional people while in town." She cast a quick glance at Jack, who was studying his phone.

Her heart sank. Case over; relationship over.

"We'll need both of you to testify against Curt Underwood and his men," Trotter said.

"Of course," Shannon said.

"Why do you need Zoe?" Jack said.

Again, everyone looked at him.

"She's been in enough danger for one lifetime," Jack offered.

"The players have all been arrested. There's no one left to pose a threat to her," Agent Trotter said.

Jack nodded but didn't look satisfied with the answer.

Okay, so he wouldn't even look at Zoe, but he was worried about her safety? How...inconsistent.

They wrapped up the meeting and Shannon turned to Zoe. "I'll be right back."

Shan followed Randy outside to talk to him. Zoe watched the intense exchange from the doorway.

"Are you okay?" Jack asked, approaching her.

She turned to him, trying to read his shuttered expression.

"Sure," she said.

"You don't sound so sure of your sure."

He was joking with her?

"I'm still processing it all," she said.

"It can take weeks or even months to recover from

a trauma such as the one you've experienced this past week. Wait, why am I telling you this? You're the counselor."

She nodded. "That's right, I am." Yet she had no idea how to communicate with the man standing in front of her.

"I've heard good things about something called EMDR for trauma victims," Jack said.

"I'm familiar."

"You could also—"

"It's you, Jack. You're what's upsetting me right now."

"Okay, I'll leave." He turned and she grabbed his arm.

"No, not you, the person. It's your behavior."

"Did I say something rude again?"

"No, that's the point. You're not saying anything. You can barely look at me."

"I can't help it. I'm going to miss you."

"We can remedy that. We can—"

"No, we can't."

"See, I'm confused. I thought you felt—"

"I do. I feel a lot…about you. Which is why this can't happen."

"For a smart guy you're making absolutely no sense here, Jack."

"I can't give you what you need."

"And what's that?" She crossed her arms over her chest, wondering where this was going.

"I will never be able to fulfill your needs emotionally, so instead, I will remove myself from your life so you can find someone who can. It was…" he hesitated "…amazing, knowing you, Zoe Pratt, spending time with you, even under the circumstances."

He leaned forward and kissed her cheek. Again.

She was stunned. Flummoxed. Nonplussed.

This incredible man was worried about her emotional needs, and since he believed he fell short, he would simply remove himself from her life. He cared about her that much.

She started to call after him but wasn't sure what to say.

Shannon approached and put her arm around Zoe. "You were busy while I was kidnapped and held hostage in the mountains," she said.

"He doesn't think he's worthy of me."

"He's not. No one is." Shannon gave Zoe a squeeze.

"That's not true." She glanced at Shannon. "If anyone's worthy, it's a guy like Jack."

"Let's go decompress at the hotel and figure out what to do about our guy trouble."

Back to work. Back to normal.

Jack had a hard time sitting still, focusing. He paced to the window overlooking Puget Sound.

"I'm not sure about Quantum Enterprises. There's something about the CEO that makes me think they'd be difficult to work with," Heather, Jack's assistant, said.

Everything struck him as difficult lately.

"I could set up an introductory meeting if you want to check it out for yourself?"

"No, I trust your judgment." Besides he didn't have the bandwidth to sign on with difficult clients. He wasn't sure what he had the energy for these days.

"Okay," Heather said. "Unicom Properties wants to know when you'll be testing their system."

He turned to Heather. "If I tell them, then they'll try to prepare. That defeats the purpose of my service."

"Good point."

Jack's phone vibrated. He glanced at a text from Zoe. He looked away. Glanced back at the phone.

"SAR?" Heather asked.

"What?"

"You keep looking at your phone. Did you get a search-and-rescue alert?"

"No. It's a female."

"O-kay," she chuckled.

"I don't understand females."

"Want me to…?" She motioned.

He handed her his phone. She read aloud, "'I have never felt so cherished, understood or safe with a man.'" Heather looked up. "What's the confusion?"

"I don't understand what that means."

"Uh…boss? I think it means she loves you."

He paced to his bookshelves and analyzed the binding on a hardcover edition of a coding textbook.

Love? Even after he'd told her he was broken, that he couldn't give her everything she needed?

The phone pinged with another text. He turned to Heather. "Read it, please."

"She's asking you to meet her at Serenity Lake Overlook tomorrow." She stood. "You've only got one meeting tomorrow. I'll handle it. I'll put off the Principality meet and greet until next week and tell Unicom March 1."

"Why March 1?"

"To throw them off track so they won't be prepared."

"But—"

"Nothing is more important than love, boss." She handed him back his phone. "Even a man as brilliant as you must know that."

* * *

Zoe checked her phone. 12:17 p.m.

He wasn't coming.

She paced the area overlooking Serenity Lake. Jack knew where to find her, both from her text and the fact he was probably still tracking her phone location.

Which meant he'd chosen not to come.

Well, she never would have forgiven herself if she hadn't tried, hadn't reached out one last time.

She accepted the fact you couldn't fix another person, couldn't give them the confidence they needed or make them feel something they didn't.

Yet Jack felt love for Zoe. He'd admitted as much. He just didn't believe himself good enough to make her happy.

"Oh, Jack," she said softly. Zoe believed in her heart that he was exactly the type of man who would be a good life partner. He was honest to a fault, caring of others and had a high moral compass. A wonderful combination.

He'd even seemed to open his heart to God during the short time they'd spent together.

Was she crazy for feeling this way? *No*, she reminded herself, *you can't control your feelings, you have to name them and embrace them.*

She had fallen in love with Jack Monroe.

Crossing her arms over her chest, she gazed out across the gorgeous aquamarine lake below. It was beautiful here. Even after all the trauma of the past week, beauty ruled over darkness.

If she left town in a few days with a wounded heart, she'd still focus on the things she'd learned, like the fact it was okay to rely on another person for help. She didn't have to do everything on her own.

She had relied on Jack.

A text vibrated and she glanced at her phone, hopeful. It was Shannon, checking in. Zoe was optimistic for her friend since Shannon and Randy had been spending time together. Randy had begged for Shannon's forgiveness, both for suspecting her of being involved in the drug scheme and for having to lie to her about his motivations. He said he loved her so much he'd consider quitting the DEA to be with her.

Now that was true love.

Zoe responded to Shan that Jack was a no-show, and pocketed her phone. She decided to say one last prayer of surrender. Interlacing her fingers and closing her eyes, she said, "Dear Lord, I know I've done my best to open his heart, to make him feel safe and loved. If it's not meant to be, then I surrender my pain to You and pray that You help Jack find peace, love and happiness. Amen."

She took a few slow, deep breaths.

The sound of a barking dog filled her heart with joy. She turned just as Romeo raced up to her. She dropped to her knees and embraced him.

As she buried her face into his fur, she thanked God for what she hoped was about to happen.

Jack joined her and she stood, offering a smile. "You're eighteen minutes late."

"Nineteen actually. Please forgive me. There was an accident in Darrington and I tried texting but couldn't get service in the pass."

He reached out and took her hand. The warmth shot clear up to her heart.

"I'm glad you waited," he said.

"Me, too." She squeezed his hand and gazed across the lake, marveling at the beauty below. "I like it here."

"It's the view," Jack said, studying her. He offered a smile and pulled her into a hug. "Is this okay?"

"It's perfect."

"Perfect. As good as it is possible to be." He broke the hug and looked directly into her eyes. "Your text… I wasn't sure… I mean, after what I said about not being able to make you happy."

"Look at my face." She cracked a wide smile. "This is my happy face, and it's how I feel when I'm with you."

"Oh, good. I mean my assistant interpreted the text—"

"My text needed an interpreter? Wow, I'm honored."

He actually smiled, indicating he understood she was joking around.

"I needed her assistance because I wanted to confirm I wasn't misreading things," he said.

"You weren't."

"That's a first."

She chuckled and searched his eyes. "What about your plan to sell your company and go on adventures? I'll be honest, Jack, I'm not the type to pick up and leave for months at a time."

"I think…" he offered a half grin "…this adventure will be better."

He kissed her, a warm kiss filled with promise, devotion and love.

* * * * *

Isabelle Trent woke with a start. She lay still, trying to figure out what had jarred her just as the sun was beginning to make its way above the horizon. She'd forgotten to pull her curtains closed before she'd fallen into bed with a half-finished prayer on her lips.

Maybe it was just the light that had disturbed her.

A faint cry reached her. A cry that sounded like...a baby? A kitten?

The sound grew louder, and it came from the wraparound porch.

Finally, she identified it.

A baby.

With a soft gasp, Isabelle hurried forward to unlock the French door and step outside.

At her feet, an infant was strapped into a carrier. "Oh, my sweet little one." Isabelle released the straps and scooped the tiny body, blanket and all, into her arms.

Movement from the edge of the porch caught her attention. "Hey, who's there?"

The slow-moving sun only revealed the silhouette of a man simply standing there. Not moving. Just watching. Unease crawled through her. "Hey, is this your baby?"

Still, he stayed silent. He looked back over his shoulder one more time, then seemed to make up his mind about something. Her nerves jangled and alarm shuddered through her. He took a step toward her and Isabelle spun. Holding the infant in the crook of her left arm, she twisted the knob with her right hand and pushed the door open just wide enough for her to slip through. She shut the door and locked it.

He moved as though to leave, then turned back, dark eyes on hers. He came toward the glass door, reaching for the knob. Isabelle whirled and raced to her bedroom to snatch her phone from the nightstand. She dialed 911 and hurried back to the den area to see the dark-clad figure pacing in front of her door. Quick as lightning, he spun and slammed a fist on the wooden part of the door. The noise jarred the infant, who let out a wail.

"911. What's your emergency?"

"Someone's trying to get in my house."

Don't miss
Peril on the Ranch *by Lynette Eason,*
available July 2021 wherever Love Inspired Suspense
books and ebooks are sold.

LoveInspired.com

Get 4 FREE REWARDS!

We'll send you 2 FREE Books plus 2 FREE Mystery Gifts.

Love Inspired Suspense books showcase how courage and optimism unite in stories of faith and love in the face of danger.

FREE
Value Over
$20

YES! Please send me 2 FREE Love Inspired Suspense novels and my 2 FREE mystery gifts (gifts are worth about $10 retail). After receiving them, if I don't wish to receive any more books, I can return the shipping statement marked "cancel." If I don't cancel, I will receive 6 brand-new novels every month and be billed just $5.24 each for the regular-print edition or $5.99 each for the larger-print edition in the U.S., or $5.74 each for the regular-print edition or $6.24 each for the larger-print edition in Canada. That's a savings of at least 13% off the cover price. It's quite a bargain! Shipping and handling is just 50¢ per book in the U.S. and $1.25 per book in Canada.* I understand that accepting the 2 free books and gifts places me under no obligation to buy anything. I can always return a shipment and cancel at any time. The free books and gifts are mine to keep no matter what I decide.

Choose one: ☐ **Love Inspired Suspense Regular-Print** (153/353 IDN GNWN) ☐ **Love Inspired Suspense Larger-Print** (107/307 IDN GNWN)

Name (please print)

Address   Apt. #

City   State/Province   Zip/Postal Code

Email: Please check this box ☐ if you would like to receive newsletters and promotional emails from Harlequin Enterprises ULC and its affiliates. You can unsubscribe anytime.

Mail to the **Harlequin Reader Service:**
IN U.S.A.: P.O. Box 1341, Buffalo, NY 14240-8531
IN CANADA: P.O. Box 603, Fort Erie, Ontario L2A 5X3

Want to try 2 free books from another series? Call 1-800-873-8635 or visit www.ReaderService.com.

*Terms and prices subject to change without notice. Prices do not include sales taxes, which will be charged (if applicable) based on your state or country of residence. Canadian residents will be charged applicable taxes. Offer not valid in Quebec. This offer is limited to one order per household. Books received may not be as shown. Not valid for current subscribers to Love Inspired Suspense books. All orders subject to approval. Credit or debit balances in a customer's account(s) may be offset by any other outstanding balance owed by or to the customer. Please allow 4 to 6 weeks for delivery. Offer available while quantities last.

Your Privacy—Your information is being collected by Harlequin Enterprises ULC, operating as Harlequin Reader Service. For a complete summary of the information we collect, how we use this information and to whom it is disclosed, please visit our privacy notice located at corporate.harlequin.com/privacy-notice. From time to time we may also exchange your personal information with reputable third parties. If you wish to opt out of this sharing of your personal information, please visit readerservice.com/consumerschoice or call 1-800-873-8635. **Notice to California Residents**—Under California law, you have specific rights to control and access your data. For more information on these rights and how to exercise them, visit corporate.harlequin.com/california-privacy.

LIS21R